"I wish you would say what you are thinking,"

Andrena said. "Or do whatever it is that you mean to do to me."

Mag's hands tightened again on her shoulders, but looking down into those heavily lashed blue-black eyes, he seemed unable to think of anything but the sensations storming through his body.

"There is one more thing I would ask," he said.

"What?" Her little red tongue darted out to dampen her lips.

"Sir Ian delights in teasing his friends and flirting with comely women. Prithee, do not encourage him."

"Mercy, sir, do you think Ian would go beyond the bounds? I do not."

"Nevertheless, you must not encourage him. I don't like it."

"Well, that is plain enough," she said with a rueful look.

Shifting his right hand from her shoulder to cup the back of her head, he gently touched her lips with his. When she pressed forward, inviting more, he murmured, "You are *mine* now, lass. If you want to flirt, flirt with me."

"Deliciously sexy...a rare treat of a read...*Highland Master* is an entertaining adventure for lovers of historical romance."
                                                    —RomanceJunkies.com

"Hot...There's plenty of action and adventure...Amanda Scott has an excellent command of the history of medieval Scotland—she knows her clan battles and border wars, and she's not afraid to use detail to add realism to her story."
                                                    —All About Romance

TEMPTED BY A WARRIOR

"4½ stars! Top Pick! Scott demonstrates her incredible skills by crafting an exciting story replete with adventure and realistic, passionate characters who reach out and grab you...Historical romance doesn't get much better than this!"
                                                    —*RT Book Reviews*

"Captivates the reader from the first page...Another brilliant story filled with romance and intrigue that will leave readers thrilled until the very end."
                                                    —SingleTitles.com

SEDUCED BY A ROGUE

"4½ stars! Top Pick! Tautly written...passionate... Scott's wonderful book is steeped in Scottish Border history and populated by characters who jump off the pages and grab your attention...Captivating!"
                                                    —*RT Book Reviews*

Other Books by Amanda Scott

AMANDA SCOTT

The Laird's Choice

FOREVER

NEW YORK   BOSTON

This book is a work of fiction. Names, characters, places, and incidents are the product of the author's imagination or are used fictitiously. Any resemblance to actual events, locales, or persons, living or dead, is coincidental.

Forever
Hachette Book Group
237 Park Avenue
New York, NY 10017

www.HachetteBookGroup.com

Printed in the United States of America

First Edition: December 2012
10 9 8 7 6 5 4 3 2 1

Forever is an imprint of Grand Central Publishing.
The Forever name and logo are trademarks of Hachette Book Group, Inc.

The publisher is not responsible for websites (or their content) that are not owned by the publisher.

ATTENTION CORPORATIONS AND ORGANIZATIONS:
Most HACHETTE BOOK GROUP books are available at quantity discounts with bulk purchase for educational, business, or sales promotional use. For information, please call or write:
Special Markets Department, Hachette Book Group
237 Park Avenue, New York, NY 10017
Telephone: 1-800-222-6747 Fax: 1-800-477-5925

To Frances Jalet-Miller
(dear, wonderful Francie)
with many, many thanks!

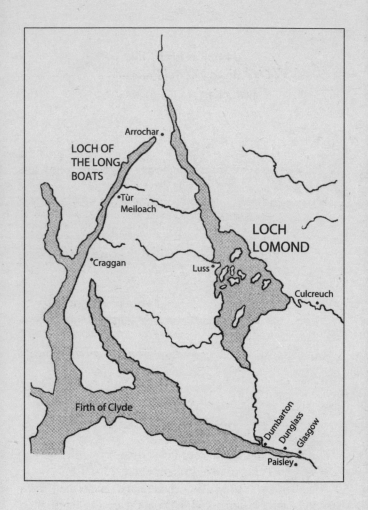

Author's Note———————

For readers' convenience, the author offers the following guide:

Bealach = BYAL uch, a mountain pass (*na Duin* = by/ of the mound or hill)

Clachan = village

Collop = fee for passage over someone else's land, usually plural (per head)

Fain = eager, eagerly

Forbye = besides, in addition, furthermore, however

Gangplank = the board or ramp that provides access from dock to galley

Gangway = walkway between rows of oarsmen's benches on a gallcy

Garron = small Highland horse, very strong, agile enough for the landscape

Lachina = Lock EEN a

Lina = LEE na

Lippin (as in Lippin Geordie) = trust, trusted

Owf = not crazy but a little out there

Plaid (great kilt) = all-purpose garment formed from length of wool kilted up with a belt, the excess length then flung over the wearer's shoulder

...the noo = now

Tarbet = isthmus, an arm of land connecting two bodies of water

Tùr Meiloach = Toor MIL ock

The Laird's Choice

Prologue ──────────────────

Arrochar, Scotland, early August 1406

They're coming, my love! I must go."

The woman lying on the ground—nearly hidden by darkness, shrubbery, the thick bedding of pine boughs on which he had laid her, and the fur-lined cloak that he'd spread over her—opened her eyes and smiled wearily.

"Keep...safe."

Had his hearing been less acute, he would not have heard his beloved wife's soft murmur. As it was, he feared that he might never see her again.

"I'll come back for ye, *mo chridhe*," he said. The certainty in his voice was as much for himself as for her.

"Aye, sure," she said. "I wish I could keep the bairn with me, though."

"Ye ken fine that it wouldna be safe. If she cried, they'd find ye both, and I'll take her straight to Annie. She has a wee one of her own and milk aplenty for two."

"I know," she whispered. "But guard our wee lassie well."

"I will, aye."

With that, he drew more shrubbery over her, but he

could linger no longer. Sounds of pursuit from the north were louder, too loud. In the distance to the south, he could hear the raging river that might be their salvation. Reluctant though he was to leave her, he dared not let them catch him or all would be lost.

Turning toward the last stretch of hillside he had to climb before descending to the river, he shifted the strap of his baldric and felt the reassuring weight of the sword and spear across his back. In the cloth sling he carried across his chest, his wee daughter nestled, sound asleep, one tiny ear near his beating heart.

Cradling her in one large palm, he moved through the woods with the silence gained only by a hunter-warrior's lifetime practice in such an environment. Pale rays of a slender summer moon slipped through the canopy to light his way.

He allowed his pursuers to see him only once, as he hurried across a clearing in the moonlight. He knew they would easily spot his movements there from below.

In the trees near the crest of the hill, he heard the river's roar, still distant but louder. However, sounds of pursuit were louder, too. His enemies numbered a dozen or more, all warriors like himself. Doubtless, others hunted him all across his lands.

His mind raced. Thanks to a late thaw, snow still capped nearby mountain peaks. But the days had been warmer for a fortnight.

Although he had not seen the river for weeks, experience told him it would be running high, still in snow spate. The glen that it had cut was steep-sided and narrow, but below where he stood, the river's course flattened for a short way.

With luck, he could cross it there in a manner that his pursuers would be unlikely to emulate. His primary concern was the babe he carried.

She was silent, still sleeping. But if she cried, they would hear her. Also, the river would be too deep and too turbulent—in its long, plunging course—to cross without swimming. That fact was the very one that might save them, though. He tried to imagine how, carrying her, he could get them both safely across.

The answer was plain. He could not. But safety lay only on the other side, on the sacred ground of Tùr Meiloach.

He carried his dirk, his sword, and his spear. He had also brought his bow from the castle but had left it with his lady wife. She had kept her dirk, too.

Although she had assured him she would keep safe until his return, he held no illusions. In such matters, he had never doubted her, nor had she ever proven wrong. But as weak and exhausted as she was now, she could not defend herself against so many had she every weapon in Scotland at her disposal.

Her only hope, and thus his own, was that he succeed in getting their bairn to safety. Then he could return for her.

Reaching the swiftly flowing river at last, unable to hear his pursuers over its roar, he wasted no time in deliberation but untied the sling. Then he pulled his spear from its loop on his baldric, uncoiled the narrow rope he'd wound around his waist against any such need, and fashioned a knotted cap with it for the blunt end of the spear. Working swiftly, he found two suitably curved lengths of bark, bound the swaddled babe inside a bark shell and then securely to the center of his spear. Then, hefting the result, he gauged the distance, hesitated only long enough to hear male voices above the din of the river, and let fly with the spear.

He knew he had chucked it far enough, that his arc was high enough, and that his aim would be true despite the added weight of the babe. But if the high end of the spear struck a tree branch, or if he had misjudged the position of the babe on the spear, she might land too hard. The spear might also hit a boulder. He knew that the thicket where he had aimed it boasted little such danger. But the Fates would have to be in a gey gracious mood for such a daring act to succeed.

If it did, the spear's point would bury itself in pine duff and soft dirt, the knotted rope cap at its top end would prevent the babe in her swaddling and sling from hitting the ground, and the bark shell would prevent any other damage.

Then, if he made it across the river to her, all would be well. Muttering prayers to God and the Fates, he hurried to the upper end of the river's flat section, arriving just as the sudden, unmistakable baying of a wolf struck terror into his soul.

His pursuers' shouts were loud enough to tell him they were topping the rise, so he knew they had not seen him throw the spear. Also, he could at least be hopeful that the river's noise would prevent their hearing the babe's cries when she squalled. And she surely would, if not now then later, unless...

That thought refused to declare itself. He had to focus on his own actions now and draw his pursuers as far from his lady as he could. If they thought he was dead, so much the better. But they would have to see him in the river first.

Accordingly, he waited until he saw movement on the steep hillside above him. Then he leaped onto a moonlit boulder that jutted into the roiling flow.

Hearing a shout above, knowing that they had seen him, he flung himself into the torrent. Although the shock of the icy water nearly undid him, he ignored it and swam hard. Letting the current carry him, he also fought it to swim at an angle that would, he prayed, carry him to the opposite bank before it plunged him over the hundred-foot waterfall into the Loch of the Long Boats and out to sea.

When the river swept him around a curve, he swam much harder for the distant shore. His pursuers could not move as fast as the water did. And, if anyone was daft enough to jump in after him, he would see the fool coming. He also knew, though, that if he mistimed his own efforts, the sea gods would claim him.

Minutes later, nearing the shore and battered by unseen rocks beneath the surface, he dragged himself out and lay gasping in unfriendly shrubbery to catch his breath. Then, creeping through the shrubs, he prayed that the hilt of the sword still strapped across his back would look like a branch if anyone saw it moving. As fast as he dared, he made his way to the shelter of the trees and back up the river glen.

He heard only the water's roar. Then, as that thought ended, he heard the wolf bay again, a she-wolf by its cry. Finding a path of sorts, he increased his pace.

The usual fisherman's trail lay underwater. So this was a deer trail or a new one to the river from Malcolm the sheepherder's cottage. In any event, the warrior's finely honed sense of direction told him that the cottage stood not far away.

He soon reached the clearing, where he saw a pack of wolves gathered close around the spear. The weapon with its precious burden had landed perfectly.

The wolves' heads turned as one at his approach, their teeth viciously bared.

He halted, terror for his child again clutching his throat. When the leader lowered to a crouch and crept slowly toward him, he could almost hear its growl. The others watched, their narrowed eyes gleaming reddish in the pale moonlight.

The warrior stood still. Hearing a faint sound above the river's rushing roar, he recognized it for his daughter's wail of hunger... or pain.

It stopped as suddenly as it had begun.

The lead wolf stopped, too, still in its threatening crouch, ready to spring.

The warrior drew his sword and took a step forward, mentally daring the beast to charge him. He had counted a half-dozen in the pack. But now he saw other dark, beastly shadows moving through the trees behind them, too many to count and far too many to kill before the pack would take him down.

The lead wolf, unmoving, bared its teeth again.

The man stood watching it, sword ready, long enough for the icy chill of his wet clothing to make him shiver.

Then, abruptly, the wolf rose, turned away, and vanished into the forest.

The others followed.

The baby remained silent.

Chapter 1

Tùr Meiloach, Scotland, mid-February 1425

Dree, what's amiss?" fifteen-year-old Muriella Mac-Farlan demanded as she stopped her spinning wheel and pushed an errant strand of flaxen hair off her face.

Tawny-haired Andrena, now six months into her nineteenth year, had stiffened on her stool near the fireplace in the ladies' solar. Dark blue eyes narrowed, head atilt, listening but with every sense alert, Andrena remained silent as she set aside the mending she loathed.

"Dree?"

Standing, holding a finger up to command silence, Andrena moved with her usual athletic grace to the south-facing window, its shutters open to let in fresh, sun-warmed afternoon air that was especially welcome after the previous night's fierce storm. She could see over the barmkin wall to the steep, forested hillside below and others rolling beyond it to the declivity through which the river marking their south boundary plunged into the Loch of the Long Boats and on out to the sea.

When Muriella drew breath to speak again, the third person in the room, their seventeen-year-old sister,

Lachina, said quietly, "Murie, dearling, possess your curiosity in silence for once. When Dree knows what is amiss, she will tell us."

After the briefest of pauses, and not much to Andrena's surprise, Lachina added, "*Is* someone approaching the tower, Dree?"

"I don't know, Lina. But the birds seem distressed. I think someone has entered our south woods—a stranger—nay, more than one."

"Can you see who they are?" Muriella demanded. Resting her spindle in its cradle, she moved to stand beside Andrena at the window.

"I cannot see such a distance or through trees," Andrena said. "But it must be more than one person and likely fewer than four. You see how the hawks soar in a tight circle yonder. Such behavior is odd even for goshawks. Forbye, if you look higher, you'll see an osprey above them. I'm going out to have a look."

In the same quiet way that she had spoken to Muriella, Lachina said, "The woods will be damp after such a furious storm, Dree. Mayhap you should tell our lord father what you suspect, or Malcolm Wylie."

"What would you have me tell them?" Andrena asked with a wry smile. "Would either of them send men out to search for intruders merely because I say the birds are unsettled?"

Lina grimaced. They had had such discussions before, and both of them knew the answer to the question. Andrew Dubh MacFarlan would trust his men to stop intruders. And his steward, Malcolm Wylie, would look longsuffering and declare that no one could possibly be there. By the time either decided, for the sake of peace, to send men out to look, there would *be* no one. Andrena had suggested once that their men had made more noise than the intruders did. But her father had replied only that if that was so, her intruders had fled, which was the best outcome.

"I'm going out," Andrena said again.

"Surely, men on the wall will see anyone coming," Muriella said, peering into the distance. "Both of our boundary rivers are in full spate now, Dree. No one can cross them. And if anyone were approaching elsewhere, watchers would blow the alarm. In troth, I think those birds are soaring just as they always do."

"They are perturbed," Andrena said. "I shan't be long."

Her sisters exchanged a look. But although she noted the exchange, she did not comment. She knew that neither one would insist on going with her.

Instinct that she rarely ignored urged her to make what speed she could without drawing undue attention to herself. Therefore, she hurried down the service stairs, deciding not to change from her green tunic and skirt into the deerskin breeks and jack that she favored for her solitary rambles. It occurred to her that she would have no excuse, having announced that strangers had entered the woods, to say that she had not thought anyone outside the family would see her in the boyish garb.

Andrew did not care what his daughters wore. But he did care when one of them distressed their mother, who had declared breeks on females to be shameful. Moreover, the mossy green dress would blend well with woodland shrubbery.

From a rack by the postern door, Andrena took her favorite cream-colored wool cap and twisted her tawny plaits up inside it. Then she donned the gray wool shawl hanging beside it and took down the dirk that hung by its belt under the shawl.

Fastening the belt so that the weapon lay concealed beneath the shawl, and leaving her untanned-hide boots where they lay on the floor, she went outside barefoot and crossed the yard to the narrow postern gate.

Four of the dogs, anticipating a walk, sprang up and ran to meet her.

Catching two by their collars, she said to the wiry red-headed lad eyeing her as he raked wood chips near the gate, "You must keep them in for now, Pluff. If anyone should ask for me, I'm going for a walk. But I don't want to take the dogs."

"Aye, m'lady," the boy said with a gap-toothed grin. Setting aside the rake, he ordered the dogs back to their naps and unbolted the gate for her, adding, "Just gie a shout when ye come back and I'll let ye in."

Smiling her thanks, she went through the gateway and heard the heavy gate thud shut behind her and Pluff shooting the bolts. Looking skyward as she crossed the clearing between the barmkin and the woods, she saw that the circling birds had moved nearer. Whoever it was, was still two hills away but was definitely moving toward the tower.

Looking over her shoulder, she saw one of their men on the wall and waved.

He waved back.

Satisfied that her sisters and at least two of their people knew she was outside the wall, she hurried into the woods. She had her dirk and the wee pipe she always carried in the pocket that Lina had cunningly woven for it in the shawl.

Thanks to Andrew's teaching, Andrena was skillful with the dirk and, if necessary, could use the wee pipe to summon aid. Since she did not expect anyone in the woods to see her, she doubted that she'd need any help.

＞

He was out of breath from running. But he knew that in dashing away from his pursuers earlier, he had left evidence of his flight for a regrettable distance before he was far enough ahead of them to take precautions.

As it was, he needed to find cover and catch his breath. That his pursuers lacked dogs to track him was a rare boon from the ever fickle Fates.

He had been both careless and foolhardy, and it irked him. He had sensibly managed to keep his wool plaid with him, even as he swam, knowing he would need its warmth. Scaling the cliff from the stormy loch had been necessary, since he could not stay on the shore and in the rainy darkness he'd seen no safer way to go.

After reaching the top of the hurtling waterfall, sleeping for a time, and waking in foggy dawn twilight, it had come as a shock to find that he could not travel farther south without fording the damned river.

To be sure, he *had* seen this area from the water, including the distant sharp ridge of peaks beyond its cliffs and forested hills. The two great waterfalls had been full even then, but he had assumed he'd be able to cross the river somewhere.

However, it raged furiously down through its bed, tumbling over and around boulders and rocks in its path—too deep to ford, too wide and dangerous to swim.

He had followed it inland until he had seen and recognized the three men.

Now the fog had cleared, and the sun shone in a cloudy

sky. He was well away from the river, deep in ancient woods—a magnificent mixture of tall beeches, oaks, thickly growing conifers, and where it was dampest, spindly birches and willows. The woodsy scents filled him with a heady sense of freedom. But his pursuers were not far enough behind yet for safety.

Although he had not entered such dense woodland for nineteen long months, he had hunted from the time he could keep up with his lord father and knew that he retained his skills, had even heightened most of them. Quietly drawing deep breaths and releasing them, he forced himself to relax and bond with the forest while he listened and waited for its creatures to speak to him.

Thinking of those creatures and the fact that he had come ashore north of the waterfall, he was nearly sure that he must be in Tùr Meiloach woods. He had heard men warn that the place was rife with danger, either haunted or bewitched. Some swore that it was a sanctuary for true MacFarlans, others that it was a taste of hell for unwary strangers. Wondering which it was would do him no good now, though.

It occurred to him that although he had moved carefully and in near silence for the past quarter-hour, the denizens of the forest remained remarkably still. He had not listened for them earlier, knowing that the din of the river would cover any sound they made and being more concerned about eluding his pursuers.

As if it had intercepted his thoughts, a hawk shrieked above. Then an osprey replied with its shrill whistle, declaring the woods its territory. It would, he thought, have better luck taking fish from the nearby Loch of the Long Boats and should leave the woods to the hawks, which were better-suited for hunting in dense foliage.

All thought ceased then, because he sensed someone in the woods north of him moving as silently as he did. Had one of the devils got round him? Was one north of him now and the other two south? He had seen only three men earlier on the far side of the devilish river. They had swung across it on a rope tied to a high branch of an ancient beech rooted in what looked from a distance like solid rock.

The three carried swords and dirks. When he'd recognized them as Pharlain's men, he knew they were seeking him.

A soughing of leaves above drew his glance to a female goshawk on a high branch. The canopy above her was thick. But he knew that hawks, even big ones like the gos, with two-foot wingspans, were perfectly at home in the Highland woods. He had occasionally delighted in watching one take prey by flying at speed between trees that left insufficient room for it. To fit through, the bird seemed to fold itself, wings and body, into a thinly compressed, arrowlike shape and to do it without missing a single sweeping beat.

The hawk above him fixed a fierce yellow eye on him. Then, as if that glance were all it required, it opened its wings and swooped down and away.

He eyed the gos's erstwhile perch. It was high, but in the dense canopy above it a man might rest unseen for hours. A rustle of disturbed shrubbery south of him, accompanied by a man's muttered curse, made the decision easy. He paused only to conceal his plaid in the shrubbery.

⌒

Andrena heard the curse, too, and froze in place to listen. She had sensed the trespassers' approach more easily with each step, because the woods were her home, their every sound familiar. She had noted the eerie silence, had seen the goshawk as it shot through the trees in front of her without making a sound.

The hawk's presence might have frightened nearby small creatures to silence. But it would not account for the unusual quiet of the forest at large. It seemed to hold its communal breath, to be waiting as she was for the intruders to reveal their nature.

So still was it that in the distance to her right and far below, she could hear waves of the loch, unsettled from the storm, hushing against the rockbound shore.

The strangers were much closer.

Sound traveled farther through woodland than most people realized, and her ears were deer-sharp. The intruders were a score of yards away, perhaps more, but an effortless bowshot in the open. She would soon see them.

Noting movement in shrubbery near the ground, she saw that at least one creature had managed to follow her from the tower. Lina's orange cat eyed her curiously through slender branches sprouting new leaves.

Without a sound, the cat glided off ahead, doubtless prowling for its supper.

Andrena moved on, too. She heard no noises specific enough to identify but she knew now that there were at least two or three men. Careful to stay hidden but watchful, she also knew that her sweeping gaze would detect any movement.

A large shadow passed between two large-trunked beeches ahead to her left.

Going still, she watched as a stranger stepped between the two trees. Two others followed. All three wore saffron tunics, kilted plaids of dull red and green, swords slung across their backs, and dirks at their belts.

So much, Andrena thought, for Murie's certainty—and their father's—that no one could ford the wild river south of their tower without plunging into the loch and out with the tide. Either the three men had forded it or they'd found other means of trespassing onto Andrew's land without his or his men's knowledge.

~

The man in the tree suppressed a curse when he saw the lass. Who the devil, he wondered, would be daft enough to let a girl wander out alone in such dangerous times? His eyes narrowed as she carefully shifted her shawl and he saw the long dirk in its sheath suspended from her narrow leather girdle.

If she had an ounce of wit she would at least try to keep it hidden, because if the louts searching for him saw it, and they would, they might kill her just to teach her a lesson.

Knowing that they might sense *his* presence as easily as he had sensed hers, he decided that he ought to do what he could to prevent that. Fixing his gaze on a leaf midway between the three men, now only five or six yards away, and the girl moving toward them—ten paces from his tree—he let his mind go blank.

The last thing he wanted was for anyone to sense him watching them.

~

The men had moved much faster than Andrena had expected, stirring irritation with herself as well as with them. Having expected to get her first look at them from the next rise, she realized now that she had taken longer than she had intended. In truth, she had paid more heed to the forest creatures' silence than to its most likely cause, that the men were nearer than she had judged them to be.

Lina would say, and rightly, that having formed an image in her mind of what would happen, Dree had let her thoughts wander and, thus, had failed to think through all the possibilities of what *might* happen before coming out to investigate.

Hoping that Lina would not learn what had happened, Andrena considered what to do next. She was close enough to the tower for people on its ramparts and wall to hear her pipe if she blew it, so she slipped it out of its pocket into her hand.

The hawks still lingered nearby, as well.

It occurred to her that she would offer help without hesitation had the men simply been storm-tossed onto the shore and missed their way. Perhaps if she . . .

What the devil was she doing now?

He tensed as he watched her step out into the path of his three pursuers. At least now he knew he need worry no longer about their sensing *his* presence. The louts had seen her, and the Fates knew that she was stunning enough, even with that ridiculous boy's cap covering her hair, to stop most healthy men in their tracks.

She walked with unusual grace on the uneven forest floor and did so without glancing at her feet. Her posture was regal, and the soft-looking gray shawl did little to hide a curvaceous, womanly body.

Hearing a scrabbling on the bark below, he glanced

down and saw her absurd cat clawing its way up the tree toward him. He could even hear it purring when by rights it should be flying, claws out, at the villains approaching its mistress.

"Forgive me, good sirs," the lass said in a clear, confident tone, her voice as warm and smooth as honey. "Doubtless, you have lost your way and entered our woods unaware of whose they are. I fear that my father, the laird, requires that men present themselves at Tùr Meiloach before trespassing hereabouts."

"Does he now, lassie?" the tallest of the louts said, leering at her. "And how might we reach yon tower without stepping on your father, the *laird's,* land?"

"We be searching for an escaped prisoner, mistress," the second man, dark-haired and midsized, said sternly. "Ye shouldna be out here alone like this."

"I'll see her tae safety," the tall one said. "Come along, lass. I dinna think ye belong tae the laird at all. A laird's daughter wouldna wander about all by herself. Doubtless, when we tell him ye've been pretending tae be his daughter, ye'll find yourself in the suds. But I'll no tell him if ye plead kindly wi' me."

"I would willingly direct you to the tower," she said. "It lies—" Breaking off when he grabbed her right arm, she stiffened and said icily, "Let go of me."

"Nay, then, I'll ha'—"

Putting two fingers of her other hand to her lips, she whistled loudly.

"Here now, what the—"

A sparrow hawk flew from a nearby tree right at his face, flapping its wings wildly and shrieking an angry *kek-kek-kek* as it did.

With a cry, the man flung up an arm in defense. Shearing away at the last second, the bird swooped around and struck again. Flinging up both arms this time, the lout released the young woman, who stepped away from him.

The cat had reached the branch on which the hunted man lay stretched. It walked up his body to peer over his right shoulder into his face, still purring.

Short of grabbing it and dropping it on one of the men below, he could do nothing useful. So he ignored it.

Had he had his sword with him or even the lass's dirk, he might have dropped in on the conversation. As it was, he hoped they would realize from her demeanor that she was as noble as she claimed to be and were wondering, as he did, why men were not already rushing noisily to her aid, summoned by her whistling.

He had barely finished the thought when three goshawks arrived silently, all much larger than the sparrow hawk. The lout already intimidated by the small hawk took off running, back the way he had come. The other two tried to shoo the birds away. But the birds screamed then as if they were new parents and the men had disturbed their young.

"Our hawks are exceedingly territorial, I fear," the lass said matter-of-factly.

$\sim$

"Call them off, ye devilish witch!" the tall man yelled at Andrena while flapping his arms as wildly as the birds flapped their wings. Since he was also trying to protect his eyes with his hands, his flailing elbows had little effect.

"They are scarcely *my* birds, sir," she replied, elevating him with that single word far above his deserved station in life. "They just know that I belong here and you do not. Had I brought my dogs, they would act in a similar way, as I am sure your dogs do when someone threatens you. I cannot call them off. But if you two follow your friend back to where you came from, they *may* stop attacking you."

The hawks, acting more helpfully than hawks usually did, continued flying at the two despite their waving and shouts. One of the men reached for his sword.

"Don't touch that weapon if you value your life," she said, raising the wee pipe, still in her right hand, to her lips. "If I blow this pipe, our men-at-arms will come. So I should warn you that my father wields the power of the pit and gallows. Our hanging tree stands right outside our gate, and he will not hesitate..."

The man was staring beyond her, his mouth agape.

Glancing over a shoulder, she saw that with the racket the hawks had made, she had failed to hear the osprey arrive. The huge bird perched nearby, looking even more immense when it tensed, puffed its feathers, and glowered at the intruders.

Andrena said, "She has much worse manners than the others. So do *not* challenge her."

"We're a-going," the dark-haired one said. "But tell your father that if he finds our prisoner, he must send him back tae the laird in irons."

"I shall give him your message. But you must tell me who your laird is. I cannot pluck such information from your mind."

"Aye, well, I thought ye'd ken who we be. The missing chap be one o' Pharlain's galley slaves, taken in fair capture whilst raiding."

"Then doubtless my father will do as you wish," Andrena said mendaciously. Andrew would more likely help the man on his way.

The osprey, balefully eyeing the intruders, spread its wings and twitched its talons menacingly.

Abruptly, the men turned and followed their erstwhile companion.

The goshawks, one of the few hawk species that will hunt together and now a veritable flock, swooped after them.

Andrena stood for a time, listening, to be sure they were well on their way. Then, hearing a loud purr at her feet, she looked down and saw the orange cat. It walked across her bare feet, rubbing against her shins.

"Where did you spring from this time?" she asked.

The cat blinked, then continued around her and back toward the tower.

Turning to follow it, Andrena found herself face-to-muscular-chest with a huge, broad-shouldered, shaggy-bearded, half naked stranger. He wore a ragged, thigh-length, saffron-colored sark, the ripped left shoulder of which revealed a bad abrasion and bruising that extended along his upper arm.

Startled nearly out of her wits, she snapped, "Where did you . . . ? That is, I never even knew that you were—"

"Hush, lass, they may still be near enough to hear you." His voice was deeper than her father's, and mellow, unlike any she might imagine coming from a villain.

"They are halfway across yon hills to the river by now," she said.

"They may be, aye. But I want to be sure."

"Then follow them. But how did you get so close to me, especially as big as you are? Faith, you're a giant, and

I can always—" Breaking off, aware that she was talking too much, she said, "You must be their missing prisoner, aye?"

His twinkling gaze met her frowning one. "They would identify me as such, aye. But I disapprove of slavery. So I don't see the matter as they do."

"I suppose not. But—" Breaking off when she saw how steadily he gazed at her, she eyed him askance. "Are you *not* going to follow them, then?"

"Nay, for I cannot leave a wee lassock like yourself out here alone. I'll see you safely to your gate first."

"Thank you, but I don't want or need your escort," she said firmly.

"Aye, well, you need not look so displeased by the notion," he said. A wistful smile peeked through his unkempt beard as through a shaggy hedge. "Unless you fear that your da will hang me for escaping," he added.

"He will not do that. He feels no love for Parlan Pharlain."

"Then why do you hesitate to go home? Art afraid he'll punish you for coming out alone and learning how dangerous that can be?"

"He won't do that, either. By my troth, although he will not hang you, you are the one who should be leery of him."

"Why should I?"

"Because, since you managed to escape from Cousin Parlan and must therefore be Parlan's enemy, I fear that Father will insist that you marry me."

Chapter 2 _____

Mag Galbraith smiled. He couldn't help it.

She was gazing up at him, looking into his eyes, and hers were such a dark blue that they looked black. Her long, thick lashes were black, too, but her delicately arched brows were deep golden brown. They knitted together when she said, "You do not believe me, but you should. My father can be most persuasive."

"We'll talk as we walk," he said, moving to retrieve his plaid from where he had hidden it. As he slung the length of still damp fabric over his injured shoulder, he added, "Art sure your devilish birds will continue to harry those louts away?"

"Most likely," she said. "We'll tell our lads on the wall about them, though, lest they try to sneak back. I was surprised they had got so close...and you, too."

"I did see that I'd startled you."

"And are amused to have done so," she replied. "But where were you hiding? I thought no one but those men had entered our woods."

"Dense woodland conceals much and is always dangerous," he said, indicating that she should lead the way.

"Your father should not let you wander here alone. One can never know when one might encounter menace."

"I usually do know when others are near me," she said, turning obediently back the way she had come. "I can sense danger, too."

"'Tis true that hunters, woodsmen, and warriors can sense such things," he said as he followed her along a nearly indiscernible path. "Their fathers and commanders train them to use all of their senses and to keep them well honed. Forbye, you are neither woodsman nor warrior."

"I do not know what that has to do with using one's senses. My father trained me just as yours must have trained you. He encourages me to roam our woods, to know every rock and rill, and to keep a close watch for danger."

"Next you will say he encourages you to carry that dirk of yours."

"Aye, sure, he does," she replied. Glancing back at him, she added, "Why should he not when he gave it to me himself?"

"The man must be mad."

"Mayhap you will tell him so," she said with an edge to her voice. "I would not advise such a course, because his temper is uncertain at the best of times. It will be bad enough when we tell him that three of Parlan's men—nay, for you must count as a fourth, must you not? So *four* men successfully invaded our woods. I know I said that he would not be wroth with you—"

"Because he'll want me to marry you, aye," he said, smiling again.

As he did, he realized that it was unusual for him to smile twice in the space of less than a few minutes.

He could not remember a time during the past nineteen months when he had smiled at all.

⁓

Despite the smile and the engaging twinkle in his light brown eyes, Andrena told herself that he was just another man like any other. Wrinkling her nose at the smell of wet wool, she looked back again to say, "You look as if you've been in a fight, and, by the smell of that thing you carry, it is soaked through with sea water."

"This *thing* is my plaid," he said, hefting it slightly off his otherwise bare and exceedingly muscular but badly scraped shoulder. "I hear water gurgling, though, so there must be a burn nearby where I can rinse the brine out of it."

"It will have to be stretched to dry if it is to cover you afterward," she said. "How did it get so wet?"

"I had it on over my sark when I dove into the loch last night from your friend Pharlain's galley," he said.

"He is *not* my friend, and you cannot have swum with a plaid wrapped round you. However, if you swam ashore below our cliffs, I can understand why you look so battered and why that sark is in tatters. Some of those scrapes are bleeding and need attention, especially the one from your left shoulder down your arm."

"The sark was ragged before I dove in, but I'll admit it is more so now."

"I wish you'd tell me who you are and how and why you came here."

"Since we are apparently going to be married..."

When he paused pointedly and with another twinkle, she gave him the look that could usually silence even her sister Muriella. But he met it without a blink. Except for his persistent, rather annoying tendency to let his amusement show, the man's thoughts failed to reveal themselves in either his voice or expression.

"'Tis good that the thought of marrying me amuses you," she said. "I could enjoy it more, though, if I thought such amusement might last beyond your discovery that I am right about my father. Are you going to tell me who you are?"

"My family and close friends call me Mag," he said. "Pharlain and most others call me Magnus Mòr."

"Meaning 'Big Magnus' or 'Magnus the Mountain,' I expect, rather than that you have a son, a nephew, or a younger cousin who shares your name."

"'Tis the first one," he said. "I have nae bairns, and I doubt that any kinsman also bears my name. But how did you guess that?"

"From the way you said it. Also, you *are* gey big. The top of my head barely reaches your armpit. Forbye, had you been father or uncle to a Magnus named *for* you, you'd have said Magnus Mòr MacFarlan. But you are not a MacFarlan, are you?"

"Do you know every MacFarlan?"

"I do not, but I do know that you are not one of ours. And since you were a galley slave of Parlan's . . . How did you come to be his prisoner?"

"By being in the wrong place at the wrong time," he said.

"Aye, sure, that explains it," she said dryly.

⟨⟩

His words were true enough, Mag thought, but he did not want to explain himself further . . . not yet. "How far is it from here to your tower?" he asked.

"How do *you* know it is a tower?"

"You said the word twice whilst you were speaking to those louts."

"Twice? Faith, do you count such things? Nay, do not answer that. Instead, tell me where you were that you could so easily hear all I said."

"I was above your head in the beech tree," he said. "With your cat."

"That cat is my sister Lachina's, not mine," she said. "Since I am sure you did not carry him up there with you, he must have followed you."

"Aye, and stretched himself across my shoulders, purring, to watch you with the louts," he said, taking advantage of the widening path to walk beside her.

Her expression lightened in response to the comment. But he had hoped to see her smile, and she did not.

Instead, she said, "'Tis unusual behavior for him, especially with a stranger. And you still have not told me much about yourself."

"Nay, I have not," he agreed. "Nor have you told me *your* name."

She cocked her head, eyeing him rather than watching where she walked, which was a daft thing to do, he thought. She seemed to be assessing him, so he prepared himself to catch her if she tripped and waited for it to happen. But she walked as confidently as if her feet knew every pebble and declivity along the way.

"I am Andrena MacFarlan," she said. "Andrew Dubh MacFarlan is my father. You know who *he* is, do you not?"

"I thought you must be kin to Andrew Dubh. I ken fine that Pharlain believes him to be his archenemy. In troth, though, I've heard nowt of Andrew's making mischief against Pharlain."

"Nay, 'tis Parlan who makes mischief against us. He killed my brothers and stole my father's land years ago. Then he declared himself chief of all MacFarlans. Before, he was just my father's cousin Parlan MacFarlan. Afterwards, he declared himself a direct descendant of the original Pharlain and entitled to call himself so."

"Not *Mac*Pharlain, though, as would be proper for such a descendant?"

"Nay, and Parlan's is not the true male line. He is my father's cousin, no more. Our mutual ancestor, the original Pharlain, was a grandson of the third Earl of Lennox and his countess, who is also an ancestor of ours. Their son and heir signed a charter as MacFarlan, and so our name has remained. The rest is Cousin Parlan's way of making himself more important. It also justifies, in his own mind, his usurpation of my father's lands and chiefdom by base treachery and murder."

"I believe you," he said.

"Do you truly believe me, or do you say so just because you dislike Parlan?"

⁓

Andrena glanced up at him as she asked the question and eyed him more narrowly when he did not answer her. He continued to look straight ahead but said after a time, "I meant what I said, my lady. I will admit, though, that my dislike of Pharlain may have encouraged my belief in all that you say."

"That is honest, at all events."

"Aye, and I should also tell you that I do know more

about this place and its people than I've led you to believe."

"Then you were gey brave to enter these woods and come so far," she said. "But why did you lead me to believe otherwise?"

"Sithee, I wanted to hear what you would say about your father and Pharlain. I've heard several versions of what took place at Arrochar two decades ago, but each new version seemed more mythical than the previous one."

"Why 'mythical'?"

"You do know the meaning of the word, do you not?"

"Aye, sure; it implies either a fanciful account of the facts or a purely imaginary tale," she said. It occurred to her that she might normally take offense at such a question. That she had not done so was doubtless a result of his nearly stoical nature. She believed he had asked the question only because he wanted to be sure that she'd understood him. Other men she knew would have asked it in a tone indicating certainty that she did *not* know.

He continued to walk silently beside her. But she was curious to know more about him and what he was thinking. Trying to keep her voice as neutral as his had been, she said, "Did you think that *we* were figures of myth?"

"You will admit, I think, that Tùr Meiloach has a mythlike reputation. Its very name means a small tower guarded by giants. Forbye, 'tis said to be dangerous, even deadly, to trespass here. Men swear that birds and other beasts of the forest are wilder and more vicious here than elsewhere and that your bogs reach out to grab unwary strangers and drag them under. They say that your terrain is replete with rivers too wild to ford—a fact that, like your birds, I saw for myself. But they also speak of deep chasms with walls that crumble at a man's touch and bury him. I've even heard that whole armies have vanished here."

"Then why did you come?"

"It was not by intent," he admitted. "I thought the galley was still far enough south of here for me to make landfall in Colquhoun territory. But the storm had carried us farther north than I knew. In the pitch darkness, with waves battering me as I swam, it was hard to tell where I was."

"Are you a Colquhoun, then?" She knew any number of Colquhouns, who were their nearest neighbors to the south.

"Nay, I'm not." His gaze met hers.

"Is your home near them?"

"Aye, in places, and near MacFarlans, too. I'm a Galbraith. But let us stop now before we ford yon burn. I want to rinse out my plaid and tend my scrapes."

She watched him stride to the gurgling burn and drop to a knee beside it. She knew who the Galbraiths were. But, despite their being neighbors of a sort, she had never met one before. Their lands lay over the mountains, along Loch Lomond and south of the MacFarlan land there. The Galbraiths also owned an island castle in the loch, near the ancient sanctuary of Luss, where many MacFarlans lay buried.

"I have heard my father speak of Arthur, Laird of Galbraith."

"He is my father," Mag said, glancing back over his shoulder as he pressed his plaid into the stream with one hand.

"Then your family lives on Inch Galbraith and in Glen Fruin," she said.

"We have a tower on the inch, the land on west Lomondside, and more on east Lomondside in Strathendrick," he replied as he switched the plaid to his left hand so he could splash water on his injured shoulder with his right. Still trailing the garment in the water, he knelt to duck his head in the icy stream. Then, shaking the water from hair and beard, he slicked his hair down and combed it with his fingers.

"That's got most of the salt out, I think," he said.

She could tell nothing from his voice or what little expression his beard let her see, so she said, "I thought the Laird of Galbraith was one of Parlan's allies."

"My lord father would say he is not. He would insist that he just follows the dictates of our liege lord, the Earl of Lennox."

"Aye, sure, for that is what Parlan says, too, and other Loch Lomond lairds, according to my father. And, although the King ordered Lennox's arrest two months ago, Lennox is still allied with his good-son, Murdoch Stewart, and Murdoch's two scurrilous elder sons. But if Parlan took you prisoner, you must have been in some sort of fray against him. Did you fight against your father, too?"

"We are not going to discuss politics or my activities of nearly two years ago," he said, taking his plaid from the burn as he stood and shaking it out.

"Do you want help wringing that dry?" she asked.

He smiled again. Truly, he had a charming smile. One wanted to smile back at him, even if one had no idea what he might be thinking.

" 'Tis a kind offer," he said. "But I am accustomed to doing it myself."

As he spoke, he held the plaid high, letting its rectangular length drape nearly to the ground. Gathering the fullness of it into his right hand below where he held it at the top in his left, he pulled his right fist slowly but steadily downward, forcing water from the length of wool in a veritable cascade.

With an envious sigh, Andrena said, "I wish I could strip water from a sheet or a garment as easily as that."

"Aye, well, I've had much practice."

"If you rowed a galley up the loch in last night's storm, you must have had to row against the wind," she said. "And if you swam ashore and climbed one of our cliffs, you must have been exhausted afterward."

"I was, and battered, too, as you see. Your coast is as unfriendly as men claim it is. I did sleep, though, after I reached the top."

"Good sakes, how could you sleep out in that storm as you were?"

"I wrapped myself in my plaid and slept under a rocky outcropping with thick shrubbery betwixt me and the worst of the storm."

"In a wet plaid?"

He raised his eyebrows. "Lass, men sleep out in wet plaids all the time. On cold nights especially. Wet wool retains a body's warmth better than dry wool does."

She was skeptical about that. But something else concerned her more. "Your pursuers got here the same way you did, did they not? What if they'd found you?"

"They swam ashore but not until after dawn. And they

landed on Colquhoun's side of yon great waterfall. Doubtless they'd expected me to make for home."

"Then how did they cross to this side?"

"I saw them swing across it on a rope from a tree limb. Sithee, I'd had to wait until dawn myself to see well enough to travel. I do respect the tales I've heard, mythical or not—and even more so now that I've seen those birds of yours."

"They swung across it on a *rope*?"

"Aye, and perforce left it attached to its tree. So they cannot get back without following the river to its headwaters, unless there is another way across."

There was, of course, but she was not about to reveal it to him. Nor would the Colquhouns tell Parlan's men about it. In fact, if the Colquhouns caught Parlan's men, those men would sorely regret trespassing on Colquhoun land.

"How much farther is it now?" Magnus Mòr asked.

"Not far. As for those men, they will have to climb down one of the cliffs."

"I don't envy them that endeavor. Climbing down a cliff is much harder than climbing up one, even by daylight."

"Parlan's galley will not wait long for them either," she said. "The Colquhouns take strong exception to unwelcome boats lingering in their waters."

"They are friendly enough to Pharlain, lass—or Parlan, as you call him. I have seen that for myself."

"Aye, sure, when Parlan is not threatening them. But to send men ashore on Colquhoun land without permission and wait offshore to pick them up again? With or without a prisoner, that would not sit well with the Laird of

Colquhoun. And, unlike most other lairds hereabouts, he has never answered to the Earl of Lennox."

"Perhaps not, but he does not go out of his way to annoy Lennox, either."

She did not reply, for she was crossing the burn. Moreover, she knew that what he said about Colquhoun was true.

⁓

Mag watched her lift her kilted-up skirts higher to cross the burn, stepping from rock to rock with the same easy confidence that she had shown all along. She had lovely feet, trim ankles, and shapely calves.

She still wore the silly cream-colored cap, and he wished she would take it off. He wanted to know if her hair matched her eyebrows or was lighter. He wondered, too, about her willingness to discuss matters concerning men whom he doubted she had ever met. Most women had no interest in such matters, nor—in his opinion—should they have. But she was unlike any woman he had ever known.

His sisters were not at all like her. Of course, all three were married by now unless Lizzie, the youngest, had turned up her nose at the man their father had chosen for her. She was a contrary lass but a charming one, and she usually got away with her contrariness.

"You can see our tower now," the lass said.

He had been enjoying the way her backside twitched from side to side as she strode ahead of him. Looking up now, he saw the brownish-gray stone tower ahead, framed in an opening between trees. A deep clearing separated the tower's barmkin wall from the woods. He saw, too, that men on the wall walk had seen them. They held bows at the ready, arrows nocked to drawn bowstrings.

"Tell them to stand down," he said just loudly enough for her to hear him. "I come in peace and bear no weapons, as you have seen."

"I do not control those men any more than I controlled the birds," she said. "My father is too canny to allow his guards to lay down their arms merely because someone outside the wall bids them do so. Even if it is one of his daughters," she added. "Someone inside will tell them that no danger threatens."

He opened his mouth to ask how anyone inside could know such a thing. As he did, the narrow gate opened and a maiden with long, flaxen plaits and eyes that he could see were light blue, even at that distance, hurried out, crying, "Dree, you've been gone for an age. We've been watching the birds and decided to go and find you. But who is this? Faith, he looks like one of the giants that guard Tùr Meiloach."

"He is called Magnus Mòr," Andrena said. "This is my sister Muriella, sir."

"But you are injured!" the lady Muriella exclaimed. "How came that about, sir? Did the birds attack you? Prithee, tell me what happened!"

"Murie, dearling, do let Andrena and her companion enter."

He had been staring at the flaxen-haired lass, only faintly aware that another young woman had followed her through the gateway. The new one's voice was lower, more dignified, and her gray tunic and skirt suited her calm demeanor. Her eyes were an intriguing bluish-gray hazel. Looking from one to another and then to the lady

Andrena, he could see the strong family resemblance. Andrena was the tallest, the lady Muriella the shortest of the three.

"Lina, this is Magnus Mòr Galbraith," Andrena said. "This is my sister Lachina, sir." To the others, she added, "Parlan has been holding Magnus Mòr prisoner as a galley slave. He escaped last night during the storm."

"But surely, one man seeking sanctuary did not distress those birds," Muriella said. "We saw them, Dree, and we both felt—" Glancing at Mag, she broke off and looked sheepishly at Andrena. "As I said, we decided to meet you."

"Aye, but do let us go inside, Murie. As you have noted, our guest is not at his best and will doubtless be grateful for food and drink. Go and ask Malcolm to arrange it, will you? And tell him, too, that three of Parlan's men were after him. I must find something to make him more presentable before Father sees him."

"Very well," Muriella said. "But do not talk about anything important until I return. I want to hear everything that happened."

"Indeed, my lady," Mag said, "there is no reason to fuss, because—"

"If you mean to suggest that you should try to make your way home without sustenance or weapons," Andrena interjected, "pray put that notion out of your head. My father does not let strangers roam our land at will. You must ask his permission if you want to cross it safely."

"Then take me to him, if you please," he said, following her through the gateway. The men on the wall had returned to their duties, evidently having decided to accept the lasses' approval of him without question.

"If you truly want to see Father, looking like a scruffy

poacher, I will take you to him," she said. "But you'd do better to eat and furbish yourself up a bit first."

"I have salve to put on your scrapes, sir," the lady Lachina said. "Also, that plaid is wet and your sark is badly torn. I can improve them, as well."

"I'd be grateful, my lady," he said, realizing that it would be daft to avoid Andrew Dubh and dafter yet to present himself looking like something their wretched cat had dragged out of a bush.

⁓

Andrena hoped that Magnus had decided to be sensible. But as had been the case from the moment she'd found him blocking her path, she could tell nothing about his thoughts or feelings. She was more accustomed to men— and women, too—who wore their feelings on their faces and in their voices.

Leading the way into the tower with Magnus and Lina following her, she wondered what he had made of Murie's comments.

She had little time to ponder such thoughts, though, because when they reached the main stairway, Lina said, "Let us go to the solar, Dree. That sark I mended for Malcolm's Peter still sits in my mending basket. Peter is large enough, although not as tall as Magnus Mòr. Moreover, Peter has two other sarks, so he will not mind if Magnus wears his until I can provide Magnus with one of his own."

Nodding, Andrena led the way up the winding stairway to the second landing above the great hall. Two rooms opened from the landing. One was their parents' bedchamber, the other the ladies' solar.

Inside the solar, Lina went to her usual place and

opened the woven-willow kist that sat beside her stool. "Here it is," she said, taking out a large, gray tunic. "Before you put it on, sir, scoop some of the salve from this pot and smear it on the worst of your scrapes. It will speed their healing."

Andrena watched with amusement as Magnus warily took the wee pot and lifted the lid to sniff its contents.

Murie, entering as he did so, laughed and said, "It won't poison you, sir. Lina's potions always do exactly what she says they will do."

"I'm sure they do," he said. "But, I must also hope that the contents will not permanently stain this borrowed sark."

"Any stain will wash out," Lina said. "I just hope that Peter's sark is long enough to protect your modesty, sir."

"I haven't got much left to me these days, my lady. I would be grateful, though, if you have a place where I may see for myself if it will do."

"Stay here," Andrena said. "We'll go onto the landing and return when you declare yourself properly clad."

"Wait," Lina said, diving into another kist. "Try this, as well, sir. It should be long enough to wrap round yourself and kilt up in the usual way."

The length of gray and cream-colored fabric she held out to him was one that Andrena knew Lina had intended to make into a dress for herself. But Lina's offering it was no surprise. Nor would it trouble her to have done so. She enjoyed weaving and sewing and was always thinking of new patterns to create. She and Murie talked often of possible dyes for the threads and yarns that Murie spun and Lina wove into fabrics and stitched into garments. Both were highly skilled.

Visibly stunned by Lina's kindness, Magnus accepted

the length of wool fabric that she held out to him, and the sisters went out to the landing. Shutting the door, they stood quietly until he bade them enter again.

When they did, Andrena saw that the sark was long enough, barely, and that he had arranged the gray and white plaid and kilted it up with his belt.

"This wool is exceedingly soft," he said, stroking it.

"We have our own sheep and do our own carding," Andrena explained. "Lina is particular and will not accept wool that does not feel right to her. That length of fabric is lambs wool."

"I thank you for lending it, my lady. I'll see that it gets better treatment than my last one did."

"If you are ready now, sir," Andrena said, "I'll take you to my lord father."

"I am, aye," he said.

"He'll be in his chamber," she said. "It lies just downstairs."

She led the way and rapped on a door at the next landing. Hearing her father's voice from within, she pushed the door open.

"We have a guest, sir," she announced as she entered the small room. A large rectangular table took up most of the space, and her father sat behind it with his book of accounts. "This is Magnus Mòr Galbraith," she said. "He has been a—"

"—a prisoner of Parlan's for this past year and a half," Andrew Dubh said, pushing back his stool and getting to his feet. "Come ye in, lad, and tell me all about yourself. By the size and look of ye, ye should have escaped that villain eighteen months ago. But afore ye explain yourself, tell me this: Are ye married?"

Chapter 3

Hesitating briefly at the threshold, Mag decided that for the moment, he would be wiser to ignore Andrew Mac-Farlan's provocative question than to answer it. Accordingly, keeping a wary eye on his host, he entered the chamber, saying, "It is an honor to meet you, my lord."

Despite MacFarlan's welcoming demeanor, Mag remained cautious, knowing that Andrew Dubh, in his prime, had been one of the Highlands' greatest warriors. He still looked fit and a decade younger than the fifty years he was surely nearing. His dark brown hair showed no hint of gray, and the only evident wrinkles were laugh lines at the outer corners of eyes that were as dark blue as the lady Andrena's.

Hoping that he faced a friend and not a foe, Mag assured himself that MacFarlan's greeting had not been a challenge, despite having had the ring of one. After all, his daughters had offered hospitality. That fact alone would prevent the laird's treating him badly. Highlanders extended hospitality as a matter of honor, offering it even to their worst enemies. He would be safe enough while he ate and slept under MacFarlan's roof. But that would not stop the man, if he were so inclined, from ordering him killed the minute he left Tùr Meiloach land.

"How came ye here to us?" MacFarlan asked.

Andrena said, "He escaped from one of Cousin Parlan's galleys during last night's storm, sir. He dove into the loch and came ashore below our cliffs."

"Did he, indeed?" her father said, beaming at her. "Then ye'll ken fine why I would talk privily with him. Forbye, your sisters will want to hear the whole tale from ye straightaway."

Meeting Andrena's gaze and reading the query in it, Mag gave a slight nod to show that he was content to be alone with her father. So obviously was she a lass who knew her own mind that he half-expected her to ask MacFarlan to let her stay. But she curtsied and left without another word, closing the door after her.

Andrew Dubh raised his thick eyebrows. "D'ye think she fears I'll eat ye, lad?"

"I doubt that, my lord. What I do think, because she said so herself, is that she suspects you will urge me to marry her."

"I see that ye be a plainspoken man," Andrew said with a chuckle. "Well, I be another m'self. I'll tell ye to your face that if ye be willing, I'd urge that very course. Ye're Arthur Galbraith's fourth-born son, are ye no?"

"I am, aye, sir, although only three of us remain now."

"Aye, 'tis true. I'd forgotten that your brother Will died in the fracas your lot had two years ago with Parlan, or Pharlain, as the traitor likes to call himself."

"Nineteen months ago, to be exact," Mag said.

Andrew's eyebrows rose again. "Ye say that with nae expression, lad. I'd expect ye to show bitterness, even fury, toward the villain who killed your brother."

"I don't like Pharlain, sir. But I have a more vital matter on which to expend my energy now. Also, I learned quickly as a prisoner that one is wiser to conceal one's emotions. Otherwise, one's captors will exploit them."

"Ye've gained wisdom then. That be nae bad thing for a man. Forbye, your father still has two other sons. But I'm thinking our Dree may no have told ye of the impediment for others that I've approached on her behalf, fathers and sons alike."

"She mentioned only that you seek a marriage for her."

"I thought so. Sithee, when I came to Tùr Meiloach, a number of me own lads followed, if not straightaway, then as soon as they'd taken Parlan's measure. Ye ken the man, so ye'd ken fine that he's nae one for a sensible man to trust."

"I'd never trust him. But tell me about this impediment of yours."

"'Tis just that I've only daughters now—that traitor, Parlan, having stolen Arrochar and murdered my three sons, not one of them yet of age to fight. So—"

"He tells everyone that you abandoned the place to him."

"Aye, sure, he does. And what else was I to do, with my sons already dead in a surprise attack by an army greater than mine and our wee Andrena a newborn babe in arms? I had a bolt hole, o' course—as any man of sense must in these perilous times. So my lady and I snatched up our babe and fled here to Tùr Meiloach, which has ever been a sacred and safe haven for true MacFarlans."

"As Pharlain tells the tale, he saw you plunge into the river, which swept you over the falls. He suggests that only the magic of wee folk or witches could have seen you to safety after that."

With a wink, Andrew said, "Aye, well, it was dark with but a sliver of a moon. He didna see all that he might have seen."

"I've not come this way before," Mag said. "From Inch Galbraith, the usual way to the Highlands is along the west shore of Loch Lomond. One then crosses the narrow tarbet to the Loch of the Long Boats and goes through the pass northwest of Arrochar. I do know of a pass west of Glen Luss and an ancient one from the tarbet itself. But both routes are apparently so treacherous now as to deter travelers."

"I ken the Lomondside routes well, lad. As chief of the MacFarlans, I used to be keeper of that pass and controlled the tarbet of Ballyhennan, too."

"As Pharlain does now," Mag said. "But, I tell you, sir, I've heard talk about the river guarding your north boundary and know that it is as wild as the one I saw for myself that serves as your south boundary. I'd like to know how you forded the northern one with only a sliver of moon to light your way."

"I'll tell ye one day," MacFarlan said. "But now, about the impediment... Sithee, with only daughters to inherit, and being determined to win back my lands and chiefdom as I am, I need powerful allies and warriors to aid me. The Earl of Lennox wields great influence despite his arrest and allies himself with Murdoch, second Duke of Albany, and his thievish elder sons. At Lennox's order, all of my neighbors save one have as good as joined Murdoch in his quest to unseat our King."

"That one being the Laird of Colquhoun, or so I have heard," Mag said.

"Aye, and even Colquhoun prefers to keep the peace

and takes no side in any fight. Your da were like that at first, too, seeking to please all. Now he seems fixed with Murdoch, Lennox, and Parlan. As I see it, I owe allegiance as chief of Clan Farlan first to the King of Scots, *not* to the treacherous dukes of Albany or their equally underhanded kinsmen. That includes Lennox, be he my liege lord or none."

"Years ago, according to my father," Mag said, "the first Duke of Albany governed the kingdom legally in his brother the King's stead and did so for much of his reign. Then Albany continued to rule after the English captured Jamie Stewart and the old King died. Noblemen believed that they had to follow Albany then and his son, Murdoch, after Albany died. Both men dealt ruthlessly with defiance."

"Aye, but now Jamie has come home, taken his rightful place on Scotland's throne, and has shown us all that he means to keep it," MacFarlan said. "So, I owe my allegiance to him. Forbye, he has ordered all landholders to produce their charters to justify possession of their lands. Parlan cannot produce one, because I hold the royal charter for Arrochar and other Clan Farlan lands."

"Then you need only show it to the King."

"That willna be enough, lad. In any disagreement over estates or a chiefship, the weight of judgment will most likely go to the man with a string of strong sons to support him. As I have none, I must have strong, loyal good-sons who will take the MacFarlan name. *That* be the impediment I mentioned."

"I can see that it would be," Mag said dryly.

"I ken fine that I canna expect the eldest son and heir of another laird to agree to such a demand. But a younger son with ambition and knightly skills...Och, I've put me foot in it, though. The lass didna call ye *Sir* Magnus, did she?"

"Nay, although two years ago, Lennox did offer me a knighthood but only if I would agree to serve him and Pharlain. I refused, which may be what annoyed them and how I ended up rowing Pharlain's galleys."

Eyeing him speculatively, MacFarlan said, "Then, what d'ye say?"

Mag met his steady gaze with ease. "I have no immediate objection to marrying your daughter, sir, or to allying myself with your clan. But there is one matter that we must discuss before talking further of a marriage."

"Sakes, lad, I'll tell ye plain, I'd have little respect for a man who accepted such an offer *without* discussion. Yonder stool will bear your weight, so pull it up. Then sit ye down, and we'll talk of this thing. Ye're no married already or ye'd have had an objection. So that canna be the hitch."

"Nay, but it will mean postponing any marriage for a time, at least."

"Spit it out then."

Mag wondered if he was making a mistake. But his long experience with men and warriors told him Mac-Farlan had been sincere about his loyalty to young Jamie Stewart. So he pulled up the stool, sat, and said, "It's like this, sir..."

⌒

Andrena returned to the ladies' solar, and as she opened the door, she heard Muriella say, "Dree, at last! Now tell us just what happened!"

"You might at least wait until I am in the room," Andrena said.

Lina said, "You told us when you left that you were just going out to see what you could see. But Murie sensed sometime after that that you had run into trouble. You must have seen them. Why did you let them see *you*?"

Muriella chuckled. "Dree wanted to know why they were in our woods, of course. You had your wee pipe in hand, did you not, Dree?"

"Aye, sure," Andrena said. "So I knew I could summon our men. But when one of the louts grabbed my right arm, I could not raise the pipe, so I whistled instead. You may imagine my astonishment when the hawks swooped down. I suspect they sensed my anger and indignation just as I had sensed their distress. We know that animals here do sense that we mean them no harm. Those hawks amazed me nonetheless. The osprey came down, too, but I'd wager that it was just curious."

"Aye, or feared that the goshawks had developed a taste for fish," Murie said. "But tell us about Magnus Mòr."

"You said he was Parlan's prisoner," Lina said. "Was he one of the three that you met, or were they seeking him?"

"Wait now," Murie said. "You must tell it just as it happened to you, Dree. We want to learn about Magnus Mòr as you did. The story will make more sense that way, and I will more easily remember all the details."

"You never forget anything," Andrena said.

"I know. But I remember things the way I hear them. So prithee, do tell it just the way it happened to you."

"Aye, sure," Andrena said. Taking her customary backstool, she ignored the basket of mending that sat beside it and began with her departure from the tower. In telling her tale, she skimmed glibly over her warning to Magnus that Andrew would urge him to marry her.

Even so, Lina said, "Father *will* likely ask him to do that unless Magnus is Galbraith's heir."

"He is not," Andrena said.

"Go on," Murie urged. "This will be a grand tale to tell at ceilidhs."

"Have the goodness to wait until I am actually married to the man before you tell such a tale to *anyone*," Andrena said.

Murie stared at her. "Do you *want* to marry him?"

Lina said, "We need not discuss that now. First we should know that Father has asked him and that Magnus Mòr has agreed."

"Nay," Murie protested. "One wants to be prepared! If the notion is a horrid one, Dree must be able to say so without inflaming Father's temper."

"Do you want me to tell my tale, or would you rather plan my future?" Andrena asked in a tone that told Murie which choice would be the wiser one.

"I want to hear all that Magnus and you said and did before we met you."

Andrena told them what she could, trying to remember just what they had said to each other. Her ability to repeat an entire discussion verbatim was not as exact as Murie's was, but she thought she acquitted herself well.

"You have told us what you said to each other," Lina said when she had finished. "But what did you think of him, Dree? And what does he think of you?"

"And how could you have just turned and found him standing in your path as you say you did?" Murie demanded. "Surely, you *knew* he was in that tree."

Andrena grimaced. "I must have had my senses so narrowly attuned to those three men that I failed to realize he was there," she said. "I failed to notice that your cat had climbed up to him, too, Lina."

Lina frowned. "That is unlike you, Dree. Of the three of us, you have the keenest ability to sense when others are near, especially when you are alone in the woods. To hear that a man as large as Magnus is could lie on a tree limb right over your head without your knowledge disturbs me."

"It would disturb me, too, if he had wished me ill," Andrena said. "I do think I'd have sensed him then."

"Mayhap your abilities are fading as you get older," Murie suggested.

"Do you think that yours have?" Andrena asked her.

Murie thought briefly before she said, "In troth, my memory has grown stronger. But I get chances every day to test it, and you don't often meet strangers. My awareness of what others may be feeling or thinking seems to be as it always has been. But, in that respect, my ability has never matched yours."

"Nor will my memory ever match yours," Andrena said. "Now that I think of it, though, weren't you going to visit Annie Wylie today?"

"Aye, but after you went into the woods, I stayed to be sure that all was well with you. Annie will be as happy if I visit her tomorrow."

"I asked Murie to stay," Lina said. "I can sense your feelings, Dree, but only when your emotions are truly on end or when you are desperately sick."

"I always know when you are getting angry," Muriella said with a grin. "I learned even before I could talk to avoid getting near you at such times."

"Was there ever a time when you did not talk?" Andrena asked her. "I am sure that I cannot remember such a peaceful time."

"Aye, that faulty memory of yours would be the reason, I warrant."

Lina burst into a peal of laughter.

As always when Lina laughed, Andrena laughed, too. "A point to you, Murie," she said, still chuckling.

⁓

Knowing by Andrew's expression that he had captured his full attention, Mag said, "I learned of a plot to assassinate the King, sir. I must warn him at once."

"God have mercy," Andrew muttered. Rallying, he said, "Ye've nae cause to rush off, lad, even so, unless this plot be in motion now."

"I don't think it is," Mag said. "I know only that Pharlain is involved in such a plot. The main beneficiary of its success would be Murdoch, Duke of Albany, so I assume that Murdoch and his sons are also involved. Pharlain mentioned a meeting of Parliament that will take place next month and which his grace will attend."

"Aye, sure, for Jamie summoned the lords to meet in Perth on the twelfth day of March—less than a month from today—did he no?"

"If you say so, sir. I did not know the date. Nor do I know their plan. What I did hear is that his grace will not live beyond the last day of this Parliament."

"Since the first Duke of Albany's death five years ago, powerful nobles have got used to taking their own road," Andrew said. "Albany kept them in line, but Murdoch is lazy. He let his sons and other nobles wreak lawlessness throughout the land. Then Jamie returned, arrested Murdoch's eldest son, Lord Walter Stewart, and clapped him up on the Bass Rock, ignoring Murdoch's indignant complaints. I say Murdoch should count himself lucky that Jamie didn't clap him up, too."

"Lennox is evidently still active, despite *his* arrest," Mag said. "'Tis no surprise, though, when his daughter is Murdoch's wife."

"Nor is it anything new," Andrew said. "He demanded that his Loch Lomond lairds support Albany when it meant going against the *old* King. Has it occurred to ye, lad, that your father is likely up to his chin in this conspiracy ye've uncovered?"

"That did cross my mind, sir," Mag admitted. "But I reject the notion that he would act secretly against his King. It was my father, after all, who taught me that my loyalty must be first to our family and clan, next to Lennox as our liege lord, and last but nonetheless most strongly to the King of Scots as chief of chiefs."

"I expect that noblemen are rediscovering their allegiance to his grace in numbers equal to the number of lords Jamie arrests and punishes," Andrew said. "Forbye, if I were Jamie, I'd withhold my trust until each man had proven himself."

"But you do see that I must warn him. And if Parliament is meeting so soon, I must lose no time. God knows how long it will take me to track his grace down."

"It willna take as long as that," Andrew replied. "News of his comings and goings flits across the country with the speed of birds in flight. Ye need only go to Dumbarton or Glasgow to learn where he is and where next he'll be a-going. I can tell ye he stays at religious houses, rarely at royal fortresses. He said too many such English castles served as his prisons."

"Even so, sir—"

"What better way to avoid Parlan's men?" Andrew interjected. "To hide in plain sight be the best plan, and ye're too big to hide long, any road. We'll say ye be a cousin come to visit, one of me lady's Galbraith kinsmen."

"*Is* your lady a kinswoman of mine? I've no ken of such a connection."

"Aye, for my lass be kin to the Comyns and nigh everyone in the Highlands and elsewhere, one way or another," Andrew said glibly. "Nae one will question it. Now, then," he added briskly. "It willna take long for me to find a priest, and ye seem willing enough to have the lass. As for Andrena, she'll do as I bid her. But I'd have ye wedded afore ye leave. That road, if aught happens to ye in your travels, I'll have good reason to request Clan Galbraith's help against Parlan. Sithee, Arthur's own grandchild would then stand to inherit at least a third of what I leave."

Mag met his gaze and held it for a long moment before he said evenly, "I did say that I had no great objection to marrying. But I'll not take an unwilling bride, sir. With all due respect to you, I'd have her tell me herself that she is willing."

"Ye've already said she's expecting me to arrange such a marriage."

"She said she *feared* that you would urge one between us. I thought she jested and paid her words no heed. But I do know that she expressed no willingness to obey such urging. I'll talk with her on my own, sir, and I'd like your promise not to speak to her about this until I've had a chance to do so."

Andrew shrugged and said, "Ye should easily reach the King, wherever he is, within a sennight. If ye leave here Friday morning, say, ye'd reach the Firth of Clyde by midafternoon on Saturday. Ye could ride on then Sunday morning to wherever his grace may be. To reach Perth from Glasgow be a matter of but four days unless ye dawdle. And ye dinna seem to me like a man who does."

Mag remained pointedly silent.

With an exaggerated sigh that turned quickly into an air of virtue, Andrew said, "I'll see about finding that priest whilst ye arrange to have your talk with our Dree. It be nigh to suppertime, but whether ye talk now or in the morning, she will offer nae hindrance. Ye can wed when the priest arrives."

Andrena and her sisters, likewise realizing that the supper hour was nearly upon them, had retired to the bedchamber they shared, to prepare for the meal before Magnus Mòr emerged from Andrew's chamber.

Although Andrena was curious to know what was transpiring between the two men, her curiosity was as nothing to Muriella's.

"What if Father does persuade Magnus to marry you, Dree?" she demanded before the bedchamber door had shut behind them. "What will you say?"

"Dree kens her duty," Lachina said.

"Aye, sure, I do," Andrena said. It was true. She had known from childhood that it would be her duty to marry in a way that would strengthen Andrew's hand against Parlan.

"Duty," Murie said scornfully as she began to loosen

her flaxen plaits. "I want to know what you think of Magnus Mòr."

"What should I think of him?" Andrena asked her, picking up a looking glass to tidy her own hair. "I met him only this afternoon and barely talked with him."

"But what did you sense about him?" Muriella asked.

"Naught to tell me what sort of man he is," Andrena said with a sigh. "I told you, I sensed nothing about his presence, let alone his character."

"He was kind enough to see you safely home," Lina said, taking her usual seat. Since she rarely seemed to have a hair out of place, she had little tidying to do but had taken off the apron she wore when sewing. "He looked rather shabby," she added. "But one would expect that in an escaped prisoner from Arrochar. I like him, Dree. He is polite, and he lacks the arrogance we so often see in men we meet."

"Wait and see what Mam thinks of him," Murie suggested.

"Speaking of Mam," Lina said, "we should decide how we mean to celebrate the anniversary of her birth next month. It will soon be upon us."

"It will, aye, but we can talk about that later," Murie said. "This is vital now, because if Mam takes against Magnus Mòr, Father will look elsewhere for your husband, Dree. He rarely goes against Mam's wishes, as we all ken fine."

Andrena did know that her father respected the lady Aubrey's opinion. She decided that she need not worry about Andrew urging Magnus to marry her until her lady mother had met him. That she could scarcely think of anything else while she finished preparing for supper was a fact that she did not share with her sisters.

It was just as well, too, because when they joined their parents at the high table in the great hall for the evening meal, she barely recognized Magnus in the handsome gentleman who stood on the dais beside Andrew. But for his size—and the plaid and a linen sark Lina had provided—she would *not* have known him.

In place of the scruffy erstwhile prisoner she had brought home was a well-scrubbed, neatly shaven gentleman four or five years older than she was. He was talking with her mother when the three sisters approached. As they stepped onto the dais, he finished what he was saying and turned toward them.

Only the amusement in his golden eyes was familiar.

Responding automatically with a smile, Andrena wondered at herself. She had meant to maintain an air of careful dignity. But his twinkle was irresistible.

Reminding herself hastily that she had not yet greeted her lady mother, she made her curtsy, saying, "Good evening, Mam. I hope you enjoyed a pleasant day."

"I did, dearling, thank you," Lady Aubrey said in her quiet way. "Not one as eventful as yours, though. I merely paid my customary visits to our people and found everyone well and busy. Naught of excitement amongst them. Then I came home to learn that you had brought us a most charming guest."

Taking her place beside her mother, Andrena exchanged a glance with Lina and saw that her sister's reaction matched her own.

Muriella nodded knowingly, but Andrena did not need the younger girl's silent assurance to know that Lady Aubrey approved of Magnus Mòr.

At the end of the meal, Lady Aubrey said, "You men

will excuse us, I know, for you doubtless have much to discuss. Come, my dearlings," she added to her daughters. "We will adjourn to the solar."

Whether by mutual consent or because Andrew rarely opposed his lady, Andrena knew that she would have no further conversation that day with Magnus. She thought it odd, though, that her father had said naught to her even to hint of nuptials and wondered if her mother would be the one to break the news to her.

In the solar, however, Lady Aubrey asked Muriella to entertain them with one of their favorite tales while they attended to their various domestic tasks.

Andrena resigned herself to her mending but soon found herself chuckling at Murie's tale about a "wee, wee trickster" who outwitted a fairy queen. Murie had a nearly magical knack for telling a story. When she had finished, she took up her lute and began to play for them.

The men did not join them, and Lady Aubrey suggested their retirement at the usual hour.

Although Andrena lay awake for what seemed hours, trying to imagine marriage to a huge man with a decided twinkle in his eyes and little else yet to recommend him, she awoke the next morning at her usual early hour.

Gray dawn light peeked through the shutters. When she opened them to look out, fog blanketed the yard and everything beyond the wall. The outside world was therefore still and eerie, but fog would not dissuade her from her morning walk in the woods. She dressed quickly in her deerskin breeks, boots, and jack. She wanted to think, and to do so before the rest of the household awoke and began the new day.

Chapter 4 _____

Mag had awakened early, too. Discovering that servants had set bread, meat, and ale on the dais table, he helped himself to some of each, ate his meal, and went out into the foggy yard. The first person he met there was a thin lad of eleven or twelve with freckles and a mop of red hair who introduced himself simply as Pluff.

Having taken a long, measuring look at Mag, the boy said. "Ye'll be the one as be a-going tae marry the lady Andrena. I seen ye return wi' her yesterday. I didna think the men would let ye in, but the lady Lina and the lady Murie did say it were right tae open the gate. So we did. Some say the wee folk did bring ye. But Lady Aubrey did tell her woman that ye be a friend and we should treat ye well."

"Who is Lady Aubrey?"

"Pluff's eyes widened. "Why, the laird's lady, o' course. She always kens friend from foe," he added. "But I never heard tell o' her picking husbands afore."

"Then she may be mistaken this time," Mag said, realizing that he ought to have guessed at once from "her woman" who Lady Aubrey was. But he'd thought of her as Lady MacFarlan and would address her so until she commanded otherwise.

"Nay, she's never been mistook," Pluff replied. "Men do say the lady Aubrey can see things that others do not."

"Do you mean that she has the Sight, that she can see things in far places?"

"Nay, for that'd mean she sees faraway doings as they come tae pass. She only sometimes kens what *will* come tae pass later. See you, they say that her name means ruler o' the elves. And elves be wee folk. So, likely they tell her things the wee folk ken. I'll tell ye this much. I ha' never known her tae be wrong when she speaks so."

Ever resistant to notions of second sight, wee folk, and similar fantastic creations, Mag changed the subject. "What are your duties here, Pluff?"

"Mornings, I look after the dogs unless someone asks me tae do summat else," the boy said. "I muck oot the byre and tend the postern gate, too. But at this hour, I need only tae let the lady Dree oot and in again after she's had her walk."

"Then your duties are lighter than usual today," Mag said. "No lady would walk out in such a dense fog."

The boy shrugged. "Lady Dree goes out in all weather, sir. She left nigh a half-hour ago. She says she can think better outside the wall."

Mag frowned. "She went alone?"

"Nay, she took Old Bess wi' her."

"Old Bess?"

"Her collie. Lady Dree loves all the beasts, but Bess be her favorite."

"A dog would be of little use if her ladyship suffers a mishap in the fog."

"Aye, sure, Old Bess would. She be gey smart."

"I think I'll take a walk myself," Mag said.

The boy gave him another measuring look. "Wi' respect, sir, I'm thinking that Lady Dree kens our woods better nor any stranger could. I reckon ye've heard tales about bad things that befall strangers here at Tùr Meiloach."

"I can look after myself," Mag said with a reassuring smile.

The boy nodded. "Right then. I'll let ye oot. But when ye lose yourself, dinna be telling the laird that I had aught tae do with it. D'ye want tae take one o' them other dogs wi' ye? Any one o' them could lead ye home if need be."

Mag shook his head and turned toward the gate. Its outline was barely discernible, but he had a nearly infallible sense of direction and a good memory for the location and layout of any place he had seen.

"Which way did her ladyship go?" he asked the boy.

"She doesna tell me," Pluff said with another shrug as he opened the gate.

When it thudded shut behind Mag, he paused to get his bearings. The fog was thick enough to blanket both the sun and the landscape, but he could make out the darker area of woodland beyond the clearing easily enough.

Despite dense, swirling ground fog, he could see his feet and freshly made imprints of smaller ones heading back the way they had come the day before.

He followed them into the woods, where they disappeared on the damp pine duff. But he detected a narrow trail that seemed to lead toward the cliffs.

Except for ragged tatters of fog drifting eerily down through openings in the canopy and wispy shreds curling through shrubbery, it was clear enough in the woods to see his way. The creatures were silent, as was usual in such weather, and he could hear waves distantly hushing against the loch shore below.

He hoped Andrena had kept to the woods. But when the path continued to take him toward the cliffs, that hope faded. If his sister Lizzie were to behave in such a potentially dangerous way, he would have something stern to say to her.

The thought drew the hint of a smile to his lips. He had seen naught yet to suggest that the lady Andrena was anything like Lizzie. Andrena herself had said that her father expected her to know every rock and rill of Tùr Meiloach's lands.

Doubtless, she believed that she did know every one.

The thought was not reassuring. He was nearing the edge of the woods and could see that the fog had drifted in farther there and was even denser than it had been in the yard and the clearing. Concern rippled through him.

Surely she would not have gone far beyond the safety of the trees.

Reaching the edge of the woodland and noting that what little he could see of the area beyond was damp, rock-bound granite, covered with pebbles and gravelly sand, he paused to listen but heard only water lapping against the shore far below. He doubted that he had walked a half-mile from the tower. But when he had rowed on the loch, he had not studied the clifftops thereabouts with particular care.

He could see the ground before him well enough to know that he was not stepping into oblivion, so he began to make his way toward the precipice. He could sense open space ahead and sensed another human presence as well, sufficient to hope that if he kept going straight, he would find her. A faint extension of the woodland path did seem to lead that way.

When a shadowy figure took eerie form in the drifting gray mist ahead, its shape made him think he had mistaken the presence of some unknown lad for the lady Andrena. But when the figure shifted position slightly, he noted that its shape was too enticingly curvy to be masculine. Also, a shaggy dog sat silently beside her.

Mag's heart nearly stopped beating at the realization that Andrena had to be standing dangerously near the edge of the cliff. Facing away from him, as she was, she was surely too near the edge to risk startling her by speaking her name.

Tamping down the concern he felt for her safety and the annoyance that such concern stirred in him, he reminded himself to speak calmly if he did speak. He wondered if she would sense him watching her. She had seemed surprised that she had not done so the day before. But she stood unaware, gazing into the thick fog.

The dog likewise sat still, although Mag saw its ears twitch and its head turn slightly toward him. He hoped it would not bark. Dogs rarely did bark at him, and he had petted those he'd met in the yard the day before. However, Pluff had said the collie was intelligent, so one might expect it to growl a warning.

Looking down, he realized that although he had been walking on solid fog-damp granite for some time now, a patch of the gravelly pebbles lay a foot or so away. Moving with care, he disturbed them enough to make them rattle.

She turned toward him then and stiffened when she saw him.

Andrena had been thinking about him, so it was as if with that slight rattle of stones, she had conjured him up before her. A frisson of unease stirred at the sight of him, because once again, she had failed to sense his approach. To be sure, she'd been deep in thought. Nevertheless, she ought to have felt his presence behind her.

The sensation she experienced now was what she might have felt in her father's presence if she had displeased him. But she could not tell a thing about Magnus Mòr's feelings from his demeanor. Surely, if he were angry—not that he had any right yet to *be* angry with her—she would sense his displeasure. Even so, she could not imagine any other reason for the brief chill of trepidation she had felt.

She glanced down at Bess, who was wagging her tail and practically smiling at him. "You might at least have warned me," she muttered to the dog.

"I thought she might bark or growl," Magnus said. "Are you not dangerously close to the edge of that cliff?"

Relaxing, she said, "It lies a yard or so ahead of me. You can just make out the shape of that boulder there," she added, gesturing. "One can safely go that far even in dense fog. I came here because I like listening to the waves whisper whilst all else is quiet. One can enjoy such silence only when a fog is thick enough to keep the birds in their nests and the other creatures still. Sithee, I came out here to think."

"Has the tower no place inside quiet enough for contemplation?"

"I like it here," she said, feeling wary again. "The fog

does not trouble me. I could find this spot safely in pitch blackness."

"Do you often wear lad's breeks?"

Squaring her shoulders, she lifted her chin. "I do. In troth, I prefer them for my solitary rambles. Does that trouble you?"

"Nay, I like the look of them, although I would not recommend them in company, especially female company. Do you mind if I stay here with you?"

"You may if you like," she said. Although she would have preferred to enjoy her solitude longer, she was uncertain of his mood and did not want to be rude. He seemed to have accepted her explanation, but her wariness lingered. After all, her father wanted her to marry the man, and she had no idea yet about what sort of husband the large, powerful-looking Magnus Mòr Galbraith would make.

Evidently taking her mistress's calmness as approval of Magnus Mòr's presence, Bess moved to greet him more enthusiastically.

Bending to stroke the dog's head, he looked up and met Andrena's gaze. "I'll go back if you want me to," he said. Then, straightening, he added, "It occurs to me, though, that if you are willing, this might be a good place to talk privately."

She nearly said that she could not imagine what they would talk about. But she stopped the untruthful words before they could leave her tongue. "I'm willing, sir. I ken fine that you must wonder at my father's plan and think he is daft."

"Nay, for his plan makes sense to me. I am sure now that Pharlain wrested Arrochar and its lands from

Andrew by force and by stealth. Also, I can understand why your clan accepted Pharlain rather than demand his banishment."

"Do you? Our clan has a well-deserved reputation for wildness, so I own, I used to resent their failure to support my father when he needed them. I did not understand that, at the time, most of his finest warriors were involved in unrest elsewhere and that Lennox..." She paused, uncertain of how much she should say about the earl, who was also the Galbraiths' liege lord.

"Dissension was everywhere then," Magnus said quietly. "The earl acted in his own self-interest, just as most other nobles did."

"How old were you when my father lost his lands?" she asked bluntly.

He smiled. "When Pharlain took Arrochar nineteen years ago, I was just six. But I've learned much about those times. Unrest prevailed throughout the country. Recall that the English had captured a very young Jamie Stewart and that his father, the King, died of grief when he learned of it. That left Scotland with a mere boy—an English captive at that—as our King. And *his* heir was his uncle, the first Duke of Albany, who was and had been for years acting as Governor of the Realm."

"You sound as if you approve of what Albany did."

"Nay, I am not so bold as to approve or disapprove of what is now history. I have no way to know how I would have acted had I been of age or wielded power at the time. The fact is that Albany was gey powerful and Scotland needs a powerful ruler. We have too many greedy nobles, each determined to win as much power as he can for himself. Few seem to spare any thought for the health of the realm."

"But the first Albany has been dead for five years. And no one can possibly think that his son Murdoch is as canny, as strong, or as capable as *he* was."

"True, but what Murdoch lacks in wisdom, his son Lord Walter Stewart makes up in slyness, deceit, and ruthlessness," Magnus said as he leaned his backside against a handy boulder. "Doubtless, Walter would seek to be King of Scots or rule in the rightful king's stead, as Governor of the Realm, just as Albany of old did."

"Aye, perhaps, but Jamie is back," she said. "And he locked Lord Walter up on the Bass Rock soon after he got back, so Walter can no longer harm him."

"You must know better than that," he said. "Jamie's enemies seek to oust him, and Walter, prisoner or not, stands next after Duke Murdoch to inherit. But Jamie may hold his throne despite them and their supporters. He seems determined to do so, and from all that I've heard about him this past year, he is a canny lad. He has already won over Douglas, Scott, and other powerful Border lords."

"My father thinks they are untrustworthy."

"Aye, well, most Scots wait to see who will benefit them most before taking sides. If Jamie can hold his throne for another year, he should be safe enough."

It occurred to her that few men of her acquaintance would so casually have discussed the King's uncertain position with her. Those who might would speak to her lightly, as if she were a child, or would soon change the subject. Only her father and mother ever took time to explain things to her.

As if Magnus Mòr were somehow hearing her thoughts, he said, "You seem to know much more about political matters than one would expect a woman to understand, especially one who has grown up in such a place as Tùr Meiloach."

"Noblemen's actions can affect all of us," she said. "My sister Muriella hears many things, because she talks to everyone she meets and encourages them to tell her much of what they know or hear. She remembers it all and repeats it to the rest of us."

"Everything?"

"Aye, Murie never forgets. She views conversation as storytelling, and since she means to become our clan seanachie, she takes pride in her ability to collect news whenever it comes her way."

"Have the three of you lived here at Tùr Meiloach all your lives?" he asked, looking and sounding as relaxed against his boulder as if they sat by the hall fire.

"Aye, sure," she said, wondering if he was truly as content to stay and talk there as she was. He certainly seemed to be. Despite the damp and the hardness of his chosen position, he seemed oblivious to any discomfort.

"You must lead a gey isolated existence," he said. "How can you know so much about what happens in the outside world?"

"We aren't immured in our tower, sir. To be sure, Father rarely leaves Tùr Meiloach, knowing well that Cousin Parlan will learn of his absence and try to seize Tùr Meiloach's lands as well as those of Arrochar. But people do visit us, and my mother has often taken us to visit her kinsmen. Also, the people south of us—"

"The Colquhouns?"

"Aye, the laird is a friend, although he does not make a song about that friendship for all to hear. He was frank enough from the outset to say that he values his peace and would liefer not have to go against Lennox to support my father."

"Then how does his friendship aid you?"

"Colquhoun owns land from our southwest boundary to the Firth of Clyde, as you must know. He discourages all travel across his land, demanding large collops from would-be travelers, especially those who want to meet with Father."

"I *did* hear that Colquhoun charges much to cross and guards his cattle well."

"He does, aye. But he charges us naught and aids us when we want to travel. I have been to Glasgow many times and even once to Stirling. My mother insisted that we learn how to behave in other people's homes. We are not peasants, after all, sir. She believes it is her duty to accustom us to noble society."

"Do you enjoy town life?" he asked.

"Not much," she said. "I hope that does not disappoint you. Sithee, I love it here at Tùr Meiloach."

"I just want to know more about you, lass. Above all, I want to know what you think about this scheme of your father's. Do not simply say that you are his obedient daughter. I want to know your true thoughts on the subject."

She almost blurted out her frustration at not being able to sense his emotions or his thoughts even from his expressions. Perhaps, if she was honest...

Nay, then, she could not be. She and her sisters had long since learned the wisdom of keeping their unusual abilities to themselves. Besides, even if she could explain hers, she would have no way to know if he believed her or was being honest with her in return.

In fact, if he had heard all that the men seeking him had said to her the day before, he had heard one of them call her a witch. Moreover, he had admitted knowing more about her family than he had first seemed to know. Having lived with Parlan's men for more than a year and a half, Magnus Mòr had doubtless heard many truths and untruths about all three MacFarlan sisters...and their mother.

"What is it?" Mag asked. "I can see that my words stirred your thoughts."

"I am not sure that I can explain why they did or that you will believe me if I try," she replied without hesitation.

"You have given me no cause to doubt your word, my lady. Until you provide such a cause, I will believe that you are telling me the truth or at least what you believe the truth to be. Is that fair enough?"

"Aye, sure," she said. Her tone was doubtful, and she remained silent long enough to make him wonder if she would reveal her thoughts to him.

She glanced back toward the loch, as if seeking inspiration there.

He saw that the fog behind her had thinned. Above her head, a small patch of blue sky was visible through the mist.

Returning her gaze to him, she drew a deep breath and said, "Sithee, sir, my sisters and I share a bond closer than that of most sisters."

"'Tis understandable that you would, growing up here as you did," he said. "Do you fear you'll see less of them if you marry me?" When she hesitated, he added, "Surely, you know that Andrew expects me to stay here at Tùr Meiloach."

She nodded, her expression solemn, and he realized that he could now see how close to the edge she stood. He felt an urge to tell her to move nearer to him but ignored it, not only because he wanted to hear her opinion of their possible future together but also because he doubted that she was in real danger. Clearly, though, she lacked the strong respect for great heights that he had.

At last she said, "Your own home lies not far from here, on Inch Galbraith, so I expect I would see my family often enough even if you decided that you could not bear to live at Tùr Meiloach."

This was no time to admit that his father had disowned him, leaving him uncertain that he *had* a home. "Tell me more about your family," he said.

"Why, when you have revealed so little about yours?"

"Because you seem reluctant to tell me how you feel about this marriage notion of your father's. Whilst you decide how you feel about that, it would be helpful for me to learn something about the rest of your family."

"In troth, sir, I'm wondering why you don't object to my father's having decided your future for you," she said.

This time, it was Mag who paused to reflect before replying.

~

Andrena watched him, trying to figure him out

"I do see some benefit to myself in such a marriage," he said at last.

Evidently he had no objection to marrying her. His voice was even, his face expressionless. But he must have objections. Faith, she had objections to such a marriage, despite having known for years what her father planned to do.

Worse, how could she know if he meant what he said when she was unable to sense his emotions the way she did those of other people? That she could not even hazard a guess as to what the man might be thinking or feeling was most unfair.

"What is it?" he asked. "Something has disturbed you."

She wanted to grind her teeth. She could not read him. But apparently he could read her with ease.

"I have said naught that should make you think I am upset."

"By our lady," he said as calmly as ever, despite the epithet. "You fear that your father will force us to marry. And you don't think much of the notion."

She did grind her teeth. "You are mistaken."

"Am I? I don't think so."

"By my troth, sir, I don't *know* what I think. I have known about my father's plan for as long as I can remember. I know it is my clan duty to marry a warrior. However, until you came along, he had found no one willing to marry me who met his requirements. So I gave the matter little thought until now, but my father will *not* force us to marry. Forbye, you say you see a benefit for yourself. What is it?"

"I see more than one," he said, surprising her. "First, any younger son needs a wife with property or wealth. But, also, I find you intelligent and most intriguing. I believe you would suit me well as my wife, *if* you are willing to marry me."

"You do not object to adopting the MacFarlan name?"

"Nay, I'm willing enough. I was born a Galbraith, and I'll always be one. But I've nae great objection to taking the name of MacFarlan."

"What about your family?"

He hesitated and then said, "What they might think won't trouble me."

"Doubtless you think calling yourself MacFarlan will protect you from Cousin Parlan," she said musingly, eyeing him to see if he would take offense.

"It may help for a time," he said with a shrug. Then, folding his arms across his chest, he added, "But that was not the chief benefit that leaped to my mind."

"What was?"

"I think I'll leave discussion of that subject for a more appropriate time."

His gaze caught hers then and something in his brought heat to her cheeks that seemed to radiate through her body, as well.

But she still could not tell what he might be thinking.

With a small sigh, she said, "We should go back now. But you should know that I will not disobey my father's wishes."

"Then *you* should know this, lass. If I think for a moment that you dislike the marriage, I will *not* agree to it."

"Even though it will benefit you?"

"Despite *all* the benefits," he said. "Perhaps we should discuss this more and get to know each other better before we return to the tower. I'd like to walk high enough to look over the route I took yesterday. Pharlain's men may have returned."

"Nay, they have not," she said.

"How can you be sure?"

She hesitated and then said glibly, "Our men will be on the watch for them. They will not allow what happened yesterday to happen again."

Then, before he could quiz her more on that subject,

she stepped toward him and said, "I'll show you, if you like, since the fog is lifting. A burn not far from here feeds into the south river. From the hilltop above it, we can see much of the area you crossed and mayhap even catch a fish or two for the midday meal."

"I brought no pole," he said, pushing away from the boulder to stand upright.

"You won't need one. I keep a cache nearby that will supply us."

He nodded, gesturing for her to lead the way. As he did, the way he looked at her made her suspect that he knew she had not revealed the true reason that she was sure Parlan's men had not intruded on Tùr Meiloach land again.

If he did suspect it, he would be right. But she doubted that he was ready to hear that the birds or beasts would warn her of intruders in the forest.

Striding ahead of him into the woods, she headed southeast. Before long, the incline steepened, and shortly afterward, they came to the merry burn. It ran through a narrow rocky chasm above them for some distance before widening and wending its way southward through an entanglement of hills to the river. Leading the way up a rock-and-pebble-strewn path near the water, she continued until they came to a half-hidden shelter in the shadow of overhanging boulders.

Entering it, she found her spear and one that her father often used. When she emerged from the shelter with them, she saw his eyes widen.

"You do know how to *spear* salmon, do you not?" she asked with a smile.

Chapter 5

Mag was delighted to see her smile but astonished to see the spears. "You are ever surprising, lass. I'll admit that I'd expected poles. I have not taken a spear in hand for many months, but I'll wager that I can still spear a fish or two if I must."

"You must, aye," she said, still smiling. "I keep such caches scattered about, because I don't like to carry things unless it is necessary. I often carry my dirk, but I ken fine that a woman bearing more noticeable arms may seem to seek trouble."

"You think of your fishing-spear as a weapon?"

"Aye, sure I do. Don't you?"

"I do, but I've never known a woman who could throw anything straight."

"I'll hit any sensible target you choose except a forest creature," she said evenly as she leaned the second spear against a nearby boulder.

"Another time, perhaps," he said, watching her as she turned back to face him. Wondering if he'd offended her, he added, "I just want a view of the landscape I crossed yesterday. If the fog has lifted enough, I'd like to see the loch, too."

"Go ahead," she said. "From the crest of yon ridge across the burn, you will have a fine view southward to the river and west to the Loch of the Long Boats."

"Will you not come with me?"

"Nay, I've no need to look to know that no enemy threatens us now."

He wondered if she truly had such confidence in her father's men. He had noted the pause earlier before she had assured him that men would be watching for intruders. The previous day, clearly, they had failed to see him or his pursuers. Most likely Andrew Dubh had made his displeasure known. No leader of men wanted to learn of enemy intrusion from any but his own people. The wildly inclement weather over the last few days was surely not sufficient excuse.

Andrew had seemed to take the incident in stride, though. If he had spoken to his men, Mag knew naught of it.

Finding a place where he could leap across the burn, he climbed swiftly but cautiously, recalling the tales he had heard about Tùr Meiloach's terrain—its dangerous instability and the equally dangerous beasts that inhabited it. The lass proved to be right about the view from the ridge, because it was spectacular, the sort of panorama on which one could feast one's eyes.

Mist still clung to the ground and to trees here and there but was thinning rapidly. A thick finger of fog hovered over the river to the south, and a thinner layer coated the loch. But he detected no movement and could see no boats on the loch. Nor would any boats have set out through such a dense morning fog. Pharlain's men were skilled, but they were not daft.

Although the view invited him to stay, he did not linger, because the lass was more enticing and he wanted to see her smile again. He could see her now below in the still misty declivity, standing on a flat granite slab that jutted into the burn. She had clearly put him out of mind and focused her attention on her fishing.

He was about to scramble down again when she drew back her spear.

Pausing to watch, he admired the figure she made, standing there like a huntress. As the thought crossed his mind, her spear flashed down and back up, a large salmon wriggling indignantly near the tip. She swiftly brought the fish to ground and ended its struggles in a single blow with a rock. Then, she gently removed it from the spear and slipped a string through its gills before sliding it back into the water and tying the string ends to a stout branch of an overhanging shrub.

Shifting the dirk on her belt, she glanced up, saw him, and waved.

His long vision was excellent, and he could tell that the salmon's death had saddened her. Not a true huntress then, he decided. He saw no hint of victory even now as their gazes met. Descending almost as quickly as he had climbed, he found her seated near the water on the jutting rock slab.

"I saw your catch," he said. "You handle that spear right skillfully."

"Thank you. My father taught me."

"Do you use it for hunting, as well?"

"Nay, I hunt with my bow, but only rabbits and only when I must. I dislike killing any of our beasts. I don't mind so much with the fish, but this one was such a splendid chappie that I hated to see him die."

"Men must eat, lass. Women and children, too."

"I ken that fine," she said, returning her gaze to the water. "My father taught me many skills, so that I can look after myself and, if necessary, anyone else who needs looking after." Looking back at him, she added, "I confess, though, that I wanted to fish today just to show you I can."

"I see nowt amiss in that," he said, picking up the spear that she had leaned against the boulder. "Your skill is impressive. But it will not long remain so if you do not practice regularly."

"I know that, too. But I've got my fish. It is your turn now."

He nodded, hoping he was not about to make a fool of himself. He had not so much as touched a spear during his imprisonment. Hefting the one he held, he saw that it was well-crafted, smoothly polished, and perfectly straight. Its point was razor sharp and well-barbed. He would have no excuse if he failed.

She scooted out of his way. "Stand yonder, at the edge. 'Tis the best place."

Accepting her recommendation, he stepped to the edge of the slab and saw that the burn widened just below it, drawing fish into a near whirlpool there. He watched for several moments, noting passage of a few large trout as well as salmon.

She kept quiet, watching him.

He drew back the spear, chose a target, nearly went for it, but drew back. Hefting the spear again, he drew breath and, finding a new target, brought the spear down hard, pulled it back, and flipped its tip upward as soon as it pierced the fish.

Hers was bigger, but his was a fine specimen. He

looped the two together on her string and dropped them back into the water to keep cold.

"We should go back now," she said. "Forbye, I hope you broke your fast before you came out."

"I did, and I am not ready to return. Don't you want to take more fish?"

"Nay, others will be fishing—hunting, too. We do not lack food."

"Then we can discuss your thoughts regarding this plan of your father's," he said, sitting on the slab beside her. "You say you don't know what you think but will obey Andrew Dubh. I would liefer know the cause of your uncertainty, lest you submit to his will and soon regret your decision."

"I will discuss whatever you like," she said amiably. "But I would like to choose a topic of my own first if I may."

"What is it?"

"You seem much more even-tempered than most men I have met," she said. "I did think that you might take offense earlier when I suggested that you might take our name only to protect yourself. But you did not seem to do so."

"I was not offended," he said, mentally rejecting his initial brief surge of annoyance as taking offense. "You had reason to question my agreement with your father. As for being even-tempered, I must admit that I was a fire-brand in my youth. My brothers could easily stir a blaze in me with their teasing. But a prisoner learns quickly that a hot temper is *not* an asset. In troth, had I had better control of my temper before that fracas, I'd likely not have fallen captive. But tell me what your sisters think of our possible marriage."

"Lina likes you. I think Muriella would like me to know you better."

"Doubtless, they both would like that, as would I. They call you Dree?"

"They do, aye. Muriella gave Lina and me our nicknames when she first began to talk, because she couldn't say our names. She also called herself Murie. Our mother tried to persuade her to say Muriella, but she refers to herself so only when she is in the sort of company that demands formal behavior."

"She seems gey sprightly, more so than the lady Lachina."

Andrena smiled. "Murie just seems so, because Lina is so practical. As you have seen, Lina is a skilled weaver and needlewoman. She is also a fine musician and the peacemaker amongst us. Murie is a dreamer and gey creative. She, too, is skillful with music but prefers to make up her own tunes and songs. She also spins threads, yarns, and stories. And, as I mentioned before, she remembers everything she hears or sees. Sometimes one wishes that her memory were less retentive."

"I see," he said with a smile, thinking of Lizzie, who also often remembered things that her brothers wished she had not. He nearly said so but stopped himself. Not only had he grown accustomed to keeping his thoughts to himself, but also, now that Andrena was talking, he did not want to divert her.

"What I doubt you will understand as easily is the bond that the three of us share," she said. "When one of us is upset or ailing, the other two sense it even if they are not with her. Yesterday, when you and I returned to the tower, you will recall that they were about to set off in search of me. They had been watching the birds, and they both sensed my emotions when I reacted to that lout who grabbed my arm. They sensed them again when I turned and found you in my path."

"When I startled you, you mean."

"Aye, you did," she said. "But we talk only of me, sir. You have yet to tell me much of interest about yourself or your people."

"There is nowt much to tell," he said. "I have two brothers and a father on whom I have not clapped eyes in more than a year and a half. My mother died when I was small, but I had four sisters. One died young, two married before I fell captive, and the fourth has likely married by now." Meeting her gaze, he said gently, "I'd liefer talk more about you, lass. I want to know what you think."

"In troth, sir, I think we should go back. We can talk as we go, if you like, but my sisters and my father will begin to wonder where we are. And if my lady mother begins to worry, you will soon get a taste of my father's temper."

"Then, we will go at once," he said, suiting action to words.

⁓

As Andrena rose to accompany him, she decided that he had agreed too easily to go. He seemed amiable enough, so she wondered why he resisted talking about his family. It was, after all, common Highland custom to exchange details of one's clan and family whenever one met new people. Visitors or overnight guests often recited their ancestry for generations to ensure that others did not mistake them for anyone else. The larger the clan, the longer the introductory discussion might take. But Magnus Mòr had merely enumerated members of his immediate family: two living brothers, three living sisters, one father, and no mother.

Under other circumstances, she might have pressed him harder. But amiable as he was, something about him made her feel as if it would be rude to insist that he tell her more about his brothers and sisters. If so, it would be ruder yet to ask about their spouses, the circumstances of his mother's death, the scope and violence of his temper when it did flare, and other such intriguing details.

Overall, she decided as they walked silently downhill toward the tower, there was much to recommend Magnus Mòr Galbraith as a husband. Despite his having suffered capture and imprisonment, he seemed confident of his skill with weapons and would doubtless hold his own in battle. More intriguing was the twinkle in his eyes, the way his smile lit his face, and the natural good manners he displayed.

When she moved to step down from one boulder to another, she unexpectedly felt a gentle hand at her elbow. Her first impulse was to reject the notion that she needed his help. But the thoughtful gesture warmed her, so she thanked him.

He smiled then, and she half-expected him to speak, but he just gestured for her to go ahead of him. He reminded her of a gentle giant in a tale that Murie had told, a giant who always acted kindly, moved with the lithe ease of a cat, and spoke more softly than a whispering wind. That giant revealed more martial traits when his friends were threatened, and Andrena was sure that Magnus Mòr would, too.

When he still had not spoken by the time they reached the track that she had followed the day before, she said, "What was it like to be Parlan's captive?"

"Unpleasant," he said. "But to survive, a man finds his way wherever he is."

"That," she said, glancing back at him, "is not much of an answer."

~

Mag had been watching her well-shaped backside twitch under the soft deerskin breeks and wondering how long it would be before she felt compelled to speak. But he had not expected her to put him on the spot so quickly.

Amusement stirred at that thought, and honesty, as well. The fact was that watching her stride ahead of him had been stimulating him in more ways than he wanted to contemplate. She had startled him right out of that pleasant reverie.

Moreover, had he not, only a short while before, been thinking that she was not only stunningly beautiful but intriguingly strong-minded and that life with such a woman could only prove interesting, not to mention sensually and mentally invigorating? Now, here he was, taken off his stride by a question that he ought to have expected before now and a flat refusal to accept his glib reply.

"In troth, I'd liefer not talk about my imprisonment," he said. "But you do have a right to know that nowt of importance happened to me there. Once I learned to keep my wits about me, to control my temper, and to avoid setting anyone else's temper aflame, I got by. It was unpleasant, but it did me no lasting harm."

"You stayed there for a year and a half," she said.

"Surely, as big and powerful as you are, you ought to have been able to escape long ago."

"One of the disadvantages of being larger than most is that the guards kept a closer watch on me. Also, some louts believe they must challenge anyone who looks more powerful simply to prove that he is not. I learned to keep my wits well-honed, and I made friends with other prisoners, even with some of Pharlain's henchmen. Recall that a number of the older ones served your father. They are not all as loyal to Pharlain as he thinks they are."

"But you must have wanted to escape," she said. "Sakes, when you did escape, you chose the worst possible weather for it. You might have drowned."

"Aye, but thanks to the devilish winds and rough water, they had taken off my chains. I swim well, and they were not expecting me to try. Nor could they follow me in such blackness. The wind had blown out our torches and the lantern they kept swinging from the bowsprit. One can tell the difference between water and land even in such darkness, but one cannot see the hazards. They had, perforce, to keep their boat well away from that rockbound shore until dawn."

"But why didn't you escape before? There have been other stormy nights."

"Aye, sure, but chains must always be a deterrent, and we were rarely on the loch in bad weather. Also, after a captive settles into a routine, although the notion of escape does often tickle his thoughts, he does not dwell on such notions without a stronger incentive to escape than to stay put."

"Mercy, I should think escape would be the first thought in one's mind."

"Only if one sees more benefit in trying to escape and accepting whatever punishment comes if he fails than in staying where he is."

"You didn't *want* to escape?" She stopped, turned, and stared at him.

"I didn't say that," he replied, coming to a halt. Shifting his gaze toward a nearby stirring of leaves, he thought briefly and said, "Sithee, a man must consider the odds. One chap who tried to run sacrificed a foot as a result. Pharlain said it would keep him from running again, and it did. The poor chap died of infection."

Her face paled. Then, frowning thoughtfully, she said, "Did your clansmen not seek to free you? Could they not have paid a ransom or some such thing... or fought for your release?"

"They may have done such things," he said. "Pharlain might not have told me if they had." He doubted that anyone had offered to pay a ransom. Nor, he thought, would his father or brothers have inquired about his health. But he was not ready to confide that to her... not yet. Mayhap a time would come, or not.

She was still frowning. "My father aids his people whenever he can. I know that if one of our lads were captured, Father would do all he could to win the man's freedom... or the woman's, come to that," she added firmly.

"He would, aye," Mag said. "He does seem to be that sort of a man. But if you think that our dallying will annoy him, mayhap we should make haste."

She gave him a quizzical look but turned and strode swiftly along the path, offering him that splendid view again. However, his enjoyment of it faded under the weight of knowing that he owed her answers to her questions. He suspected that what had stopped him might be fear of her reaction, rather than simple reluctance to discuss painful facts. That might mean that he feared he might lose her, though.

She made no further effort to converse, and he soon saw the tower rising above the trees. The gate opened before they reached it, and Andrew Dubh stood just inside, waiting for them.

The lass did not seem surprised to see him.

⁓

Andrena knew from the look on her father's face that he expected them to have news for him. Feeling contrary and annoyed with both men, she bade him a cheerful greeting and asked if her mother was in the solar.

"Sakes, I dinna ken where she be. I've been wondering where the pair of ye were." He was not looking at her but at Magnus Mòr, who remained silent.

"I walked to the cliffs," Andrena said. "Then we speared a pair of fine salmon near my cache on the home burn and came home."

"Well then?" Andrew said, still looking at Magnus, who hefted the string of fish for him to see. Fixing a piercing gaze on Andrena then, Andrew said, "Ye ken fine what I want to hear, lass? Will ye agree to marry this fine lad?"

"I will, sir, because he is kind and considerate and I ken fine that you might have provided someone much worse. But I'll tell you plainly, I am by no means sure that this is the best notion you've ever conceived."

But Andrew was grinning. "'Tis a fine plan," he insisted. "Ye'll see. I've sent for the priest to come as soon as ever he can get here. I didna tell him *why* he's to come, so likely he'll be imagining last rites or such. Forbye, he'll be pleased to find a wedding awaiting him instead.

"But now, lad," he said to Mag without giving Andrena a chance to respond, "I were thinking ye might want to send word off to Inch Galbraith, too, so that your kinsmen can see ye wed. If so, we should send someone straightaway. Sithee, the priest be at Balloch, so he might arrive as soon as tomorrow evening."

"We can discuss that further without detaining her ladyship, sir," Magnus said in his amiable way.

Andrena gave him a look that should have given him second thoughts about marrying her. Then, bobbing a curtsy in the general direction of her father, she made her escape. As she left, she heard Andrew say that they could discuss whatever Magnus wanted to discuss and to come along to his private chamber.

Stifling a sigh, she went in search of her sisters.

~

"What is it, lad?" Andrew asked as he led the way across the yard.

"By your leave, sir, I would wait until we know that none will overhear us."

"Aye, sure," Andrew said. But he kept silent only until he had ushered Mag upstairs to his small chamber and shut the door. Then he said, "Out with it now, lad. What remains to discuss?"

"I doubt that my lord father or brothers would come if we invited them," Mag said quietly. "You must know that my father most likely supports Murdoch, Lennox, and Pharlain. He may not approve of this marriage."

"Arthur Galbraith is still your father," Andrew said.

"He is also the chief of your clan. You have a duty to seek his blessing, lad, if not his permission to wed."

"Neither is necessary," Mag replied. "See you, sir, my father disowned me before I was captured. To the best of my knowledge, he made no effort to seek my freedom. Nor did my brothers." The ache in his soul that he had long since ceased to notice stirred again as he said those words. But he had had much practice in concealing such feelings and suppressed the ache with relative ease.

Andrew, still regarding him sternly from under dark and bushy eyebrows, remained silent for another moment or two before he said, "I'll admit that I did wonder what went amiss, because I'd heard nowt of Arthur's trying to free ye. I tell ye, though, lad, having lost sons of mine own, I canna believe that the man didna care. He has aye got a fierce temper, though. Also, he was deep in grief then over the loss of your eldest brother, Will, as ye must ken fine."

Mag drew a steadying breath before he said, "He blames me for Will's death, my lord. Had I not persuaded Will that Pharlain and his lot were wrong to side with the men determined to keep Murdoch in power and do nowt to bring the rightful King home, Will would never have been in that fracas with me and my men."

"Ye were ambushed, were ye no?"

"We were, aye. But, in troth, we went in search of trouble. I was fierce in my desire to bring Jamie home from England, and knowing of the rift in Clan Farlan, we'd hoped to persuade some of Pharlain's men to abandon him and join us."

"Look here," Andrew said. "Ye were no letting Pharlain keep ye in near slavery just so ye could spy on the gallous snaffler, were ye?"

Mag smiled wryly at the thought. "No, sir, I was not. I'll admit that I did keep my eyes and ears open, but that was necessary for my own survival. Pharlain made no secret of his hope that I'd step out of line far enough to give him cause to hang me. I think the only reason he did not invent such a cause was that some of his men had begun treating me with respect. I fear that you and the lady Andrena think that, because of my size, I possess the mythical powers of your mythical giants."

"The plain fact is that when ye decided to escape, ye did so straightaway."

"Does it seem so?" Mag asked, considering the point. "Mayhap it does. But I learned of Pharlain's part in the conspiracy over time by piecing together bits of information gleaned from numerous sources. When I could no longer doubt the conspirators' foul intent, I realized that I had to warn his grace as soon as I could. I admit that I then seized the first opportunity that offered. Even so, nearly a sennight passed without providing any such opportunity."

"Then the sooner ye be wedded and on your way, the better," Andrew said.

"I have not told Andrena that my father disowned me, sir, but I should. Not only do I dislike keeping it from her—"

He broke off because Andrew was shaking his head. "Ye've nae cause to tell her straightaway," the older man said. "Forbye, ye may find that, for all your strong belief to the contrary, your father will be gey glad to see ye."

"With respect, sir, he made it plain that he does *not* want to see me again. I know that you mean for Andrena and me to live here, but—"

"I do, aye, so ye've nae need to burden the lass with

Arthur's opinions or his rants. 'Tis best to keep your own counsel in this, lad. She canna read your mind."

Mag agreed, whereupon Andrew told him that it was time for the midday meal and the household would be gathering in the great hall.

They went downstairs to find all three sisters on the dais with Lady Aubrey.

Andrew strode to his place at the table there and, facing the lower hall, raised both arms for silence. When everyone was quiet, he said, "This braw laddie, Magnus Mòr Galbraith, has asked our Andrena to marry him, and she has agreed. I have sent for the priest, who will marry them as soon as he arrives from Balloch."

Cheers broke out, accompanied by the general foot stomping that indicated strong approval, and glancing at Andrena, Mag thought she looked pale. But he had no time to think about it, because the lady Lachina approached him.

Smiling, she held out a length of red-and-green wool to him. "I thought you might like this plaid to keep," she said. "These are our own colors, and since my father has said that you mean to take the MacFarlan name…"

"He takes much for granted still, I'm thinking," Mag said gently.

"You will soon come to see that he assumes that others will always do as he bids them," she replied. Then, with a glance toward her mother, she looked back at Mag and added with a wry look, "Most of the time."

⁓

Andrena, standing by her mother and trying to conceal her own unease at her father's grand declaration, watched

Magnus while he talked with Lina, his animated gestures revealing his pleasure in the new plaid. She heard him promise that he would return the gray-and-white one directly after they dined and Lina's reply that he could do so whenever he found it convenient.

Lina added, "Your own old plaid should be ready for you tomorrow, sir. You will then possess one for formal occasions and one for every day."

Andrena knew that Lina was also making him a new linen sark of his own, so that Malcolm's Peter could have his own old mended one back.

Telling herself that it was useless to be wondering if she was doing the right thing by marrying Magnus, since her father's announcement had effectively put everything in train for the marriage, she wondered instead if the priest would come as quickly as Andrew Dubh expected.

Beside her, Lady Aubrey's thoughts had clearly taken a similar path, because she said quietly, "I expect the priest will arrive before nightfall tomorrow, my dearling. But I think it will be wiser to wait and marry on Wednesday afternoon."

Chapter 6

During the meal, Mag thought Andrena seemed unusually quiet. His hearing had become more acute during his imprisonment, and he had developed the ability to listen to one person while keeping an ear out for other remarks that might be of interest or importance. So, while he listened respectfully to all that Andrew said to him, he remained alert to voices from the ladies' end of the table.

He knew Andrena's voice now. Despite questions from Muriella about what he and Andrena had done that morning, he heard only a word or two from Andrena. Quieter, less audible comments from the lady Lachina evinced naught more until Lady Aubrey said she thought the wedding should take place on Wednesday.

Quietly, Andrena said, "It must be as my lord father and you wish, Mam."

Andrew Dubh was describing the bounties of Tùr Meiloach, the number of sheep and cattle grazing on shielings spread high and low across its acres, the number of men-at-arms, drovers, tenants, and others. He also listed the dangers that lack of attention to their boundaries might bring now that Pharlain's men had successfully trespassed and crossed so much territory unharmed.

Although Mag listened and responded to what his host said, he decided that Andrena's submissive attitude, while praiseworthy, seemed uncharacteristic even to one who had known her for only a short time. Recalling Lachina's earlier remark about their mother—and the boy Pluff's comments that morning about Lady Aubrey—Mag wondered if everyone at Tùr Meiloach stood in awe of her ladyship.

"Ye'll want to bathe afore the priest comes," Andrew said.

Smiling reminiscently, Mag said, "I did so before retiring last night, sir. Your steward, Malcolm Wylie, suggested I might, and I must tell you that it was a great pleasure to sink into a tub of hot water again. Pharlain's notion of bathing is to throw a chap into the loch wrapped in chains to see if he can swim in them."

"I did note that ye'd tidied your hair and shaved off your beard," Andrew said. "If ye've nowt else to occupy ye the noo, I've summat to show ye."

"I am yours to command, sir."

"Aye, well, we'll see about that, won't we?" Andrew replied with a grin. "Sithee, it does occur to me that if ye mean to seek out his grace, the King, ye'll need to arm yourself."

Before his imprisonment, Mag had rarely gone anywhere unarmed, so he was glad Andrew had raised the subject. He had not thought the time right yet to inquire about weapons.

"What sort d'ye like to carry?" Andrew asked.

"I miss my sword most of all," Mag said. "But I was accustomed to carrying a dirk and often a spear or a bow and quiver, as well."

"I can provide whatever ye need, but I've nae horse large enough to carry ye, only garrons," Andrew said. "Colquhoun will accommodate ye, though, if ye want to ride to Glasgow. His own sons are tall men. Sakes, Ian is nigh as broad across the shoulders as ye be yourself."

"I'd reach Glasgow faster by boat," Mag said, refusing to let his thoughts linger on the image that leaped to mind of the scrawny, prank-loving lad he recalled as Ian Colquhoun growing into a tall man as broad-shouldered as himself.

"Talk to Colquhoun when ye reach Craggan Tower," Andrew said. "When he hears that ye've married our Andrena, he'll likely aid ye however he can."

"I'm not sure I should tell him why I'm going to Glasgow," Mag said. "Does he support the King or Murdoch?"

"I trust the man. But ye'll want to decide about that for yourself."

That was true, but Mag knew Colquhoun would be easy to read. He worried more about Andrena's reaction when she learned he would leave right after they wed.

～

Lost in her own thoughts, Andrena paid little heed to her sisters' low-voiced conversation. She was glad she would not have to marry the next day. But marrying in two days was not much better.

It had struck her when her father made the announcement that *thinking* about marrying a man who would aid Andrew in reclaiming his lands and title was one thing. Actually *doing* it was something else altogether.

In the past, whenever her sisters had asked her what

she thought of the notion, she had replied that she knew her duty. The man involved was some unknown person hovering in a distant future and had never seemed to matter. She had trusted Andrew not to pick a fool.

Magnus Mòr had already shown that he was no fool. He was not only larger than life but a living, breathing man about whom she knew next to nothing and could deduce little more. Nevertheless, and despite his amiable manner, she had a strong feeling that he would prove harder to manage than Andrew was.

She had enjoyed their morning together, but a lifetime? What would happen if she decided *after* she married him that she loathed the man? What if she told the priest before the ceremony that she was not ready to marry anyone? She had learned while visiting her mother's kinsmen that a Scotswoman could refuse any marriage if she was willing to face the consequences of her decision.

By law, no one could force her to marry.

But the consequences could be dreadful. What if Parlan seized Tùr Meiloach, killed Andrew, and turned her mother and sisters out? What if Parlan took them all prisoner, as he had taken Magnus Mòr?

If she married Magnus, the Galbraiths might help them defeat Parlan and reclaim Arrochar and Loch Sloigh, their clan gathering place in the mountains north of Arrochar. Then Andrew would control the pass and the tarbet again, and Parlan would be just another clansman—if Andrew didn't hang him for his treachery.

Lady Aubrey declared that it was time the ladies retired to discuss what Andrena would need for her admittedly hasty wedding. Starting at the disruption of her reverie, Andrena looked from her mother to Lina and Murie.

Both of her sisters were grinning at her.

"I'll wager I can guess what you were thinking," Murie said with a chuckle. Lowering her voice and indicating Magnus, she added, "He is as big as a mountain but cheerful withal. We like him, Dree."

Glancing at him, Andrena saw his lips twitch and knew that he had heard Murie's comment. By the frown on her mother's face, she deduced that Lady Aubrey was not as amused by that comment as Magnus was.

Lady Aubrey said quietly, "Make your curtsy to your lord father, Muriella. Then hie yourself ahead of us to the solar."

"Aye, Mam," Murie said contritely. Excusing herself with equal politeness to her father, she led the way upstairs.

A fire crackled on the solar hearth, and someone had shuttered the windows and lit two candles. Andrena opened the south-facing window to see that, outside, the sun still shone. The air remained as crisp as a wintry day.

"May I leave the shutters open for a time, Mam?" she asked.

"Aye, sure," Lady Aubrey said. "Lina, what do you think Dree should wear for her wedding?"

"I know just the thing," Lina replied.

Turning back to the window, Andrena stopped listening. She would wear what they decided she should, so her thoughts flew elsewhere. Having been to two of her cousins' weddings, she recalled promises they'd made to be obedient to their husbands. Therefore, according to Holy Kirk, God would want her to obey Magnus.

What if she thought he was wrong about something?

The thought steadied her. When had she ever failed to

express her opinions? Moreover, the man had shown no inclination to dismiss anything she'd said to him.

Just one thing, a small voice in her head reminded her. He had certainly dismissed her assurance that Andrew would urge him to marry her.

Stifling a sigh, she assured herself that Magnus, knowing that he'd been wrong about Andrew, was smart enough to have learned from the incident.

She continued to argue with herself, knowing she would do none of the things that her inner voice suggested. She would obey her father because she had known she would from the day she'd first understood what he would ask of her.

"Your sisters will see to your clothing, Dree," Lady Aubrey said. "So come now with me to my chamber, for I want to talk with you. I shall also want to talk with you, Muriella," she added sternly, "*before* you leave to visit Annie."

Casting a sympathetic look at Murie but more curious about what their mother would say to her, Andrena followed Lady Aubrey across the landing to the bedchamber she shared with Andrew. The hearth there boasted no fire, because the room habitually retained smoke.

The window was open, so the room was chillier than the solar. But Andrew objected to sleeping in a smoky room. He explained, whenever anyone dared to raise the subject in his presence, that he was quite capable of keeping his lady wife warm in bed. If such comments embarrassed her ladyship, Andrena had seen no sign of it.

Now, however, Lady Aubrey lit several candles in their dishes and then shuttered the window. "What think you of this marriage, love?" she asked when she had latched the shutters and draped a warm, pink woolen shawl over her shoulders.

"In troth, Mam, I know not what to think of it or of Magnus Mòr Galbraith. He conceals his thoughts and feelings too well."

"Mayhap he hides naught, my love. Mayhap he is as he seems to be—a large, placid, kindly gentleman. One might easily find a worse husband."

Holding her mother's gaze, Andrena said, "He eluded those men of Cousin Parlan's easily yestermorn. Even so, any hunted man must feel great anxiety, even fear of capture. Mam, he took shelter in a tree, and whilst I was telling those men that Father would take strong exception to their trespassing on our land, we stood right underneath him. Yet I felt *no* sense of his presence. Mam, you *know*—"

"I do know that you can usually sense such things, Dree," Lady Aubrey interjected. "But you know me as well. I believe this match will be a good one. Good not only for your father and Clan Farlan but also good for you."

"Will we be happy together, Mam?"

"Now, how would I know that?" her mother said, smiling. "That is for you to determine, not me. I *can* tell you that no marriage is happy all of the time. But if you will try to understand Magnus and do your best to help him understand you, I believe that your marriage will endure and prosper."

"Will Father win back his lands and title?"

"I can never foresee things at will, Dree. I am too close to your father to do so, in any event. You know that, because I have told you so before. That may be why you cannot sense things about Magnus. Mayhap the Fates have chosen him for you. If so, they may allow him to hide his feelings until he wants to reveal them."

"I hoped that if you could tell me *anything* about him, you would know if he can help Father defeat Parlan."

Lady Aubrey shook her head. "I believe he will try, because he seems to be a man of his word. But like any such gift or curse, mine is ever unpredictable."

"But my abilities have not been," Andrena protested. "Not until now, with him. What if being with him destroys my gifts altogether?"

"I believe, as your father does, love, that yours are but finely honed instincts. Whatever it is that keeps you from sensing Magnus's emotions and therefore his presence when he is near you lies in him, not in you. If he is not as placid as he seems to be, then he contains himself better than most people do. That's all."

"But—"

Lady Aubrey lifted a finger, silencing her before adding gently, "You sense things the way most creatures do—and many humans to a lesser degree. You were just born with a stronger ability than most. Your sisters share many of your gifts, some as strongly, others not. Perhaps Magnus shares them, too. Men, especially hunters and warriors, often have a stronger awareness of other people or beasts nearby than women do. They also have an ability to creep up on prey or enemies."

"But I—"

"Think of that fawn you nearly stepped on two summers ago. You had no sense of its presence before you stepped over that log, because the fawn revealed nothing. Mayhap Magnus Mòr has acquired that same ability."

"I don't know how a man may acquire a fawn's ability to keep predators from sensing its presence," Andrena said. "But perhaps you are right."

"I am always right," Lady Aubrey said, smiling again. "Now, what do you know about a wife's duties to her husband in their bedchamber?"

"Only what my cousins chattered about at their wedding feasts."

"Then, let us talk about that. Your husband will bed you right after your wedding feast, and a wife should know her part in that. I shan't keep you long, though. I know you need time to prepare. I did suggest to your father that Wednesday is a more auspicious day for your wedding than tomorrow. But if the priest arrives by midday... You know how impatient your father can be."

"Aye, Mam," Andrena said as she drew up a stool and sat down. "So, prithee, tell me what I must know."

The priest arrived an hour after supper the following evening.

When Andrew said it was too late to hold the ceremony that night, Mag felt relief but also surprise, because Andrew had been so eager to get them married quickly. Mag decided that Lady Aubrey must have exerted her influence.

He had scarcely laid eyes on Andrena since the previous day's midday meal, so he supposed she was preparing for the wedding. Many people were superstitious about such rites and believed it was bad luck for a groom to set eyes on his bride on their wedding day, before the ceremony. Since Andrena had shown no sign of being superstitious, he thought it more likely that the women feared Andrew might insist on an immediate ceremony despite his lady's wishes.

Mag was with him when the priest arrived, so he stayed long enough to be courteous, then excused himself.

"Aye, sure because heaven kens when ye'll sleep again after tonight, eh, lad?" Andrew said, clapping him on a shoulder. "Forbye, I've near talked your ears off this day and a half past, telling ye about Tùr Meiloach. Ye should take time to ponder what I said, though, lest ye have questions for me afore ye leave."

The priest looked from one man to the other, his curiosity plain. But Andrew said naught to relieve it, and Mag had learned enough about his host to believe he would keep the assassination plot against the King to himself. Priests were famous for spreading news and gossip acquired outside of the confessional. At least, Mag hoped they never shared people's confessions.

Having little to do to prepare for his wedding, he soon slept and awoke to the gray twilight of a misty dawn outside his open window.

Donning his sark and his old plaid, he decided to explore the barmkin yard. He had no sooner stepped outside than he heard shrieks of pain.

Following the sound, he found the lad Pluff in the clutches of a muscular brute, who was flailing him with what appeared to be a leather scabbard.

"Hold there," Mag said in a calm voice but one that carried easily to the other man's ears. "That's enough of that, I think. You disturb the morning's peace."

The man paused but said gruffly, "Ye've nae call tae be telling me when's enough. I ha' charge o' this lad."

"Nevertheless, you will release him."

"He deserves every lick," the man insisted. "I told him tae muck oot the byre afore he tends them blasted dogs, but he'd liefer play wi' the dogs."

"There are better ways to earn the respect of your minions," Mag said.

"Aye, well, the willsome bairn deserves *this* way."

"I'll talk with him," Mag said. "I do not know you, but you do know that I am Magnus Mòr. You also know I am to marry the lady Andrena today, aye?"

"Aye, sir, I do," the man said with a grimace. "I be Euan MacNur. And I didna mean nae disrespect. But more oft than not this bairn sets his mind on things other than his chores. When I saw the state o' yon byre this morn—"

"I have said that I'll talk with him, and I will," Mag said. "You will come with me now, Pluff," he added.

"Aye, sir," Pluff said, looking relieved. As they strolled across the yard together, he said, "Thank 'e, sir. I feared he might kill me this time. He's a dour man, is Euan Mac-Nur, when he's peevish or crabbit."

"Is what MacNur told me the truth?" Mag asked him.

Pluff shrugged. "I'm tae feed the dogs and see tae them as soon as I get up, but I'm also tae help him in the byre. Sithee, some days he be more short-tempered than others. I dinna ken why."

"Has he told you to muck out the byre *before* you tend to the dogs?"

"Aye, sure. But he's doesna usually get up as early as he did today. So I have time tae do both."

"If you failed to see to the byre first, then you are the one in the wrong, Pluff. That is, unless the laird himself told you to see first to the dogs. Did he?"

Pluff had begun to look uneasy. Darting a wary glance up at Mag's face, he seemed to take solace from what he saw there. He said, "It wasna the laird wha' told me, sir, but the lady Murie. Sithee, the young ladies favor the dogs. Often Lady Dree comes oot afore MacNur does. She expects me tae feed the dogs first, so they be ready tae go wi' her if she wants them."

"I see," Mag said.

"I thought ye might," Pluff said with a sigh of relief.

"What I see is that you need to discuss this dilemma of yours with MacNur."

"What's that... me dilemma?"

"This dilemma is that more than one person in authority has given you orders in such a way that you cannot obey one without disobeying another."

"Aye, sure, but Lady Dree be the one I should obey, aye?"

"But you are in MacNur's charge. So you must tell him how it is and seek his advice. To do that, you must first apologize to him for failing to follow his orders," Mag added, emphasizing the last five words.

"Apologize tae him? But I—"

"You must, for you were in the wrong," Mag said, drawing him to a halt. "You want to be a man-at-arms one day, right? And mayhap to lead other men?"

"Aye, sure, I do," the boy said, looking up at him earnestly. "I'm already a fair shot wi' me bow and arrows."

"Then you must learn to take orders, Pluff, and carry them out faithfully. One day, if you work hard enough, you may be captain of a nobleman's guard. You seem a likely enough lad to accomplish whatever you set your mind to do. But if you cannot follow orders yourself, you will never be a good leader of men."

The boy fell silent for a time. Then, looking up at Mag, he said, "Ye're right, sir. I should ha' talked wi' Euan. But if Lady Dree be wroth wi' me—"

"You may tell her that you and I have discussed the matter. She can be as wroth with me as she likes, laddie. She will have that right after we've married."

Pluff grinned then, saying, "I dinna envy ye that, sir. Lady Dree's got a right sharp tongue when she's vexed. I ha' heard it for m'self."

"Aye, so likely I'll be crushed by her fury in no time," Mag said.

The boy laughed. "I dinna think *that*." Then, sobering, he added, "Thank 'e again, sir, though it wouldna surprise me if Euan MacNur thinks I've no been punished enough and gives me more chores tae do."

"If he does, you will do them without complaint, Pluff."

Giving the lad a moment or two to ponder that statement, Mag added, "Speaking of chores, it occurs to me that a man getting married is supposed to have someone stand up with him. But I have no friend here to do it and no time to send for one. Do you know any man who might be willing to support me today?"

Pluff frowned. "There dinna be many gentlemen hereabouts, sir. Mayhap the Laird o' Colquhoun or one o' his sons would do it. But the wedding be at midday, and it would take gey longer tae send 'em a message and get someone here."

"I ken that fine," Mag said. "The chap need not be a gentleman, though. I have not been one myself these many months past. I'd just like to have someone at the wedding who is willing to stand by me and wish me good luck."

"Mayhap Malcolm Wylie would stand up wi' ye. He's getting on in years, but he's one as would ken how tae behave withal."

"But I've barely met him. In troth, Pluff, I've been here such a short time that I've not talked with anyone more than once except the laird and Lady Andrena."

"Ye've talked wi' me," Pluff pointed out. "*Twice.*"

"So I have," Mag said, eyeing him thoughtfully. "Perhaps you might see your way clear to supporting me then."

Pluff's jaw dropped. "Me?"

"Aye, sure, why not?"

"But I'm naebody, and ye were just vexed wi' me. And I've nowt tae wear!"

Chuckling, Mag said, "Brush your hair and you'll look fine to me. But I'll ask Lady Lachina if she has aught she might lend you to smarten you up."

"Aye, then, I'll do it. But I'd best be getting back tac MacNur. Likely, he'll be fain tae get even wi' me for bringing ye down on him."

"Then get to it, lad."

Watching him dash across the yard, Mag smiled and wondered what Andrena and her family would think of his groomsman.

As he turned toward the tower, he saw Lady Aubrey emerge from the main entrance. Seeing him, she waved, and he strode to meet her.

"I'm glad to have found you, Magnus," she said. "I noted yestereve that you wear no jewelry. I expect that Parlan confiscated whatever you had."

"I wore none then, either," he said.

"Well, you'll need a ring for Andrena. I thought you might like to have my mother's ring to give her, if that would suit you. If not, Dree can wear it until you find a more suitable one."

"I cannot imagine one she would like better," he said. "But I'll let her decide. I thank you, my lady, for thinking of the lack. I found myself a groomsman, but I'd meant to tell Andrena I'd look for a ring in Glasgow."

"Well, this will do for now," she said, handing him a gold band with a small yellow stone set in it. "But who is—?" Breaking off on a gurgle of laughter, she said, "Don't tell me you asked that incorrigible scamp, Pluff, to stand up with you."

"Is he incorrigible?"

"Oh, aye, the most delightful laddie, and gey smart. He will be strutting about for weeks now. But how kind of you, sir! I knew I would like you."

Speechless, Mag quickly collected his wits, thanked her, and escorted her back inside before going in search of the lady Lachina.

~

Andrena's wedding was over almost before it had begun.

She thought that such a hasty ceremony in the great hall was hardly worth the priest's time but wondered, too, if Magnus would hold her to her promise to be meek and biddable. The priest had looked sternly at her while she repeated her vows.

Magnus's eyes had twinkled throughout.

She knew he was pleased with his choice of a groomsman.

Red-headed Pluff stood beside him, straight and proud, wearing a clean shirt that was too big for him. He did his duties with stern sobriety until Andrena smiled at him.

Then he grinned, noted the priest's frown, and stiffened again swiftly.

Her sisters stood with her at first but stepped back when the priest beckoned the bridal couple to the make-shift altar. Pluff remained at Magnus's side, and Andrena wondered why until the boy handed him a ring.

Looking now at the flattened gold band that Magnus had put on her finger, she recognized it from its delicate engraving and the small yellow cairngorm set in it as her grandmother's ring. To have it for her own delighted her.

When he slipped it on her finger, his hands were warm and gentle.

Her thoughts flew then to her mother's description of what would happen in their marriage bed. Looking up at him while the priest presented them as Magnus Mòr MacFarlan and his lady wife, and seeing the ardent look in his eyes when his gaze met hers, she felt heat flood her cheeks.

She thought that his cheeks looked a little pink, too.

When the cheering died away, he leaned close and murmured, "I hope you don't mind that it's your gran-dame's ring. I can look for another in Glasgow if you'd liefer have one of your own."

"I love it," she said, adding with a saucy grin, "You may buy me other rings if you like, and necklaces, brace-lets...I'm gey partial to emeralds. Sithee, I saw one once, deep green like the forest in early summer. I'd like to have dozens."

"Greedy wench." He shook his head, then sent a wide-eyed Pluff to join the men in the lower hall and guided her from the erstwhile altar to the high table, where a feast awaited them. Then he said quietly, "Evidently your father neglected to tell you that I've nae wealth of mine own yet to share with you."

"He did tell me," she said. Watching his expression, she added, "But you look like a man who will provide well for me, sir. In troth, I have every confidence of that. You would not want to turn your wife into a threaping scold."

The only change in his expression was the twinkle that lit his eyes again.

She realized as she said the words that, although the thought had not crossed her mind before, she meant every word of what she'd said up to the part about turning into a scold. She did not know what sort of husband he would make, but he was strong, solid, and likable. She was sure he would not let her starve.

They took their places at the center of the high table, flanked by Andrew and Lady Aubrey, with the priest and Andrew's captains at his right and Andrena's sisters to the left of her mother. They all faced the lower hall, where cheering and stomping had broken out again. The din faded away when the priest raised his arms to signal for silence and the grace before meat.

During the feasting, three musicians played lutes and a harp near the foot of the dais. Andrena nibbled this and that, but so aware was she of the large, silent man beside her that she could not concentrate on her food.

After a time, a tingling stirred deep within her. Before she had acquired the full sense of it, Lina leaned past Lady Aubrey and murmured, "We should go, Dree. The men are plotting, I think, and will doubtless snatch Magnus Mòr away at any minute. If you are still here..."

"Not to worry, my lady," Magnus said quietly. "I'll let no harm come to her."

Andrena recognized the wisdom of Lina's warning. "They would not purposely harm me, sir," she said. "But you must know our clan's reputation for unruliness. That reputation has naught to do with Parlan but much to do with our history. They will abduct you, strip you, and carry you to our chamber. If I'm nearby, someone might knock me over in the melee. I refuse to be the cause of some poor man's hanging just because he's in his cups and stumbles into me. I must go."

"Then go, lass, but do not fear for me. I don't 'abduct' easily."

Chapter 7 _____

Mag watched the women leave and saw with relief that Andrew did not mean to let his men tease or harass Andrena...at least, not until she was safely in bed and under the covers. As for himself...

He saw them preparing for him, six large men, although none as large as he was. Even so, and although he was sure he could keep them from capturing and carrying him, he likewise knew that someone might be hurt in the struggle. He did not want to begin his relationships at Tùr Meiloach with mayhem.

Accordingly, he nodded for the gillie standing nearest him to fill his goblet with wine from the jug. When the lad had obeyed, Mag stood and raised the goblet, saying in a voice that carried above the din of music and conversation, "Be all now upstanding, for I would offer a toast to my lady wife on our wedding day and mine own heartfelt thanks to the great clan that fathered her. I ken fine that I am new to your midst, but I swear to you all that I'll give you nae cause to regret your chief's invitation to become one of your own."

The six men watched him. And, although they raised goblets and cheered with the others when the cheering broke out, their purpose remained clear.

Looking right at them, Mag said, "I am fain to match with any who would test my skills, but we'll do it in the yard at a more appropriate time. Also, the wheel stair here is gey narrow. If you crack my skull whilst you are 'helping' me to my marriage bed, you will do my lady nae favor. If I crack one of yours, I'll be doing the clan none, either. Forbye, I'll welcome assistance with my unclothing, but I'd liefer see to it *after* we reach the room allotted to the purpose than let you lot *try* to accomplish it whilst attempting to carry me up yon stairs."

Stomping, laughter, and ribald comments greeted his words. The men drank to his toast. Then, with a roar, the six and many others charged toward him.

Andrena, looking in astonishment around the bedchamber that she and Magnus would occupy, said to her mother, "This is the old munitions room. How did you accomplish such a transformation so quickly?"

"Annie Wylie and I have been anticipating this day for nearly nineteen years, my dearling. We spun and wove the wool for your bed curtains years ago, and I worked the design on them for many evenings after you girls had gone to bed."

"The bed is huge!"

"Aye, we had to rearrange things quickly, because we wanted Magnus to sleep comfortably, without his feet hanging out. So the men built a larger frame, and we increased the size of your featherbed and bedclothes to fit it. Annie and I added fabric to the bed curtains, too, so they will close when you want them to. You still lack curtains for your window, but you like to sleep with the shutters open, and I hear that Magnus leaves his open, too."

The room was near the top of the tower, just under the ramparts. Andrena knew that in winter, a number of their men had slept on the floor there.

"Is that why Father has built more cottages outside the wall?"

"'Tis one reason. He also wants to increase our guard near the high passes. It concerns him that those three men of Parlan's suffered little for their trespass. Ways do exist at either end of the ridge, after all, where small parties of men might slip through the passes. In winter, men guarding those passes will need warm cottages near their posts. But make haste, my dearling. You do not want them to catch you out of bed when they bring Magnus to you."

"We'll hear them coming up," Andrena said.

Lina laughed. "We may hear them, aye. But if they've stripped his clothes off on the way, he'll have no reason to enter that room across the way. So hurry!"

She and Murie helped Andrena undress and gave her a robe to wear while she sat and let her mother brush her hair. Although she was nervous, she made no protest when the women slipped the robe off her and urged her into the huge bed.

No sooner had she drawn the coverlet to her chin than clamor erupted in the stairwell. Wishing she could dive under the covers and hide until the noisemakers went away again, she remained stoical. But her heart pounded in her chest.

The door to the bedchamber banged open, and multiple hands and bodies thrust Magnus through the opening. He clutched a ragged sark to his loins.

Lina and Murie shrieked and covered their eyes. A roar from the priest, following close behind the men, silenced everyone. Even so, many of the men accompanied Magnus and the priest into the room. Others crowded in the doorway.

"Ha' the goodness tae recall their ladyships' presence here!" the priest bellowed fiercely. "Ye'll silence yourselves till I've said the blessing. Then ye'll clear a path so their ladyships can depart with dignity. And ye'll take your own leave when they go, or I'll put the curse o' me ancestors on every one o' your gallous souls! D'ye hear me now, the lot o' ye?"

They fell silent so quickly that the one who said, "Aye, the devil hisself could hear ye," stirred a chuckle or two.

Andrena noted that one such chuckle came from her newly wedded husband.

The priest hastily blessed the bed and the couple about to share it. The men who had entered the room made way for Lady Aubrey, Lina, and Murie to leave, then followed them, revealing Andrew near the door as they did. He lingered long enough to say while the priest shooed men from the landing, "Ye've my blessing, too, the pair of ye. We'll no look to see either of ye afore midday tomorrow."

Then the door shut, and Andrena was alone with her naked husband.

⁓

She was his. The thought was a heady one, because she was beautiful and he liked her. One part of his body liked her so much that it was already eager to merge with hers, so eager that he feared he might frighten her. One look at the lass told him that she was not frightened yet, despite the recent din and rowdy company.

She had propped herself against a pile of pillows. She had also pulled the coverlet up so far that it covered her to her chin. But she regarded him calmly.

Late afternoon sunlight still lit the small room, although now that they were alone, he saw that it had just seemed small with so many crowded into it and because of the large bed. He supposed he should be grateful to the priest for shooing everyone out so quickly and not allowing the ruckus to grow as wild as it might have. It was not unheard of for a bedding audience, usually all men by that time, to demand that the couple perform for their entertainment. Not that Mag would have allowed that. He was just glad that no one had suggested it.

Eyeing his lady wife thoughtfully, he said gently, "D'ye ken what we're expected to do here, lass?"

"Aye, Mam told me."

"What did she tell you?"

Blushing rosily, she said with a calmness that seemed careful now rather than natural, "She said many things. Above all, she said I must let you guide me and trust you to be gentle with me."

He nodded, wondering what details Lady Aubrey had provided and deciding they did not matter. His cock strained under the wadded-up sark he held against it.

"You should get rid of that thing," she said.

He bit his lower lip to stifle the laughter that surged within him at the first "thing" that came to mind, and which he definitely meant to keep. He thought he would be wiser *not* to explain that he had been thinking of anything other than his sark, though. His bride might not appreciate the humor.

Instead, he obeyed her, tossing the sark onto a nearby stool.

~

Andrena gasped at the sight of him. Surely her mother was wrong. Something that large could *never*... Thought ceased.

He was about to get into bed.

She scooted nearer the wall side of the bed to make room for him.

The bed shifted with his weight until he was near enough for her to feel his warmth despite his body's having been unclothed for some time. Late afternoon sunlight brought no heat with it, but his body, still inches away from her, radiated warmth as if someone had slipped a huge hot brick into the bed.

When he slipped an arm behind her shoulders and eased her closer, she welcomed his warmth.

"I heard you gasp, lass. Art fearful?"

"Nay, just concerned that we won't fit together as Mam says we should."

"Men and women are made to fit together," he said. "Sometimes it takes a bit more work and patience than other times, but we'll find our ways."

His deep voice was like a low-pitched, comforting hum near her ear. She had not realized how tense she was until she felt her body begin to relax.

"What else did your mam say?"

She tried to think and wished her memory for discourse were as reliable as Murie's was. The things her

mother had described to her had seemed difficult to imagine doing with him. At last, remembering Lady Aubrey's
primary advice, she said, "Why don't you just show me
what to do?"

Mag's body leaped at the suggestion. The most eager part
of him had relaxed as they'd talked. Now, if possible, it
seemed more eager than before.

"Art comfortable as we are now?" he asked her.

"Aye, you're as warm as a hearth fire."

He smiled. "I would like to make you feel warm all
over," he said.

"Don't you think you should kiss me first? You did not
do so when the priest presented us to everyone. My cousins' husbands kissed them straightaway."

"Did they? I warrant their priest told them they might.
When ours did not, I decided to wait. Forbye, the men
in the hall were already rowdy, so it seemed sensible to
follow the priest's lead. I can make up for that lack now,
though."

Looking into his eyes, she pursed her lips expectantly.
The very way she did it made him smile. It also told him
that no one had ever thoroughly kissed her. He looked forward to remedying that lack as well.

Leaning up on his left elbow, he bent toward her and
touched his lips to hers.

"Good sakes," she muttered against them. "Your lips
are even warmer than the rest of you. You may well *bake*
me in this bed."

"Shhh," he murmured back. He kissed her more
firmly, then teased her lower lip with his tongue while he

moved his free hand under the covers to cup one breast. When she gasped, he slipped his tongue between her lips, just far enough to give her a hint of his intent. When she responded by pressing her lips harder against his, he eased his tongue in further and moved his thumb over the tip of her breast.

Her body arced upward, and her lips parted.

Keeping her mouth occupied with his, he waited for her to relax, then moved his hand to her belly and then slowly, tantalizingly, back up to her other breast. Both were firm and silky, and each filled his hand as if God had meant for them to do so.

⸏

Andrena savored every movement of that teasing hand, astonished by the sensations that its slightest motion stirred in her. Never before had she felt such things. Lady Aubrey, although having declared that coupling could be pleasurable for both parties, had not begun to describe *how* pleasurable it might be.

His kisses stirred similar sensations, making her body feel as warm all through as his did... even warmer. It was as though hers caught fire here, there, everywhere, from just the slightest touch of his lips, tongue, or a finger.

When he'd thrust his warm tongue into her mouth, although she had never heard of anyone else doing such a thing, it seemed right for him to do so.

His hand moved lower, nearing the fork of her legs. He stirred her feelings more with each new thing he did until she was writhing with desire for more. But when he slipped a finger inside her, her body tensed.

"Easy, lass," he said.

"I'm not a mare," she said with an unexpected chuckle that she knew came more from taut nerves than aught else. "I did not know you were going to do that."

"You worried about our fitting together," he murmured. "It will help if I stretch you out some before we try more passionate things."

"My father did say that we should stay abed until midday tomorrow," she reminded him. "Will it take as long as that?"

"Nay, it will not," he replied. "Not only will I be starving long before then, but you will be, too. Also, I must be up and about before midday, because I must leave early Friday morning for—"

"Leave!" She stared up at him in astonishment. "Where are we going?"

"*We* are not going anywhere, but I must go to Glasgow and mayhap some distance beyond," he replied calmly. "Your mother knew. I thought you did, too."

His finger had stopped moving, and she wished it had not. He had said only that he could buy her a ring in Glasgow. But Glasgow could wait until the morrow.

"You will do as you must," she said. "Mayhap you will tell me more before the time comes. Meantime, prithee, teach me more."

~

He needed no further invitation but used his lips, mouth, hands, and fingers to stir her passions until he knew she was as ready as any maiden could be for her first coupling. Moving gently over her, keeping his weight on his elbows and knees so he would not crush her, using one hand, he eased himself in. Then, positioning himself carefully, he made sure that his right hand retained access to her enticing breasts.

Once in, determined to cause her as little pain as possible until her body had time to adjust to his, he fought his own urges for stimulation and release, to remain gentle. She was breathing heavily and too quickly. To distract her, he bent and touched the tip of his tongue to her left ear, tickling it until she wriggled.

Moving more purposefully then, he attuned himself to her movements and expressions, hoping that Lady Aubrey had not told her she must never complain if he hurt her. He knew that many mothers told their daughters to endure their connubial duties. He wanted Andrena to enjoy them.

When she showed no sign of pain and began to arc against him, he slowly increased his pace until instinct took over. The sounds she made then told him that he was causing her some pain, but she moved with him and her actions encouraged him to let himself go. After he reached his peak and plunged over it, he lay back against the pillows, sated, and pulled her close again.

～

Andrena snuggled against him, although she was thinking that, like the wedding, their physical coupling seemed shorter than it ought to have been.

"Ah, lassie," he murmured, "I hope I did not hurt you too much."

"'Tis a strange aching only," she said. "You are so big; it astonishes me that it did not hurt more. You must be gey good at such coupling."

A new thought occurred to her, and she turned her head to look at him. "Have you done this with many women?"

"That, lady wife, is a question that no bride should ask her husband. Content yourself with your belief that I am good at it, and be done."

He was smiling as he said it, so she smiled back. But once again, she wished she could understand him the way she understood most other people. How ironic that she should marry a man she could barely read at all. How unfair!

"What is it?" he asked abruptly, his smile gone.

"'Tis naught," she said. "I doubt you would understand."

"Perhaps I would not," he admitted. "I know I will not if you do not at least try to explain it to me."

"Not tonight," she said. "I want to think more about it first. I am no longer a maiden now, am I?"

"Nay, lass, you are my wife."

"And you are my husband, sir. But I feel all sticky. Is it permitted that I get up and cleanse myself?"

"Aye, sure," he said. "I'll help you, and you can help me afterward."

"The ewer and basin are on the washstand yonder," she said, pointing. She could not easily get out of the bed until he did.

He got up and strode across the room, and she watched him, enjoying the play of his backside and thigh muscles as he did. His body was magnificent.

He glanced back and grinned at her. "You coming?"

⌒

Her blushes made him smile. He knew she had been watching him and savored the thought that she had wanted to watch. Sakes, just being with the lass brought him more pleasure than he had known in years.

She got out of bed, and it was his turn to stare, because she made a splendid figure. Her tawny hair fell to her hips in a mass of soft, somewhat tangled waves on which the fast lowering sun's light danced in golden glints. Her waist was narrow, her breasts full and firm, her hips wide enough to bear many children, and her arms and legs well shaped and strong looking. Her skin, as he knew for himself, was as smooth as satin and delightful to stroke, caress, kiss, or just to touch.

When they had cleaned themselves, they returned to bed and lay beside each other in comfortable silence until she said casually, "Will you tell me now about this trip of yours to Glasgow?"

"The reason I go is not one that I should talk about."

"Did you tell my father?"

"Aye, sure, I had to."

"Then you should tell me," she said. "I am your wife, and I understand about secrets. Still, if you don't trust me…" She left those words hanging in the air.

He turned onto his side to face her. "What about your sisters? You have told me plainly that the three of you are gey close."

"Aye, we are. They know much about me. If I am distressed, they will know and plague me to tell them why. But if I am not distressed, I need tell them naught."

"That sounds like a threat, madam wife. But mayhap I misunderstood you. Prithee, tell me you do not mean that if I refuse to tell you why I go, it would distress you so that you would feel obliged to tell your sisters."

Her lips twitched wryly, making him want to kiss them again and thus easing his irritation. She said, "I am not petulant, sir, nor petty. They would surely plague me. But

I need tell them only that it is not my tale to tell, and they will desist."

"Will they indeed?" he said, letting her see his disbelief.

⁓

Andrena knew that Lina would desist. But she also knew that Murie would *not* stop plaguing her in such an instance until commanded to do so in no uncertain terms, and for once she could see that Magnus was annoyed. "They may not stop straightaway," she admitted. "But if I promise you to tell no one, that does include Lina and Murie. Is it such a great secret that I must not know it, either?"

He was silent, giving the question thought. Then he said, "I have a message for the King, one that I must get to him as soon as possible."

"Then I *should* go with you," she said. "Think how much safer you would be traveling openly as my husband than as a lone warrior. A large one, forbye, who matches the description that Parlan will have bruited everywhere, along with his demand that whoever sees you must return you to him at once. As *my* husband—"

"Nay, lass," he said. "I will go faster without you. That very danger you mention is reason enough for you to stay here."

"How then," she asked, "do you propose to travel?"

"I will walk if necessary. But Andrew tells me that Colquhoun will provide a horse if he does not transport me to Dumbarton on one of his galleys."

"Aye, he might do that, but he'd be more likely to if I were with you. The Laird of Colquhoun likes me," she added with a smile.

"I expect that most healthy men of any age would like you," he said. "But I trust that you will not plague me about this. I may have an even temper, but a lass who pinches and pokes at me to do what she wants me to do will rarely prosper."

"I see. Well, I am neither a pincher nor a poker, sir. I am your wife and have vowed to obey you. Still, if you change your mind, I'd be fain to go with you."

His eyes narrowed. "Why is it that your meekness arouses my suspicions?"

"I haven't a notion," she said, relieved to know that she *had* aroused feelings in him beyond passion and amusement—his suspicion now and his annoyance when he thought she'd issued a threat. "I am all obedience, sir. Mayhap, whilst I am in this mood, you will teach me more ways to pleasure you. I still ache too much to repeat our earlier exercise, but perhaps you know other pastimes just as delightful."

"I do," he said.

"Good, but I should tell you that I am beginning to sense that I did not eat nearly enough earlier. Do you suppose anyone will think to bring us supper?"

Mag managed to distract her from thoughts of food for another hour or so. By then he was hungry, too. Since Andrew's parting words had suggested that no one would intrude on their privacy, he decided to forage for food himself.

Getting up, he found his old, mended sark in a kist near the wall and put it on. For the ceremony, he had worn the soft new plaid that Lina had given him. But it had disappeared somewhere on the stairway. Although his pursuers abandoned their earlier intention of carrying him to his marriage bed, they had nevertheless managed to denude him while hustling him upstairs. He'd kept his new sark by main strength. Now it was as ragged as the old one had been.

He did not have far to go, though, because a rosy-cheeked maidservant waited on the landing below theirs, far enough away to avoid overhearing them but near enough to send her for sustenance. Informing him that her name was Tibby, she hurried away and returned shortly afterward with a tray.

"The laird said I collected enough food for four people, sir," Tibby said. "But by the size o' ye, I hope I ha' brung enough."

Smiling and assuring her that she had brought plenty, Mag relieved her of the tray and returned to his bedchamber.

As he shut the door, he noted that his bride was looking thoughtful.

"Have you decided to confide your earlier concerns to me?" he asked. "The ones that you feared I'd not understand?"

"Nay, not tonight," she said. "Just now, I was thinking about your journey and the plans we should set in motion to prepare for it."

"What plans? I'll just take one of Andrew's lads along, one whom Colquhoun knows and who will know how to get us across the south river."

"Father or Malcolm usually sees to that," she said. "But they do not do it alone, so other men do know the way. Forbye, you should decide what you will tell such men. How much can you confide to them and to Lord Colquhoun? Also, you need more clothing if you are to visit the King."

"Sakes, lass, his grace won't care how I look. He will care only about what I must tell him."

"As a warrior, you doubtless spent little time in noble society, sir," she said. "His grace, the King, may welcome you but only if his minions deign to tell him that you desire an audience. And then only if he knows who you are. In troth, if he does know, he will also know that Galbraiths have befriended his enemies. In any event, he will receive you more readily if you look as if you belong in his company. You must have *some* baggage if only to make yourself look respectable. Fear not, though. I shall attend to that tomorrow with my sisters' aid. Lina will know just what a gentleman requires for such a journey."

"I want to travel light, Andrena."

"Aye, sure, you did say that you may have to travel beyond Glasgow to find his grace. He moves frequently, or so my cousins and Colquhoun have said. Sithee, I have not yet had the honor of meeting his grace. I have heard, though, that you should not look for him at royal castles, such as Stirling or Edinburgh."

"So your father told me," Mag said, glancing at her as he set the tray on a table near the west-facing window. "He said his grace prefers religious houses, because fortresses remind him of the English ones in which he was held captive."

When she seemed disappointed that he knew what she must have been about to tell him, he eyed her more closely, wondering if she took such interest because she still hoped to go with him or was just acting as a normal wife might act.

Since he hadn't had a wife before . . .

Andrena noted the look but was more interested in the food he had brought. Besides, she had already said some things that ought to make him think.

The rest, she decided, she could leave to her father. Andrew was unlikely to miss the chance to lay his own predicament before the King and even less likely to trust an untested Galbraith—good-son or not and no matter what message Magnus carried—to plead *his* case for him. In the morning, she would pack her things.

Chapter 8

As they supped, Mag asked Andrena to tell him about her kinsmen and more about her life at Tùr Meiloach. She complied willingly, but pointed glances that she sent his way now and again told him that she was resisting a strong desire to demand that he reciprocate by telling her more about his family and Inch Galbraith.

Since he was sure that their wedding night was *not* the time to tell her that his father had disowned him, even if he were inclined to defy Andrew's advice not to do so, he was grateful for her reticence. They soon returned to bed, where he hoped he had redeemed himself by showing her new ways that he could pleasure her and a few ways by which she could return the favor. To his surprise, he then slept deeply and, for the first time in many months, without one bad dream.

He awoke at his usual early hour Thursday morning. Andrena was still asleep with her head resting in the hollow of his shoulder, her soft breath warm against his skin. So he lay quietly until he felt her begin to stir. He saw her eyes open, then widen, and he knew she had abruptly recalled where she was.

Without moving her head, she looked up, saw that he

was awake, and said, "Good morrow, sir. You make a nice warm pillow."

"I hope I am good for more than that," he said. "Did you sleep well?"

"I did, but I'm wide awake now. What shall we do until midday?"

"I am getting up," he said. "I doubt that I've ever stayed abed so long at one time as we have since our wedding feast. I want a brisk walk and a large breakfast. Then I must speak with your father."

"He will have much advice to offer you, aye," she said.

"Before I do any of that, though, I mean to kiss my lady wife," he said, suiting action to words. That action led to more action, and by her eager response he deduced that she was not still sore from their activities the previous evening.

"Have you a maidservant who attends you, lass?" he asked when they were ready to get up and dress.

"My sisters and I share Malcolm's daughter, Tibby," she said. "I warrant she is waiting for me to shout."

"She fetched our supper yestereve. Mayhap she, too, expects us to stay abed until noon."

"Tibby knows me better than that," Andrena said. "Come to that, so does my father. May I walk with you, sir? I should take the dogs out and let them run."

"Aye, sure," he said. "The sky is clear, and the sun will soon be up. I want to walk along those cliffs and see how far one can see when it is clear."

They dressed and went down to the hall, where they found a number of people up and breaking their fast. Andrew was not among them.

"I usually take an apple and a roll with me when I walk," Andrena said.

"Well, I require more food than that," Mag replied. "We'll break our fast properly first and then take our walk."

"Father will be busy in the yard by now or out with some of his men. We should have plenty of time to eat and walk before you need meet with him."

His gaze met and studied hers. She looked utterly guileless, but...

⁓

Andrena always enjoyed a brisk walk and was able to keep up with Magnus, although she could tell that he was shortening his stride to match hers. They walked silently for a time, and as she listened to birds chirping and squirrels chattering, she recalled the silence of the woods the morning she had met him.

It was hard to believe that a mere four days had passed since then.

As they neared the cliffs, she knew from the sound of waves against the shore below that the tide was ebbing. From the clifftop where they had stood before, she saw only one galley on the loch.

"I think that is a Campbell boat from the west shore," she said.

"Aye, it is," he agreed. "You can tell by the boar's head on its banner."

"Faith, you can see that banner well enough from here to recognize the boar's head on it as the Campbells'?"

"Aye, sure, cannot you?"

"Nay, and my long sight is excellent, sir. I can see some yellow and a black device, but many boating clans use yellow as their background color. Faith, but even the Lord

of the Isles' little-black-ship device sits on a yellow background, and several clans have bear's heads, which must
look much the same as a boar's."

"Aye, well, that is the Campbell boar's head," he said.
"I can see it clearly. As for bear's heads, the Galbraith
bear looks up. The Campbell *boar* looks down."

"I surrender," she said, smiling up at him.

"Good lass. Mayhap you can surrender more, later."

Both grinning then, they walked farther along the
cliffs but soon turned back toward Tùr Meiloach, where
they found Andrew waiting for them in the yard.

"Couldna sleep, eh?" he said.

"We are not slugabeds, sir," Andrena said. "You ken
fine that I am up with the sun if not before. And Magnus
likes to walk as much as I do."

"Ye're well suited then, just as I said ye'd be," her
father said, nodding. "Have ye told her yet about your
journey, lad?"

"I did, sir. I'd like to discuss that more with you, if you
will."

"I'll leave you to your discussion then," Andrena said.
"I must show myself to Mam. Then, I have things I must
do to help Magnus prepare for the journey."

"Aye, go along then," Andrew said. "We willna keep ye."

⁓

Watching her stride away across the yard, Mag wondered
again about her meek behavior. He'd noted that she had
said "*the* journey," not "his journey."

Andrew said, "Ye'll want to know how ye should
approach Colquhoun. But ye needna fret about him,
because our Andrena's a prime favorite of his."

"I've met Colquhoun, sir," Mag said. "And Andrena is not going with me."

"Aye, sure she is," Andrew said. "I ken fine that ye've a message of import for his grace, but if ye gain audience with him, ye must also explain the state of affairs here. Tell him that I am the rightful Chief of Clan Farlan and keeper of the pass. If he honors the charter that proves it, I'll be fain to put my whole clan behind him. But Andrena kens the way of things here far better than ye could after such a short time at Tùr Meiloach. She can therefore better explain it to his grace, too."

"Surely, all I need to tell him is that you hold the true charter," Mag said. "For that matter, you can soon show it to him yourself."

"Aye, and he comes here to see it," Andrew said testily. "When d'ye think he'll do any such thing? He kens fine that Lennox holds sway here, so he must believe that, like Lennox himself, all the MacFarlans be against him. Ye could tell him that that isna so, but I'll wager he'd listen with a closer ear to Dree. Moreover, lad, if ye be thinking ye'll gain his ear on your own, I can tell ye, ye'll have a better chance with a toothsome lass at your side than without one. Our Jamie, though he does honor his vows to Queen Joanna, has a keen eye for the lassies."

"If you want me to take Andrena, I will," Mag said. "But what if I must travel far beyond Glasgow to find his grace?"

"Sakes, d'ye think my lass canna sit a horse? Ye'll hire nags in Glasgow for the pair of ye. Aye, and that reminds me that ye'll need gelt, because I ken fine that Parlan didna leave ye any. Now then, d'ye want to take Dree with ye or no?"

Mag met Andrew's fiery gaze and said, "I thought you would not want her to go, sir. I shall enjoy her company."

He wondered then if Andrena had somehow persuaded her father to take her side. Had he been able to imagine how she could have managed it since learning of his intended journey, his suspicions would have been strong. As it was, he knew she had been with him since then and had had no such opportunity.

～

Andrena found her mother in the solar with Lina and Murie. When she entered, Murie said, "Why did you not tell us that Magnus is leaving tomorrow?"

Looking at her mother, Andrena said cautiously, "Mam?"

With an understanding smile, Lady Aubrey said, "Your father told me that Magnus is going to Glasgow, dearling, and that he would need more clothing than he has now."

"I wish we could all go," Murie said. "It has been months since we visited our kinsmen. Mayhap you will introduce Magnus to them."

"I doubt that," Andrena said. "Even if he lets me go with him, I doubt that we'll stop anywhere on the way. We'd go to Dumbarton, of course, and perhaps places beyond Glasgow. It must be as Magnus decides, though."

"Surely, he will not leave you behind so soon after marrying you," Lina said. "He must want to present you to *his* family. It seemed strange that he would so willingly marry without their knowledge and consent. Imagine how Mam and our father would react if any of us did that." She glanced at their mother, but Lady Aubrey was attending to a knot in her stitchery and did not respond.

"I don't need to imagine that, because none of us would *do* that," Andrena said. "If you want to know about Magnus's family, Lina, you must ask him. At present, though, I do need your help to decide what he should take. I must tell you that he is likely to find himself in noble company, so he will want to dress well. His new sark was sadly damaged yesterday when the men undressed him."

"I heard about the sark," Lina said. "I am making a linen one for Father, which is almost finished. I can adjust it to fit Magnus. I have his new plaid, too. One of the maidservants found it on the stairs." She shook her head. "Men."

"Well, don't blame him," Andrena said. "You saw what they did to him."

"I know," Lina said. "Don't fret about his clothing, Dree. A Highlander is always presentable in his plaid, is he not, Mam?"

"He is, indeed," Lady Aubrey agreed. "Magnus will want breeks, too, if he must ride a horse. I don't know what we can do about that, but I'll ask Malcolm to see if anyone has breeks that might fit Magnus. He will care more about comfort than fashion when he rides. As for you, Dree, if you do go with him, you should wear your amber dress to meet his gr—his grand and noble friends. Your russet-colored one will do at Craggan Tower," she added, making it clear—to Andrena, at least—that Andrew had revealed Magnus's true intentions to her.

Satisfied that the problem of Magnus's clothing was in capable hands, Andrena excused herself and returned to the chamber she shared with him. Her own clothing was there because Tibby had moved it, so it took only a short time to collect what she would take with her if Andrew acted as she expected he would.

Packing quickly, she managed to fit everything tidily into two straw baskets with long straps that gillies could use to sling them over a shoulder. They would also serve to strap them to a sumpter pony if they rode beyond Glasgow.

When she had finished, she rejoined her mother and sisters in the solar, certain that Magnus would look for her there if he wanted her. The women attended to their usual tasks and duties, and the rest of the morning passed swiftly. Andrena did not see Magnus or her father until they all gathered for the midday meal.

When the two men joined the women on the dais, Andrena could deduce nothing from either man's expression. Magnus seemed to eye her speculatively, but he took his place next to her father without pausing to speak to her.

Sitting between her mother and Lina, she listened to see if Andrew or Magnus would volunteer any information about the forthcoming journey. When they did not, she kept her attention firmly on her food.

Afterward, though, when Lady Aubrey stood to signal that the ladies should return to their tasks, Andrena nearly sighed with relief when Murie walked up to Andrew and asked him if Magnus was truly leaving the next day.

"Aye, he is," Andrew said. "'Tis likely to be just for a short while. He'll be taking our Andrena with him, mayhap to meet the King of Scots himself."

Andrena allowed herself a sigh of relief then.

Shifting her attention to Magnus and finding his steady gaze on her, she felt an odd shiver of apprehension. His expression was as bland as ever. She could see no sign of the sort of displeasure that might stir such a sensation in her, so why...?

"I *knew* your journey would be exciting," Murie said. Turning to Magnus, she said, "You must pay close heed to all that you see and hear, sir, because we'll want to know every detail you can recall about his grace. Oh, how I wish I could go, too."

"Well, ye cannot," Andrew said. "They dinna want to be burdened with your chatter all the way. Run along with your mam now, Murie-lass. She's beckoning."

Magnus had not taken his eyes off Andrena even while Murie was speaking to him. He was still watching her, so she stepped toward him, past her father, and when she faced Magnus, she said quietly, "I am to go with you, then."

"Aye, madam wife," he murmured. "But I think you knew that already."

"I did suspect that Father would want me to go," she said. "Forbye, if you wonder how Murie knew about—"

"I expect Andrew must have told your mother."

"Aye, he did, and my sisters expressed a belief that I should go with you. But I do know that the decision rests with you, sir. If you don't want me—"

"Nay, lass, I'd like you to go. In troth, I wish we could leave today. But your father insists that tomorrow will be better, because we'll have had more rest. In troth, I do not want to fratch with the man."

"Is the message you carry so important then, that hours might matter?"

"It may be," he said. "I'll wager that you've already packed your things."

"I have. But Lina does need time to provide you with another sark. You are gey hard on your clothing, are you not?"

Mag's gaze had drifted to Andrew, but at these words he looked at her with words of defense leaping to his tongue. They never left it, because the teasing look in her eyes told him she was well aware that his sarks had reached their present state through no fault of his own.

He realized that he could not present himself to Colquhoun, let alone to Jamie Stewart, looking like one of the scaff and raff. Expecting the lady Lachina to produce a new sark and whatever else the women might collect by way of suitable clothing for him before the morrow was already demanding miracles.

However, the women proved equal to their tasks, so when he and Andrena descended to the hall to break their fast early the next morning, everything was ready for their departure. After promising Andrew faithfully that they would return to report to him as soon as they had spoken with James, they set out southward with four of Andrew's men to accompany them.

Malcolm's lanky son, Peter, carried Andrena's two small baskets. A stouter, somewhat older gillie called Jonas carried the larger sumpter basket containing Mag's clothing. Malcolm had even found him a pair of breeks.

Their party included Andrew's personal manservant, Sorley MacFarlan, and young Pluff, along with Andrena's two favorite dogs. Malcolm had provided a basket of food for the day, which Pluff had slung over a shoulder.

Andrena was barefoot although Mag knew she had packed a pair of silk slippers and her boots. Someone had found horse-leather boots with the hair still on to fit him, and he was trying them out. The rough leather was uncomfortable, but his feet were tough, and he knew that the leather would soon reshape itself to them.

He had wondered at Andrew's decision to send his personal servant along but had not questioned it since Andrena had not.

Pluff was visibly and audibly delighted to have been included. The dogs were fresh and boisterous. At one point, the lad set off running after them, despite the basket of food he carried.

When Sorley called him sharply to order, Mag said, "Hand me that basket, rascal. If our dinner ends up in a burn or scattered across the forest floor for the beasts to devour, I'll feed you to them, as well." When Pluff obeyed him with a grin, Mag added quietly, "Let the dogs run, lad, but don't let them go far."

"Aye, sir," the boy said, darting off again and shouting for the dogs.

"Ye shouldna be carrying that basket, sir," Sorley said. " 'Tis the lad's duty."

"He can have it back when he's run off some of his energy," Mag said. He noted that Sorley did not offer to carry the basket himself.

⁓

Andrena ignored them all. The woods were peaceful, but the dogs' rowdy presence had stilled many of the forest creatures. As soon as the men fell silent, though, a squirrel chattered in the distance, and birds began to twitter.

They walked without speaking until she heard the dogs again a short distance ahead. First came a growl, next a sharp bark, and then a cacophony of sound.

"Mercy, they've cornered a badger!" she exclaimed, lengthening her stride.

"Sakes, how can you know that?" Magnus demanded.

"I know the way they bark when they corner one," she replied, hoping the answer would satisfy him. "Hurry!"

"Lass, if they've cornered a badger..."

But she was no longer listening. Picking up her skirts, she began to run. Aware that he was right behind her, she focused her senses ahead.

Breaking into a small clearing, she saw Pluff on the other side, watching something beyond him, every inch of his wiry body aquiver with tension.

Slowing to a stop, she put two fingers to her lips and gave a sharp whistle, then another. "Step back slowly toward me, Pluff," she said, keeping her voice calm. "The dogs will come away to me, but you hold their leashes."

"There be a right enormous badger a dozen feet from me in them bushes, me lady," Pluff called without turning. His voice shook. "I never s-seen one so big."

She whistled again and then called the dogs. "Rowdy! Bess! To me!"

Hearing the familiar sound of steel leaving leather behind her and feeling a large, firm hand on her left shoulder, Andrena stood her ground and said, "You won't need your sword, sir. The badger will go now that I've called off the dogs."

His grip tightened, and despite her assurances, he moved her easily aside and stepped in front of her. But the dogs had reached Pluff, and she had seen the lad bend to leash Bess. Both dogs were still excited, not to mention disappointed, since they lived in the certainty that they could demolish any enemy.

Pluff, with Rowdy now also leashed, had relaxed.

As Magnus moved quickly and quietly toward the boy, sword at the ready, she said, "It has gone, sir. It will not trouble us further."

He glanced back at her but went on until he stood beside Pluff.

She followed, despite knowing that Magnus had meant for her to stay put.

~

Mag realized that Andrena was right about the badger. Both dogs were still looking that way, but their defensive attitudes had eased.

"I'm right sorry ye didna see that brute, sir," Pluff said. He was, Mag noted, holding both leashes firmly in both hands, as if he feared that the dogs might try to bolt after their prey again. "I swear tae ye, it were as big as a sheep."

Mag raised his eyebrows.

"Well, a sma' sheep," Pluff assured him.

"And a fierce one, I make no doubt," Mag said. "You were wise to stop where you did, lad. A cornered badger is a gey dangerous beast."

"I were more fearful for the dogs than for m'self," Pluff said stoutly.

"I believe you. But you still had the good sense to keep well away and let the dogs do as they would. Many men would have thought they should aid them."

"They'd be right daft tae try."

"They would, Pluff," Andrena agreed, coming to stand beside Mag.

He gave her a look that ought to have sent her right

back to where he'd left her. But he was not surprised when she grinned in reply.

"I hope you did not fear for my safety, sir," she said. "I am well acquainted with the beasts of this forest and have great respect for them. I know better than to do anything daft. But the dogs are not always so cautious, especially Rowdy."

Mag slid his sword back into its baldric and put his arm around her shoulders. Then, he said, "I ken fine that you know this place better than I do, lass. But when I take out my sword, I'd liefer not have a woman standing between me and my target."

"Then we understand each other," she said lightly. "I will remember that, if you will *try* to remember that I have looked after myself for years in these woods."

"Fair enough," he said, giving her shoulders a squeeze and hoping he could keep to that agreement. Watching her run toward an angry, frightened badger as big as a small sheep was not an experience he wanted to repeat.

When Sorley and the two gillies joined them, Sorley said, "We be nearly tae the top o' the last hill now, sir. When we get there, I'm thinking we might pause tae eat our midday dinner. Then we'll send young Pluff and the dogs back wi' Jonas. Peter will go on wi' us tae carry her ladyship's baskets, and I'll take yours, sir."

Mag agreed but wondered why they were keeping one gillie and sending Pluff and the other one back. He said nothing until they had all eaten and Pluff and Jonas had departed with the dogs and the empty food basket.

As everyone else strode downhill toward the river, Mag moved closer to Andrena and said, "I can understand sending Pluff and the dogs back. But why send that gillie, Jonas? I doubt that Sorley is accustomed to carrying sumpter baskets."

Andrena smiled at him but said only, "You'll see."

~

As they continued downhill toward the river, Andrena noted the way Magnus scanned the distant riverbank, just as she and doubtless the other two men were doing. They all sought signs of trespassers there, or any Colquhouns.

Magnus's expression was as placid as usual. But a few minutes later, he moved up to walk beside her and said mildly, "I think you should know, lass, that when I ask a question, I'd liefer hear an informative answer than an impertinent one. Why did Sorley send Jonas back?"

She had a strong urge then to test him, to see if she could make him reveal more about himself to her. Deciding that, as his wife, she had every right to know more about him, she said, "If I send Sorley and Peter on ahead and ask you to tell me more about your family than that they are Galbraiths and your father their chief, will you give *me* informative answers, sir?"

He was silent. The urge to press him more grew stronger by the second.

"Well?" she said, looking straight at him.

He pressed his lips together hard enough to make a muscle twitch in his jaw and stir a dimple to life in his lower left cheek. But he said only, "I'd liefer you not quiz me about my kinsmen now, lass, and answer my question instead. I don't make bargains in such matters. And I do want an answer."

Gritting her teeth, she fought to stifle her need to see if she *could* anger him.

Abruptly, Sorley said "Look yonder, sir. In them trees lochside o' that tall evergreen wi' the sticking-up, bare point on it. Two o' them."

"I see them," Magnus said.

"I see them, too," Andrena said. "Do you recognize them, Sorley?"

"One o' them might be young Ian. I dinna ken the other."

She looked at Magnus. "Can you see them both well enough to describe them to me, sir?"

He nodded. "The one on the left is wearing a plaid that looks mostly blue with perhaps some grayish green, over a saffron-colored sark. He's got graying dark hair and is carrying a bow and a quiver of arrows. He wears boots and carries a dirk. The one on the right wears a white shirt and a finer-looking plaid of darker blue and green. He's carrying a sword in the same manner as mine. I cannot be sure how tall he is, but if the shrubbery on that side is as it is here, he'd be six feet or more."

"His hair, what color?"

"Brown, I think, to his shoulders. But he's wearing some sort of knitted cap and stands in the shadow of the trees, so it's hard to tell."

"His eyes?"

He looked at her then. "I've got good long sight, lass. But not that good."

She chuckled. "No matter. That's Sir Ian, Sorley. We'll lower the bridge."

Chapter 9 ─────────────

Mag watched as Sorley and Malcolm's Peter waved at the watchers and hurried downhill toward the river. When they neared it, the two of them went off the track at an angle through the trees, making their way westward without any trail that Mag could discern. He and Andrena followed them.

He saw at once that the dense shrubbery was deceptive, because they eased around trees and shrubs without hesitation. Taking care not to break any branches, they came in time to a huge evergreen that overlooked the river roaring furiously down toward the great waterfall just west of them. The tree looked as if its dense branches nearly touched the ground.

Sorley and Peter set down their burdens. Then, straightening, they took another long look at the rugged, heavily forested land across the river. The two men who had been watching them were close enough now to see clearly. Mag had met Ian Colquhoun frequently in years past, before Ian won his knighthood, but had not seen him since. Ian's skills in the tiltyard and on the battlefield were well known, though.

If Andrew was right to trust Colquhoun, Mag thought

they might also trust Ian's integrity and loyalty to the Crown. However, his strongest memories of the younger Ian were of a teasing, prank-loving laddie, so he was reserving judgment.

Just how far either Colquhoun would go to aid him or Andrew Dubh was anyone's guess. Colquhoun's land was his own, though. And, like Andrew, he wielded the power of the pit and the gallows. Also, he did not answer to Lennox.

Mag looked at Andrena, who was waving and smiling at the two. Catching her eye, he said, "Your father told me that we can trust the Colquhouns, lass. Forbye, he also said that Colquhoun prefers peace over annoying Lennox and resists taking sides. Moreover, I heard at Arrochar that Pharlain views Colquhoun as insignificant if not as an ally. His son Sir Ian is a knight of the realm and should be loyal to the King, but I'd liefer tell neither of them more than we must."

"I believe we can trust their loyalty, sir," she said soberly. "I have not seen Ian in more than a year or the laird since last summer. But they are both honest men and straightforward. If they cannot help us, they will say so and they will do us no harm. Sithee, Gregor Colquhoun, a close kinsman of theirs, is captain of the guard at Dumbarton Castle now, and Dumbarton, as you know, is a royal fortress."

"Aye, but if you are thinking that a Colquhoun being captain there means that his grace trusts the man, you should know that it speaks more for the man's connection to someone in power than for his being a Colquhoun. The powerful one in question is more likely to be Murdoch or Lennox, is it not?"

She shook her head. "Not now. Murdoch's son, Lord Walter, *was* Keeper of Dumbarton. But, after his arrest last year, the King named his own uncle, Sir John Stewart of Burley, as Keeper. Burley is loyal to him, and so is Gregor Colquhoun."

"Likely you're right," he said. "I can tell you Pharlain expects no trouble from Dumbarton, but that may be because his plans center on the upcoming Parliament in Perth." He saw Peter climbing the huge tree. "Is there truly a bridge hereabouts?"

"Aye," she said. "Watch now."

When the lad shouted, Sorley did something inside the dense lower foliage.

To Mag's astonishment, a log bridge some two-thirds as long as the tree was tall began lowering slowly on ropes toward the water. Peter seemed to be gripping at least two thick ropes, and Sorley, below him, did likewise. Mag went to help, and when the older man made way for him, Mag saw that a system of hooks, ropes, and pulleys that stretched up the tree's trunk helped control the bridge's descent.

Continuing to scan the opposite shore, he saw the two men moving hastily toward the place where the bridge's far end would come to rest. That sight told him as plainly as anything could that the Colquhouns had not revealed to Pharlain or his men the location of that bridge. Had his erstwhile pursuers known of its existence, they'd have lowered it to get back across the river.

He could see now that the log had planks attached to it and even boasted a taut-looking rope railing. When it was down, he went back to Andrena.

"That bridge cannot accommodate horses or other livestock," he said.

"True," she agreed. "But we have what we need, and doubtless you see now why we sent Jonas back with Pluff and the dogs."

"Not entirely. But I'd guess that both lads are unaware of the bridge's location and that your father wants to keep it that way."

"Aye," she said. "'Tis likely they know or can guess that some sort of bridge exists. And I believe they are trustworthy. But Father wants as few people as possible to know its exact location and how to lower it. By sending the lads back together, it is unlikely that either will suggest trying to see where the bridge is. But one curious man alone with an opportunity to learn its location might hide and watch."

He nodded. "I understand that. What I do not understand is why you refused to tell me that when I asked you about it."

⁓

Andrena hesitated. Temptation stirred again to say something saucy or to tell him the truth in some other way that would test his temper more. But the bridge was in place, Peter was descending, and Sorley was watching them.

The last thing she wanted was to anger Magnus enough to *feel* his anger with others watching and listening. Accordingly, she reached out to touch his arm and said frankly, "I *should* have told you, sir. I am used to keeping silent about it. But since Father himself is sending us across the bridge, I should have explained. Forgive me?"

"Aye, sure, I do," he said, putting a warm hand atop hers on his arm but holding her gaze with his. "I think there was more to it than that, though."

"We should go across now and quickly," she said, wishing she knew how it was that he seemed to understand her thoughts and motives more easily than she could discern his. "We'll talk more about that later if you like."

"We will," he said, putting his arm around her shoulders again.

When they reached the bridge, she led the way across, trying as she always did to ignore intruding thoughts of what might happen if she slipped.

The planks were wide, though. And the rope railings gave one a sense of safety even if she touched them only for reassurance and doubted that they'd help much if she tried to grab one as she slipped. Telling herself that she had made it across many times before and would do so many times again, she nevertheless breathed a sigh of relief when she set foot back on solid ground.

Sir Ian Colquhoun—lanky, slim of hip and broad-shouldered—stood waiting at the end of the bridge, grinning, his light blue eyes atwinkle as he said, "You've grown even more shapely since last I saw you, Dree-lass."

"So have you, sir, so much that I scarcely recognized you," she said, grinning back. "Nor would I have expected you to meet us here yourself."

Still grinning, he said, "Some of our lads in a coble caught three of Pharlain's men on the shore below your cliffs a few days ago and presented them to my sire. That put him in a pelter until they persuaded him that they'd done no harm and that your evil hawks had run them off. So, to amuse myself, I offered to serve as a guard here for a time. We saw you crest yon hill, and I am pleased to say that I recognized *you* easily, lass. So we hied ourselves down to bid you welcome."

"Are you home for a long time now or just for a visit?"

"I'll stay for a while. I hope that you mean to stay, too, this time."

Hearing Magnus clear his throat behind her, Andrena remembered her manners and said, "I should present my husband to you, sir. This is Mag—"

"Maggy!" Sir Ian exclaimed joyfully, clapping Magnus on the back. "By heaven, I thought it was you. Nay, to put it more exactly, I hoped it was. To think of *two* men as big as mountains wandering about uncaged would be too much. But after my gaze fixed on our lovely Dree here, I clean forgot—"

"It is good to see you, too, lad," Magnus interjected. "As for caging, you will delight to know that Pharlain kept me so these nineteen months past."

"The devil he did! I do recall hearing something about you falling captive in that fray when your brother Will was killed. But it never occurred to me that they'd keep you longer than ten minutes after they caught you. Sakes, I thought you'd have flung them about as freely as ever Samson scattered the Philistines."

Receiving no reply to these light words, he added nonetheless cheerfully, "So you've married Dree, have you? I swear my father knew nowt of such a wedding, so you must tell us all about it. But how may we serve you?"

"Andrew Dubh suggested that we might request hospitality from your lord father overnight," Magnus said.

"Sakes, we refuse hospitality to none. Forbye, you and our Dree are more welcome than most. Father will be delighted to see you again."

"I assured Magnus that we would be welcome,"

Andrena said with a smile. Casting another to her husband, she added, "I doubt he believed me, though."

Ian chuckled. "As I recall it, *you* nearly always come to Craggan Tower because you are going elsewhere. Is that how it is today?"

"It is, aye," Andrena said. "We're for Glasgow. We'll ride if we must, but Magnus would like us to get there as soon as we can. We were hoping we might beg a place in one of your galleys if the laird will permit it."

"He will, aye," Ian said. Shifting his gaze to Magnus, he said, "Do I ask what is speeding you to Glasgow now, Mag?"

"You don't if you would please me, not yet," Magnus said. "As I recall, though, you were always a curious buckie. So, prithee, keep your questions to yourself until we join your lord father. I'd liefer not explain twice."

"As ye will, Maggy-lad," Ian said with a mocking bow and mischievous grin.

Andrena glanced at Magnus. If the absurd nickname troubled him, she could not see it. But recalling how he had cleared his throat after she had greeted Ian, she realized that there might be another, easier way to test his temper.

The exchange reminded Mag so much of the younger Ian Colquhoun that he wondered just how much of that cheeky lad remained in the young knight. Ian was just two years younger than he was and an esteemed knight of the realm. But he should still, Mag decided, show proper respect for someone who was older, more experienced, and able to match him with any weapon.

However, warning Ian to mind his manners was not the course to follow when they needed help from the Colquhouns. Accordingly, while they saw Sorley and Peter back across the river and watched them return the bridge to its nest, Mag ignored Ian's evident determination to flirt with Andrena.

He also ignored her mischievous reciprocation.

Thanks to speculative looks she threw *his* way, Mag knew she was enjoying herself and suspected that she hoped to pay him back for reproaching her about the bridge. Fair enough, he decided, slinging his basket over his good shoulder. But young Ian, despite his power to provide or refuse them aid, had better watch his step.

Ian and his man willingly carried Andrena's baskets, and the distance up to Colquhoun's tower in Glen Craggan was less than two miles. So, despite the rugged terrain, their party traveled swiftly and reached the tower in its shady glen, between two towering slopes, before sunset.

Ian summoned gillies to attend to the baskets and took his guests into the great hall. There they found the laird sitting with his lady by the large fireplace.

Both rose eagerly to greet them.

A fit-looking, well-formed man in his midforties, the laird looked much as his son would look in twenty years. Ian was taller by an inch or two, but the laird looked able enough to hold his own in battle.

His lady was plump and comfortable-looking with graying light brown hair that showed under a plain white veil. She let her husband do most of the talking but punctuated his comments with smiles, nods, and murmurs of agreement.

"By heaven, lad," Colquhoun, said, looking Mag up and

down after they had exchanged amenities and Mag told him of their marriage, "I'd wondered what had become o' ye. D'ye mean to say ye were Pharlain's prisoner for two years?"

Ian said, "It must have seemed that long, sir, for it was nineteen months."

Ian's manner, Mag noted, was now properly respectful. Perhaps he reserved his impudence solely for his friends.

"'Tis much *too* long," Colquhoun said dourly. Despite the stern tone, his expression was sympathetic. "I'd warrant Pharlain did *not* treat ye kindly."

"I got on well enough, my lord, once I learned to keep my mouth shut."

"Never a bad course to follow," Colquhoun agreed. "But how did ye come to marry Andrena? I'd no notion Andrew expected to celebrate a wedding. I do ken fine that he hoped to find Dree a husband willing to take the MacFarlan name. Never tell me ye agreed to that, though. Your father—"

"With respect, sir, perhaps we might delay that discussion for another time," Mag interjected, having no wish to discuss his marriage, his father, or anyone else in his family just then. "We are going to Glasgow, and Andrew Dubh said he keeps horses with you."

Feeling Ian's keen gaze on him, he was unsurprised when the younger man said, "What they'd like is a galley, sir. This journey is one that Mag believes must be done in haste."

Colquhoun's gaze sharpened then. He turned to his lady, saying, "Dree will want to refresh herself before we take supper, madam."

"Aye, sure," Lady Colquhoun said with a warm smile

for Andrena, who shot Mag a look that he easily interpreted as a plea to suggest that she stay.

"You come along with me, my dear," Lady Colquhoun said. "We'll give you and your handsome new husband the room that you shared with Lina and Muriella some months ago."

"Thank you, my lady," Andrena said. Shooting a more speculative look at Mag, she added, "Before we go, though, I do think the laird and Ian should know that Magnus, having been Pharlain's prisoner for so long, has grown understandably mistrustful. In troth," she went on, still looking at Mag, who controlled his temper with difficulty, "I am risking his ire by saying so. But my father trusts you all in all, my lord, or he would not have sent us here."

Knowing that she meant her words for him more than for Ian and Colquhoun only increased Mag's annoyance. He would decide whom to trust on his own, and his lady wife would do well to learn not to speak for him or about him without his leave—certainly not in any such way as she just had.

⁓

Andrena felt a chill up her spine as she said the last few words, and her gaze avoided Magnus's as if of its own accord. She realized that although she had never sensed his feelings as easily as she sensed most people's, she'd had no trouble reading the look he'd given her when she spoke of his mistrust.

Glancing at Ian, she saw his eyes dance. So he had noted Magnus's anger, too. Nevertheless, Ian's smile was as warm and reassuring as his mother's when he said, "I think Mag knows he can trust us, lass. He has done so before. We need only persuade him that he can safely do so now."

"Aye, lassie, so run along and let us talk," Colquhoun said.

She drew a deep breath and exhaled slowly. Although she still could not read her husband, the Colquhouns were easy. Both men were completely at ease with the notion of earning his trust again.

As she turned away, she looked again at Magnus. His gaze was steady, his expression calm. But she was sure that he would have something to say to her about what she had just done.

To her surprise, she looked forward to that conversation.

Mag watched her leave, then turned to meet his host's gaze and was unnerved to see a look of sympathy. Whether it stemmed from Andrena's having just reduced him to nursery status with her concerns or something else, he would wait for Colquhoun to tell him if he chose to do so.

Ian, for once—and wisely—kept silent.

Colquhoun said, "Ian, fetch yon whisky jug from the corner shelf and mugs for us three." When Ian nodded and crossed the hall, leaving his father and Mag in relative privacy, Colquhoun said for Mag's ears alone, "I ken fine what your father said to ye two years ago, lad. Arthur told me himself. And I told *him* what I thought of such cruel foolishness. I'd no be surprised to learn that he's had a change of heart. But I also ken fine that, if he has, he's done nowt to reveal it."

"Thank you for telling me, sir. That makes it easier to tell you what I must."

"I think I can deduce some of it," Colquhoun said. "I did think ye'd escaped and kept away just because Arthur had disowned ye. But doubtless Ian told ye we had trespassers some few days ago."

"He did, aye."

Colquhoun nodded. "They crossed to the Tùr Meiloach side of the river afore we could catch them. But by watching the shore from land and loch, we got them on their return. When they said they sought an escaped prisoner of Pharlain's, I told them they'd nae business on Colquhoun land and that I'd hang any of Pharlain's lot that we found here in future. But I'm guessing ye'd be the prisoner they lost. Ye must have come ashore in that fierce storm Sunday night."

"Aye, sir."

"So your wedding was a hasty one. As I said, I ken fine that Andrew was seeking a husband for Dree. But that outrageous demand of his—"

"I did agree to accept the MacFarlan name, my lord."

"I canna say I blame ye, lad. But that will offend your da."

"I did not do it in defiance, if that is what you think."

"Nay, what I'm thinking is that ye've had a bad two years of it. But it's over, and ye'll no let Pharlain catch ye again. Forbye, ye've doubtless learned things as a prisoner that will stand ye in good stead in times to come. I willna plague ye to tell us more than ye want to tell now. But if ye ever want to sit down and talk about Pharlain and those devilish long months, I'd welcome the discussion."

Ian brought the whisky and handed them each a mug.

It was as well that he did, because Mag had had no idea what to reply or if he could even speak. His throat had closed with an unfamiliar ache. Had he been ten years old, he might have wept.

But he was not ten, and he never cried. He swallowed the feeling and managed a calm, "Thank you, my lord. I will remember that."

"Good, now tell us about this journey of yours. Whither d'ye go?"

"South, toward Glasgow," Mag said. "I must find the King."

"Ye may not need to go as far as Glasgow. They'll likely have ken of his grace's whereabouts at Dumbarton Castle. I'll send ye in one of my boats, and ye'll take Ian with ye lest ye need his sword or aught else of him."

"Thank you, my lord."

"Ye ken fine that my castle of Dunglass lies three miles upriver from Dumbarton and that much closer to Glasgow. So, unless ye'll find his grace sooner by riding from Dumbarton, ye'll stop in the harbor there just long enough to learn where to find him. If ye do ride from Dumbarton, Gregor Colquhoun will see to the galley. He can just send it and our oarsmen on to Dunglass."

"He is the captain of the guard at Dumbarton, aye?"

"Aye, sure. Now, have ye plenty o' gelt if ye must go far to find Jamie?"

"I do, sir, aye. Andrew Dubh gave me plenty. See you, I have information for the King, and Andrew commissioned me to speak for him, too."

"I ken fine on what topic that must be," Colquhoun said, nodding. "If he can set that charter of his before Jamie, it ought to help. Neither of our two dukes of

Albany cared a whit for charters other than to seize them to expand the Albany holdings. But our Jamie believes in the rule of law."

"Aye, so I have heard," Mag said. In the silence that followed, he sipped his whisky. Feeling its warmth spread through him, he began to relax.

Colquhoun said, "I needna ask ye about Andrew, and I'd not keep any young man long from his new bride. But I suspect that Dree's declaration afore she left us concerned the information ye mean to share with Jamie."

"Aye, sir, it does," Mag said, meeting his gaze.

"Ye've nae reason to trust either of us with a matter of such import, lad. So I'll no press ye to do so. But if we can help, we will, without question or concern."

Mag thanked him again but was grateful when Ian changed the subject to general, more political matters. It was good to catch up on news of who was doing what to whom. It was even better to relax for a time without being quizzed about his imprisonment or his family.

Ian did mention Mag's brothers, saying he'd heard that Rory had served Lennox before the earl's arrest and that Patrick served Murdoch's youngest son, James Mòr Stewart. He'd heard earlier that Rory served the earl but had not known that Patrick, the youngest of Mag's brothers, had had the sense to serve the only one of Murdoch's sons whose pleasant manner and harmless behavior exempted him from all suspicion of treachery. Mag was relieved to hear it.

Colquhoun announced that they would not change clothes for supper, so the men went on talking and joined the women when they came down to the hall dais.

Mag wondered if the laird had hoped thereby to protect Andrena from a well-deserved husbandly rebuke. He realized even as the thought struck him that he needed only to have excused himself had he wanted to scold her.

The wary look she gave him when she stepped onto the dais suggested that she was uncertain about his mood. It was good if she was. A man didn't want his wife explaining him and his feelings to others, whatever her reason might be. Nor did he want her flirting with cheeky knights like Ian Colquhoun.

At the table, Andrena invited the Colquhouns to attend the festivities planned for Lady Aubrey's birthday. They accepted with delight, and the meal continued without incident. The conversation remained general or focused on events that had taken place in the area since the previous summer.

Mag enjoyed his supper and the whisky that followed Lady Colquhoun's withdrawal with Andrena to the solar. An hour later, he followed a gillie upstairs to the chamber where Andrena waited, and considered what he would say to her.

Andrena had excused herself to her ladyship twenty minutes earlier.

Throughout supper, she had tried to decide if Magnus was seriously displeased with her, or not, for what she had said to the laird and to Ian.

She had wanted only to assure Magnus that he could trust the Colquhouns. The brief, freezing look he had shot her then told that he was annoyed. Yet that look passed as quickly as it had appeared, and she had not *sensed* any other hint of his anger. Shortly before supper, though, while she talked with Lady Colquhoun, she had sensed deep sadness in him and wondered what had caused it.

Alone in the room she would share with him, she had doffed her clothes, cleaned her teeth, and donned the green silk robe that she had brought because it was warm and easy to pack. Then she sat on a handy stool and began to brush her hair, listening all the while for Magnus's footsteps outside the door.

Despite her precaution, she did not hear him coming until the latch clicked, startling her so that she dropped her brush. Snatching it up, she jumped to her feet as the door opened, unwilling to be sitting when he entered. He would tower over her, and she felt vulnerable enough already.

He entered, glanced at her, and shut the door. Then, taking off his belt and his plaid, he hung both on a hook by the door, pulled off his boots, and without saying a word, went to the washstand in only his sark.

"Are you so angry that you don't mean to speak to me?" she asked.

"If I'm ever angry enough that you need be wary, you'll know it, believe me."

In that moment, she did know it.

Turning toward her, he said, "Don't you think I have reason to be irked? How would you feel if I introduced you to friends of mine and took the liberty of providing them with my version of your feelings about *them*?"

"When you put it that way…" She nibbled her lip. "By my troth, sir, I meant only to help. I wanted you to understand how much Father trusts them. But I also wanted to see how they reacted, so I could tell whether you and I should trust them as much as he does."

"I agree that you are likely right and both men are trustworthy," he said.

She relaxed.

"However," he went on, stirring her tension again, "you cannot *know* we can trust them simply from the way they received what you said. Sakes, lass, they both reacted only with surprise that you would say such things about your own husband."

Standing had not helped. Nor was the slight space between them helping.

He loomed over her, large and authoritative. Even so, she could not tell what he felt. He radiated calm.

So why, she wondered, did he make her feel so vulnerable?

She wanted to explain that she *could* tell when people were sincere, that she could sense even small reactions and what people were feeling when they made vows or agreements. But she'd rarely spoken of her gifts or, as her mother called them, her extraordinary instincts. Not only were they inactive where he was concerned but he'd also dismissed what little she had revealed about them. She was reluctant to tell him more.

When he turned back to the washstand, she felt immediate relief and decided that her uneasiness had been due merely to guilt at having said what she had.

Then he turned and stepped toward her, making the tension leap again. Other feelings leaped, too, sensual ones less familiar to her.

When he put his hands on her shoulders, those feelings

increased tenfold. Warmth from his hands, and trepidation, sped throughout her body.

She could scarcely breathe.

He was her husband. They barely knew each other. Yet, if he decided to punish her or couple with her, he could do either one. In *any* way he chose.

Chapter 10 ⸻

Mag knew the instant he touched her that he had made a mistake. Her eyes were huge, their black pupils nearly obscuring her irises. Her expression was wary, as it deserved to be, but her lips were full and inviting.

A man making things clear to so enticing a bride should, he decided, keep his hands to himself until he established that clarity. Sakes, but he ought never to have hung his belt up with his plaid. A more experienced husband would likely have kept it in hand, if only as a warning of what an angry man might do to an erring wife.

With a mental grimace, Mag told himself to stop thinking like a dafty. He would never take a belt to any lass, let alone to Andrena. Sakes, but he had even stopped MacNur from giving that scamp Pluff a well-deserved leathering.

She licked her lips as if she might be nervous. But she seemed more curious and uneasy than anxious. Uneasy was good. She should be uneasy.

"I should not have said what I did," she murmured, looking down and then up into his eyes. "I did not think before I spoke. But you are right when you say that I'd dislike it if you said something like that about me to someone I'd just met."

He nodded, his fingers contracting on her shoulders. He did not speak, because he no longer wanted to punish her. But what he wanted to do would teach her nowt save the strength of his desire for her, desire so strong that she might easily see it as a weapon or a means, at least, of controlling him. He gazed into her eyes, wishing he could peer through those dark pupils to the thoughts in her mind.

"I wish you would say what you are thinking," she said. "Or do whatever it is that you mean to do to me."

His hands tightened again on her shoulders, but looking down into those heavily lashed blue-black eyes, he could not seem to think of anything but the sensations storming through his body. His cock, having lain dormant for nineteen months before getting a taste of what it had missed, wanted much more and was urging him to forget everything except what the lass offered to remedy the lack.

Forget punishment, it seemed to shout. *Just dominate the woman in bed!*

Seizing on *her* last few words, he said, "I am not going to do anything dreadful, lass. I just want to be sure that you understand what you did, why I didn't like it, and to know that you won't do such a thing again."

"I won't, sir; I promise," she said. "It was gey thoughtless of me."

"Then we'll say no more about it."

She sighed, and he knew that she *had* been worried, perhaps even afraid of what he might do.

"There is one more thing I would ask," he said.

"What?" Her little red tongue darted out to dampen her lips.

"Sir Ian delights in teasing his friends and flirting with comely women. Prithee, do not encourage him."

"Mercy, sir, do you think Ian would go beyond the bounds? I do not."

"Nevertheless, you must not encourage him. I don't like it."

"Well, that is plain enough," she said with a rueful look.

Shifting his right hand from her shoulder to cup the back of her head, he gently touched her lips with his. When she pressed forward, inviting more, he murmured, "You are *mine* now, lass. If you want to flirt, flirt with me."

Her lips curved against his as if she were smiling, so he scooped her into his arms and took her to bed.

Andrena savored his lovemaking but felt as if something were missing, as if he were not wholly with her. Her previous experience of sexual matters had consisted only of occasional flirtation and rudimentary knowledge gained from watching animals. So she could not measure how he compared to or differed from other men.

She did know that she had easily sensed the strength of a man's desire for her then. Indeed, most men who desired her had made no secret of their feelings.

But Mag had said naught of having tender feelings, or any feelings, come to that—except that he had disliked Ian's flirting with her. She had known then from the hungry look in Mag's eyes that he'd wanted to take her. But although he pounded strongly into her now, it seemed only physical, and she was unsure how to respond. Unable to gauge his emotions, she felt adrift in a world no longer her own.

For all she knew, he was still furious with her.

After he reached his climax, he lay beside her and pulled her close so that her head rested on his chest near his shoulder. Listening to his slowing, steady heartbeat, she waited for him to say something. The next thing she knew, he was asleep.

Irritation stirred. She felt like giving him a good shake to wake him. But she could think of nothing sensible to say if she did. While she tried to think of a pithy way to explain how she felt, she fell asleep herself.

Saturday morning, they got up early and joined Colquhoun and Sir Ian on the dais to break their fast. While they ate, gillies carried their belongings to the wharf.

Outside, the sky was gray, heavy with overcast. A brisk wind from the south raised frothy waves on the loch. Andrena wore her fur-lined cloak and her boots, so she was warm. But the voyage would be slow unless the wind shifted or died down.

The longboat provided little comfort for passengers, but Mag drew her to a bench near a small cabin near the prow. There, the cabin wall and the boat's high stempost and sloping plank sides protected them from the wind. Warmed through by his body heat, lulled by the low, steady beat of the helmsman's drum and the rhythmic stroking of the oars, she gazed idly out over the backs of the oarsmen. She could see all the way to the towering, mist-curtained mountains that cradled the loch's head. No other boat or sail was in view.

Magnus was silent, apparently lost in his own thoughts.

Continuing her idle musing, she wondered what, other than flirting with Ian, might anger Mag enough for her to sense it in her usual way. In any case, she knew she would be wiser not to anger him while they traveled with Ian and his men. A tickling awareness stirred that angering Magnus was unlikely ever to be *wise*.

She tried to imagine just asking him about his feelings and persuading him to describe them for her. When they made love, she felt an aching desire for him throughout. But as stoical as he was, despite the strength and power of his lovemaking and the pleasure he brought her, she could sense no identifiable emotion in him. She knew she would find it hard to express her increasingly tender feelings for him unless she could sense his eagerness to accept them.

A new thought stirred. What if he didn't have any feelings for her? Faith, what if he felt no tender emotions? Not only might being a prisoner of Parlan's have killed such feelings in *any* man, but she had heard of warriors who possessed strong feelings only for war and fighting. Such men used women only when they felt lustful. What if Magnus was like them?

Worse, what if he'd married her only to acquire some MacFarlan land? How would she know? He might even be spying for Parlan. Who would know?

Common sense told her that she was imagining things. Mag did reveal his amusement. He was protective of her, and she believed that his gratitude to Lina for his new clothing was sincere. At last, aware that he was dozing as he held her, she fixed her gaze on the scenery and wondered where they would find his grace.

~

Mag dozed but remained aware of the longboat's progress and eyed the loch behind them regularly through slitted lashes to be sure that no one followed them.

Ian stayed with his helmsman for a time but joined Mag and Andrena to share the midday meal that his father's kitchen had provided.

Mag noted with satisfaction that the younger man behaved toward Andrena with propriety. Doubtless he did so to set an example for his men. But, whatever the reason, Mag approved of the change in his behavior.

The longboat entered the Firth of Clyde at midafternoon and reached the harbor serving the royal burgh and castle of Dumbarton shortly afterward.

Dumbarton Castle sat atop a two-hundred-foot rock of basalt that jutted up in a sheer wall above the influx of the river Leven to the river Clyde, thus forming an imposing peninsula in the east angle of the confluence. A full mile around, the enormous rock stood starkly alone in the landscape. The castle entrance was on its north side, where one followed an ascending footpath through a series of iron gates.

It took one of Ian's oarsmen, sent ashore at the harbor, just minutes to learn that Jamie Stewart was staying at nearby Paisley Abbey, southwest of Glasgow.

"'Tis our good luck that he is so near," Ian said. "He visits Paisley often, though. Sithee, his father lies buried before the high altar in the abbey kirk, and Jamie was gey fond of the old King."

Ian sent the same man back to the castle to tell Gregor Colquhoun that, since the tide was receding, Ian would take the galley on to Dunglass, the Colquhoun stronghold farther up the Clyde. "You'll be glad to stretch your legs by walking to Dunglass," he told his henchman cheerfully. "We'll meet you there." To Mag, he added, "Dunglass is three miles nearer Paisley than Dumbarton is."

"I'd surmised as much, aye," Mag said, having no objection to the plan.

Less than an hour later, Dunglass loomed ahead. Mag had not seen it from the water before, having always approached from the landward side.

The riverside stronghold boasted a twenty-foot curtain wall with the Colquhoun arms marking a turret at the southwest corner. A wharf and jetty extended from the gate a few yards east of that turret, and the hoarding above the wharf held men-at-arms who eyed them suspiciously until Ian waved and extended their Colquhoun banner, rendered limp by lack of wind.

The gate opened, and men hurried to the wharf to aid their landing.

As Ian's captain brought the galley alongside the wharf with a flourish, Mag said to Ian, "Andrena and I will take horses from here if you will lend them, lad. You'll want to stay with your boat."

"Nay, Maggy, me lad. Not only do I have orders from my father to render you every assistance, but taking horse from here would also mean riding all the way to Glasgow and back westward to Paisley. We keep horses across the river. So we'll cross in the morning. As you've seen, I have thirty oarsmen. They are also skilled men-at-arms and gey loyal. We'll take eight of them with us."

"Only eight?" Mag said, raising his eyebrows.

"Since you have been serving Pharlain, who never heeds any rules including his own, you may be unaware of the restrictions Jamie imposed on the size of noble retinues, last year during his first Parliament. A knight may take only eight men in his tail. A lesser laird, a prior, or a gentleman may take only six. Forbye, earls may have a score of men and a lord, a bishop, or a mitered abbot a dozen. We'll leave the rest of my lads here to look after the boat and to rest."

"How did Jamie determine how many men a tail should have?" Mag asked as they prepared to disembark.

Ian shrugged. "No one knows, but his intent was clear. He wants to keep nobles of any rank from leading armies to wreak havoc all over the country as so many of them did before his return. He also wants to end private wars between nobles and clans, and hopes that such restrictions will aid him toward that goal."

Standing, Andrena said, "It is not only Parlan who ignores such rules. From what I ken of Murdoch, Lennox, and their followers, few of them obey, either."

"They obey the rules when they know the King is nearby," Ian said. "Some say he learned the art of ruthlessness from his uncle, the first Duke of Albany. So, unless we meet the Abbot of Paisley, I doubt we'll see any group larger than ours today. 'Tis the abbot's loss if he does *not* meet you, Dree," he added, grinning.

Andrena smiled back and then shot a look at Mag as he stood up beside her.

Mag wanted to think she looked wary and hoped she was not challenging him. But he was nearly certain that she was just trying to get a rise out of him.

To his surprise, the thought both warmed and amused him.

⁓

Having smiled automatically in response to Ian's compliment, Andrena felt instantly guilty, because she had decided not to encourage him. Seeing amusement in Mag's eyes reassured her, and she gratefully accepted his hand when he offered it to help her step from the ship to the wharf.

They spent the night at Dunglass, and Sunday morning at dawn, two Colquhoun cobles ferried their eleven-member party across the river to a small village harbor there. Magnus and Ian hired horses and sumpter ponies. Then they were all off again, wending their way along the east bank of the river White Cart as it meandered through ever-rising hills.

Mag and Ian chatted desultorily as they rode, and Andrena listened. The ride was uneventful, and the sun peeked over the eastern hilltops just as the steeple of Paisley Abbey's kirk came into view beyond a rise in the path. Cresting the rise, they saw the abbey and its grounds stretched along the riverbank below them.

The gates beside a stately gatehouse stood open. Passing between them, Andrena feasted her eyes on the extensive gardens surrounding the abbey buildings.

They dismounted in the courtyard, where a lay brother directed them to a guesthouse of considerable size. While Ian arranged to stable their horses and accommodate his men, the guest-master came outside to greet them, enveloped head to toe in the cape and hood of the Cluniac Black Monks who served the abbey. Had the stately gatehouse and the elegant stone wall surrounding the abbey not reminded Andrena that Paisley's Benedictine order was Cluniac, the guest-master's unmistakable aristocratic bearing and manner of speech would have done so.

Hands clasped inside his capacious sleeves, he said to Magnus, "I am Brother Elias, my son. How may we serve you?"

"We request chambers for the night, Brother Elias. I

am Magnus Mòr MacFarlan and this is my lady wife. We come from Tùr Meiloach, in the Highlands between Loch Lomond and the Loch of the Long Boats. We also request audience with his grace, the King, to whom I bring an urgent message. We represent Andrew Dubh, true Chief of Clan Farlan and a fierce supporter of his grace."

"You and your retinue are welcome," Brother Elias said. "I will relay your request to his grace's steward. Despite its urgency, I cannot promise that his grace will grant you an audience. He usually does so for anyone who makes effort to seek him out, as you have. But he reserves Sundays for prayer and contemplation. We celebrate High Mass at midday and encourage our guests to attend. Afterward, yeomen will serve dinner in your chambers. We are a silent order," he added. "If you have other wishes or concerns to express, prithee do so through me. You may make simple requests of our lay brothers and yeomen. And they may speak to you. If his grace agrees to see you, he will do so tomorrow after early Mass."

"His grace is fixed here for some time then," Mag said.

"His grace's people do not share knowledge of his movements or plans, my son. His grace will remain here until he departs."

They thanked him, and when Ian rejoined them, a yeoman showed them to two spacious chambers across a stair landing from each other. The man pointed out amenities, including a hogshead of wine. When he added that her ladyship might be more comfortable in a chamber reserved for visiting noblewomen, since his grace's entourage included two other noble wives, Mag said, "My lady wife will stay with me. But we will not both fit in that bed. If you can arrange for a pallet…"

"I will do so, sir, and I will bring hot water," the yeoman said. "Dinner will be ready when you return from Mass. Will you dine together here, or separately?"

Ian and Mag looked at each other.

"Together," Andrena said firmly.

The yeoman annoyed her then by looking to Mag for confirmation.

~

Peripherally noting Andrena's stiffened expression, Mag nodded with a smile in response to the yeoman's question.

The man paused long enough to ensure that they desired nothing else. Then he departed, leaving the three of them standing by the open door.

"They expect us to attend that High Mass, Ian," Mag said. "We'll meet you on the landing in an hour."

"Aye, good," Ian replied. "I want to see where they've put my men to be sure they are content." Grinning, he added, "Shall I rap if I get here before you?"

"If that happens, practice patience," Mag said.

Ian chuckled, winked at Andrena, and vanished down the stairs.

Mag shut the door and watched as she surveyed the room. Light came through two windows, each no wider than his two hands placed side by side. But the chamber was comfortably furnished and contained a small fireplace with a full wood basket beside it. The table boasted a white linen tablecloth and four cushioned back-stools. A side table held silver candlesticks, tankards, goblets, plates, spoons, and bowls.

"The linens on this bed are delightfully fragrant," Andrena said. "I expected a tidy monk's cell. This is nicer than our bedchamber at home."

"The abbey frequently welcomes royal and noble guests," Mag reminded her. Hearing male voices outside the door, he added, "That must be our hot water and mayhap our sumpter baskets."

He opened the door to a pair of lads bearing water pitchers and the baskets. When they had gone, Mag poured water into the washstand basin and said, "Wash up, lass. I want to look around whilst we're here."

She smiled. "I'm glad. I was thinking—"

"I ken fine what I suggested to Ian, but I feel the presence of too many priests to indulge my lust now," he admitted.

"I, too. Moreover, someone will soon be bringing your pallet."

"Mine?" He chuckled at the look of astonishment she gave him.

In response, she shook her head at him.

When she had washed, they went down to the courtyard, strolled quietly through the gardens, and met Ian without returning to the landing. They attended High Mass in the splendid abbey kirk, enjoying the ceremonial procession of the abbot, his train of attendant Black Monks, and the rest of the elaborate liturgy.

The time passed faster than Mag had expected. Even so, his stomach informed him several times toward the end that he had not eaten enough earlier. When they exited the kirk, they found the lord abbot awaiting them.

Greeting them and learning their names, he said cheerfully, "Prithee, enjoy your stay, my children."

"Thank you, my lord," Andrena said. "During Mass, I saw women holding strings of beautiful beads whilst they prayed. Where may one purchase them?"

"Those are Paternoster beads, my lady. One counts one's prayers on them, and our people string them here. I would be fain to gift a string to you. Later this afternoon, we look forward to seeing you at Vespers."

When they were beyond the abbot's hearing, Ian said, "Is that how you force your husband to buy jewels for you, lass?"

She smiled. "He may buy me whatever he likes, sir. But the beads are to be a gift for Mam on her birthday. I think she will like them. She does not hold by all the teachings of the Roman Kirk. But she does take interest in such matters."

So it was that they attended Vespers before supper.

In their room afterward, Andrena admired the string of amber beads that one of the lay brothers had given her on her way out, with the abbot's compliments.

Mag had dropped two silver groats in the collection basket, earning a smile from the monk.

"Thank you, sir," Andrena said as they'd walked away, and Mag nodded.

While serving supper in their room, their yeoman hinted that they should attend Complines, too. "Mercy, more prayers?" Andrena murmured after he left.

"Not for me," Ian said, helping himself to bread. "The abbot said we should enjoy our stay. Forbye, it is dark already and I warrant they'll have us up before dawn. I'll look in on my lads, but I don't mean to linger with them."

"We'll go out with you," Mag said. "There should be a moon tonight."

They accompanied Ian to the stable entrance and then quietly followed a pathway around the abbey kirk. Although it was dark, a slender thread of a moon showed itself in a declivity northeast of them. The sky had filled with stars, too, so they had light to see their way. The silence was comfortable, but Andrena realized that Mag had talked little since their arrival.

When they returned to their chamber, they found that someone had left a pallet on the floor by the bed, already made up with fresh sheets and blankets. A stone cresset on the table provided light, with flint and a tinderbox nearby.

~

As Mag lit a candle at the cresset, Andrena watched him.

"Magnus, I wish you would talk to me," she said into the silence. "You have barely spoken to me all day other than to ask me to pass food to you at the table."

Letting wax drip into the candlestick's socket—for she knew from the scent that it was wax, not tallow—he held the candle and waited a few seconds for the wax to set around it before he let go and looked up with a smile.

"What would you have me say, lass?"

"Are you angry with me?"

"I told you before that you would know it if I were."

"Mayhap you did, but I can scarcely tell *what* you are feeling from one minute to the next."

"Nay, how should you? But if I were wroth with you, I would say so. Otherwise, I am just myself. I am comfortable with silence. But if you want to discuss something, you need only tell me. I fear that during these past months, I lost the habit of initiating conversation. Sithee, Parlan did not encourage talk, especially amongst those of us who served him against our will."

"It must have been horrid," she said. "Did he keep you in chains?"

She *would* want to talk about Parlan. But he had asked for it, hadn't he?

Even so, he did not like talking about himself. When he was younger and less experienced, he had enjoyed boasting about his successes and had hounded his father and brothers to judge his skills and teach him more. Now, though...

"Well, did he?" she said.

"Sometimes," he admitted.

"Magnus."

"I wish you'd call me Mag, lass, especially when we're alone. When you said Magnus just then, you sounded exactly as my father did just before he'd take leather to me."

She bit her lower lip, but he'd detected a near smile.

"What?" he demanded. "Do you laugh at me?"

Then she did laugh but shook her head hard as if to assure him, even so, that she did not laugh at him.

"It *sounds* as if you are laughing at me."

"I promise, I'm not," she said, visibly struggling to contain her amusement. "I...I just have a vivid imagination. And the image of you over *anyone's* knee..."

Breaking off again, red-faced and nearly choking as she tried to suppress more laughter, she looked at him helplessly.

"I was a lad then," he said. "But you ken that fine."

Finding breath at last, she gasped, "I do...But I can't... picture you then." After a deep breath, she added, "I know only how you look now. When I try to picture you as a boy, I see you as you are now, only...only smaller."

He supposed the image of him as he looked now but bent over his father's knee would be humorous to a lass who did not know Galbraith. That Mag's own memories of such events were not ones he cherished would scarcely impress her though, not while she was irritated with him for not talking more with her.

He did like to see her laugh, even if she was laughing at him.

She was eyeing him differently now. He could tell that she had thought of something else, something that she was unsure she ought to mention.

He stepped closer and put his hands gently on her shoulders. "What is it, lass? By my troth, I am not angry or even a wee bit annoyed. Forbye, if I *had* been angry, my anger is quickly over. Even when I was a lad, that was true. I would roar at something or someone and then be laughing minutes later."

"I have not seen you laugh," she said, frowning as if she were trying to recall when he might have done so. "It surprised me when you chuckled before."

"I don't laugh much anymore," he admitted. "I like watching you laugh, though. Just now you look as if you are fretting about something and don't want to tell me what it is. If you want more conversation, you must feel free to speak."

"I'm not afraid of you," she said. "I'm just not certain that I ought to speak my thoughts aloud yet."

"Sakes, but now you must," he said with a smile.

"I suppose so," she agreed. "Sithee, you know that my father wanted me to meet the King with you."

"Aye, I ken that fine," he said. "I agreed to it."

"You did," she said. "But you have not said anything

to me about the message you have for his grace. I did not ask you about it when you first spoke of it, because we fell into that discussion about whether I would even come with you or not. And I haven't liked to inquire since, because I ken fine that the information may be unsuitable for me to know. But unless you mean to meet privately with his grace and then invite me to join you, which might *not* suit him..."

"I'll admit that I did not consider that," he said when she paused. "I have never been one to share confidential matters with the women in my family. My sisters rarely keep anything to themselves. But you have promised to respect my confidences, and you have given me no cause to doubt that you will. Moreover, your father clearly trusts you to speak for him." He paused reflectively.

She was silent.

Hands still on her shoulders, he gazed into her beautiful face. Then, bluntly, he said, "Parlan has been plotting with others to kill his grace."

"Who are the others?"

"Murdoch and his two elder sons, most likely. Also Lennox, I suspect."

"That's why you escaped then, to warn the King?"

"Aye, but you and your father persist in giving me credit I do not deserve. I escaped because opportunity finally presented itself, and I dared not ignore it."

"Even Ian said he'd have expected you to escape straightaway."

"Mayhap I would have, had I seen a chance to do so. But I was injured, often chained, and didn't care much then about where I was or who had chained me."

"Will you tell me more about that?"

"Some other time, perhaps," he said. "I dislike talking about it."

She nodded. "Mayhap we might think of something else to do then, other than talk. Because if we do talk, I'll likely ask you to tell me more."

He smiled. "I think that bed may be large enough for me to keep your mind off of that subject for a time, at least."

⌒

Mag did keep Andrena's mind sensuously, even ardently, occupied for a time. But, although he was inventive and stirred eager responses in her everywhere his lips, warm hands, fingers, cock, or agile tongue touched her, she felt afterward as if much was still missing from the experience.

He murmured softly to her about how silky her skin felt and how her long hair enticed his fingers to stroke and toy with it. But the strongest reaction from him was a groaning sigh as he gave way to his own needs and began pounding into her. After he reached his climax, he fell asleep as usual, despite the too-small bed.

She did not expect further discussion after their coupling. But she did wish he would tell her more about himself. That topic was of greater importance to her than the contents of his message for the King, despite her belief that had he failed to share the message with her, it would likely have caused problems later with his grace.

Bereft of her abilities as she was with Mag, she was at a loss for a way to overcome his reluctance to share his more private opinions and feelings.

He was easy enough to talk to about most things. So, why...?

The answer came before the question fully formed in her mind: *His* feelings were not the issue. *Her* abilities were. She could not keep pressing him to share thoughts and emotions that disturbed him without fully explaining her strange ability to sense such things in others, something she had never had to do before. Her parents had known she was different from the start. Her sisters shared most of her abilities.

She had nearly explained as much when Mag had insisted that she would *know* if he was angry. Before she had met him, if she angered someone, she knew it as soon as it happened, even if the person's expression remained as blank as Mag's so often did. If an opponent in an argument reacted negatively or grew emotionally fixed on his or her idea of how a debate should result, she could tell as easily as if the person were to tell her so. But Mag defeated her and apparently without effort.

She wished that she had discussed him more with her mother. Lady Aubrey understood her gifts better than most people did and had liked Mag from the start. Perhaps, Andrena thought drowsily, she should talk with her when they got home. When a hint of doubt followed the thought, she realized she could not do it.

Mag had not mentioned her mother, only her sisters. But since it was wrong to discuss things he told her with Lina or Murie, it must be just as wrong—sakes, it would be base betrayal—to reveal her private issues with him to Lady Aubrey.

She was thinking about that when she fell asleep, and it was the first thing on her mind when she awoke. Mag stood naked by one narrow, unshuttered window, staring outside. His expression, as usual, revealed naught of his thoughts.

Although she would have liked to ask what he was thinking, she kept still, enjoying instead the sight of his splendid body in the pale dawn light.

⁓

Mag felt her watching him and knew she had wakened. But she did not speak. Therefore, she was likely thinking about him or whatever still lay between them. He turned, saw her smile, and wished they had time to couple.

"People are up and about, lass, outside as well as in," he said. "Someone rapped on the door just minutes ago, doubtless to let us know that we should break our fast. I left plenty of water for you. But beware. 'Tis icy cold."

Pushing back the covers, she said, "Do you suppose the King washes with icy water whilst he is here?"

He shook his head. "I doubt it. From what I've heard, Jamie likes comfort."

"Well, he can't have got much of it as the English king's prisoner, which is a lack that you also experienced, as Parlan's captive."

"Aye, but nineteen months hardly equates to nineteen years."

"Even so, you should each have some understanding of the other."

She was right. But he did not know what to say, so he did not reply.

Chapter 11 _____

Andrena would have liked to pursue the subject, but the air was chilly. She hurried through her ablutions and then donned her amber-colored tunic and skirt while Mag kilted up his new plaid. She was tucking her plaits neatly into her coif when a rap heralded the arrival of the yeoman with breakfast.

When Ian joined them at the table, the yeoman said to Mag, "Brother Elias said I might tell you, sir, that his grace will see you directly after early Mass. Also, if you agree, Sir Ian is to accompany you and her ladyship. See you, his grace likes to meet the knights of his realm whenever he can. Do you agree, sir?"

Hesitating briefly, Mag said, "I do, aye."

"Thank you, sir. Brother Elias will come for you in half an hour's time."

The guest-master arrived promptly and led them to the elegant, high-ceilinged hall that James of Scotland used as his audience chamber at Paisley.

When they reached the tall, heavily carved door, Brother Elias said to Mag, "I will enter first, sir. Then you, Sir Ian, and your lady wife will follow me in. Prithee, wait then by the door until his grace nods for you to approach."

"We will, aye," Mag said.

When the guest-master announced their names, James nodded.

Andrena knew, as did most Scots, that the King would be thirty-one at the end of July. Even seated, as he was, she saw that he was shorter than his more Viking-like Stewart kinsmen. His body was what Scots called "square-built": heavy shouldered, thick through the torso, and solid. His dark-auburn hair touched his shoulders, thick, wavy, and unadorned. Despite the black velvet robe of state he wore over a red tunic and black leggings, his legs were fully visible. Their muscular thighs reminded her that he had a reputation for being skilled with all weapons and impressively athletic. Men also said he was imaginative, played nearly every known instrument, wrote verses on any subject that sprang to his royal mind, and was a master chess player.

His dark eyes remained serious and watchful as Andrena approached with Mag and Ian until she smiled and sank into a deep curtsy before him. Returning her smile, James stood, saying. "Welcome to Paisley, my lady."

"It is an honor to meet your grace," she said.

"You may rise," James said and then turned to Mag. More sternly, even severely, he said, "Brother Elias announced you as Magnus Mòr MacFarlan. But my steward, Sir William Fletcher, tells me you were born with a different name. Would you like to share the facts of that discrepancy with me?"

Mag felt a sudden urge to clear his throat. Curbing it, he said with his usual calm, "By my troth, your grace,

I meant no deceit. I gave the guest-master the name I'd agreed to take when I married the lady Andrena MacFarlan, at her lord father's request. Forbye, I ought to have explained to Brother Elias before he brought us in that I was born Magnus Galbraith of Inch Galbraith and Culcreuch."

"Then Will Fletcher was right," James said. "He'd heard that MacFarlan of Tùr Meiloach had devised such a requirement for any man who sought the hand of his eldest daughter. He did not mention, though, what a beauty her ladyship is."

Aware that Andrena's gaze had shifted to him, Mag smiled, saying, "She is indeed, your grace, to my good fortune." He was tempted to praise Jamie's queen in return. But having never laid eyes on her grace, a keepsake from Jamie's English captivity and one that all knew he loved deeply, Mag kept silent.

James might, he thought, be the sole King of Scots in history to show sexual interest in only his wife. Some did say that his royal sire had been faithful to Queen Annabella Drummond... in his later years, at least.

"I'm told that you bring an urgent message, Magnus Galbraith MacFarlan," James said. "Will you impart it to me now?"

"I'll leave, if you like," Ian said quietly to Mag.

Mag hesitated.

"Does Sir Ian not enjoy your confidence?" James asked.

"He is, as yet, unaware of what I will tell you, your grace. It is information gleaned whilst I was a prisoner of Pharlain of Arrochar."

"So, you have also endured imprisonment, have you?"

"Aye, your grace. But just nineteen months of it."

"Imprisonment is imprisonment," James said sourly. "It changes a man, through and through."

"It does, aye," Mag agreed.

"I will make your decision for you, then. Sir Ian will retire until you have shared your message with me. However, before you leave us, sir," he added, looking at Ian, "I will hear from your own lips whether you, as a knight of my realm, and your lord father as Chief of Clan Colquhoun, stand with me or with those who oppose my right to the Scottish throne."

Ian stepped forward. Removing his gloves as required when swearing fealty, he dropped to a knee before James. Looking into his dark eyes, Ian put his right hand over his heart and said solemnly, "I, Ian Colquhoun, do swear to you on my honor as a knight of this realm and heir to the chiefdom of Clan Colquhoun, for myself, for my heirs, and for all others who be loyal to me and to my chief that we are now and ever will be loyal to you as rightful King of Scots."

Then, extending his bare hands to James, he bowed his head, adding, "Loyally do I pledge that we will render unto your grace the services due unto you from our estates—now and, God helping, to the end of our days."

Gripping Ian's hands and placing one atop the other between his own, James said, "You are sure, then, that you speak for your father and for your clan."

"I am, your grace," Ian said, meeting the royal gaze. "My lord father and I have long been of one mind in this."

"Then I do accept your pledge, Sir Ian Colquhoun. Will your father attend my Parliament in Perth on the twelfth day of March?"

"If you want him, he will be there."

"I do want him, and you, too."

"We are yours to command, my liege," Ian said.

James released Ian's hands. "I welcome your support, sir," he said. "Doubtless, the lady Andrena will welcome your escort now as you leave us."

Mag saw Andrena stiffen. But the movement was so slight that he doubted Jamie had noticed. In any event, Ian's words and demeanor had strengthened his increasing belief that he could trust the younger man—in most ways.

Accordingly, Mag said quietly, "With your permission, your grace, I have no objection to Sir Ian's staying to hear the message I bring. My lady wife and her father know of it. And hearing Ian swear his fealty to you so earnestly has persuaded me that he should know what I have learned."

James looked from Mag to Ian to Andrena, meeting each steady gaze with a stern one. Then, to Mag, he said, "As you will, sir. What news do you bring?"

"That Parlan MacFarlan, who usurped the Clan Farlan chiefship from Andrew Dubh MacFarlan and now calls himself Pharlain after an ancient leader of that clan, has engaged with others to do harm to your grace at your forthcoming Parliament. He expects Murdoch or his eldest son, Walter, to become Governor of the Realm or even King of Scots before the end of May."

James's expression did not alter. Nor did he immediately reply. Then, flicking his gaze toward Andrena and back to Mag, he said curtly, "Lennox?"

"I cannot speak for the earl, sir," Mag said. "Logic says he must be involved, though. Pharlain has been thick with him for years."

"Murdoch, too, if only because his wife is Lennox's daughter," James said. "Sithee, I have summoned this Parliament to call my nobles to account for their actions. Doubtless, many of them will deny what they've done. Certes, my cousin Murdoch will. He'd liefer I ken nowt of his doings or those of his father, my uncle Albany, during my absence and, too often, in *my* name. Many things that I've heard about Murdoch's elder two sons and their minions seem especially shameful."

"What have they done, sir?" Andrena asked.

James grimaced. But not, Mag thought, because the lass had questioned him.

～

Andrena shot a glance at Mag to see if her question had displeased him. When his lips twitched as if he would smile at her, she felt warmed all through.

She turned her attention back to Jamie Stewart.

"Many things I've heard make unsuitable tales for a lady's ears," he said. "I will recount one, though, because, having sickened me, it stays ripe in my mind. One of my cousin Walter's minions, offended by the way a woman in his charge spoke to him, ordered her shod with horseshoes."

"What did you do?" Andrena asked, feeling sick herself at the image.

"I ordered the same done to the villain who ordered her punishment, and then I hanged him. His cruelty crippled the poor woman for life."

"Mercy," Andrena murmured.

"Just so, my lady," James said. "Such horrors should never be visited on innocent commoners in my realm.

They depend on their lairds and masters for their livelihood and security. But, during my long absence, my nobles evidently acquired a greater taste for exploiting their dependents than protecting them."

"Not all of your nobles, my liege," Ian said.

Andrena nodded her agreement.

"Not all," James admitted. "But I want to know who did and who did not."

He looked at Mag. "I do thank you for your timely warning, sir. But I must know more and will expect you to learn as much as you can, and quickly."

"I will, your grace, by my troth."

"Whilst we both consider what course you might take to accomplish that task, you had further business to lay before me, I think."

"Aye, sir, regarding the chiefship of Clan Farlan and control of the MacFarlan estates. I speak now for Andrew Dubh MacFarlan, whose cousin usurped his title and seized his patrimony by force after you fell captive to the English. We heard that your grace demands to see the charters granting lands to your nobles, to prove their entitlement. Andrew possesses such a charter, an ancient one, for the MacFarlan estates. Pharlain does not."

"MacFarlans have shown little loyalty to me," James said to Andrena.

She nodded, saying, "Parlan and his men obey Lennox, your grace. In times past, my father did, too. He fell out with him when Lennox supported the first Duke of Albany in seizing the governorship of the realm shortly before your cap—"

"I see," James interjected. "What are Andrew Dubh's sentiments now?"

"He is now and has always been fiercely loyal to your grace," Andrena said. "I ken fine that I may not kneel and swear an oath of fealty to you as Sir Ian did. But 'tis said you are a man who passionately believes in honor and duty. If you would accept my word in my father's stead, I would pledge it with all sincerity."

"Will Andrew Dubh attend my Parliament?"

"In troth, your grace, I doubt that he will. See you, he fears that Parlan will seize Tùr Meiloach, too, if he should learn that Father had left. So he never does. Come to that, other nobles would likely oppose his presence in Perth. Many of them no longer consider him to be chief of our clan."

"I do accept your word in your own behalf, my lady. I ken fine that women can be as honorable as men, and as honest. As for your father's fealty, I must hear that from him. But I accept your word that he will swear to it when he can. I wish I could accept your word for the charter, too, but I cannot. Until I establish a rule of law throughout Scotland, so that people can know and understand the laws they must obey, ruthless men will continue to hold lands by 'right of the sword.' "

"I understand, sir," Andrena said. "My father will understand, too. He has kept Tùr Meiloach safe for nearly two decades since Parlan seized the rest. I warrant he will hold it as long as he must."

"Next year, I will visit the Highlands to meet with chiefs there and anyone else who wants his say," James said. "Andrew can present his charter then."

Turning back to Mag, he said, "I have thanked you for your warning, sir. It occurs to me that as you were Pharlain's prisoner, you risked all to warn me. So it pains me to say that whilst I *will* be careful, your warning can do no good without legal evidence connecting specific men to the plot you discovered. I may suspect many who are involved. Indeed, I believe I could make a near-accurate list."

"Some *have* made themselves obvious, your grace."

"To establish a rule of law, I must show that even the Crown must obey our laws. I cannot punish, let alone hang Murdoch, his sons, Lennox, or Pharlain without unequivocal evidence of each man's involvement in the conspiracy. Sakes, Lennox must be eighty years old by now. Think of the outrage amongst our nobility, *especially* the guilty, if I should hang such a graybeard without proper evidence."

Ian said, "Does not his being liege lord of so many clans whose chiefs have either declared against you or refused to declare *for* you speak for itself?"

Hearing Mag's breath catch, Andrena glanced at him. As usual, she could read nothing in his expression.

～

Mag was angry but knew that Ian had merely spoken the truth. Doubtless he had forgotten, however briefly, that the Galbraiths were one of those clans.

Jamie was shaking his head. "Before I hang anyone, I must have evidence strong enough to persuade the lords of Parliament to agree to dire punishment."

Andrena said, "What sort of evidence must you have, sir?"

"Documentation—letters and such—or witnesses who can corroborate what Magnus has heard. Such evidence will be gey hard to get. Sithee, my lady, for years, the dukes of Albany and other powerful nobles abused their power to seize land unlawfully and bestow it on others to entice them into their thrall. The new owners dare not cross them lest they be next to lose the land. That must stop."

"You have stopped some of it already," Ian said.

"I have, aye," Jamie agreed. "But, I must stop the rest, and many of the worst offenders, like Murdoch, are mine own Stewart kinsmen. Sithee, after the English captured me, my nearest heirs seized control of the realm, and not one made a push to win my release. I *want* to hang all of them. But I must do it legally."

The men talked more about acquiring what James needed, much of which would require setting spies amongst Murdoch's men, Lennox's, or Pharlain's. From Mag's knowledge of Pharlain, he knew that such plans were fraught with peril.

He considered and rejected other ideas, listening with only half an ear to Ian and Jamie. Then Andrena said, "Pray, sirs, which clans have declared *against* his grace? Would their members not be the most likely ones involved in this plot?"

Mag froze and got a rueful look touched with ironic amusement from Ian.

James said, "It matters not whether they have *declared* themselves against me if they are *acting* against me, my lady. But I can easily imagine that each of the clans loyal to Lennox has at least a few members involved in this. Therefore, the clans to watch would include the Grahams, Lennoxes, Buchanans, Galbraiths, and mayhap even the odd Cunningham or Campbell-MacGregor."

Mag's father loomed in his mind's eye. His memory

spilled angry words from Galbraith's mouth, declaring that Jamie Stewart was too young to be King of Scots and would never be as strong as his uncle Albany. Mag dared not speak.

⁓

Andrena stared at Mag, startled by the jolt of fear that she'd felt from him when James named the suspect clans. Surely, Magnus was not fearful for himself, although he was certainly a Galbraith, or had been. His attitude toward his captivity, despite reluctance to talk about it, seemed to be that it had happened, was over, and he would fight against going back. But he did not fear Parlan. Of that she was sure. So his fear must be for his clan, and she could not blame him for that.

Aside from the strong awareness of Mag's presence that she felt now whenever they were together—doubtless because of his size—she had paid small heed to him while the men talked with James. But she did sense his nearly paralyzing fear.

It enveloped her, and yet, when she looked at him, she saw no evidence of fear in his demeanor. He watched Ian as Ian made a suggestion, something about setting men to watch the suspect clans. Ian seemed oblivious to Mag's unease.

James was watching Mag closely.

When Mag's gaze shifted to the King, James said, "As I have noted, sir, the Laird of Galbraith numbers amongst the clan chiefs who have not declared one way or another. Do you swear fealty on his behalf as Sir Ian did for the Colquhouns?"

"I'll willingly swear my fealty, your grace," Mag said.

"But I've seen nowt of my father since before my capture. I cannot speak for him or for Clan Galbraith."

"Then you will learn Galbraith's sentiments as fast as you can, sir, and report them to me. The clan will do as he bids them. But he may know more than we do about this plot, and Parliament meets just over a fortnight from now. If he does know aught of importance, you will persuade him to stand witness against the others."

"Aye, your grace," Mag said with a nod.

His speech was terse, his demeanor calm. But Andrena could still sense remnants of his fear. That alone attested to its strength.

James said, "Get word to me as soon as you know Galbraith's intentions. I ride to Stirling today and to Perth on Thursday week." Lifting one hand slightly as if to signal their dismissal, he paused, saying, "Mark me, gentlemen. We must all accomplish much in little time. Your loyalty won't be worth a cat's whisker to me if their villainous plot succeeds." Then, with a flick of his hand, their audience ended.

Ian and Mag gave the respectful nods of acceptance that Highlanders allowed themselves by way of a bow to authority, and Andrena made her curtsy. Then she and Mag left the chamber together with Ian following.

In the courtyard Ian sent a lay brother to tell his men that they would depart before the midday meal, and they asked Brother Elias for food to take with them.

When Andrena was alone with Mag in their bedchamber, she made sure the door had shut tight before she said, "You seemed disturbed when his grace named the Galbraiths, sir. Art fearful that they may be involved in this plot?"

He was stripping off his new plaid and sark, replacing them with the well-worn ones. Meeting her gaze, he said, "I've nae cause to be fearful, lass. I ken nowt of what they've been about for these two years past."

"That seems more reason than not to be fearful," she said, unpinning her coif. "In any event, we must go to Inch Galbraith straightaway, must we not?"

"I promised Andrew Dubh that we'd return to Tùr Meiloach as soon as we'd seen Jamie, to tell him what happened. You ken fine that I did, for you were there."

"Father would understand, sir. After all, the King has ordered you to learn *your* father's sentiments and if the Galbraiths will support him."

"Nevertheless, I told Andrew that we would return to him first. So we will."

Unable to think of an argument that she could imagine would sway him from that course, Andrena finished changing her clothes and prepared for departure.

~

By the time Mag and Andrena descended to the yard, Ian had gathered his men, and the horses were ready. The sumpter ponies were soon loaded, as well.

Mounting quickly and in silence, they rode out together through the tall gates, which shut with a clang behind them.

Once on the trail along the winding river toward the harbor, however, Ian said, "We'll cross to Dunglass and take the galley to Dumbarton, Maggy. We can get beds and horses from Gregor and ride on tomorrow to Inch Gal—"

"Nay, then," Mag said. "I promised Andrew Dubh we'd return straightaway."

"But he expected you to be away for some time, seeking Jamie, did he not?"

"Nae matter," Mag said. "I promised we'd go straight back. I'll see my father afterward. I can reach Inch Galbraith soon enough from Tùr Meiloach."

Ian did not give up as easily as Andrena had. But Mag prevailed.

Andrena began to suspect that his main reason for going right back to Tùr Meiloach was to deposit her there. Then he could go to Inch Galbraith by himself.

She would just see about that.

Nothing occurring to delay them, they reached the village harbor shortly before midday and found the two cobles where they had left them. After returning the horses and sumpters to the stable and loading their gear, Ian's men rowed their party across the Clyde to Dunglass. The galley sat quietly at the castle wharf.

They boarded the galley straightaway and were soon off again and away.

Andrena had kept an eye on Mag, hoping he would not notice how closely she watched him. Whatever had frightened him had released its grip, and she was almost sorry that it had. She had hoped the incident meant that she was finally beginning to connect with him. If so, it was going to be a slow process.

Instead of the bench they had occupied coming south, from which she had been able to watch the landscape only as it passed behind them, she moved to one at the stern near the helmsman. From there, she could see where they headed. She had thought Mag was right behind her. But when she turned to sit, she saw that he and Ian had paused on the gangway to talk. Since it looked as if they might talk for a while, she turned her thoughts to Jamie Stewart.

She had liked him and had felt a swift connection to him, as if they thought the same way about many things. She could not have explained that bond to anyone but her sisters or their mother. But she had understood that Jamie spoke his thoughts as he thought them. He did not seem to have a devious thought in his head. He had liked her, too. Even in his comment about her beauty, she had sensed only sincerity, not a hint of the lustful scrutiny she was used to sensing in many men that she met.

She believed that Ian was likewise sincere in his fealty to Jamie and that Ian had spoken truthfully about being of one mind with Colquhoun. She wished that she could reassure Mag that he could trust the Colquhouns all in all, and Jamie, too.

She did believe that they should visit Inch Galbraith straightaway, because to ignore a royal command was more than unwise. That was especially true with Jamie, because it was important for them all that he learn to trust them.

The galley passed below the looming rock of Dumbarton less than an hour later. The river Clyde began to widen then until they had officially entered the firth.

Ian ordered the sail up to ease the labor of his oarsmen. Then he and Mag disappeared into the tiny forward cabin, and two hours later, the galley turned north out of the firth and into the Loch of the Long Boats.

The weather cooperated more than it had on their journey south. With the winds behind them, Ian signaled for his helmsman to ship oars. A pleasant silence ensued after the men obeyed, leaving only the noise of the wind in the huge sail.

Mag strode down the gangway to sit beside Andrena, saying as he did, "Ian has been showing me his maps and rutter, lass. So, I hope you have not been lonely. I hope, too, that you understand why we must return to Tùr Meiloach."

"I understand that the King presented you with a dilemma, sir," she said. "But to ignore a royal command..."

"I told Jamie that I would learn what he wants to know, and I will. Sithee, lass, the fact is that your father still wonders if he can trust me. It would not do to break my first promise to the man."

"I do see that, aye. What sort of a man is *your* father?" she asked. "I would like to have some ken of him."

He hesitated, frowning. But at least the frown was one of reflection, not annoyance, so she stifled the urge to press him when his silence lengthened.

Then, with a rueful grimace, he said, "You do deserve to know more about him. Sithee, we argued before my brother Will was killed and I was captured."

"Ian said Will died *when* you were captured. So Parlan's men killed him?"

"They ambushed our party, aye. Will was one of the first to fall."

Again she felt his emotion. Looking at him, seeing the bleak look in his eyes, she knew that she was not sensing his pain in her usual way or at its full strength.

"It must be terrible to remember such a thing," she said. "Then to be captured and be unable to see to his burial or be with your family—"

"They would not have wanted me," Mag said. "In troth, lass, I'm not sure that my father will want to see me now."

"Mercy, I should think he would be ecstatic to see you."

His lips pressed together and he did not reply.

She wanted to ask him many more things, chiefly if he was going to take her with him to Inch Galbraith. But she did not want to argue with him, not now. Moreover, he had shut his eyes and seemed to be more in a mood for dozing than for conversation. So she occupied herself with the passing landscape instead.

After a time, the journey began to grow tedious. She wanted to move, stretch her legs, and perhaps seek conversation. She knew that Ian would gladly chat with her, and Mag was sound asleep. He would not object if she just talked with Ian.

When she stood and shook out her skirts, he did not stir.

The men were rowing again, the helmsman's low drumbeat signaling each powerful stroke. She made her way carefully for a short distance, but the swaying of the boat made footing uncertain. Deciding to wait and let Ian come to her, rather than walk the length of the gangway to him, she went to stand by the helmsman with the high sternpost wall solidly behind her.

From there, she could see land on both sides of the galley. It was a distant view to the west, a much closer one to the eastern shore, on her right.

As she peered into the distance ahead, she felt a sudden slight but increasing sense of danger. Searching the loch shore northward, she noted a steeply sloping point of land that jutted into the loch.

The prickling sense of unease grew stronger.

Her gaze swept the forward area, seeking Ian. The door to the wee cabin near the stempost stood open, and she could see his lanky figure inside.

Feeling increasing urgency, she hurried back to Mag, meaning to shake him.

He opened his eyes before she touched him. "What's amiss, lass?"

"Sir, you must warn Ian that enemies lurk ahead. They lie in wait for us."

He straightened, frowning. "That must be a wheen o' blethers, Andrena. How could you know such a thing?"

"I cannot explain *how* I know," she said honestly. "But I do, and you must tell Ian. Tell him, too, to slow this galley. They mean to ambush us. Prithee, Magnus, believe me. The men *must* prepare for attack."

Chapter 12 ————————————

Mag examined Andrena's anxious expression and tense demeanor and knew she believed what she was telling him. Although his time at Tùr Meiloach had been short, he had seen and heard enough to know that some things were inexplicably different there. Much of what he'd heard, even seen for himself, he had dismissed. But Andrena had given him no cause to think she was untruthful.

"I'll talk with Ian," he said, getting to his feet. "You keep out of sight, lass, until we know what is what."

Striding along the gangway with the ease of one accustomed to moving about on any vessel, he noted that Ian had seen him and was coming toward him.

"What is it?" Ian asked when they met.

"Andrena suspects an ambush ahead. She indicated that headland yonder and said she thinks an enemy may be lurking there. I don't know how she could know such a thing. But she insists that we must slow down."

"Then we will, and we'll prepare in case she is right," Ian said. "I've heard enough about the MacFarlan sisters of Tùr Meiloach to know that I should heed her warning. Forbye, if she is wrong, we lose nowt, and if she is right, we'll be better off than if we *do* nowt, especially since, if she is right, the most likely person to ambush us is Pharlain."

"That did occur to me, too, aye," Mag said dryly.

"Let me warn my helmsman," Ian said. "Then we'll ponder a bit."

"Have him maintain the drumbeat," Mag advised. "If anyone *is* there, they've already heard it."

Nodding agreement, Ian whistled to alert his helmsman and then gestured with his hands. The oarsmen shipped their oars, leaving the wind alone to move the galley forward. The steady, low, rhythmic beat of the helmsman's drum continued.

Mag watched the headland as they slowed, and saw no hint of danger.

Turning back to Ian, he saw that the younger man's eyes were dancing.

Ian said, "I'm thinking that since Colquhoun land lies less than a mile past that point, we must take advantage of that fact. We fly the Colquhoun banner, so if they stop us, we'll say that only Colquhouns are aboard. Dree shall be my sister."

"What am I then?" Mag demanded. "I'll tell you straight out that I've no intention of swimming ashore and leaving my lady wife to *your* protection."

His eyes still alight, Ian said, "What you are, my lad, is recognizable to Pharlain's men, even if Pharlain is not with them. I don't suppose Dree told you how *many* boats are lurking yonder."

"She did not, nor did I ask," Mag said, wishing Ian would call her by her Sunday name instead of her nickname. "Do you not know the coastline here?" he demanded. "As I recall, that headland would conceal only two, mayhap three small galleys. Moreover, I'd warrant from mine own experience that Pharlain would tuck no more than two into such a place—not so near your lord father's wharf as it is."

"True," Ian said. "Our lads watch from the peaks, and carry horns. But if a boat takes shelter for a short time, and no one disembarks, they would do nowt."

"Most of Pharlain's men would recognize me," Mag admitted reluctantly.

"Then stay out of sight, Maggy. Mayhap in yon wee cabin. If you sit on the floor in the map corner, we'll leave the door open. It will then look empty inside."

"Andrena should conceal herself, too," Mag said.

"Nay, then, she should not. If they *are* ambushers, they've had men out keeping watch for us. They might fail to tell one man from another, but they *would* notice a female aboard. We'll tell them she's a Colquhoun."

"Most of Pharlain's men must know the MacFarlan sisters," Mag protested.

"Not by sight," Ian said. "Whilst Pharlain may confer at times with Lennox or Murdoch, Andrew Dubh MacFarlan does not. Nor has Pharlain, to my knowledge, mixed with nobles who support the King. In any event, I don't mean to let his men board this galley. Moreover, I always carry my horn. One thing we can count on, even at this distance, is that if I blow it, Colquhoun galleys will put out from our wharf so fast that it will terrify Pharlain's lads."

"Mayhap it will," Mag said. "But your boats won't be fast enough or sufficient in number if Pharlain's men bear evil intent. Forbye, I'm not hiding in yon wee box of a cabin. I'll take an oarsman's place and keep my sword with me."

"Sakes, you'll stick out like a mountain amidst my lads!"

"Some of them are nearly as tall," Mag said. "If I sit amidst them and keep my head down, mayhap slouch a bit, Pharlain's lads won't notice me. They'll be concerned about your father's men ashore. Also, most of Pharlain's lads ken nowt of the coastline this far south. I'd suggest easing out away from the headland. Give yourself room to maneuver, and make them come to us."

When Ian nodded and signaled to his helmsman, Mag moved to where he could keep an eye on the headland. Although he retained doubt about Andrena's suspicions, the sight of two galleys emerging from behind the headland just minutes later, flying Pharlain's banner, surprised him less than he had thought it would.

Looking at Ian to see Andrena beside him, he said, "Lass, you should sit."

"In troth, sir, you are the one who should keep out of sight," she said, frowning. "Striding about as you are, they will certainly see you."

"I know," he said, stepping off the gangway and keeping the prow between himself and the pair of galleys. "Just *don't* let them get a close look at your face."

Unbuckling his belt, he pulled off his plaid. To Ian, he said, "That lad on the third bench is not as large as I am, but his hair is the same color and length. Have him put my plaid on. That way, if they've seen me, they'll not wonder where I've gone."

Ian summoned the man, while Mag retrieved his sword from under the bench where he had dozed earlier. Then he took the oarsman's place on the third bench.

⌒

Andrena watched Mag take a seat among the oarsmen and wondered what he was thinking as he did. That it must have reminded him unpleasantly of his rowing Pharlain's galleys she could not doubt. Yet she saw no sign of that.

It occurred to her then that having his sword at hand must make a difference. Even so, her heart ached to watch him. No son of a man as powerful as the Chief of Clan Galbraith should lower himself to row *anyone's* galley.

He glanced up then, caught her gaze, and grinned.

"By my faith," she muttered. "The man is enjoying himself!"

Beside her, Ian chuckled. "Aye, sure, he is, lass. True warriors—and Maggy is one of the finest—approach any engagement with eagerness."

Looking at Ian, she saw that he, too, was grinning. "You're enjoying it, too!" she said accusingly.

His light-blue eyes still brimming with laughter, Ian said, "Why not? I have my horn, and our lads patrol our boundaries carefully. If I blow for aid, they will relay my signal to our men-at-arms and to the tower. Fear not, lass."

"You must not call me 'lass.' Magnus dislikes your flirting with me."

"Who's flirting? Since we cannot hide you, you're going to be my lady sister."

"Which one?" she demanded, aware that he had three.

"It will have to be Alvia. Sithee, Susanna is married and Pharlain may know that Birdie is visiting her and her husband at their home near Ayr."

"I don't look at all like Alvia."

"True. But with your plaits dangling loose from under your veil as they are, you do look like a maiden. Forbye,

Alvia is with my mother's sister at Balloch, and I doubt that any of Pharlain's men know her by sight. So Alvia you shall be."

"Those boats are coming fast."

"Aye, they are. I think we'll ease back toward them now, if only to make them think we meet willingly and to be sure they recognize the Colquhoun banner."

He gestured his orders to his helmsman and then urged Andrena toward the bench where she'd sat earlier with Mag. Raising his horn to his lips then with his right hand, he blew two short blasts as he slipped his left arm around her shoulders.

"Just to let them know at home that we are near," he said, giving her shoulders a reassuring squeeze.

She could feel Magnus watching them. When she looked back, her gaze collided with his. His set expression gave her a distinct chill of unease.

~

What the devil was the man up to now? And what the devil was she about to be smiling at him and letting him put his hands on her?

Knowing he could not let such feelings show to anyone on the approaching galleys, Mag lowered his gaze to his still motionless oar. But when an image formed in his mind of himself behaving as he knew his lord father would have behaved had a cheeky knight ever put an arm around Lady Galbraith, he let that image linger.

The vast unlikelihood that any knight knowing his lordship would dare take such a liberty nearly made him smile. That touch of amusement was slight, but it eased his displeasure. He had learned the advantage of finding humor in odd places while in Pharlain's custody, and the device had helped him survive at Arrochar.

Anger and amusement simply did not mix. So, if one could see humor in a bad situation, one could nearly always control one's baser impulses.

However, to let one's captors *see* one's amusement was dangerous. Still, such a lapse added less risk to a situation than discovering that an opponent was a serious match instead of one a man could easily defeat.

He wished he could still see the oncoming galleys, but with his back to the prow as it was, he could not. Glancing toward the nearby shore, he saw that it was closer than before, which meant Ian had begun to lessen the distance between them and the enemy boats.

Wondering how close they were to the headland, Mag glanced back over his left shoulder and saw a man on its crest waving a yellow banner. Since Pharlain's men were unlikely to have set foot on Colquhoun land again so soon, the flag-waver was likely a Colquhoun, acknowledging Ian's horn.

Mag noted, too, that Ian had drawn the enemy pair far enough offshore for his galley to keep to the landward side of both when they all met and passed each other.

If Colquhoun's wharf was not in sight, it would be shortly.

"*Now*, lads!" Ian shouted. "Put your backs into those oars. Encourage them to come after us!"

Setting his thoughts aside, Mag focused on his oar.

~

Andrena also saw what Ian had done, and with alarm. "We're gey close to shore, sir, and fast closing with those two boats."

"Aye, sure, lass. But I ken every snag and pool along here. I'll wager that neither of Pharlain's helmsmen kens our coast as well as I do."

"But they're turning, and they've only to follow us to know they'll be safe."

"Perhaps, but I'll control where we go."

She saw that he held his horn in his right hand near his thigh. His sword was in its baldric across his back, his dirk hung near her on his left hip, its hilt angled upward toward his right. His eyes still danced with eager antici-pation.

Parlan's boats kept seaward of the Colquhoun galley as it inched nearer the shore. With its oarsmen rowing again, its sail and jib both full, it moved swiftly.

Parlan's boats had had the wind against them, which must have played a part in Ian's tactics. As they passed the two, the pair turned more sharply to follow them, but Ian's galley easily maintained its advantage in speed.

As they left the other two behind, she saw that both were longer than Ian's and had more oarsmen. Ian had thirty men aboard, but with only five benches to a side and two oarsmen on each, just twenty men rowed at a time. She was sure that each of Parlan's boats carried twice as many oarsmen as theirs. His boats therefore carried more weight, but she knew that when they regained speed, the power of so many oarsmen would more than make up for that extra weight.

"They'll be faster than we are when they reach speed again," she warned Ian.

He grinned. "Aye, sure they will, for all the good it may do them. I have a plan, lass ... sorry, Dree."

"You must know, sir, that it irks Magnus to hear you

call me 'lass.' It will irk him just as much, if not more, to hear you call me 'Dree.' "

"Aye, it will," he agreed, still grinning.

"Art daft, Ian? Surely, you do not *want* him to be angry with you."

With a roguish shrug, he said, "As lads we were ever taunting each other and coming to cuffs. I'll wager that neither of us has changed much since."

"Is that why you call him Maggy?"

"Aye, sure it is."

As she shook her head at him, they heard a bellowed, "Colquhoun boat! Damn your impudence! Hold water, or bear the consequences."

⁓

Mag's senses went on high alert at the shouted order from Pharlain's galley and Ian's shouted, "Hold water!" Recognizing the first voice as that of Pharlain's eldest son, Dougal, he wondered if Ian knew Dougal's voice, too.

"Give me your cap," Mag muttered to the man beside him as they dug the long blade of their oar into the water and held it hard.

Without debate, the man snatched off the cap and handed it to Mag.

A glance assured him that the high sternpost and the port side sloping down from it still blocked his view of both enemy galleys, so no man on either could see him. Gripping the oar with one hand, he fingered the knitted cap over his hair with the other in such a way that strands of hair dangled over his face.

His beard was gone, and his hair was lighter than it had been during the long months of rare washing. Also,

Dougal MacPharlain paid small heed to the captive oars-men, deeming them the responsibility of his father's oar-masters. Even so, Mag knew that his size would be a noticeable disadvantage if the other boats got close.

Slouching lower, he prayed that Dougal would not board Ian's galley.

The man beside him sat straighter, trying obviously to look taller.

While the Colquhoun galley slowed to let Pharlain's boats draw nearer, Ian stepped onto the gangway where men on the two enemy galleys could plainly see him and shouted, "I am Ian Colquhoun, son and heir of the Laird of Colquhoun and a knight of this realm, traveling on lawful business. By what right do you seek to stop a Colquhoun boat in Colquhoun waters?"

"By right of recovering missing and lawful property of Arrochar," Dougal MacPharlain shouted back. "We seek an escaped captive and would search your vessel to see that he has not found concealment aboard."

While Dougal bellowed, Ian's helmsman signaled to his men to feather their oars. They obeyed, turning each blade parallel to the water just above its surface.

The wind began slowly to ease the galley forward again as Ian shouted back, "You're daft! We Colquhouns do not make slaves of our oarsmen. So I can see for myself, standing here, that none be aboard this galley save loyal Colquhoun men-at-arms and one lad who will soon be a Colquhoun kinsman. You have nae right to interfere with us, least of all whilst we're within sight of our home wharf."

"The devil we don't!" Dougal shouted. "I ordered you to hold water!"

"A knight of the realm does not take orders from the likes of you, Dougal MacPharlain. Forbye, unless your da has taken to making war on innocent women as well as obstructing men who tend to their own business, you'll keep your lads on your boats and be about *your* business elsewhere."

"We did see ye had a female aboard. Who might she be?"

"Why, me sister, of course. The man to whom she is about to pledge her troth is here, as well. If you'd like to attend their betrothal feast, I'll ask my lord father to invite you. For the nonce, you'd do better to go in peace."

"I've the right to search your boat," Dougal shouted.

"Aye, sure, if you insist, you may search it at yon wharf. You may likewise take a dram o' whisky with me, my lord father, this strapping lad who will soon wed my sister, and all yonder who wait to welcome us home," Ian added, gesturing.

"Nay, nay, we'll search ye here."

"You heard me blow to tell them we're nearly home. 'Tis why you see so *many* gathered ashore. Forbye, we've three boats at that wharf and lads eager to engage with your lot. If I blow this horn again, you won't like what happens."

Mag listened but heard no more from Dougal. It irked him to leave all in Ian's hands. But he had to admit that, so far, the lad had done well. He'd be wise, though, to keep his impudent hands off of Andrena.

⁓

Andrena was holding her breath, hoping the other boats would leave. She had stayed put when Ian jumped onto the gangway and then had winced when he'd invited Dougal MacPharlain to take whisky with the Laird of Colquhoun.

She could see that the group on the wharf had grown larger. Men were boarding longboats there and would soon row out to aid them if necessary.

Dougal was Parlan's eldest son and his heir. She knew that he expected to be Chief of Clan Farlan one day. But whether he would dare to engage...

Then she heard him shout to Ian, "If ye find our prisoner or learn of his whereabouts, I'll expect ye to send word straightaway to Arrochar."

"Certes, I will, aye," Ian said. Glancing at Andrena, he rolled his eyes heavenward.

"You should be flogged for the lies you tell," she said when he stepped off the gangway to stand beside her.

As they watched the departing boats, he said, "I was punished for such, often, when I was a lad. But why should I tell Pharlain's Dougal aught save what I hoped would send him home again?"

"Because if he learns that you lied to him, he won't believe you next time."

"Faugh," Ian said rudely. "That lad believes what he wants to believe. So I told him what he wanted to hear."

"He wanted to hear where Magnus is. You did not tell him that."

"Nay, lass, nor would I. Didst fear that I would?"

"I did not."

Putting an arm around her, he gave her a hug. "Then, all's good," he said.

"All will not be good for long, my lad, if you persist in taking liberties with my wife," Magnus said from right behind them, startling them both.

Mag had given back the cap he'd borrowed and taken his plaid and belt from the man who had pretended to be Andrena's soon-to-be betrothed. But he had not yet donned the garment. His irritation with Ian had increased when he'd seen him put his arm around Andrena. But he had startled them, and the lass looked at him now with an expression of incipient annoyance.

"Sir Ian was expressing his relief and pleasure at having rid us of Dougal, sir," she said mildly. "Surely, by now, you must know that I think of him as nowt but a brother I never had."

"Mayhap that is so," Mag said, still eyeing Ian with disfavor. "But I have said that I dislike such familiarity. Until *I* trust him like a brother, I would fain see him keep his hands to himself."

"There is gratitude for you, Dree," Ian said with a chuckle. "But the sooner we reach the wharf, the better pleased I will be. So, take your ungrateful husband yonder and do what you can to soothe his temper."

Nodding to his helmsman, he shouted, "Nearly there, lads! Drop the jib, and we'll show them the grand style in which we land this agile craft!"

Mag growled.

"What did you say, sir?" Andrena asked softly.

"Nowt."

"It sounded as if you were about to speak."

"If you would have that lad remain in one piece," Mag said, "see that he keeps his hands off you."

"I thought his ruse was a splendid one," she said. "I did take him to task for the wicked lies he told Dougal, though."

Not trusting himself to reply, Mag gestured toward the stern bench.

Obediently taking her seat there, she said, "Do you *not* think he was clever?"

"Since the ruse succeeded, it was good enough," he said. Hoping to change the subject, he added, "Despite Ian's cheeky behavior and untimely mirth, I do think we can trust his sworn word, lass. Nevertheless, I think *you* trust too easily."

"And I fear that you trust no one at all."

"Nay, then, I am just cautious. I am also curious, though. How did you know that those boats were lying in wait for us?"

As a diversionary tactic, the question was successful, because although she ought to have anticipated it, she looked stunned. Her lips parted. She licked them and then audibly cleared her throat before she said, "By my troth, sir, I do not know how such things happen. My mother thinks my instincts are just keener than most. But I don't know how instinct could account for what happened when I beheld that headland. I just knew, somehow, that danger lurked beyond it."

"Aye, well, I want to talk more about this. But we are fairly flying toward that wharf. I hope Ian knows what he's doing now."

Her relief was nearly palpable. She said with a smile, "Watch then, because I have seen him do this before. Do Parlan's men not like to show off their skills?"

"Nay, there is little pride aboard his boats."

"I wonder if we might count that lack in our favor one day," Andrena mused. When he did not reply, she said, "Art still vexed with me as well as with Ian, sir?"

Slipping an arm around her, he drew her close. "Nay, lass, but I'm still curious. If Colquhoun would not count it an affront to his hospitality, I'd take you straight to our chamber and have a good long talk with you, right now."

⁓

Andrena had a feeling that she should bless Colquhoun for his stern notions of hospitality and good manners. Much as she wanted to discuss her gifts with Mag, she would rather do so well after this unpredictable mood of his had passed. She wanted to be sure he was not still angry that she had let Ian put his arm around her.

The laird and most of his men stood on shore, watching as Ian headed the galley straight for the wharf. At the last minute, the great square lugsail dropped, the men on one side raised their blades high while those on the other dug theirs into the water, turning the galley as if on a pivot so that it settled into place with a graceful flourish.

Men on the wharf shouted for ropes and soon made the boat fast.

Ian leaped off and extended a hand to Andrena when she and Mag used the gangplank. As she rested her hand on Ian's, he bent, kissed the back of hers, and then looked up, grinning, to say, "Thank you for your timely warning, lass."

Mag stepped off the gangplank, passed behind Ian, and to Andrena's shock, picked him up, and chucked him off the wharf into the icy loch.

After a moment's stunned silence, Ian's men surrounded Mag with a roar.

Andrena gasped.

Mag stood where he was and folded his arms across

his broad chest. He eyed each of the men in turn, as much as daring one to touch him.

Ian shouted something unintelligible, doubtless through a mouthful of water. Then a voice on shore that she recognized as Colquhoun's bellowed, "Halt there, all o' ye! The man be my guest! Leave him, and fish our Ian out of the loch!"

Someone threw Ian a line, while Mag, with a look that Andrena easily read as guilty satisfaction, politely guided her off the wharf to their awaiting host.

To her surprise, Colquhoun shook his head at Mag and said, "Ye two bairns havena changed a whit. Do I want tae ken what he did this time to stir your ire?"

"No, sir," Mag replied.

"Then we'll go on whiles he wrings himself out. Supper will be ready soon." Turning toward the path, he added, "I'm assuming from your swift return, lad, that ye found Jamie at Paisley Abbey."

"We did, aye. Take my arm on this path, lass," he added.

She did so, and the men continued talking while they walked up to Craggan Tower. As Colquhoun had predicted, supper was ready to serve when they arrived.

When Ian joined them, he sat beside his father at the table and began talking to him at once. Andrena noted that Ian's demeanor was defensive, his tone exculpatory.

Before a curt interjection from Colquhoun stemmed the flow, she deduced that the laird had no sympathy to offer for his son's unexpected swim.

"It is good that your journey took less time than you feared it might," Lady Colquhoun said gently, diverting Andrena's attention and reminding her of her own manners. "May one ask why those boats of Pharlain's accosted ours?"

"Dougal said they are missing a captive oarsman," Andrena explained.

"Your own Magnus Mòr, in fact."

Andrena smiled. "The laird told you. I thought he might. But Magnus may be displeased that he did, madam. He keeps his own counsel."

"Young men do, many of them," Lady Colquhoun said. "Our Ian may even do so at times. More oft, he says what he thinks."

"Magnus calls him 'cheeky.' "

Her ladyship's eyes danced in the same way that Ian's did as she said, "He is impudent, aye. But one hopes he does not often annoy men as large as Magnus."

"Someone told you Magnus threw him in the loch." When her hostess nodded, Andrena said, "Sithee, Mag was just annoyed. He never gets truly angry."

"Oh, my dear, all men get angry. All men have violence in them, too. It is no wiser to taunt a man with words than to poke a wildcat with a stick."

They continued to chat thus amiably until everyone had finished eating.

Mag got up then from his place next to the apparently unrepentant Ian and stepped past him to speak to Colquhoun.

When the laird nodded, Mag approached Lady Colquhoun and said, "My lady has endured three long days of travel, madam. She must be nigh dropping from fatigue. If you will excuse her, I mean to see that she gets a good night's sleep."

Smiling, Lady Colquhoun said, "I admire your

consideration, sir. I own, I had failed to notice Dree's exhaustion. But I cannot doubt your concern for her welfare."

"Thank you, madam. Come along, lass."

"Good night, my dear; sleep well," Lady Colquhoun said with a twinkle that revealed her belief that Mag had notions other than sleeping in mind.

When he offered his arm, Andrena rose but pressed her lips together to avoid saying something that might suggest to her ladyship that Mag's thoughts likely had more to do with her son's behavior than with amorous intentions of his own.

*Chapter 13*_____

Mag noted Lady Colquhoun's dancing eyes and Andrena's tightened lips and appreciated the lass's restraint. He purposely ignored Ian, believing that to see mischief in *his* eyes might result in behavior Colquhoun would deplore.

Andrena led the way upstairs, and Mag held his peace until they reached their room and he'd shut the door behind them. Someone had drawn the curtains and lit three candles so that their light cast a warm, inviting glow over the bed.

The stiffness of her back and shoulders as she moved to the center of the small chamber and stood without turning told him she was displeased. The candles' glow turned her tawny, loosely plaited hair to gold.

"We must talk, lass," he said firmly. "If you want to read me a lecture for taking you away from the dais betimes, then have your say. But you should ken first that I won't apologize unless I have done aught for which I must."

She turned then, tilting her head and eyeing him with a speculative frown.

He could not tell if she was trying to decide whether to

lose her temper or thinking something else altogether. But he had said that she could speak first.

At last, she said, "I wish you'd just say whatever it is you want to say to me."

"Sakes, I thought you were vexed with me," he said. "I've told you what I want to discuss. I feared that if we waited until after the laird and his lady retired for the night, we might be so tired that we'd say things we might wish we had not."

"I know you are displeased that I let Ian flirt with me," she said.

"I am not, for I did not see you encouraging him. The only blame for Ian's behavior lies with Ian. But I do think you trust too easily, lass. If such trustfulness encourages him, I might deem it misplaced, but that is all. I also think you trusted Colquhoun too quickly and his grace, too, come to that."

"Sakes, where did I misstep with his grace?" she asked, clearly bewildered.

"You told him more than was wise. Forbye, you spoke of his honor and sense of duty as if you had known him for years, when you met him only today. You next assured him of how your father will behave. What if Andrew does not act as you think he will?"

"But he will. And I like James. I could sense that he is trustworthy. He listens and does not censure people for what they say to him. He *wants* to know what they think, and he should know that my father stands ready to support him."

"You seem to believe that you know what men are thinking, Andrena. Can you tell me what I am thinking now?"

She hesitated, eyeing him again in that strange, measuring way.

Then, drawing a deep breath, she released it, nodded as if she had settled something within herself, and said evenly, "May we sit down, sir? The way you loom over me, I can barely think. Moreover, since the matter is one that I do not understand myself, it is hard to describe to someone else. I will do my best, but I'd liefer do it whilst we sit face to face."

"Come here," he said gently.

The look in her dark, beautiful eyes turned wary, but she obeyed him.

~

Andrena wondered what he meant to do. If only she *could* read his thoughts!

He put his hands on her shoulders as he had earlier that day.

Involuntarily, she felt herself stiffen. Her mouth dried.

His voice still gentle, he said, "You are trying to delay this talk, to divert me from it. But you must know that you cannot. You may say anything you like to me, lass, but I have told you what I want to know. What am I thinking right now?"

"I cannot tell you," she said, meeting his gaze.

"Cannot or will not?"

"Cannot," she said firmly. "I wish I could. I tried to explain how things are with me soon after we met. I told you that I can usually sense danger or when anyone else is nearby in the forest. But you dismissed what I said. You said that although warriors and hunters could do such things, I was neither one but only a maiden. You as much as called my father daft for giving me a dirk and teaching me to use it. Doubtless, you suspected that he had also taught me—or tried to teach me—to notice things in the forest as hunters or warriors do."

"I did think that, aye." He reached for the ties of her tunic and undid them.

"What are you doing?"

"This is a discussion that might go more easily if we were more comfortable," he said. "*That* is what I was thinking. And, because I see no suitable place in this room for us to sit as you suggested, except in the bed, I think we should continue our talk there. Prithee do not dally over your preparations."

She hurried through her ablutions and noted that he did likewise. From the frequent glances he gave her, she began to think that his thoughts were taking the sensual track that Lady Colquhoun's and doubtless Ian's had taken earlier.

Now that he was ready to listen, though, she did want to talk, to explain herself as well as she could, so that he might begin to trust her gifts. Therefore, she kept her smock on and climbed into bed ahead of him.

Mag did not keep anything on.

He got into the bed, plumped the pillows up behind him, and drew her close as he pulled up the covers, so she could rest her head in the hollow of his shoulder,

"Now, lass, tell me more about this. I can already see that I should have listened more and talked less the first time you spoke of such things."

"Aye, you should," she agreed, snuggling closer. "But I don't blame you. I have never tried to explain my abilities to anyone before. Faith, sir, for years I did not know that they were odd. They just were what they were, and I did not question them. I did tell you that my sisters and I share a close bond."

"You told me so, aye. Others have also mentioned it."

"Lina and Murie were coming to look for me that first day because they knew I had suspected intruders. Also, they sensed my shock when you startled me. They knew I was unafraid, but you have met Murie. You know how curious she can be."

"That has nowt to do with what happened today, though, aye?"

"By my troth, sir, I do not know the answer to that question. I have a special connection to the beasts of the forest that my sisters do not share. Likewise, my ability to sense other people's emotions is stronger than theirs."

"Can you tell when someone is lying to you?"

"Often. Not always. Sithee, some people lack the strong sense of guilt or wrongdoing about lying that others have. But I *can* tell if someone is trustworthy."

"Surely, not always," he said.

"Not as fast as I could tell with Jamie Stewart," she murmured. "I can nearly always tell, if the person is asked a question about trustworthiness, and he answers that question—or refuses to answer it. I could tell that the King speaks from his heart and desperately wants to know whom *he* can trust. Also, that he values trust."

"Most people do," Mag said.

"Or say that they do. The difference is important. Men who value trust also value it in themselves, whilst those who *dis*trust others are often untrustworthy themselves. One has only to think of liars one has met. To a man they are quick to insist that others lie, that everyone does. Men who never lie, on the other hand, are more easily gulled, because they expect others to speak the truth, too."

He was silent for a moment. "And you believe that Jamie values trust?"

"I do. I believe he has a keen eye for such things, too. He did trust Ian straightaway. And I believe he trusts you to speak the truth to him."

"What about you, lass? You have called me mistrustful. You have also said that such men may not be trustworthy. Do you believe I speak the truth to you?"

"You have given me no reason to *dis*believe it," she said. "Also, I was speaking of men who distrust *everyone* with or without cause. But I cannot read your emotions the way I read other people's. That has frustrated me since we met, because I usually know if I've vexed someone before the person voices displeasure. I can then amend what I've said to be sure the person realizes that I'm just speaking my thoughts without meaning to offend and that I sincerely want to know what the other has to say. Do you understand what *I'm* saying?"

"I think so," he said.

Tilting her head to look up at him, she smiled wistfully and said, "Do you *have* emotions, Magnus Mòr?"

When he hesitated, she said, "Nay, of course you do, for I have sensed some of them. I sensed your fear when his grace mentioned the Galbraiths as a clan that is unfriendly to him. And I do *not* think that fear was for yourself."

He remained silent.

"Am I wrong, sir?"

"Nay, but neither are we going to discuss Clan Galbraith tonight."

"Then you *are* concerned, mayhap about its chief and his other sons, aye?"

"I can tell you only what I told his grace. I ken nowt of their activities since my capture. But I'll admit they may be shoulder deep in the very plot I uncovered."

"I hope they are not," she said sincerely.

"I, too. In troth, though, Ian did say he'd heard that Rory had served Lennox and that our brother Patrick serves Murdoch's third son, James Mòr Stewart."

"James Mòr? I know little about him. Is he a mountain of a man, too?"

"Nowt of the sort. Nor is he fat or a great noble. Men rarely speak at all of him. I think he calls himself so to seem more important. But, lass—"

"I know. We are not going to talk about him, either. At least, you've told me about your brothers. What about your father?"

To her surprise, this time he answered her. "Just as you think you know your sire, I thought that I knew mine. Although he did play Jack-of-both-sides, I believed he was a man of honor. I don't know what he has become now. And I could not swear to what I do not know. Hence am I fearful, just as you've said."

"But not as fearful as you are grief-stricken over your brother Will's death," she said, giving his hand a squeeze. "I sensed that, too, when you mentioned him."

He made a sound low in his throat, then shifted onto his side so that he looked into her eyes as he said, "Again you are right. But tell me more about these so-disconcerting abilities of yours. We can discuss my feelings anon."

Feeling closer to him than ever before but also guilty for pressing him and for mentioning his brother Will's death, she said, "I can tell you that Jamie Stewart is fiercely determined to bring the rule of law to our unruly nation—to *all* of it—and at any cost. In troth, his determination is so fierce that I fear that it may blind him to what others think if he does not take care. But he is wise, too, I think."

"Aye, he thinks you are beautiful. But that takes only ordinary eyesight."

"You jest, Magnus. But I think you do so only to divert me from more talk of your family, because you must know I thought of your father again when I spoke of Jamie. I do believe that Galbraith will be overjoyed to learn that you've escaped from Parlan. And I think that when you tell him you spoke with the King and that Jamie expressed doubt of his loyalty, your father will be fain to assure you that he *is* loyal—and honorable, too. Then you can reassure his grace."

"Sakes, lass, do your abilities allow you to predict the future?"

"No, sir. I cannot do that. But fathers and sons must often disagree. Even so, if they care deeply for one another, they must find their path together."

⁓

Mag was glad she could not read his thoughts just then. He did not doubt her faith in her own father but feared she was equating Galbraith with Andrew. In truth, even if Galbraith said he was loyal to the King, Mag was not sure he'd believe him.

Since he was not ready to share that thought with her, he gave her shoulders a squeeze and said, "I won't know what my father thinks until I see him, will I? So, tell me about the beasts now. I saw how you whistled the hawks and the osprey to your aid. But I know not how you trained them to attack on command."

With a sigh, she rested a warm hand against his chest and said, "I do not train birds, sir. I told Parlan's men as much that day, and you heard me. But I cannot blame any of you for disbelieving me. Sithee, I know when the animals are distressed or when one might attack, just as I know such things about people. I sense emotions even at a distance, but I don't know how or why. My mother accepts my ability. My father pretends to think it is foolish talk and says he has never seen it for himself. But he trusts my opinion of people. Mam insists that he *has* seen things. He simply did not understand them or want to believe in them."

"What do you suppose she meant by that?"

"I don't know. I think something must have happened when we escaped from Parlan. Perhaps you should ask her."

Mag tried to imagine such a conversation with Lady Aubrey and decided there had to be other ways to learn about her unusual gifts or abilities.

Andrena was beginning to sound drowsy, but fingers of the hand she rested against his chest had begun idly stroking him, and he was sure that if he kept silent for long, she would press him to talk more about his family. Deciding to divert her thoughts in the way that he knew best, he began gently to untie the ribbons that held her smock closed across her breasts.

When she responded with a murmur of pleasure, he shifted position slightly to help her off with her smock, gently kissing and teasing her nipples as he did. Then, trailing kisses from her breasts, over her ribs, to her belly and lower, he felt her tense when his fingers touched the soft curls at the juncture of her silken thighs.

Leaving that hand lightly where it lay, he moved to capture her willing lips and explore her mouth with his tongue. When he knew she was ready for him below, he eased himself up, over her, and inside. Then he paused, watching her.

All three candles had begun to flicker. One guttered and went out with a soft hiss. The golden-orange glow in the room dimmed.

With a low moan, she pressed upward against him— once almost hesitantly, the second time with insistence and a tweak of his right nipple—urging him to move with her and smiling when he willingly complied. Although their coupling was short, he knew she was weary and accounted his tactic a successful diversion.

They slept, and the next day, after breaking their fast and bidding their hosts farewell, they returned to Tùr Meiloach, following the route by which they had come. Colquhoun offered to send them in a galley, saying that the shortness of their journey might mean that no one on the MacFarlan side of the river would be looking for them yet. But Andrena assured him that someone would be there.

When Mag reminded him that Parlan's men might still be on the watch, the laird agreed they would be wiser to avoid calling attention to themselves.

⁓

Andrena hoped to talk more with Mag as they went. Not only had she been glad to learn more about his family, but she also liked exchanging ideas with him and just hearing the sound of his voice.

Ian and two of his men walked with them to the river crossing, where Sorley and Peter were waiting. The bridge came down, and as they said their farewells, Ian told Mag to send word if he needed him.

"I hope you've forgiven me, Mag," he added.

"Aye, sure," Mag said, clapping him on the back. "Many thanks, lad. We'll be seeing each other again soon for the lady Aubrey's birthday if nowt else."

After they crossed the bridge, Ian and his men turned back toward Craggan.

With Mag's help, Sorley and Peter returned the bridge to its tree.

As they all began walking up the hill, Andrena suggested that Mag ask the other two to drop back enough to let them talk privately.

"Nay, lass," he said, glancing back at the two. "We'll talk soon enough about aught that you want to discuss. For now, I want to make speed. Sithee, the sooner we tell Andrew Dubh what happened at Paisley, the sooner we gain his counsel and can decide on our best course."

"Surely, your own course is to hie yourself to Inch Galbraith to talk with your lord father and present your wife to him." When he hesitated, she looked up and saw that he'd pressed his lips together. "Sir," she said gently, "I hope your need for haste does not include leaving me behind when you do go to Inch Galbraith."

He looked as abashed then as a child caught in mischief might. But he rallied to say, "I'll admit I did have some such thought before we talked yestereve. And I'll not say that I fully believe in all the gifts you claim to have. I do not disbelieve what you tell me," he added hastily. "I agree with your lady mother that you may enjoy heightened awareness in some way or another. But I remain reluctant to accept that you can tell just by meeting someone if he is trustworthy or not."

"I never claimed to do that," she said, glancing back to see how close Peter and Sorley were. Deciding they were all still close enough to the river for its roar to keep them from overhearing her, she added, "I said I can *usually* sense when I can trust someone or if a person's statements are sincerely spoken."

"I remember," he said. "Forbye, I do want you to come with me to Inch Galbraith, and for more than one reason." With a rueful twinkle, he added, "My father will behave more civilly to me if you are there, for one thing. In troth, though, I'll welcome your opinion of aught he says to us. He will likely want to be privy with me as well, though."

"I am sure he will, sir. My father would want the same thing had he not seen me for nearly two years."

"We'll talk more of this," he said. "There are things you should know before you meet him, things that I . . . that I have not told you. Even so, I'd liefer get to Tùr Meiloach quickly and talk quietly there *after* we both have rested."

"Then you expect protest, an argument, or even a scolding from me, I think."

He grinned and put an arm around her, giving her a warm hug. "I don't know what I expect," he admitted. "But I do want to think some before I give my head to you for washing, if that is what happens."

"I must terrify you, as wicked and temperamental as I am," she said with a mocking look.

"Aye, you're a threaping scauld and nae mistake, always giving me the dichens. But if I can devise a defense whilst we walk, I may just survive the fracas with most of me still intact."

She shook her head at him but understood that he needed time to think.

Although they did talk as they walked, their conversation was sporadic and desultory. They were still a mile or so from the tower when Andrena saw that her family had been expecting them.

"Look yonder, sir," she said, gesturing.

Drawn abruptly from thoughts that had scarcely begun to sort themselves, Mag stared into the dense foliage ahead and saw nothing. Then well-honed instinct asserted itself, and he sensed the approach of two or three entities.

His right hand moved to his sword, his left to shift Andrena from his path.

The grin on her face when she turned at his touch gave him enough warning to relax seconds before two of her collies burst from the foliage. Her sisters and Pluff followed, calling out greetings.

"You must have had a successful trip," Lina said. "We were surprised to realize you were returning so soon. But we are gey glad to see you. Dare we hope that you did so quickly find"—she flicked a glance at Pluff—"the man you sought and gained an audi—that is, that you talked with him?"

Giving Andrena a look that he hoped would warn her to say nowt yet about their audience with Jamie Stewart, Mag held his breath.

She said, "We did meet him. He is charming, and you would both like him. But we must speak to Father about that first and let him and Magnus decide how much to tell others. Sithee, some of it was privy between Magnus and... and him. Sir Ian Colquhoun went with us, though. And I *can* tell you about that."

Mag said, "Before you do, lass, we should send Pluff ahead to let everyone know that we will be there for supper."

The look she shot him indicated protest, but it faded quickly.

Andrena nearly told him it wasn't necessary to send Pluff. But she realized that Mag was being both cautious and wise. It would not do to let too many people learn the truth about Ian's journey with them or their confrontation with Dougal's galleys.

"Aye, then, Pluff," she said. "Run ahead and tell Malcolm Wylie that we're nearly at the gate and are nigh to starving."

When the lad had obeyed, taking the dogs with him, Andrena said to her sisters, "Two of Parlan's boats, under Dougal MacPharlain's command, tried to stop us on the Loch of the Long Boats shortly before we reached Craggan Tower."

"Mercy," Lina said. "Surely, the Colquhoun galley did not stop."

"It did, but only long enough to let Ian pretend that I was his sister."

"His sister!" Murie exclaimed.

Andrena added dryly. "Although Ian has become Sir

Ian, he has not changed much. He spun Dougal a tale as good as any of yours, Murie."

Lina said, "Ian sounds as if he were still ten years old, as full of mischief as he was then, and still reckless withal. Someone ought to teach him caution."

"I did tell him he ought not to tell such lies," Andrena said. "But he just laughed and said that Dougal and his lads *deserved* to hear lies."

"That may be so—" Murie began, but Lina interrupted her.

"Sir Ian Colquhoun is a knight of the realm. He ought never to lie!"

"You must tell him so," Andrena said. "He may listen to you. Meantime," she added casually, "Magnus chucked him into the loch."

Her sisters both burst into laughter, and Lina said to Mag, "I do thank you, sir. I have wanted to do that any number of times myself. As for Ian listening to me, Dree, you must know that he pays me no heed at all."

"Well, we mustn't stand talking," Andrena said. "Let's walk, you two."

Murie and Lina turned back toward the tower, and Andrena looked up at Mag, who was looking bemused.

"You see," she murmured. "They knew we were coming."

"Art sure that your father's men did not tell them?"

"You ken fine that Sorley and Peter are still walking behind us, sir."

"Aye, sure, but Andrew Dubh must have many others keeping watch."

"He does, aye. But not one would leave his post merely to tell him that you and I are returning with Sorley and

Peter. That they are with us would assure any watcher that all is well."

When he remained silent but held her gaze, she realized that he had reason to question the guards' competence. "You and Parlan's men did enter our woods that day without them seeing you because of the dreadful storm and the morning fog that followed it. Your pursuers also crossed Colquhoun's land to hang their rope swing. You may have noticed that it is gone now, as is the limb from which they swung."

"I did notice," he said.

Murie turned then and asked them to describe the King and what he had worn. The conversation became general after that until they reached the tower.

Mag knew that Andrew would urge him to go straight on to Inch Galbraith and likely would brook no delay. But the stakes involved in confronting his father were high, because he still had much to lose if all was not already lost to him.

He suspected, too, that Andrena's curiosity would not contain itself much longer. As she chatted away with her sisters, he felt a certain wistful envy of the ease with which they communicated, often with only a look or a gesture.

Doubtless, such ease was a result of having spent nearly every day of their lives together. It was only natural that each was able to anticipate what the others would say. Although he was still doubtful of their more unusual abilities, he wished that he had enjoyed such easy intercourse with his father and brothers.

Logic told him that such relationships had been unfeasible. His brothers were all older, often away for training or battle. Even when he'd begun to follow in their footsteps, they were beyond him in their training and impatient with him. His father, too, had had his duties and was intolerant of error or disobedience. That Mag had made little effort at the time to curb his own temper or his now admittedly naïve desire to set the world to rights had not helped.

Realizing that the three young women had fallen silent, he saw that Andrena was eyeing him thoughtfully. But she made no comment.

The tower wall came into view, and when they neared it minutes later, Andrew strode through the open gateway to meet them as he had before.

"Ye're an efficient lad," he said, gripping Mag's hand. "Come and tell me all about it now whilst Lina and Murie help Dree change for supper."

Noting Andrena's look of protest, Mag did not acknowledge it, saying only, "Aye, sir, I'll meet you in your chamber shortly. I'd liefer clean myself up first, so I can help Andrena if she needs it. She and her sisters will have time to talk later."

Looking from Mag to Andrena, Andrew nodded. "Aye, then," he said. "But dinna be all night about it. I'll tell Malcolm to order supper set back a bit."

When Mag shut the door of their bedchamber, Andrena watched him, wondering yet again what he was thinking. Despite her frustration that her father wanted to talk with him alone, she had made no protest. Nor could she think of anything else that she might have done to irk him, so she held her peace.

When he turned from the door at last, she saw to her astonishment that he looked wary, as if he again feared that *he* had annoyed her.

Her sense of humor stirred.

Although she managed not to smile or laugh, one of his eyebrows shot upward, revealing that he had noted the change in her mood.

"How do you *do* that?" she demanded.

"Raise one eyebrow?"

"Nay, I could see that you were worried about something and wondered if you feared you had angered me again. When I realized that I was being foolish to imagine such a thing, that wary look of yours vanished. Although you *have* said that you do fear my temper," she added dryly.

But I do, aye," he insisted, looking both earnest and guileless. "Even the lad Pluff warned me that ye've a mighty sharp tongue on ye when ye're wrathful, lass."

His eyes were twinkling.

She shook her head at him and said, "You are gey glib, sir. But you do not answer my question. I did not smile or, I think, reveal my thoughts in any way. Yet you did notice my change of mood. I want to know how you did *that*."

Chapter 14 ————————————

Mag yearned to hug her, and more, but they needed to talk. He said hastily, "Lass, everything that you think or feel reveals itself on your face. I don't need special powers to tell me when your mood alters. However," he added before she could protest, "just as I learned to curb my temper whilst enjoying Pharlain's notion of hospitality, I learned other things, too. And my senses became more acute."

"So you do sense things in ways of your own," she said.

"I have always been good in the woods, and I learned much in training for battle. But my hearing has grown sharper, and I see more than I used to see."

"How? In what way?"

"In many ways. Before, I tended to heed only what lay ahead of me in a forest. At Arrochar, I learned to heed everything around me, just as I do in battle. It became second nature to note the slightest look or gesture, because danger could come from any direction. My field of vision expanded. I began to see things on each side of me almost as clearly as I see straight ahead."

"Sakes, I can do that."

"Many women seem to have that skill, aye, doubtless because they must ever be watchful for their own safety. I don't mean that I could *not* see to the sides before, just that I was not as aware of seeing as much as I do now."

"What else can you do?"

He thought for a moment. "I can get the gist of more than one conversation at a time now. Before, if others began talking whilst I was listening to someone, I'd likely have to ask that person to repeat his or her words."

She said, "I can heed several conversations at a time, too. But it disturbs me that you can sense what I am thinking or feeling, whilst despite my usual ability to sense such things, I can rarely discern your moods or thoughts in any way."

Grimacing ruefully, he said, "Concealing my thoughts and feelings became a matter of survival. It was dangerous to reveal them by as much as a look, a gesture, or a sound. Pharlain could decide on a whim to hang a man or cut off a foot or a hand, which made us all try to appear as harmless as we could."

"I expect it must have had that effect. But you are no longer a prisoner."

"Habits, once formed, are hard to break, lass. But I promise to try."

"That is not what *you* wanted to talk to me about though, is it?"

Reaching for her, he drew her close and looked into her eyes. "There is more," he said. "Sithee, I saw that you were displeased when Andrew said he would talk alone with me. But that is the best course for now. I'll tell him what happened with Colquhoun and his grace, and how we met Dougal MacPharlain's boats. I'll also tell him that I must go to Inch Galbraith and learn where my father stands."

"And that I am going with you."

"That, too, aye," he agreed. "But Andrew knows something that you do not. I came here instead of going with him, because I'd liefer he not blurt that information out at supper or somewhere else before I can explain it to you."

"Then, tell me," she said, tilting her head.

Wishing he did not feel as if he were a bairn again, confessing to a sin that would earn him a skelping, he said, "I told you that my father and I argued."

"Before your capture, aye."

"I also told you that I had nowt to bring to this marriage of ours."

She frowned but said only, "Aye."

He shoved a hand through his hair, wishing that he could read her as well as she thought he could and know what her reaction would be before he told her.

Then, bluntly, he said, "What I did not tell you is that my father disowned me. So I doubt he'll want to see me now, despite his grace's command. In troth, he's unlikely to welcome either one of us."

"Why did he disown you?"

"I dared to argue against his so-called neutrality. He was just playing Jack-of-both-sides, and I said it put him with Murdoch and Lennox against Jamie's return."

"As it did," she agreed.

"His argument was that because Lennox is his liege lord, he could not defy him. But he'd taught *me* that our strongest fealty must be to the King. Murdoch and Lennox were as one in thinking that Jamie's capture kept Scotland from suffering through another governorship during his childhood, as if his capture were a boon to Scotland. When people began trying to bring him home, others insisted that his long English captivity had made him too English to sit on Scotland's throne. They said it was Murdoch's *duty* to keep the reins of government in his own hands."

"Murdoch's father did govern Scotland for many years before his death."

"Aye, but Murdoch is *not* his father. The first Duke of Albany was ruthless. But he was also politically astute. Murdoch is politically deaf and a fool, as well. People support him only because they fear to do otherwise."

"Do you think your father fears Murdoch?"

"Nay, and I'd never accuse him of such a thing. What I argued was that Albany, Murdoch, and the others should have done all that they could to free him from the English. Instead, they did what they could to keep him in England."

With a gentle touch to his arm, she said, "But that is all true, is it not?"

"Nevertheless, I was defiant, speaking so. I also threatened to do all that I could to bring Jamie home. My most grievous fault, though, is that I persuaded Will to come with me in search of men who might agree that Murdoch was a villain and Lennox a fool for supporting him. Before then, Will had agreed with Father. But Will was a fair man, willing to heed others and learn from them."

"Did your father think Jamie would be *bad* for the country?"

"I don't know." He covered the hand she had placed on his arm with his own hand, gripping hers as he said, "He was too angry then to make sense. He did believe in honor, though. I doubt that that has changed."

"You are his son, no matter what he may have thought of you then," she said. "If he is honorable, he will not abandon you. Nor will he abandon his King."

"You can say that about your father," he said. "You don't know mine."

"True, but my father does. What did *he* say?"

Mag hesitated. Then he said, "Andrew hasn't seen him in years. He cannot know him now any better than I do. Other things will likely stand between us, too. But the disowning is the worst. I wanted to tell you about that myself."

"And you have," she said, putting her free hand gently against his chest. "You believe he blames you for Will's death, don't you?"

"I know he does," Mag said, unable this time to suppress the ache in his soul as fast as he had before.

She moved her hand up to stroke his cheek. "Nay, then," she murmured. "You cannot *know* that. Did you not tell me that Parlan captured you in the same battle that killed your brother?"

"I did, but I also know my father," Mag said. "Sithee, one of the accusations he hurled at me in his temper was that I was going to get Will killed."

She gasped, her hand fell, and he felt the ache at his core grow stronger.

⁓

Andrena knew she had revealed her shock. She could see the pain that Mag felt written on his face. She also sensed brittle stress in him of strong and perhaps warring emotions. For once, she felt only relief that he could fight them down. Seeing his hurt and his grief was enough.

Had she been able to sense the full strength of his feelings, she might have burst into tears for him. Instinctively, she knew that such a reaction would not help.

Seeking the gentlest way to express herself—aware that he might suspect pity instead of the sympathy she felt for the deep pain his father's unfortunate words had caused him—she said as matter-of-factly as she could, "How dreadful it must be to carry such a memory. But I can see how you came by that hot temper you once described to me. Because of your own temper, though, you must know that all men—all people, come to that—say things in anger that afterward they wish they had not said. Until we can talk with him, you cannot *know* how he feels."

"Art sure you still want to go with me?"

"If you tried to leave me here now, I would give you your head in your lap," she said in the matter-of-fact tone she had used before.

His lips twitched, and she was relieved to see it. She had meant to startle him, but making him nearly smile was better.

"Where *did* you come by such a vulgar expression?" he demanded.

"It is what Annie Wylie threatens to do to Malcolm whenever he displeases her," she said. "I think he believes her, too."

"I have not met Annie Wylie yet, have I."

"Nay, for you would remember her. She is half Malcolm's size, and skinny, with graying red hair that must once have been as bright and as frizzy as Pluff's is. But that threat always pulls our burly Malcolm into line. Sithee, Annie is also something of a bard, which is why Murie visits her as often as she can. Annie knows all the old stories. Murie's goal is to learn them all and as many more as she can learn from other seanachies."

With a hint of amusement, he said, "Muriella is not at

all my notion of a seanachie or bard. The ones I've met have all been old men with long gray beards or young minstrels with lutes or harps."

"Well, if you value your reputation, sir, don't say that to Murie. She not only memorizes the ancient tales but makes up her own. She rarely uses anyone's name unless a tale is flattering and true. But her descriptions are terrifyingly apt, so many of her listeners can recognize themselves or others if she thinks they should."

The twinkle faded. "That, my lass, is a dangerous pastime," he said sternly. "You tell young Muriella that I'd better not hear her doing such things. Does Andrew know that she does?"

Andrena began to shake her head, then caught herself and said in surprise, "I don't know if he does. Unless Mam has told him of an occasion when Murie told such tales to amuse Mam's kinsmen during a visit, he would not know that she does it anywhere but here. And everyone here knows her and loves her."

"Knowing and loving her may not excuse a tale that falsely redounds to someone else's discredit."

"But Murie is not malicious, sir, just mischievous. People nearly always laugh, even at themselves, when she tells such tales."

"A man may laugh and be nonetheless furious, a woman even more so. If Murie strikes near the truth of something that her victim wants to keep secret..."

"I understand, sir. But I doubt that such a thing could happen here. We all know each other too well."

"Likely, you are right," he said. "But you should talk to her."

"I'll talk to Lina," Andrena said. "Murie listens to her

about serious things. She rarely heeds me, except when she detects a story in something I say. In any event, my father is likely pacing the floor by now, wondering what is keeping you. And this is not getting either of us ready for supper."

"I'll just tell him my naughty wife kept me. I'll wager he'd understand that."

"Aye, perhaps, but he'd still scold you for keeping him waiting," she said with a smile. "Do we leave in the morning for Inch Galbraith?"

"I should discuss that with Andrew before deciding," he said.

Grimacing, she said, "Then prithee go and discuss, sir. I can tidy myself. But you might pull a comb through your hair and straighten your plaid before you go."

Smiling now, he obeyed, giving her hope that she had diverted his thoughts—for a time, at least—from Galbraith's likely reception of them.

⁓

Mag found Andrew in his chamber. If the older man had expected him any sooner, he said naught of it. Gesturing for Mag to take the stool, he said, "Tell me everything, lad. What did Jamie say about me charter?"

Mag had anticipated the subject that would be paramount in his good-father's mind. Hoping to delay a discussion about Jamie's possible support until they had more time to talk privately, he said, "His grace said the same thing about your charter as he said about the plot against him, sir. Because his mind is wholly on establishing his rule of law, he demands to see the charter and requires similar evidence of the plot's existence. He cannot take my word alone for either one."

"Sakes, ye'll no tell me that he didna believe ye! The lad is nae fool."

"He did believe me," Mag said. "But to bring a case against the plotters, in Parliament, he needs to see documents and other acceptable evidence. He'd like to have witnesses willing to appear before the lords and name the plotters."

"But we ken fine who they are," Andrew said, frowning.

"Consider it from his grace's position, sir. After years of Albany's rule and Murdoch's, people believe that those in power have only to accuse a man to hang him. Jamie wants to change that. To do so he must produce evidence that the lords of Parliament will view the same way he does. Despite the many accusations laid against Lord Walter Stewart, and much as Jamie wants to hang him and his father for trying to steal his crown, he has not done so. He merely imprisoned Walter. He has taken no action against Murdoch, although the man claims still to be Governor of the Realm despite Jamie's coronation and that of the Queen."

"Murdoch is a fool."

"Aye," Mag agreed. "But a dangerous one."

"His grace needs nae witness to believe in my charter."

"He says he must see it. He believes it will prove what you say it will, but he pointed out that ownership by right of the sword remains rampant, especially in the High-lands. Forbye, he means to meet with the Highland chiefs at Inverness next year to discuss how he will establish a rule of law throughout Scotland."

"Good luck to the man," Andrew said with feeling.

"If he can bring law to the Borders and Lomondside," Mag said, 'tis likely he'll succeed elsewhere, too."

"Aye, perhaps. But he hasna established it anywhere yet."

Unable to deny that, Mag turned the subject to Galbraith. He was unsure whether to be relieved or worried when Andrew said he knew that Mag could manage his father and should visit him straightaway.

"You will not say I must cross the south river and Colquhoun lands to reach Inch Galbraith, will you?" Mag said. "I'm certain that a pass through the mountains must still exist somewhere nearer."

"Aye, sure, it does," Andrew said with a grin. "That pass be closely guarded by giants, wicked beasts, and the wee folk, though."

"And bottomless bogs, landslides, or avalanches, depending on the season," Mag said, holding his gaze. "Heaven knows what else you've dreamed up."

Unfazed, Andrew nodded and said, "Aye, aye. But our Dree kens every obstacle and danger. She'll see ye safely over the hills."

"I'm told she has ken of more than obstacles or mysterious trails," Mag said. Hoping he was not making a mistake by broaching a subject that Andrena had said he should discuss with her mother, he added, "I described our audience with his grace, sir. I must also tell you that, on our return, Dougal MacPharlain tried to stop the Colquhoun galley before we reached its wharf."

"The devil he did! Did Dougal see ye?"

"He did not. Thanks to Andrena's warning that danger lay ahead of us, I took an oarsman's place whilst we watched the headland we were nearing. I'll admit I was astonished when two galleys emerged to confront us."

"*Two*! How did ye avoid two o' them?"

"Ian Colquhoun told them Andrena was his sister and that the oarsman, who by then was wearing my plaid, was her betrothed. The ruse worked. But I am curious to know how Andrena could have suspected Dougal MacPharlain's presence. She told me she has feelings about such things but does not know why. I thought perhaps you might tell me more about that."

"Sakes, how could I? I ken fine that the lass possesses fine instincts. I've learned to trust her opinion of people she meets. She is rarely mistaken."

"Her instincts aid her with birds of the forest, too," Mag said, watching him closely. "Mayhap with some beasts, such as badgers, as well."

Andrew made a dismissive gesture. "I told ye, the place be close guarded. The lass has roamed the forest and the lands of Tùr Meiloach since she could walk, so the birds—and, aye, the beasts, too—ha' grown tame around her, is all. Now then—"

"I'd like to know *how* tame they might be, sir. You told her that you ken nowt of such things. But her lady mother believes you know more than you admit."

"I can tell ye that ye needna fret about Dree in our woods. The beasts do seem to look after her. But bless us, where has the time gone? If we dinna go down and join the others, we'll be getting nae supper. We can talk more when ye return from Inch Galbraith if ye think there be more to discuss."

Mag was sure that there would be. He was likewise sure that Andrew would try to avoid such a discussion then, too, and wondered why.

⁓

Andrena had joined her sisters and Lady Aubrey on the dais shortly before Mag and Andrew arrived. But her thoughts had remained with Mag. Anticipating Andrew's disappointment that the King had not agreed to see his charter at once, she hoped he would not blame Mag or think they ought to have done more.

When the two men entered the hall and strode to the dais, Andrew's smile for Lady Aubrey told Andrena that he, at least, was content.

Mag looked as he always did. Then his gaze caught and held hers, and she detected a twinkle in his eyes. Strongly suspecting that he recognized her curiosity, she also knew he'd do nothing to alleviate it until after supper.

Muriella, ever irrepressible, held her tongue only until they had said the grace before meat. Then, leaning forward, she said to Andrew, across both of her sisters and her mother, "Prithee, sir, will you tell us what Magnus and Andrena learned? Or must that remain a secret?"

Flicking a glance at a hovering gillie, Andrew said, "We'll no discuss that now, lassie. Mayhap after supper, your sister and Magnus can tell you more about it. I will tell ye that nowt will happen straightaway. But I ken fine that ye'll want to hear what everyone did say."

At least, Andrena thought, Murie was being more discreet than usual. She did not instantly blurt out that she had already quizzed them and learned much about his grace and Paisley Abbey. They had not discussed the charter, the conspirators, or the evidence that Jamie Stewart needed to punish them.

That might change if Mag took Andrew's words to mean that they should tell the others all they had learned.

When Lady Aubrey signaled for the ladies to leave the table, Mag also stood and intercepted Andrena. Drawing her to the rear of the dais, he said quietly, "We'll excuse ourselves now, lass. We *are* going leave early in the morning."

"Coward," she muttered. "You don't want to submit to Murie's inquisition."

"True enough," he admitted. "I think we'd be unwise to feed her hunger for every detail of our audience. You have made it plain that she remembers such details with the purpose of recounting them to others, so we cannot talk about the conspirators. Nor do I think Andrew meant us to do so. And to talk of the Arrochar charter before Jamie arranges his Inverness meeting would also be a mistake."

She knew he was right, but she also knew Muriella. "She has a knack for finding things out. But naught that she might say would go beyond our boundaries."

Without comment, he took her hand, placed it firmly on his extended forearm, and moved to bid Lady Aubrey a courteous goodnight. "We must make an early start tomorrow, madam, for we go to Inch Galbraith," he said. "Having traveled much these past days, we are, as you might suppose, fain to sleep."

"But you cannot go to bed yet," Murie protested.

"Hush, Muriella," Lady Aubrey said. "Andrena and Magnus must be exhausted. You will have to restrain your curiosity a little longer."

"But they are going to Lomondside," Murie said in what was nearly a wail. "God alone kens how long they will be gone!"

"You will contain yourself until they return," Lady Aubrey said.

"Aye, Mam," Murie said, struggling and failing to suppress a grimace.

Andrena bit her lower lip.

"Say goodnight, lass," Mag said to her.

Obeying, she turned, meaning to give her father a hug. But Mag's other hand clamped onto the one she had set on his forearm, letting her know that he would not let go. When he whisked her off the dais toward the stairway, she made no protest. But when he thrust her through their bedchamber doorway and shut the door with a snap, she turned with her hands flying to her hips to say, "Really, sir, I think—"

"If you honestly *think*," he said grimly, "that nowt that you, your sisters, or others say here goes beyond your boundaries, you need to *think* again."

Rapidly collecting her wits, she said, "I was thinking only about Murie then. She is gey persistent and will plague us both until she has a tale to tell."

"She will not plague me because she would soon hear what I'd say about such rude behavior."

"But it is her nature to express her curiosity," Andrena said. "Come to that, Annie and other bards and scanachies have urged her to do all that she can to glean the facts of such events. It is a seanachie's duty to recite accurate details so that others may learn from such experiences."

"I understand the duties of a seanachie," he said. "But your sister is not one yet, and I doubt that she comprehends the responsibilities she'll assume if she ever does become one. Meantime, neither you nor I will share information with her that should remain between us and his grace."

When she was sure he had finished, she drew a breath. Then, meeting his stern gaze, she said, "By my troth, sir, I would not have shared such things with her. I promised you that I'd tell no one and specifically not Lina or Murie. I'll keep that promise. Also, now that we are married, I won't share anything with them that is privy between us two. Mam said I must not. But in troth, I knew it before then."

"Then why did you say such news would not go beyond the boundaries?"

Guilt sent heat to her cheeks. But she knew that only the truth would satisfy him. Dampening dry lips, she said, "I...I was thinking only of Murie's persistence and how far away Parlan is, how unlikely...I did not think it all through to what you would suspect I might say to her. I...I should have." Eyeing him warily, she knew she had not said enough. With a sigh, she said, "It was a sort of a clincher, to show that it wouldn't matter if she *did* somehow find out. Also, I expect I was curious about how you would react. That was foolish. I can see that now. But—"

"Why?"

The single word stopped her. The heat in her cheeks burned, and she looked away, hoping for the first time that his temper was not as flammable as Andrew's.

"Well?"

"You don't mean why it was foolish, I expect."

"No."

Swallowing, she said, "I am beginning to sense some of your emotions. I...I think I may, in some way or other, be *trying* to sense them, to test my ability."

His jaw tightened until she saw the dimple dance in his cheek again. The sight sent a shiver up her spine.

Chapter 15 _____

Mag felt an urge to shake her but knew he dared not. Touching her would unman him as it always did, and he needed to keep his wits about him. Another instinct urged him to reassure her. But he did not want her to go on testing him.

"You've tested me often, I think," he said, keeping his tone stern. When she nodded, he said more sternly yet, "Did it work before?"

"Nay. Nor did it work just now."

"You ken fine that it displeased me."

Her mouth twisted wryly at the understatement. She said, "I think you were more than displeased. I think you were—aye, and still are—gey angry with me. I wish you'd just say so and be done."

"I think you fail to understand *why* I am displeased. You declared that your cousin Parlan lives far away, as if you think such distance keeps him ignorant of what goes on here. I can tell you of mine own knowledge that that is not so. He kens how many people live here, who they are, and how many are warriors. He is aware when people travel from here and sometimes even learns where they've been."

"Do you think he knows we went to Paisley? How could he?"

"Dougal said nowt to indicate knowledge of aught save a missing prisoner, but use your wits, lass. Your father told me only this evening that *you* know how to reach Loch Lomond without crossing Colquhoun's land. *That* suggests that the pass to Glen Luss still exists. Do you think Pharlain is unaware of it? Forbye, if I recall correctly, a high pass exists at the northern end of those mountains, too."

"Landslides blocked that one years ago, but I'm surprised that Father told you as much as he did. I can promise you, though, sir, that any such pass is well guarded and impassable to anyone but us."

"If we can cross the mountains to Inch Galbraith, Parlan can do the same to come here," he insisted. "So can anyone he sends to spy on you. Sakes, almost anyone here could be giving him information."

"But none of our people—" She broke off, aghast. "If he *has* got spies…"

"He must," Mag said. "Moreover, you must know as well as I do—and as Pharlain may have guessed—that Andrew's wild beasts, man-swallowing bogs, and other mythical protections are nae more than that. The rivers are real, aye. But—"

"Much more than the rivers are real," she said. "You saw for yourself how the birds behave, the predatory ones at all events."

"I saw hawks and an osprey respond to your whistle. You told me that you didn't train them, and I believe you. But you never explained why they answered the whistle or why you whistled at all, if you did not expect them to attack."

"You will think I am daft, sir. But I think that, just as I am aware when they are distressed, angry, or in fear, they sense it when I'm upset. And the beasts—"

"I don't think you're daft. But neither do I believe that birds sense human emotions or would respond to them if they did. As for the beasts, all I saw for myself is that a badger knows enough to be fearless after you call off your dogs."

"But..." She paused.

"Lass, Andrew told me that the beasts are tame because you've walked amongst them so often that they trust you. That certainly belies their being as fierce as his myths depict them to be. He did suggest that they seem to look after you," he added. "But I think you may have explained that yourself when you told my pursuers that the birds, at least, are simply more territorial than most."

A look of frustration flitted across her face but disappeared almost before he recognized it for what it was. "Believe what you like then," she said. "I will guide you through the high pass to Glen Luss. That trail is steep but usually open at this time of year. My father does keep men there, though, and they guard it well."

"I thought so." He stepped toward her and was glad to see that she met his gaze easily and seemed to relax. "Sithee, lass, I have one more concern," he said, stopping inches away without touching her. "I don't want to wonder if you are pinching at me to test me or because you want to fratch with me. I still don't understand what you expect to feel, or how you might know what I am thinking or feeling other than by the normal ways that most folks employ."

"You don't reveal much of yourself in *any* way," she

said. "I won't test you again, sir. But I'm not your captor, so I don't understand why you still guard yourself so closely. People break habits every day."

"They do," he agreed. "So we will try to talk more and share what we think and feel. We can practice such discussion tomorrow whilst we walk. It must be all of ten miles from here to our landing south of Luss."

"It is, aye. Also, the track up to the ridge is steep, and the pass may be snowy, so it will take us longer than it did to reach Craggan Tower. With an early start, we should reach Inch Galbraith before dark, though." Looking down and then up at him from under her lashes, she said, "Art still vexed with me?"

He shook his head. "Nay, I cannot stay angry with you. I ken fine that we are both finding our way." Putting a finger to her chin so she would not look away again, he added, "You should be aware, though, that you can stir my temper quicker than my brothers or Pharlain ever could."

"Then the sooner I can sense that I'm stirring it, Magnus," she said, meeting his gaze but moving his finger aside, "the better it will be for both of us."

"I'll tell you what will be good for us," he murmured, drawing her into a hug. "I still have a few things to show you that I think you will like. We'll find some new ones that I'll like, too."

She smiled, melted against him, and he felt the last of her tension drain away.

⁓

The warmth of Mag's body still astounded her even after a sennight of sleeping with him. She had never shared a bed with another man, but she was certain that most men did not radiate as much heat in bed as Mag radiated wherever he was. She had to push off most of her covers while sleeping with him.

That night, in bed, his lightest touch stirred her passions so deeply that for a time she forgot everything but the heat rushing through her body. She felt emotionally closer to him just knowing that he would *try* to share more of his private thoughts and feelings. That he did not yet understand what was lacking for her seemed less important. If he tried to learn what it was, surely he soon would.

Their coupling was passionate, sweaty, and introduced her to a new and higher realm just before Mag collapsed, gasping and moaning his pleasure. She wondered why he always seemed to enjoy the ending of their unions more than she did.

The best part of it for her was that the last remnants of their earlier tension had vanished by the time she curled into the curve of his body, rested her head on his chest near his shoulder, and slept.

The next morning, Mag woke her before dawn, and they set off as soon as they had broken their fast. At the last minute, Andrena tucked her deerskin breeks, her jack, and her dirk into her sumpter basket. She wore her hide boots.

Malcolm's Peter and the gillie Jonas would go with them again. Malcolm brought food from the kitchen for their journey.

"I've told Peter tae take one o' the garrons, Master Magnus," the steward said. "Ye'll none o' ye be wanting tae tote much save your weapons over yon hills. And a garron be gey agile over such rocky terrain."

The morning was misty, but the mist would burn off soon.

Peter and Jonas waited in the yard with a sturdy black Highland garron, one of the small horses bred for the terrain they would cross. Even so, Andrena was doubtful of the stout little beast's ability to negotiate the high pass if it still lay under a blanket of snow. Ben Vorlich, the great mountain to the north, still boasted a huge snowcap, and other peaks that she could see wore caps, too.

Sorley had packed Magnus's belongings, and Mag wore his own old plaid that Lina had mended, over his sark and breeks. He also wore his hairy boots.

Pluff was nowhere in sight. But Euan MacNur assured them that he would keep the dogs inside the wall until the travelers were well away.

"Pluff were here not an hour since," he said. Then, to Mag, he added hastily, "I'm no at oots wi' him, though, sir. He's been a different lad since ye talked wi' him and let him stand wi' ye at your wedding. I didna think much o' that notion, I'll admit. But the lad took a lesson from it, and I'm glad o' that. I dinna doot he'll turn up soon and be gey disappointed tae miss bidding ye farewell."

"Tell him we'll see him in a few days," Andrena said. When they were away from the wall, with Peter and Jonas leading the laden garron a short distance behind them to give them some privacy, she said, "What did Euan MacNur mean about you having talked to Pluff? What happened?"

"Nowt save a wee misunderstanding betwixt the two of them."

"Tell me," she said.

"I'll tell you this much," he said. "You and your sisters

created a dilemma for the lad by telling him to feed the dogs first thing each morning. Sithee, MacNur had told him to muck out the byre *before* he fed them."

"But they *should* eat before I take them for a run," she said.

"I think you will find that the matter has resolved itself."

She glanced up at him, saw that he was smiling, and leaned closer to give him a nudge with her shoulder as they walked.

~

Grinning, Mag gave her a quick hug and released her.

He let her set the pace and was pleased when she set a brisk one.

The woods were eerily silent. Mist still crept down through the canopy, and clung here and there to trees and shrubbery. A chilled, salty dampness filled the air, making the simple act of inhaling feel like a magical elixir.

The silence enfolded them. Their feet made no noise on the damp, duff-covered ground. Even the pony's hooves made only whispers of sound.

Mag's thoughts drifted to his father. The stakes between them were high, God knew. Certainly, he had much to lose. Come to that, he had likely already lost his family, even his clan, irrevocably

"What are you thinking?" she asked softly.

He started to shake his head, to say that his current thoughts were not for sharing. But he had promised to try, so he met her quizzical look and said, "That I may be unable to reconcile with my father or my brothers."

"Rory and Patrick," she said. "I remember their names.

But you told me only that Rory served Lennox and Patrick serves James Mòr Stewart. At least neither serves Lord Walter or Lord Alexander. *They* are the wickedest ones."

"I don't know much about my brothers anymore," he said.

"Despite that, you do keep thinking that if Lennox is involved in the plot with Murdoch and his older sons, 'tis likely that your brothers are in it, too."

Hearing her put his train of thought so bluntly, he drew a deep breath of the cleansing air and let it out again before he said, "You're right, lass. We cannot be certain of that yet. It is as likely, if not more so, that they ken nowt of plots."

"That could be true."

"Aye, sure. Sithee, my brothers, like your sisters, are gey different from each other. Will was the responsible one, the one we all looked up to and admired. He was a fine warrior and one who would speak up for his own lads when sometimes those above him did not want to hear it. He should have won a knighthood, but he never did. In troth, it was Lennox's offering *me* one that helped me persuade Will that he might be following the wrong leaders."

"You turned down a knighthood?"

"I did. Sithee, he offered it only if I would agree to serve him and Pharlain."

"Then of course you turned it down," she said. "What sort of man is Rory?"

"Amiable, cautious, and observant," Mag said. "He follows orders but keeps his head down. He would follow Will in almost anything. But if our father became wroth with Will over something *he'd* done, Rory took care never to do that thing."

"And Patrick?"

Mag shook his head. "I've never understood Patrick. All three of my brothers teased and mocked me, but he was the worst. He's a year older than I am, and for as long as I can remember, he has seemed to dislike me."

"Is he smaller than the rest of you? Might he resent your size?"

"He might resent my height, but he's taller than Rory."

"Perhaps your parents favored Patrick before you were born," Andrena said. "I remember feeling as if Murie demanded everyone's attention when she was small. I felt invisible then, as if I'd lost my importance. Faith, I barely talked to anyone, including Lina. The feeling passed the first time Murie made me laugh. But it was strong before then, because our parents both seemed besotted with her. Mayhap Patrick felt something akin to that."

"Perhaps, but he was grown when last I saw him and had not changed. To be fair, I was trying to persuade him as well as Will that we should support his grace's return to Scotland. But Patrick believed, and doubtless does to this day, that Jamie had become too English. He said that the rumors of Jamie's intended marriage to an English noblewoman proved he was unfit to be King of Scots."

"But Mam says that Queen Joanna is as much in love with Scotland as she is with his grace. Also, that she has done as much as he has to aid the common folk."

"I doubt that Patrick cares about common folk."

"What you are saying is that I am *not* going to like Patrick."

Mag chuckled. "In troth, he has been more of an irritant than a brother to me. Nevertheless, he *is* my brother, and I'd fain see him quit of James Mòr."

"Are you ever sorry you did not accept that knighthood?"

"Before my capture, I was disappointed that I had not *earned* one. Sithee, my goals were to win my spurs, gain a fortune, and find a suitable bride. Imprisonment changed those goals. When I escaped, all I wanted was to elude capture long enough to find his grace and warn him of his danger."

"That's all?"

Mag shrugged. "I hoped they'd not catch me again."

Glancing at him, she said, "I asked you once to tell me how captivity affected you. I'm thinking that I should have asked how *being captured* made you feel."

"I was furious with myself and grieving wildly over Will's death. When I learned the MacFarlans had killed him, I wanted to kill every MacFarlan that lived."

Her eyebrows shot upward. "One hopes you've got over *that* desire."

"I have," he said with a wry smile. "I still feel irritated with myself for falling into Pharlain's clutches and more annoyed now that I failed to escape earlier. I seem unable to leave the past in the past."

"Weren't you afraid to try to escape?"

"It wasn't fear, although I understood the consequences of failure. I just didn't care enough to try. Nowt mattered after Will died. I knew my father must feel the same way, and he'd already disowned me. I knew he'd do nowt to help me."

"That is his greatest crime, I think," Andrena said flatly.

"Aye, perhaps. I must find a way to persuade him to help Jamie, but I have at least three marks against me to overcome before he might."

"Three?"

"Aye, sure. First, I failed to keep Pharlain's men from murdering Will. Second, I did not try to escape my imprisonment until now. Sithee, Will's death and my capture will simply have proven to him that I was wrong to oppose Lennox and Murdoch. But my failure to escape will make him think worse of me. And third…" He paused and looked at her, wondering if he ought to tell her.

She grimaced. "Third is that you not only married me without seeking his permission but also agreed to adopt the MacFarlan name as your own."

"Aye, so in troth, the count is *four* heavy marks against me withal."

⁓

Andrena met Mag's gaze again and was surprised to see that, despite his somber tone, his eyes were alight with amusement.

"You, sir, ought to be discussing how to meet that problem straight on," she said sternly. "Not pretending that it is smaller than it is."

"It isn't larger than it is, either," he said, putting an arm around her again. "My father did say once that he would leave me Inch Galbraith at his death, because he is building a larger, more modern seat at Culcreuch on east Lomondside. We have nobbut a gey ancient square tower there now."

"Like Tùr Meiloach," she said dryly.

"Just so," he agreed. "In any event, Inch Galbraith is all that I might have inherited and thus the only property I've lost. Anything he has left after dowering three daughters, he will leave to Rory with doubtless some small bequest to Patrick, who didn't want Inch Galbraith. As the youngest son, my prospects were dim before I stumbled into Tùr Meiloach. Life has been more interesting since then."

They continued to talk as they trudged up the steep, rocky, barely discernible track to the snowy high pass known as *Bealach an Duin*. Winds had cleared the sky by then, and from the top of the pass, they looked down more than a thousand feet to the blue waters of Loch Lomond and its many wooded islands.

Across the loch, northward, the magnificent mountain known as Ben Lomond shot high, its sparkling snowy cap piercing the sky.

The wind increased as if to blow them on over the pass. Finding shelter on the downslope, they stopped to eat their midday meal.

Until they were beyond the snow, going downhill seemed more difficult than trudging up. One had to take much care not to slip.

The sun disappeared behind the ridge an hour before they emerged at the mouth of Glen Luss and turned south along the gently undulating west shore of Loch Lomond. As they passed through the sacred site of Luss, Andrena said that many of her ancestors lay buried there and learned that many of Mag's were there, too.

Southward, the land as far as Glen Fruin was Galbraith land.

From Luss, Loch Lomond seemed small, because the eastern shore was closer there, and the view was mostly forest-covered islands. A quarter-hour later, they had their first clear view of Inch Galbraith, less than a half-mile ahead offshore. The loch widened, too, so one saw mostly water beyond the islet. But the travelers came first to a shore-side clachan, where Mag shouted for someone called Lippin Geordie.

When an elderly man strode out, glowering at first and then grinning broadly, Mag stepped forward with a hand out to greet him.

"God bethankit, Magnus Mòr!" the old man said with delight, gripping Mag's hand with both of his own as he looked him up and down, "I feared I'd never clap me keekers on ye again. If Himself be expecting ye, though, I've heard nowt of it."

"He is not expecting us, Geordie. I'll need a boat to take us over and someone to look after this garron and our two lads here for as long as we stay."

"Aye, sure, Magnus. Who might the lovely lady be, then?"

"She is my wife, Geordie," Mag said.

Andrena waited for him to give her name and anteced-ents, but he did not.

Geordie looked from Mag to Andrena and back again, his rheumy eyes glinting with humor. "Is she now? I'm thinking Himself will be givin' ye a muckle scauld if no a drubbing tae match what ye got for setting Master Will's coat afire. Forbye, if the laird kens aught o' bridals, I've heard nowt o' that neither."

"I mean to cast myself on his mercy," Mag said lightly. "My lady's beauty, charm, and good sense may help him forget his fury with me."

"Aye, well, if that does pay the collops, be sure tae tell me, lad. I'll pass it on tae some others wha' might like tae ken how tae placate Himself when he's in his ire. But ye'll no want tae stand talking wi' me when ye can be home again. I'll roust out our Dolf tae tak' ye across."

"Why did you not explain who I am, other than your wife?" Andrena asked Mag when Lippin Geordie had walked away shouting for Dolf.

"Because I hope to be the first to tell my father," Mag said. "The way news travels hereabouts, if I say the words aloud, they might fly to him on the wind."

Andrena had suffered experiences that made her think the same thing about her own father, so she accepted Mag's reasoning without comment.

Geordie soon returned with a lanky man so like him in figure and twinkle that she was sure Dolf was his son. They unloaded everything from the garron into a small longboat with four oarsmen. Mag helped Andrena in, stepped in himself, and the oarsmen pulled hard for Inch Galbraith.

She could see its square tower looming above the trees. When she saw that Mag was gazing at it and had begun to look wary, she said, "Might someone on the ramparts recognize you from there?"

"Perhaps," he said. "More likely, they'll shout down to my father that a boat is coming. Then he'll go up to see for himself who it is."

"It is dusky, though, and will soon be dark. Would he know you in this light?"

He did not reply, and she realized that it did not matter if the Laird of Galbraith had warning or not. They would learn what he thought soon enough.

~

Mag felt his tension building but realized rather quickly that it was not fear for himself. It was fear that his father might say something to hurt Andrena.

The thought steadied him. By the time the boat reached the landing on the islet, he was in command of himself.

It was not Galbraith who hurried down to meet them, however, but old Hector. And Hector was smiling. Even so, as the old man shook Mag's hand, he said hastily, "We must not tarry, laddie. Himself be waiting in the great hall. And he's told everyone else to take themselves off, so you'll be alone with him."

"Thank you, Hector." Mag drew Andrena forward. "This is my father's steward, Hector Galbraith, madam. This lady, Hector, is my wife, Andrena."

"It is an honor, my lady," Hector said, with a polite nod. "I hope you will be comfortable here. If aught displeases you, pray tell me at once."

"Thank you, Hector," Andrena said. "It is beautiful here."

The old man smiled and then shouted at Dolf to help him take their things in.

Mag urged Andrena off the end of the pier and onto a pebbled path. "We'll go right to my father," he said. "Hector will stay away until he shouts for him."

The tower was smaller than Tùr Meiloach and four stories tall. Since it sat on an islet, it lacked a barmkin wall and trees grew close to the tower walls. In the evening silence, she heard chickens settling and the soft lowing of a cow.

"You have beasts on this islet? It looked so small."

"It is small by comparison with Inchconnal and the others. But we have dogs and a cow, chickens, ducks, and two pigs that produce piglets regularly. But come now. Or do you want to wash and refresh yourself before we see him?"

"We won't make ourselves more welcome by keeping him waiting, sir."

"Then take my arm," he said, extending it for her. "Give it a good pinch if he begins bellowing at me as Lippin Geordie suggested he would."

She pinched him.

"What the devil was that for?"

"Just a test," she said. "I like to test things out before I need to use them."

"Take care that you don't earn yourself a skelping just so I can decide whether one will prove salutary or not. We agreed there would be no more tests."

She grinned at him, and he smiled. But the smile faded when they crossed the threshold and saw his father standing by the fireplace.

Two years had not changed the Laird of Galbraith. He still stood straight, tall, and broad-shouldered. His dark hair and well-trimmed beard might boast a bit more silver, but that was all. He wore a hip-length black robe embroidered with silver slashing at wrists and neckline, over black leggings and short black boots.

"So you have returned at last, Magnus," he said evenly.

Suddenly tempted to remind him that he'd said he never wanted to see him again, Mag focused instead on the slender hand that rested on his forearm. Taking a breath, he said, "As you see, my lord. I hope you won't turn us from the door."

~

Andrena held her breath until Galbraith said, "You may stay the night at least. We will see what comes of that."

She wondered if the laird would begin bellowing or

maintain his stiffly stern demeanor. He was a man in rigid control of himself, but an ordinary man, not one who had suppressed his feelings in the name of survival, as Mag had. Despite Galbraith's stern look, she sensed deeper emotions in him.

Mag's posture and visible tension told her much about his feelings, too. She had come to realize that he cared deeply for his family, even his demon brother Patrick. But she saw now that he cared even more about his father than she had guessed and wanted desperately to regain his approval.

Mag said, "I did not think you would welcome us, sir. I am grateful."

"I had expected to see you long before now," Galbraith said. "Prithee, do not tell me you remained a captive of that lout Pharlain all this time."

"I fear so," Mag said. "But I'm free now. I have come because I have urgent business to lay before you."

"Indeed?"

"Aye, sir. First I must present to you my wife, the lady Andrena."

Releasing Mag's forearm, Andrena curtsied as low as she had to the King of Scots and waited with head bent for Galbraith to speak.

When he did not, she looked up to see that he was staring at Mag.

Deciding then that she had behaved meekly enough, she rose from her curtsy and stood quietly, waiting for Galbraith to acknowledge her.

Looking rather startled, he said, "I beg your pardon, madam. But if I am not mistaken...That is, I know of only one lady in these parts bearing that name."

"I am Andrena MacFarlan, my lord. My father is

Andrew Dubh MacFarlan of Tùr Meiloach, the true Chief of Clan Farlan. My mother is the lady Aubrey Comyn, a kinswoman of your late wife. When Magnus flung himself off Cousin Parlan's galley into that vicious storm last—"

Mag's hand touched her arm, silencing her before he said, "It is enough to say that I escaped, my lord, and found refuge with Andrew Dubh and his family. He persuaded me to marry Andrena for reasons of his own that you and I can discuss later. I married her of my own will, however, and expect to be as happy in my marriage as you and my lady mother were in yours."

"I hope you will be," Galbraith said. His tone was civil, not hopeful. But again Andrena sensed deeper emotion. She was uncertain what it was, but it was not anger. Nor was Galbraith indifferent to his son in any way.

"It does surprise me that it took you so long to escape," Galbraith said.

Without hesitation, Andrena said, "Had he not waited, my lord, the results might have been catastrophic. In troth, they still may be."

For the first time, she drew his full attention. "How so, madam?"

Her gaze met Mag's. "You must tell him, sir. He will hear you."

"A strange thing to say, lass," Galbraith said. "I am standing right here, and my hearing is as acute as ever it was."

"She meant no disrespect, sir," Mag said. "But she is right to say that I must explain. Dare I hope, though, that we have come in time to get some supper?"

A hint of the twinkle that she saw so often in Mag's eyes appeared in his father's eyes then and Andrena relaxed a little more.

Chapter 16 _____

Glancing toward the archway through which they had entered the hall, Galbraith bellowed, "Hector!"

"Aye, m'lord," that worthy said, appearing in the archway so fast that no one, least of all Mag, could doubt that Hector had been standing just to one side of it and had heard every word they had spoken.

"Order food for our guests," Galbraith said. "They have had a long and arduous journey today. Also, order Rory's bedchamber set to rights for them." To Mag, he added, "Rory now uses the one that was Will's. But he rarely brings Alana with him, because she complains of dampness. Alana is Rory's wife," he explained to Andrena, who nodded."

"Where is Alana living then?" Mag asked.

"Culcreuch, of course, in the old tower. She takes interest in our building."

"She should, since it will one day be their home," Mag said. "It is warmer there, too, I expect, and perhaps not so damp."

"Shall we move to the dais?" Galbraith said, gesturing toward it.

They sat comfortably at the fireplace end of the

high table. Galbraith faced the lower hall and Mag and Andrena, side by side, faced him.

While gillies scurried about, putting food and wine on the table under Hector's supervision, Mag and his father chatted about the weather. They agreed that more rain would come and that the windy afternoons portended storms ahead.

Andrena remained quiet, but Mag was conscious of her presence and wondered what she thought about his father.

At last, Galbraith dismissed Hector and his minions with orders to keep the hall clear until told to do otherwise. Then, turning to Andrena, he said, "How does your father fare, lass? And your lady mother?"

"They are well, thank you, my lord," she said.

"I do not mean any offense to you by aught that I say, lass. But I do wonder how Andrew Dubh persuaded my son to marry you."

"Do you, sir?" she asked, looking right at him. "I should think that almost any bride would find it hard *not* to take offense at such a remark. So mayhap it will surprise you to know that I do not. I quite understand that our union may irk you, especially since Magnus was unable to seek your permission beforehand."

To Mag's surprise, his father did not immediately reply to her, let alone do so as sharply as Mag had expected he would. He was even more astonished when the proud Chief of Clan Galbraith's expression softened ruefully.

"I should not have said that, my lady," he said. "You are right to point out that merely *saying* that I did not mean to offend did nowt to stop the offensive words from leaving my tongue. I hope you will accept my apology."

"Aye, sure, I will, and right gladly, sir," Andrena said.

"I ken fine that this meeting is difficult for both of you. See you, Magnus has told me how you parted. I suspect that that argument hurt you as much as it hurt him."

Mag wished he could silence her but could think of no way to do so that would not make matters worse. In truth, his father seemed to agree with her, for he was nodding. Then Galbraith said, "It does puzzle me, though, that Mag stayed at Arrochar for as long as he did. It is a hard thing to believe that a son of mine could not outwit a man like Pharlain long before now."

Mag pressed his lips together, but Andrena's chin came up sharply, and she said, "*Does* it, sir? Mayhap you have never been the prisoner of a man as ruthless as Pharlain is. Why, I heard that when one man tried to escape, Pharlain cut off his foot. He has hanged others for naught save his own cruel whim. Moreover, he keeps his oarsmen in chains, his largest and strongest men, especially."

Galbraith's gaze shifted from Andrena to Mag, but Mag met it with ease. It was a long time since anyone had leaped to defend him. And, although he could speak for himself, he—

"Furthermore," Andrena went on, "had Magnus escaped any sooner, he would not have learned about the wicked conspiracy against his grace."

"What?" Galbraith demanded harshly, looking from one to the other. "What madness is this? What conspiracy?"

"There does seem to be something of the sort brewing, sir," Mag replied.

He'd have preferred to go slowly, to avoid risk by acquiring some notion of where his father stood with regard to Jamie Stewart before mentioning the words plot or conspiracy. But it was too late for that now.

Galbraith frowned heavily at him. "Just *who* do you think is brewing this so-called plot?" he demanded.

Mag gazed back silently, determined to wait him out. He was certain that his agile-minded sire must easily surmise—if he did not already know—who the likeliest plotters were. Failure to do so, or prevarication, would suggest more than if Galbraith simply named Duke Murdoch, his sons, and Lennox.

In the increasingly heavy silence that followed, the laird fixed his gaze on Andrena again. Mag kept his on Galbraith, and Andrena kept quiet.

She did not even flick a glance Mag's way, he noted peripherally.

"Good lack, Mag," Galbraith said at last. "I can easily imagine that you *do* believe in some plot against young Jamie. You ever had a soft spot for that lad."

Mag replied quietly, "With respect, my lord, he is no longer a lad. He is thirty years old and King of Scots. Moreover, sir, during the past year, he has proven himself both able and determined to rule this realm."

"He has held his own for a time and may continue to do so, aye," Galbraith said. "In troth, I wish him well. But he is young and inexperienced. Forbye, he lived with English Harry and his son for too long to know much about Scotland."

"He seems to know what he is doing, nevertheless. And the conspirators—"

"Don't mince words, Mag. If you heard about this conspiracy at Arrochar, you obviously suspect that Pharlain is leading the conspirators. *Pharlain*?" His expression and tone both indicated utter disbelief.

"This goes much higher than Pharlain, sir," Mag

replied calmly. "Of that I am certain. What I would like to know, if I still have the right to ask you, is where Clan Galbraith will stand if they do try to execute such a plot."

"I am loyal to the King of Scots as chief of chiefs," Galbraith said stiffly. "I should think you would know that much about me, sir. I am also loyal to my liege, the Earl of Lennox, as you also should know but choose to forget when it suits you."

"I do not forget, my lord. But neither do I follow any man blindly, especially one who chooses politics and his own greed over the good of this realm."

"If you think this conspiracy of yours goes higher than Pharlain, you must be including Lennox as a party to it."

"I am," Mag said. "I also include Murdoch and his sons. I'll grant that I've not been out and about much in past months. But as I see it, Lennox has consistently followed Murdoch. And Murdoch is foolish enough to think Jamie will let him play Governor of the Realm whenever he chooses to do so. He doubtless still consults with his sons and lets Alexander and his men continue to terrorize the country with his wicked lawlessness as both he and Walter did before Walter's arrest."

"I ken nowt of any plot. But . . ." Galbraith hesitated.

This time, the glance that he cast Andrena told Mag that Galbraith wished she were not there. But Mag was not going to send her away or, if he could prevent it, allow his father to do so. Her presence had a more quelling effect on their tempers than anything else he could imagine. The last thing he wanted was to lose control of his temper again or inflame Galbraith's.

The silence grew heavier.

The gillies had gone and would keep themselves out

of the line of fire. Hector would likewise stay away until someone shouted for him. Meantime, the jug of claret sat between them. Mag lifted it and poured claret into Andrena's goblet.

Shooting a quizzical look at Galbraith, he received a curt nod in reply and filled his goblet, too. He filled his own nearly to the brim. Then, gently setting down the jug, he raised his goblet and took a sip.

"The claret is excellent, sir," Mag said, setting down the goblet but keeping his fingers curled round the stem. "You've not lost your skill at selecting wines."

"This *is* a good one," Galbraith agreed. "You seem to have a high opinion of Jamie for a man who's been chained up since his return. I should think that..."

He paused when Mag shook his head.

Mag said, "We met his grace at Paisley Abbey two days ago, sir. Sithee, after I realized they were plotting against him, I escaped during last Sunday's storm and washed up at Tùr Meiloach. When I told Andrew they were scheming, he agreed that I must warn his grace. We were fortunate to find him so quickly."

"Jamie visits Paisley often. His father lies buried in the abbey kirk."

"Before the altar, aye," Mag said. "I saw how confident Jamie is, sir, and how determined he is to bring a rule of law to Scotland. That may sound like an English notion. But we have long had laws and rules that we all should obey—not that everyone did. Sakes, Borderers and Highlanders, in particular, did not."

Galbraith's mouth twisted wryly. "You don't mean to tell me that the first Duke of Albany followed the law, do you?"

"Nay, but he did acknowledge that laws exist—aye, and applied them, too, when it suited him. I hope you won't deny that the lawlessness has greatly increased since Murdoch succeeded his father as Governor."

"Nay, because it's true. In troth, I would welcome sound laws that apply to all, as well as the restoration of a semblance of order in this kingdom. If Jamie can do that, I will hail his return and support him strongly. But only if I can do so without endangering our clan, our lands, or our family's safety."

"So you want Jamie to prove himself *before* you will support him. Is that what you are telling me?"

"I am telling you that I will support him if I can safely do so. But I won't risk infuriating Lennox, Murdoch, or Murdoch's vicious sons if I can avoid it. In troth, lad, I fear that our rebellious nobles are too powerful for Jamie to tame. If they *are* plotting to assassinate him, they will likely succeed."

"They must *not*," Andrena said. Then, when both Mag and Galbraith frowned at her, she said, "Prithee, forgive me if you expected me to sit here in silence. But I believe in Jamie Stewart. He means what he says, so he does mean to impose law and order. God knows that we all need peace and protection from those who would terrorize us. But Jamie needs help from other strong leaders, just as my father does if he is to win back *his* lands and title. See you, I believe in my father, too. I ken fine that *he* will not weigh the prospect of success against that of failure. Nor will he worry about vexing Lennox or Murdoch, let alone Pharlain. My father has great courage. But he cannot win his fight alone any more than his grace can, and he understands that. Forbye, he will support the King, because the King is liege lord over all of us, including the Earl of Lennox and Murdoch Stewart."

Silence fell again, like a rock. Mag could feel the fury that her words stirred in his father. A younger Mag would have trembled, not only for Andrena but for himself, as well, for having inflicted her irrepressible candor on Galbraith. The grown-up Mag did not tremble. But he did watch his father carefully for several moments before he allowed his gaze to shift to his outspoken little wife.

She, however, was still gazing calmly at Galbraith.

That fact startled Mag. He had been certain that she must be worried about his father's reaction to her blunt speech and afraid she had angered him. Instead, she seemed unaware that she had poked the Galbraith tiger right in his pride.

Andrena marveled at how much more easily she could sense Galbraith's emotions than she could sense his son's.

She had heard enough from Mag and seen enough for herself to deduce that father and son were much alike. But Mag's internal control was much stronger than his father's. Because it was, she realized now, Mag's emotions rarely stirred his features or his body to reflect them in any way.

Galbraith's tension was palpable. So, too, was his pride, and she suspected that her words had touched his sense of honor. She could feel Mag's steady gaze on her and could even sense his concern. Doubtless he feared that his father would lash out at her. But she knew that Galbraith would not.

When the laird drew a long breath and let it out slowly,

she shifted her gaze to Mag and said, "I think you should tell him what his grace asked you to do, sir."

Mag continued to look at her long enough to make her squirm a little before he said, "*I* think that first you should apologize for speaking to him as you did."

"That is unnecessary," Galbraith said gruffly.

Mag continued to look at Andrena.

"Magnus is right, my lord," she said to Galbraith. "I let my passion rule my tongue, and I should not have done that. My father would say I had no business spouting my opinions at you as I did. You were generous enough to apologize to me before, for what you said. I can do no less, for I *am* sorry I spoke so fiercely. I hope that you can forgive me, too, because I do not want to cause more strife."

"I do forgive ye, lass," Galbraith said. "In troth, I admire courage when I meet with it and sometimes must look hard to find mine own. Ye've given me cause to think." To Mag, he said, "What *did* his grace ask ye to do?"

Seeing no reason for further caution, Mag said, "To learn where your loyalty lies, sir. Jamie wants to know who stands with him and who will not. He is concerned especially about the Loch Lomond lairds."

"About all who answer to Lennox, you mean."

"I do, aye. He is sure that Lennox stands with Murdoch and his sons. Because Lennox's daughter, Isabella—"

"—is married to Murdoch," Galbraith said testily. "I ken that fine, lad, as who does not? A man is expected to support his good-sons, is he not?"

"One hopes that such a powerful man in his own right might seek to *guide* a wayward good-son," Mag said. "I believe the earl has decided to reject his rightful King for a villain who would rape the people of this realm, wreak terror in their midst, and seize properties to which he has no right."

Grimacing, Galbraith said, "You blame Murdoch for what his sons have done. He is too lazy to have done all that. Forbye, I have said I will aid Jamie as much as I can. I could not reconcile it with my conscience, though, to risk all we have—all that Clan Galbraith has—to support what is likely a lost cause."

"The fact is that there are too many leaders in the conspiracy they brew," Mag said. "Who is in charge? Lennox, who is doddering through his eightieth year? Or Murdoch, who is both lazy and a fool? They both want Walter Stewart to take the throne, and he is as ruthless as his grandfather, the first Albany, was. But Walter is in prison. I discount Pharlain as one who could plot such a coup, but does he support the witless, the prisoner, or the dodderer? We are missing something here. I've little time left to figure out what it may be, though. Meantime, I must tell his grace all that you have said, sir. You would not have me lie to him."

"No, I would not. I'll trust ye to relay my words as I said them."

"I will," Mag promised.

"Ye should ken one thing more, then. Pharlain sent out word that Lennox expects him to leave for Perth at next week's end. He is to take the rest of Lennox's supporters with him, in force, so they will all be at hand when Parliament meets."

"There are rules about how many men a nobleman may take in his tail," Mag said. "If everyone rides with Pharlain, they will look like an army."

"In troth, lad, Pharlain expects us to ignore those rules. He sent out word that his grace will *want* everyone there."

"You should tell his grace that yourself, sir," Mag said.

"Nay, then," Galbraith said. "Ye'll suppose I lack the courage I commended in your lady wife, but I'm not ready yet to defy Murdoch or Lennox. Nor should ye forget for a moment, as ye proceed on this path, that Murdoch and his wretched sons stand next in line for the throne if aught happens to Jamie."

"I must tell his grace what you've told me and that you are the one who did."

"I expected nae more nor less than that," Galbraith said. "I hope ye will not be off at dawn though, lad. I would have more discourse with ye. Forbye, your lady must be tired after her long walk today. Ye canna mean to inflict another such journey on her tomorrow."

"Andrena is accustomed to long walks," Mag said. "But I will confer with her before I make that decision. His grace may still be at Paisley, so I could get a message to him quickly if I take a boat to Balloch and ride from there."

⁓

Having heard enough, Andrena stood, and both men did as well. Making her curtsy to Galbraith, she said, "If you will ask Hector or one of his gillies to escort me to our bedchamber, sir, I will leave you two to talk as long as you like. If I might request a bath..." She paused, smiling at the laird.

"Aye, sure," he said. "Hector!"

"M'lord?" Hector said, appearing again in the archway.

"Her ladyship wants a bath," Galbraith said.

"I ha' put a tub in the room already, m'lord. If her ladyship be fain tae go up now, I'll tell the lads tae begin filling it."

This course being acceptable, Andrena turned to follow the old man.

"I'll go with you, lass," Mag said quietly.

"You would prefer to talk more with your father, sir," she replied. "Hector will look after me, I'm sure. I won't go to sleep before you come up."

"Aye, then, I won't be long," he said.

~

Mag watched her go, knowing he would much rather be going with her than staying to talk with his father. If Galbraith brought up Will's death or the ambush against them, even if he reminded Mag that he had warned him he would get his brother killed, Mag would willingly listen to all he said.

But if Galbraith was expecting *him* to introduce those subjects, he would expect in vain. Mag understood the task that Jamie Stewart had set for him, and confronting his father about past arguments was no part of it. Not only might that set off Galbraith's temper, or Mag's, but it would do naught to bring the Chief of Clan Galbraith to Jamie's support. It might well have the opposite effect.

Accordingly, when Galbraith continued to stare at the archway until Andrena had vanished through it, Mag said casually, "What do you hear from Mina and Jonetta, sir? And what have you done with Lizzie? Has she married yet?"

"Nay, but I'm hopeful," Galbraith said, turning to him with distinct relief.

They talked of family matters until Mag was sure that Andrena must have finished her bath and be getting ready for bed. At the next natural pause, he said, "I should excuse myself, sir. My lady will be wondering what's become of me."

"Aye, she might," Galbraith said. "She's a beauty, your lass. I'd not have expected to approve a match between our family and that of Andrew Dubh, but I think you did well for yourself." Pausing, he added, "You may tell Andrew for me that if he believes we can stop Pharlain—defeat him, that is—I'll do all that I can to help him. You might think of that as a gift on your marriage, if you like."

"I'll tell him, and 'tis more than a gift, sir. I thank you."

But, as Mag went upstairs, he knew that much as he wanted to believe his father, he had little confidence in his pledge. There was also, now that he thought about it, one tiny but hugely important detail that neither he nor Andrena had yet mentioned to Galbraith: the fact that Mag had agreed to take the MacFarlan name.

Andrena was alone, wearing her green silk robe and brushing her hair. She felt warm from her bath and was wondering how much longer Mag would be when the door opened and he walked in.

Without preamble, he said, "Would you mind if we did not go to bed yet?"

"What did you have in mind, sir?" she asked demurely.

He was looking around the room as if he had not seen it before, but he turned abruptly then with humor lighting his eyes.

"I would fain do as you suggest, lass. But you did say that you want to know me all through, so I thought I might show you my favorite place here."

"Then I don't mind at all. Must I dress again?"

He chuckled. "I would not care if you went naked, as long as you wear a long cloak until we are away from the castle. But I warrant you'd be more comfortable in warm clothing."

"The warmest clothes I brought are my deerskin breeks and jack," she said with a mocking grin. "Will it outrage your father or Hector if I wear them?"

"It might, for it astonished *me* to see you in them on the cliff that day," he said. "I thought at first that you were a lad. Do you often wear such garments?"

"Only on solitary rambles," she said. As she spoke, she realized that despite her experience with him, she still anticipated knowing how he would receive what she said, as if she could read him. This time, when she *felt* nothing but saw a slight frown, wariness stirred. "On such terrain as ours is," she explained, "it is easier to walk in breeks than to have to beware constantly of one's skirts."

"I should perhaps tell you that I disapprove of solitary rambles, as you call them, at any time. Pluff assured me that Old Bess is the only companion you need. But we both know that you often don't bother to take her along."

His tone was calm, revealing naught beyond the censure in his words. She could not tell how determined he was or if he was warning her that she must not walk alone again. If *that* was the case . . .

Pushing the thought from her mind, she said lightly, "Do you want to discuss habits of which you disapprove, sir, or show me this wondrous place of yours?"

His lips twitched, but he said, "Put your breeks on, lass. But we *will* talk more about this."

Moving swiftly to obey, she fastened her belt and shifted the dirk in its leather sheath into place. Then, as she swiftly tidied her long, thick hair into two loose plaits, she said, "Did you and your father sort things out?"

He shrugged. "If you mean did we talk about the argument, Will's death, or my agreement to take the MacFarlan name, nay, we did not. We talked of less taxing family matters. I let him guide the conversation, because I don't want to fratch with the man whilst Jamie needs him."

"The laird did not make his intentions toward Jamie clear, though, did he?"

"Clear enough," Mag said. "He'll wait to discover which way the political winds blow him."

"But he did say he would aid my father if he could."

"Aye, he did say that. And he said it again after you left. Art ready to go now?" he asked as she pulled on her second boot.

"I am, unless you truly want to cover me with a cloak."

"We'll take yours along. But you needn't wear it if you'd liefer not."

He led her down a service stair to the kitchen and outside by a postern door, then across a yard, through woodland, to the water. A small coble with two oars lay atilt on the shore, its mast up, its sail furled and tied to the spar. The loch was flat calm, like glass, the moon reflecting on its surface like a large pearl on black velvet.

Mag put her cloak in the boat, eased the stern into the

water, and gestured for her to get in as soon as the stern was afloat.

"Move to the stern seat, lass."

The air was chilly, but he wore only the sark and breeks he had worn all day, without his plaid. The boat rocked just slightly when he got in, for he did so agilely and with economy of motion.

Sitting on the midthwart, he took up the oars. As he rowed the boat away from shore, ripples swirled outward from it and water splashed from the oars, creating tiny ripples everywhere that opened into ever-widening circles, edged with silvery lace wherever the moonlight touched them.

The night was so silent and the loch so still that when she heard someone talking, it startled her. Realizing that the voice came from the clachan onshore, she was astonished that it had traveled so far.

Mag rowed efficiently, powerfully, and with steady rhythm. She soon saw that he was heading toward the islands north of Inch Galbraith. All were much larger than the islet.

The night and the view were too perfect to spoil by talking. Also, having heard someone talking ashore made her suspect that anything she or Mag said would travel to ears beyond their own.

Chapter 17

They passed the low, flat, peat-moss-covered islet called Inchmoan. Two large, steeply hilled, thickly wooded islands flanked them now and, with Inchmoan behind them, formed a triangle. As they approached the Narrows, a winding stretch of placid reed-edged water that separated the two larger islands, Mag watched Andrena. The moonlight lit her face so that he could see her expression change.

"Is that not Inchtavannach to the left of us?" she murmured.

"Aye, the monks' isle," he said. "No one has inhabited it in two decades."

"Doubtless because, although it lies in MacFarlan territory, it also lies too near Inchconnachan, where the Colquhouns own yet another stronghold. I'd wager that Parlan fears to anger them. That *is* Inchconnachan on our right, is it not?"

"It is." He glanced over his shoulder as he rowed. "You can see, ahead of us, where Inchconnachan and Inchtavannach come so close together as to seem one."

Ten minutes later, he rested the oars and let the coble drift to a halt. The moon was directly overhead. Silvery ripples circled outward for a time, but mirrorlike images on the glassy water soon restored themselves.

At first, the silence seemed all-encompassing. Then a nightjar uttered its shrill *coo-ie* and clapped its wings as if saying that its less nocturnal companions should wake up. The monotone whistle of an owl replied, followed shortly by its slow but querulous *pwooo...pwoo...pwoo*.

Dree's lips parted. Her eyes reflected the moonlight.

"What do you think of this place?" he murmured.

Andrena could scarcely breathe for a moment, let alone speak.

Before and after the night birds' exchange, the night was as still as could be. No breeze rustled the leaves, no water lapped the shores, and the image of the moon on the water exactly reproduced what she saw in the sky.

Earlier, she had been able to see lofty Ben Lomond looming high above the loch in the northeastern distance. Now, with two steep-sided islands flanking them and seeming to touch noses just ahead with their overhanging dense woodland, Ben Lomond had vanished. It was as if she and Mag had entered a magical place, the realm of fairies or other wee folk.

Breaking the silence might destroy the magic.

Mag smiled, and she was smiling, too. She tried to think of any other man she knew who might be affected so by such a place. She suspected that most men, even if such a place did affect them, would be unlikely to admit it.

Magnus not only understood it but had wanted to share it...with her.

The thought filled her soul with warmth, and in that

moment, she wanted nothing more than to feel *his* warmth enveloping her.

His feet flanked hers. Their knees nearly touched. She had only to reach...

Scarcely thinking, simply acting, she did.

His hands swallowed hers and felt as if he had warmed them by a fire. Without another word, he drew her to her feet and to him. If she spared a thought for the danger of standing up in a boat, it was fleeting. Mag would not let her fall. Nor would he let the boat tip over. She was safe with him, whatever she did.

Without a single second of awkwardness, she found herself in his embrace. First she was hugging him and then on his lap, comfortably leaning back against him, her head against his shoulder and his arms gently holding her.

His breath tickled her ear as he said, "We can talk if you like. The Colquhouns' castle sits at the southwestern tip of Inchconnachan, and there is no other dwelling nearby. The islands' woods will keep our voices between them."

"It feels like a cathedral here, or an abbey kirk, as if one breaks something precious when one speaks."

"I used to row out here when I was angry or upset and sleep overnight in the coble," he said.

"That must have been gey uncomfortable."

"Nowt o' the sort," he said. "If I hadn't just stormed out of the castle in a temper, I'd bring a cloak and a pillow. So I was content enough. If it was windy and the wind came from the south, it would roar through here and drown out my thoughts. Usually, the most one hears is the rustle of leaves in a breeze."

"It is a splendid place."

"It is, aye. In winter, the south part of the loch freezes solid. One can ride a horse across it. But no one can remember this wee strait freezing over, and it isn't deep. It just stays warmer here, though it ought not to do so. Other such sheltered places freeze even though they are much deeper."

"'Tis a magical place to be sure, then," she said with a sigh of pleasure.

His right hand moved to the side of her breast, idly stroking it. When her breathing turned to a little moan, the hand caressed each of her breasts more intentionally, then eased down toward her right hip and played over the deerskin breeks, coming to rest at last on the hilt of her dirk.

She heard him chuckle low in his throat. "I must tell you that it disorders my senses to feel breeks on such a fine hip, let alone to find a blade there," he murmured. "Why did you bring it?"

"I always wear it when I wear my breeks. Its sheath hangs on my belt."

"Have you ever used it?"

"Only to practice and sometimes to cut something—twigs from a branch, or a string or thong. I haven't ever stabbed anyone, nor would I want to unless I had to."

"Well, I've more alluring things in mind now. But, it puzzles me how I'd get these breeks off you without one or the other of us—or both—taking an icy bath."

"I don't want you to stop what you are doing."

"Nor do I want to stop. But if we go on, it will become gey awkward. So I'm thinking we'd best be getting back whilst we still can do so with dignity."

Although the open loch was as calm as the water in the Narrows, and the distance to Inch Galbraith the same as when they'd left, it seemed to Mag that the return trip took much longer. Andrena sat again in the stern of the boat as he rowed, and smiled at him, often seductively. His body responded with urgency every time.

Her tawny plaits hung loosely over her shoulders, gilded by the moonlight, inviting him to undo them and stroke their silky strands. Her breasts rising and falling beneath the soft deerskin jack tempted him, too. He wanted nothing more than to peel the damnable breeks off of her right there.

They beached at last on Inch Galbraith's shore, and he got out quickly. Pulling the coble high onto the ground, he helped her step out and stowed the oars. Then he put an arm around her shoulders and, carrying her cloak over his other arm, sped her back through the woods to the tower.

As they approached the postern door, he tried to imagine Hector's face if he should see her in her breeks and boots. In troth, though, Mag rather liked them. The dirk and her habitual solitary rambles were another matter.

Such habits could prove terrifyingly dangerous.

When they reached their bedchamber—fortunately without meeting anyone—he shut the door quietly, tossed her cloak aside, and moved to relight the candles with the flint and tinderbox on the table. Glancing at her after he lit the second candle, he saw that she had shrugged off her jack and was putting it into a kist with her other things.

When Galbraith had said that they would sleep in the room that had been Will's, Mag had feared that Will's image would haunt him there. But Dree apparently had the power to banish ghosts. He could think of nowt but possessing her.

When she straightened, he held out his arms, and she moved right into them.

He helped her finish undressing and get into bed. Then he stripped off his clothing, snuffed the two candles, and opened a shutter to let the moonlight in before he got into bed beside her.

⁓

As always, Mag's presence warmed Andrena at once. When he slipped an arm beneath her shoulders and turned on his side, she saw that enough moonlight had entered the room to let her discern his features.

His free hand touched her cheek, and he drew one finger from there down along the line of her jaw, then back to touch her lips.

She kissed it, and as if that were signal enough for him, he shifted his hand downward and captured her mouth hard with his. Responding, she pictured the mirrorlike water of the Narrows again and the magic she had felt, just being there with him. His hands on her body felt magical, too, stirring responses wherever he touched her so that the magic seemed to spread all through her. His lips and his tongue were even more magical. Even so . . .

He paused, raising his head and shifting upward to look into her eyes. "What is it, lassie?"

"Naught," she murmured, not only because she was sure he would think it was naught, but also because she did not want him to stop what he was doing.

"You seemed warm at first, even eager, but then

distant, as you did at Colquhoun's tower. Have I offended you in some way that I should know?"

She shook her head.

"I ken fine that something is amiss. What is it?"

"I want to sense what you are feeling when we couple," she said, reducing the matter to as simple a statement as she could make. "You might at least *tell* me."

He did his best, but words did not fill the void she felt inside. Even when he told her how much he enjoyed stroking her silken skin or how kissing her stirred his passions, her awareness of those feelings grew no stronger.

Unable to explain any more clearly why her inability with him was driving her daft, she exerted herself to keep him from sensing that something was still missing. Little did he know how delighted she was to see him enter a room, how safe he could make her feel, or how much his own vitality invigorated her. But those were not words she felt comfortable saying to him yet, although she had begun to care deeply for him. If only she could feel as connected to him as she did to others, she would agree with her father that Magnus was perfect for her.

She felt guilty for worrying him and knew that in doing so, she had been unfair. He doubtless still thought he had done something to displease her, when what had displeased her was the lack in herself. Even that had changed. She did know when he was pleased with her and when he was amused. She had also, she reminded herself, sensed deeper emotions of fear and anger in him. She suspected, too, that when he had chucked Ian into the loch, she had sensed his jealousy.

After Mag had reached his climax and fallen asleep, Andrena lay long into the night, thinking. She knew that she liked him far more than she had let him believe. As her thoughts faded at last toward sleep, she realized that it was far more than liking. As thoughtful, gentle, and kind as he had been, she was fast falling in love with him. Even so, the emotional bond that she wanted to feel with the man to whom she had given herself for a lifetime was missing.

Awakening to dawn light in a sweat from a disturbing dream wherein he had found himself back at Arrochar, locked in a cage, while Andrena fought with her damnable dirk against Pharlain wielding a sword, Mag fought off the lingering fear he had felt and forcibly shifted his thoughts to the new day. Becoming aware of soft breathing beside him, he carefully shifted himself so he could watch Andrena sleep.

Just watching her took his breath away and made him wonder what had spurred the capricious Fates to let the two of them meet, let alone marry.

She was so beautiful, even with her tawny hair in a tangle and her covers in disarray. He wondered if *he* had done that in his sleep. He always slept warm and rarely needed more than a coverlet. Then he saw that one of her hands still clutched the quilt and knew that she had pushed the covers off herself.

A mixture of emotions filled him, first a sense of protectiveness that wanted to cover her again against the chilly air coming through the still-open shutter. But a sense of deep desire also stirred that made him want to—

Her eyes opened, and she looked at him as he moved closer, her lips parting just before he captured them in a kiss that should have left her in no doubt of how he felt about her. Desire surged through him but not to possess her again, not yet, and not in the way she might expect. He had shown her much and taught her much.

But there was one thing that he had yet to reveal to her about herself.

As his fingers, hands, and tongue moved from her lips and breasts lower to her waist and belly, and lower yet, he stilled her brief, soft protests. Tasting her, he caught one flailing hand and smiled when she relaxed and uttered no further protest. After that, he paced himself carefully, laving her most sensitive spot, giving thought only to her pleasure but, in effect, stimulating himself, too, almost beyond bearing.

Her culmination exploded from her so powerfully that her body arced and she cried out—nay, screamed her pleasure to the winds—and immediately clapped a tremulous hand over her mouth.

He chuckled and moved to excite her again. Her body leaped again in response, but she grabbed him by the hair with both hands, saying, "Nay, no more, I prithee. Come inside me instead."

Eagerly, he obeyed. And she did not mention his emotions.

⁓

When the two of them went downstairs to break their fast and found themselves alone on the dais, Hector explained that Galbraith had gone across the water to the clachan. "He said tae tell ye he'll return midmorning, Master Magnus. He kent fine that ye'd likely sleep late."

Andrena glanced at her husband, wondering how he

would respond, since Galbraith had insisted that they stay. Mag seemed to see naught amiss in his father's absence, though. He merely thanked Hector for the information.

But when they had finished, Mag said, "Come back upstairs with me, lass."

"But surely, you do not—" She stopped and felt heat surge to her cheeks.

He smiled. "Nay, but we do have time yet before he returns, and I want to have a talk with you. We'll be alone, so you can wear your breeks."

They were going outside, then. Uncertainly, she said, "Do you mean you *want* me to wear them?"

"I do," he said.

Wary questions sped through her mind, but none made sense. Pushing them aside, she went with him to their chamber and quickly changed her clothes.

Remembering that he had objected to her dirk the previous night, she began to slip its sheath from her belt before putting the belt on.

"Leave it," he said quietly.

Something in his tone warned her that she might not like what lay ahead. But she finished dressing. When she turned toward the door, he stopped her.

"We'll stay here," he said. "I want you to take your dirk from its sheath and come at me with it as you would have if one of those louts of Pharlain's had done aught to make you unsheathe it."

"But I don't want to do that," she said. "I told you, my father taught me to use it. I could hurt you badly."

"I don't think so," he said. "But I want you to try. Since you like to carry it, I must know that you can defend yourself with it. I promise I won't let you murder me. But you *are* welcome to try."

———

Mag saw her eyes narrow and knew she was unhappy with him. But the fact that she had worn the dirk the night before while she was safely with him, rather than take it off her belt and leave it behind, had told him that she always carried it when she wore the breeks. She had not even considered leaving it. His nightmare had only emphasized the dangers that such a habit could bring to her.

"Take the dirk from its sheath now, and show me how you hold it," he said, hoping his tone would warn her that he expected obedience.

Grimacing, she flicked off the leather loop that kept the dirk in its sheath and withdrew the weapon. Andrew had at least given her a dirk short enough to manage. He had also taught her to take it from its sheath and hold it properly.

Even so, she looked worried rather than confident of her ability.

"This is foolish," she said, lowering the weapon.

"If you feel safer carrying it when you go out alone, you surely know how to use it," he said reasonably. "You need only show me that you can protect yourself, and I will agree with Andrew that you should carry it."

"I *don't* want to hurt you."

"And I say that you cannot. I also say that unless you prove that you can use that blade, you won't lay a hand on it again. Pretend that I'm Pharlain."

She licked her lips, and he could see that she was considering the idea. But she shook her head.

Realizing that the test would be useless if she worried about stabbing him, he snatched a plump pillow from the bed. "See if you can stab this whilst I hold it out before me. You won't hurt me, no matter how hard you try, lass, so come at me."

Her eyes glinted. He could see that she was getting angry, but that was fine. If she lost her temper, he would teach her two lessons in one.

Holding the pillow out with both hands at arm's length in front of his chest, tilted slightly downward, he said, "Strike it dead center if you can."

She held the dirk out from her right side, pointed upward with the blade's edge properly aimed away from her, gripping it as if it were a hammer, with her thumb atop her fist. She would do little harm to the pillow so. Not that he cared about the pillow, but Hector would. And Hector would tell him exactly what he thought about such goings-on in a bedchamber.

The thought made Mag's lips twitch.

As they did, she leaped at him, slashing forward and up with the blade.

In a flash, he let go with his left hand, held the pillow steady with his right, and caught her wrist before the blade touched the pillow.

"That's unfair," she said angrily, trying to jerk free. "Your arms are much—"

She broke off although he hadn't said a word. Nor did he let go.

Instead, tossing the pillow back onto the bed, he gently took the blade from her hand, set it on the nearby candle table, and pulled her into his arms.

"I should not have said you were unfair," she muttered

to his chest. "I ken fine that any man's arms will be longer than mine. But I also ken fine that you think—"

"You don't know what I'm thinking right now, lass, or how I feel."

"Aye, sure, I do," she said. "You are going to forbid me to walk out alone or to carry my dirk anymore."

"Only until I can teach you," he said. "We can work on that today and during our return to Tùr Meiloach tomorrow. Sithee, *mo chridhe*, I do understand your love of solitude—in the woods, on the hills, or near the sea. I often feel those same needs myself. I've never taken anyone with me to the Narrows before," he added softly.

"Do you truly think of me as your heart?"

"I do. My own strong, sweet heart, whose safety concerns me deeply."

"You disarmed me so swiftly, so easily. *And* with your left hand."

"Any warrior could do the same—many nonwarriors, come to that," he said. "A man who was angry or brutal enough could do much worse. Sithee, I stopped when I had taken your weapon. But I still held your wrist, so I could easily have spun you around and pressed your own blade to your throat."

Feeling her tremble, he eased her a little away from him, looked into her eyes, and said, "I think we should stop for now. I wanted to teach you that carrying such a weapon does not ensure your safety. Now I just want to hold you."

He did, and he caressed her. That led eventually to other things, so that the laird had returned from the mainland long before they left the bedchamber.

Galbraith was at the dais table when they went downstairs and greeted them pleasantly, even teased them about "sleeping so late." But Andrena thought he still seemed uncomfortable with Mag, and she soon sensed that the laird felt guilty about something. It did not take much imagination to guess what that was.

Looking from the younger man to the older, she was sure that if she could get them talking about their long-ago argument and all that Galbraith had said then, they would soon sort themselves out. But then Lina loomed large in her mind's eye. Knowing that her wise sister would say, as she had many times, that one must think through every possibility before acting on an impulse, Andrena held her tongue.

The impulse stirred again several times during the day, because they spent it with Galbraith while he showed them improvements he had made to Inch Galbraith and talked about others at Culcreuch. But Andrena, like the men, exerted herself to avoid mentioning difficult topics.

At bedtime, impulse stirred again to urge Mag to talk with his father. But he easily kept her thoughts occupied until both of them fell, exhausted, to sleep.

The next morning, when he said they would leave as soon as they had broken their fast, she nearly protested, and not just because she still hoped he would talk with his father. She felt limp from two delightful nights of sensual exertions and feared that she lacked the strength to walk to Luss, let alone up the steep, rugged path beyond its glen and onward. But she knew that Mag was eager to take her home so he could warn her father about Pharlain's plans and get word to the King, either by taking the message himself or perhaps entrusting that task to Ian Colquhoun.

Mag ate a hearty breakfast with his usual speedy efficiency, drank the last of the ale in his mug, and got to his feet. Glancing at Andrena's still half-full bowl of barley porridge, he said, "Finish eating as you will, lass. I want to see that the lads have collected all of our things and that the boat is ready to take us across. I'll fetch your cloak whilst I'm about it. Can you think of aught else you need?"

"Nay, for I packed everything in my sumpter basket."

Turning to his father, he said, "I'll return here before we leave, sir."

Galbraith nodded but did not speak. Nor did he initiate conversation with Andrena when Mag had gone, so she kept her thoughts to herself until she had eaten all she wanted. Then, signing to a hovering gillie that he might clear her place, she drew her ale mug nearer and looked thoughtfully at its contents.

Galbraith said, "That ale is not as fine as the claret I provided ye on your arrival, my lady. Still, it is drinkable, I trow."

Looking up with a smile, she said, "My name is Andrena, my lord. My friends and family call me Dree. I hope you can bring yourself to do so, as well."

"I am not sure your husband would approve of that."

"Aye, sure, he would," she said. "Moreover, if by some mischance, he did express disapproval, I would tell him that he must not."

A glint of humor leaped to Galbraith's hazel eyes. "D'ye often tell our Magnus that he is wrong?"

"I have not known him for long, sir. And he has rarely

been wrong. But I do not fear him or his temper, if that is what you mean."

"We Galbraith men have quick, hot tempers, Dree."

"I know that Magnus did have a fiery one of old," she said solemnly. "But he told me that imprisonment taught him the disadvantages of such. And I have seen no sign of its return." Before any second thought could stop her, she added, "He cares deeply about you, my lord. I am sure of that. And he feels—"

Breaking off when Galbraith lifted a warning hand, she heard the quick, approaching footsteps that he had heard. Giving him a rueful smile, she stood as Mag strode back into the hall.

Galbraith likewise arose, and when he did, Andrena turned to him, smiled again, and stepped toward him. When he opened his arms to receive her, she hugged him, murmuring, "I am glad I have you for my good-father."

"I think ye'll be a great asset to our family, Andrena-lass."

He released her, turned toward Mag, and then glanced back at her with a slight frown. "I am recalling only now that Andrew Dubh MacFarlan has been seeking husbands for his daughters for some time now. For the eldest... You *are* his eldest daughter, are you not, Andrena?"

Realizing what he was recalling and that Mag had told her himself that he'd not yet brought up the subject, Andrena said warily, "Aye, sir, I am."

Turning next to Mag, he said, "As I recall MacFarlan's requirements, the sticking point for most was his insistence that any husband for the eldest must—-"

"—must agree to take the MacFarlan name, aye, sir," Mag said.

"And you agreed?"

"I did, having at the time no great reason to refuse," Mag replied steadily, meeting his father's gaze.

Andrena nearly winced at the pain she sensed in the laird then. But he said, "I expect I have only myself to blame for that, lad. I ken fine that you must be on your way at once if you are to reach Tùr Meiloach before darkness falls. But we should talk more about this, I think."

"I'm willing, sir, and you know where I'll be."

Galbraith nodded, saying nothing. But his disappointment was keen enough to make Andrena wish that she could give him another hug.

She gave Mag a look that ought to have suggested that he could at least take a few minutes more to make things right with Galbraith.

He met her gaze as steadily as he had met his father's but said only, "Art ready to go, sweetheart?"

The endearment dashed away any further urge she might have had to interfere more than she had. She nodded but then decided that she ought to make at least one stop before they set out.

"I'll be along shortly, sir. I must visit the garderobe first."

"Aye, sure, I'll wait for you outside then."

She nearly suggested that he'd do better to talk with his father but bit off the words and whisked herself off to the garderobe, leaving the two men alone.

Chapter 18———————————

Mag understood what Andrena wanted him to do. But he did not think it was his place to bring up the devastating argument with Galbraith any more than it had been to hurl his agreement to take the MacFarlan name in Galbraith's face on their arrival. Nevertheless, he knew he must not leave Inch Galbraith without bidding his father a proper, courteous farewell.

As Andrena's footsteps faded up the nearby stairway, Mag turned to meet Galbraith's gaze and to note with relief the tiny smile curving his lips.

"She speaks her mind, that one," Galbraith said.

"She does, aye," Mag agreed. "Sometimes, she reminds me of Lizzie. But she is wiser than Lizzie is, I think."

"She has more years in her dish than our Liz does," Galbraith said. "I was telling her when ye returned that I think she will make an excellent addition to our family. Ye've done well to marry her, lad. I'd like to have been there when ye did, but I ken fine why ye might not have thought so. By my troth, though, if I could take back those words that I flung at ye in anger all those months ago, I would."

Mag could not think what to say. Having endured

the pain of those words for so long, simply saying that he could forgive them seemed impossible. Moreover, he could not be sure Galbraith even remembered all that he had said, and Mag did *not* intend to remind him.

"I... that is we should go now, sir. Will you go down to the pier with us?"

"I will, aye. And I meant what I've just said to ye, Magnus. I was wrong. Colquhoun gave me an earful, I can tell ye, when he heard what I'd done."

"He told me," Mag admitted. "We stayed at Craggan Tower the night before we went to Paisley. The laird lent us a galley and sent Ian with us."

Details of the trip to Dunglass and the abbey and of how they had met Pharlain's galleys on their return providing safe topics while they waited for Andrena, the atmosphere was entirely amiable as the three walked together down to the pier. The coble awaited them there on breeze-rippled water.

When Andrena saw Mag and Galbraith waiting for her in the tower's entry hall, she sensed calm between the two and hoped that it meant they had talked. The laird gave her an extra-hard hug and insisted on helping her into the boat, thus stirring her impatience to know what they had said to each other.

The journey to the western shore passed quickly. In the wee clachan, the two gillies and Lippin Geordie awaited them with the garron. As soon as the men had strapped on the sumpter baskets, they bade their farewells and left.

Andrena kilted up her skirts to make walking easier but wished that she were wearing her breeks. She had not asked Mag if he'd mind, because even if he had agreed that she could, her mother would learn one way or another that she had and be displeased. Not only might Peter and Jonas talk, but the possibility of meeting someone else in Glen Luss or on the path beyond it did exist. Come to that, many of their own people would find the fact that she was wearing breeks in her husband's presence worthy of eager discussion.

The gillies' presence also deterred her from asking Mag about his talk with Galbraith. She thought she saw her chance when they stopped to rest and get a drink from a gurgling rill. But he drew her toward a flat boulder, sat down beside her, and said, "Let us talk for a time about how you can defend yourself."

"Father said that the very sight of a blade in a woman's hand terrifies men."

"It would not terrify a warrior," Mag said. "Andrew must know that as well as I do. It is more likely that he believes you are safe on Tùr Meiloach land and won't need to defend yourself there. Or he may think that, in an unusual situation, you might use a dirk against a badger or a wolf, although—"

"I would *never* hurt an animal," she interjected. "As I told you before, I have killed rabbits, but rarely and only because we do eat them and Father insisted that I learn to shoot at moving targets. I hate killing them, though, because the poor things don't really move much and cannot defend themselves."

"But a badger, a wildcat, or a wolf...?"

"They don't attack me. Wolves, after all, are usually nocturnal hunters, and badgers are dangerous only if cornered. Wildcats are the same. I often see them in my rambles, because they haunt rills and burns in search of prey. But although they may look right at me, they soon melt away into the shrubbery and vanish."

His eyes twinkled. "You are making an excellent argument to persuade me that I should keep that dirk. Not only have you said that you don't need it to defend yourself against the beasts of the forest, but you have also told me that you don't want to hurt anyone. Do you think that you *would* stab a man if you could?"

She opened her mouth to tell him indignantly that of course she would. But she shut it again with the words unsaid. The fact was that she had not thought about *having* to stab a man, because she had never felt threatened at Tùr Meiloach, even by the three intruders seeking Magnus. The three had angered her but not frightened her. She had had her dirk then and not spared it a thought.

Meeting his now-serious gaze, she said honestly, "I don't know if I would."

"Good lass. I would not have believed any other answer. I have another question, though. When you sensed danger lurking behind the point on the Loch of the Long Boats, how was that feeling different from what you felt about those men who were searching for me?"

"I was not afraid of those men," she said. "I had sensed the birds' distress earlier, so I knew someone had entered their territory who did not belong there. But I sensed no threat to myself from them, then or later."

"Even when that lout grabbed your arm?" he demanded.

She thought back to that moment. "I was furious that he would dare touch me. But I felt no fear of him."

"By God, you *should* have," he said. Then, more gently,

he added, "I will admit that if lack of fear kept you from taking that dirk out of its sheath, I am glad you felt none. What he might have done if you *had* put a hand to it—"

"Faith, sir, the birds would—"

"I don't want to hear about the birds! Tùr Meiloach is not magical. Your father has merely convinced his enemies by craft and trickery that it is."

"Faith, I've made you angry again."

"Of course, I'm angry. I have not let myself care about anything for a long time, but I care about you more than I've ever cared about *any*one. I don't possess many things in this life, lass, but what I do possess, I mean to keep and protect."

Heart pounding, she stared at him, wondering if she had heard him aright.

~

The stunned look on her face recalled Mag to the other men, now watching them. "Sweetheart," he said quietly, "I'm glad the hawks flew at those men, but I don't understand *why* they did. And I'm concerned that their doing so has made you feel as if you have no need to defend yourself. Just being a woman gives you a huge disadvantage. Even a weak man is likely to be stronger."

"I do know that, sir."

"Aye, but you may not know how you can use that to defend yourself. Sithee, most men will expect you to obey them and to fear their strength. So if you lack opportunity to defend yourself with a weapon, or otherwise, you should stay calm but wary. If you appear unthreatening and wait for your opportunity, it will come. Otherwise, you may make your opponent angry with you, perhaps too angry to remember that he won't win praise for killing a lass."

~

She would have liked to assure him that the birds of Tùr Meiloach *would* protect her. But she could not explain their behavior, because she did not understand it any better than he did.

"You said you would teach me *how* to use my dirk," she reminded him.

"We can talk about that as we go," he said, getting to his feet and signing to the gillies. Walking beside her, he added, "The lads will follow us, but it doesn't matter if they hear us or not. The first thing you should know is that your eating knife is a more effective weapon for you to carry than that dirk is."

"Mercy, how could it be? That knife is too small to be a weapon."

"Small enough to hide, aye. Sithee, lass, if a man attacks you with a weapon, no matter how quick you are, you won't have time to draw your dirk. You may not even see him coming, so he could slit your throat before you knew the danger. However, if he grabs you—to abduct you or otherwise harm you—and tries to force you to the ground or carry you off, if you have a wee, sharp knife that you can draw secretly, you may be able to hurt him enough to get yourself away."

"But surely if he sees that I have a dirk and might cut him with it—"

"The worst thing you could do is to wear that dirk of yours where men will see it and talk about it. If an enemy knows you have it, he won't give you a chance to get it out of its sheath. Remember that I let you draw it and offered an unmoving target that I held with both hands. Even so, I easily disarmed you."

"Aye, you did," she agreed, gritting her teeth to avoid reminding him of how furious and helpless he had made her feel. The most irritating thing now was that she knew he was right.

"Can you really teach me to defend myself?"

"The first thing to learn is to avoid confrontation, but I can also teach you ways that may help against an attacker. The one lesson I want you to take to heart right now, *mo chridhe*, is that the best way to defend yourself is *not* to put yourself in harm's way. When I saw you step out of the shrubbery that day, to confront those three louts..." He paused, cleared his throat, and said, "You were safe before, and you stepped *into* danger. Count yourself fortunate that I could not reach down from that tree and snatch you up across my knee. I wanted to, and I was not your husband then. But I am now. You would be wise *never* to do such a daft thing again."

The shiver that shot up her spine then told her that he meant every word.

⁓

Mag saw that she understood and hoped she would remember his warning, because if Andrew did get the help he sought and went to battle against Pharlain, danger would threaten every acre of Tùr Meiloach. The thought that, under such circumstances, she might slip off on one of her rambles and run into dangers of which she now had little ken threatened to curdle his liver.

True to his word, he described ways to avoid danger

through caution and by verbally disarming trouble-makers.

A longer-than-usual-lull occurred in their discussion when she insisted that the dirk made her *feel* safer whether it *made* her safer or not. He decided at that point that silence would serve him better as a response than words could.

However, his silence failed to make her reconsider her words, as he had hoped it would. Instead, she said, "You and the laird seemed more at ease with each other before we departed."

"We were, aye. But I want to think more about our conversation before discussing it. Right now, we're talking about you and your devilish dirk."

"Aye, sure. But you should know that he cares as deeply about you as I think you do about him, sir. Also, he fears that you won't ever forgive him."

"I ken fine that he never said such a thing to you, Andrena."

"He did not have to," she said. "I asked him to call me Dree, as most of my family and close friends do. He said he was afraid that you would not like that. If he does not care about *you*, why would he care what you think?"

"Has he called you Dree?"

"Aye, once, but then you came in. He did not do so again."

He felt the beginnings of a smile tug his lips but stopped it by saying, "Do *you* think I would object to his calling you Dree?"

"Nay, I do not, and I told him so. I also said that if you did, I would tell you to your head that you were wrong."

He chuckled. "What did he say then?"

"He asked me if I often tell you, you are wrong. He also warned me that Galbraith men have fearsome tempers."

"I see. That brings us back to where we were, though, does it not? If you do not want to stir *my* temper, Dree, you will heed what I have said to you today."

With an exaggerated sigh, she said, "I ken fine that you know all about such things, but I cannot imagine that an eating knife can provide much protection."

"I will show you how when we get home," he promised. "Meantime, we can talk more about ways for you to avoid stepping into trouble."

She sighed again, but he noted as they continued up the steep path toward the pass that she seemed more fully engaged in their discussion. She also had some interesting ideas of her own about how to defuse verbal conflict.

"I've watched Lina do that sort of thing for years," she explained. "Murie and I frequently disagree. But often, before a difference can grow into an argument, Lina intervenes so deftly that we forget we were in disagreement."

"Diversion is useful in warfare, too," he said. "And as a defense tactic. A good way to divert any attacker is to make him think you have reinforcements coming. Often, you need only plant a seed of that possibility in his mind."

Noting that the suggestion seemed to intrigue her, he added firmly, "It is still better to run if your enemy outnumbers, outweighs, or can otherwise subdue you. Sakes, lass, that is no more than common sense, especially on Tùr Meiloach land, where you know the territory better than an attacker from elsewhere could."

They talked about defense and similar topics until they neared the high pass, where it was necessary to concentrate more on where they put their feet. As they made their way through the pass, Mag saw shadowy figures watching from the crags, showing themselves but never approaching. When he pointed one out, Andrena waved and said, "Aye, sure, that's Calum Beg. He has a cot near here, and although the slope above it looks like naught but scree and boulders, he grows barley in patches there. Calum also tends sheep. His sons watch the pass, too, but see few intruders. Sithee, numerous men have disappeared along this route, which deters others from following it beyond Glen Luss."

Her casual manner made his hair stand on end. Clearly, Andrew had not left the safety of Tùr Meiloach solely to his tales of fairies, bogs, and evil beasts.

Andrena felt vaguely aware that she had given Mag a shock. His expression seemed merely to have frozen, but when his wide-eyed gaze met hers, she was sure.

"We didn't murder them, sir," she assured him with a grin. "'Twas but one way that MacFarlans who wanted to join my father were able to disappear from Arrochar without Pharlain or his men following them. They would say that they were going to try to sneak in through Glen Luss, and..." She spread her hands.

"I see."

She wondered if he did, but he went on to talk about situations in which she might find herself at a physical disadvantage. By the time they reached the gates of the tower, he had given her much good advice. She still thought he worried too much.

Andrew met them at the gate and demanded to know what Galbraith had said about aiding him against Pharlain.

"He will help if he can," Mag replied.

In the face of Andrew's patent disbelief, Andrena didn't blame her husband for adding hastily, "He did say that, sir."

Catching her father's eye, she said, "He meant it, too, sir. I cannot be as sure that he will support his grace, though. He admitted fearing that the rebel leaders are too powerful for the King to defeat. But his promise to aid us was sincere. He said only that he'd want assurance from you that you expect to prevail."

When Mag shifted uneasily, she looked up to see bleakness in his eyes.

Andrew saw it, too, for he said, "Ye didna believe him, eh, lad?"

With a grimace, Mag said, "By my troth, my lord, I *want* to believe him. But I do not know if I can or not."

Andrew nodded and turned back to Andrena. "But ye did believe him, aye?"

"I did," she said firmly. "He meant what he said, sir. I am sure of that. I don't know him well enough to judge whether he is one who changes his mind easily—"

"Nay, nay, the man be as obstinate as a goat. If he said that he meant it, 'tis more likely that he does than does not. Your da does still be a man of honor, lad."

Mag nodded.

But Andrena was learning more about him each day. And she doubted that Andrew's words, or hers, had reassured him.

"Ye'll come wi' me now," Andrew said to Mag. "We'll let our Dree visit the womenfolk and get herself tidied up for supper."

"With respect, my lord, I did find more clothes for

myself at Inch Galbraith. So I'd liefer have a bath first and change into a fresh shirt and breeks."

"Aye, sure, ye do that. I'll tell the lads to haul up our biggest tub and hot water to fill it. But we can talk whilst they do that. We willna need Dree, though, so she had better show herself to her mam and her sisters."

Andrena glanced at Mag to see if he would object to Andrew's decree, but he said, "Go and see them, lass. We won't be long."

"I hope not," she replied, smiling. "I'm nigh starving."

~

Following Andrew to his chamber, Mag hoped the older man would not try to persuade him that he knew Galbraith better than Mag did. But on entering the room, Andrew went straight for the jug of whisky and two mugs. Pouring whisky into each and handing one to Mag, he said, "Sit, lad. Put your feet up if ye like, for ye've had a hard few days of it. But if Galbraith and Colquhoun will both aid us, I'm fain to craft some strategy with ye, against Parlan."

Mag sat, collected his thoughts, and said, "I did learn something you should know. He sent word to my father and other Loch Lomond lairds, ordering them to gather their men, because he means to travel to Perth in force. I think that that order, added to what I told my father, persuaded him that a plot *is* brewing."

"Aye, sure," Andrew said. "That Parlan means to travel with an unlawful army makes it plain. We must think on this and see if there be summat we can do to reduce that army's size. If Galbraith will refuse to provide *his* men—"

"He did not say he would refuse," Mag said. "However,

I'm nearly certain he was unaware of the plot before I told him. The rub is that he believes the order for them all to ride together to Perth might have originated with Lennox."

"I wouldna doubt that it did, though it sounds gey unlike Lennox to take such a risk whilst he's under arrest. But to ride as an army against *his grace*? Arthur willna be party to that, lad. But tell me now, how did ye get on with him?"

"As you predicted, sir. That is to say, he did apologize for what he said to me two years ago. But 'tis hard for me to trust his word."

"He did betray your trust," Andrew said. "Still and all, if our Dree says ye can trust him now, ye can."

"Perhaps you will be kind enough, this time, to explain why you are so sure of that," Mag said. "You seem to trust her knowledge, just as she seems to trust the beasts hereabouts to protect her. I am not so trustful of either thing and would like to know why I should be."

He settled comfortably on the back-stool then and sipped his whisky without taking his eyes off his host. This time, he was determined to get an answer.

For the first time in their acquaintance, Andrew looked disconcerted.

~

Andrena lingered in the solar with her sisters and mother just long enough to explain that they had talked with Galbraith and he'd promised to help Andrew if he could. She made no mention of his grace or the conspirators.

She had begun to describe their return journey, when Muriella said, "But that cannot be all that happened, Dree.

Surely, there was something more, something extraordinary that stirred your emotions to a fever's pitch."

Andrena frowned. "I do not recall such a thing, Murie. Our journey each way took a full day, and we spent only two nights at Inch Galbraith."

"Aye, well, 'tis yestermorn that I'm thinking about," Murie said. "Something happened then near dawn, because I awoke to the strangest sensations. Sithee, I had a strong awareness, stronger than any I've had before, that you were in raptures. Lina felt it, too. And you know that for her to feel your emotions is not as common as it is for me."

Feeling heat flood her cheeks, Andrena glanced at Lady Aubrey, saw the twinkle in her eyes, and looked hastily at Lina, whose expression was quizzical. To Murie, she said, "I do not know what to tell you, except that Mag and his father are no longer at odds with each other. I was gey delighted about that, I can tell you."

"Doubtless, that is what it was then," Lina said, nodding and returning her attention to her tambour frame.

"Aye, perhaps it *was* only that," Muriella said. "It felt as if it would be a much more interesting story, though. I was fain to hear what it might be."

"The tale of Magnus and his father is not one that you may bruit about," Lady Aubrey said. "It is too personal, and Magnus would dislike your telling it to others."

"I won't," Murie said with a sigh. "It is not only too personal. It would also hold small interest for people seeking diversion from their own dull lives, from their sorrows, even from their fratching and their feuds."

Andrena smiled. "I don't think anything that I do or that Magnus does would divert anyone from feuds or fratching."

"You never know," Murie said with a teasing grin. "A good story can be gey powerful if the right person tells it."

"By which you mean if the storyteller exaggerates the details to mythical proportions," Lina said, giving her younger sister a stern look.

"Aye, sure, exaggeration adds to a story's power and makes any tale more memorable," the undaunted Muriella said with a shrug.

Andrena sighed. At least she had diverted Murie from further demands to know what had excited her yestermorn. She did not mean to share details of her sexual experiences with her sisters—ever.

~

Andrew drew a breath and let it out, giving the still-silent Mag hope that the older man would at last tell him what he wanted to know.

Andrew said, "Ye must have heard much talk of us at Arrochar."

Mag nodded.

"Mayhap talk about me daughters or me lady wife?"

Recalling Pluff's comments but seeing no need to tell Andrew that the most interesting information about Lady Aubrey had come from the lad, Mag said, "I heard only that Lady MacFarlan sometimes sees things that others do not see."

"Aye, but rarely, mind. Forbye, when we left Arrochar, I agreed to go only because she said we must get our wee babe, Andrena, to safety or I'd have nae hope of ever regaining what Parlan had taken. Sithee, our own two lads were dead by then, and we knew it. We had a secret way out of the castle, so we hied ourselves south toward Tùr

Meiloach, which has long been a sanctuary for true Mac-
Farlans."

"Is that tale real, sir, or merely a folk tale?"

"'Tis real. My lass said that all would be well if we
could cross the river, that Tùr Meiloach would protect us
if we could reach it. That was enough for me."

"You said that Andrena was a baby. How small?"

"Nobbut two days old." When Mag uttered a sound of
protest, Andrew raised a hand. "I'll tell it me own way or
not at all. It was a dark night with but a thread of a moon
to guide us. My lass made it nigh to the river afore she
fell. Out of childbed betimes as she was, she'd spent what
strength she had to get that far. I was frantic, I dinna mind
telling ye. But she insisted I must go on, that we'd lose all
if I failed to cross the river. I swore I wouldna leave her
and the bairn."

"'Nor should ye,' the woman says to me. 'Ye'll take
her across with ye.' Her words near sent me wild. But
she promised me she'd be safe, and I could hear Parlan's
men ever nearer. So I put my lady under the shrubbery,
wrapped in her cloak. Then I snatched up the bairn in her
swaddling and dashed on to the river."

Mag's mouth was dry. He drank some ale.

"The water was savage, in full spate," Andrew said. "If
ye've no seen it up close, I can tell ye it be wilder than the
river south of here. But having seen its great falls from
the loch, ye'll ken how it plunges down over high, sheer,
unclimbable cliffs. Parlan's men were close behind me by
then. I had nae time to think."

Reminding himself that Andrena and Lady Aubrey
had survived, Mag stifled further protest, fearing that if
he spoke, Andrew would refuse to say more.

Andrew eyed him quizzically, then relaxed and said, "I have me doots that ye'll credit what I tell ye next. Sithee, I'd heard seanachies tell the ancient Roman tale of Camilla's da and his spear. D'ye ken that one?"

Mag nodded and fought down a chill that threatened to shoot up his spine. "You bound your own wee daughter to a spear and chucked her across the river?"

"I did, aye, over the river to a clearing in the woods beyond." He paused. "Only afterward did I hear the wolves."

The chill swept through Mag unchecked then. But a heavy double-rap on the door interjected itself before he could reply.

"Aye, Malcolm, what d'ye want?" Andrew demanded curtly.

The door opened to reveal not only Malcolm but the burly Euan MacNur gripping a terrified-looking Pluff by the back of his jacket.

Chapter 19 ———————————

Andrena found Tibby and a tub half-filled with hot water when she reached the chamber she shared with Mag, but no Magnus. Waiting only until men had brought up the last of the hot water and a pitcher of cold to cool it, if necessary, she shooed them away and took advantage of the tub.

With Tibby's help, she washed quickly, expecting Mag to show up at any time and feeling shy at the knowledge that he would walk in on the two of them without knocking. Then she was out and dressed in her favorite kirtle, its amber color reminding her of autumn leaves. Tibby had pinned up Andrena's plaits in a pile atop her head. Strands that had escaped them were damp from her own hasty washing of parts she could reach and from Tibby's energetic scrubbing of her back.

"I'll take them pins out now, m'lady, if ye'll sit on yon stool," Tibby said.

Andrena was moving to do so when the door opened and Mag strode in.

"Prithee, leave us now, Tibby," he said, holding the door wide.

"Aye, sir," Tibby said, fleeing without so much as a glance at her mistress.

Reaching up to take out the hairpins herself, Andrena said as he shut the door, "I think you frightened her. Is aught amiss?"

"I sent her away so I can get my bath before we eat supper. I'm sorry if I gave her a fright. Young Pluff has got himself in trouble again," he added with a grimace. "You recall, do you not, that he was not at hand either to bid us farewell on our journey or greet us on our return."

"I do now that you speak of it," she said. "What did he do?"

"Apparently, he slipped away to visit a friend."

Pins out, she began to undo her plaits. "What friend?"

"Her name is Annabel. If I heard aright, she is Mac-Nur's daughter."

"But MacNur's Annabel lives at Arrochar with her mother, Mae," Andrena said, frowning. "The tale I've heard is that, when MacNur decided to leave ten years ago to join us here at Tùr Meiloach, Mae refused to come with him."

"Aye, so the lad told us. But he did so only because when he finally admitted he'd gone to Arrochar, Andrew demanded to know why the devil he had."

Having stripped off his clothing, Mag got into the tub.

Briefly and warmly distracted by the fascinating play of his muscles as he did, Andrena gathered her wits. "I thought you and Father must be plotting tactics."

"So we were, aye," he said, picking up the soap and lathering himself. "But MacNur brought Pluff up because he thought the lad had lied to avoid punishment. He went straight to MacNur on his return and told him that Pharlain is arming his men as if he's preparing for war. Pluff told MacNur that he feared they meant to attack here," he added as he soaped his hair. "He also told MacNur that Pharlain means to leave Arrochar by week's end. When MacNur told Andrew that the lad could not possibly know such things, your father demanded that Pluff explain himself or take a leathering right then and there from *him*."

"So Pluff admitted that he went to Arrochar to meet Annabel?" Andrena, said, finding it as hard to believe as MacNur had. "How could he even know her? Annabel cannot be more than thirteen, if that, and she has never lived here."

"Pluff said they are the same age. He said that MacNur had been irritable about something and that things the man said had helped the lad figure out that MacNur still had family at Arrochar. Pluff asked around, and when one of the men told him that MacNur's wee daughter lived there with her mam, he got it into his head that what he calls MacNur's being peevish or crabbit must be due to missing them. So Pluff decided to find out if they also missed MacNur. If they did, Pluff said, he meant to help them escape from Arrochar to Tùr Meiloach."

"Mercy," Andrena said. "He is lucky Parlan did not catch him. Faith, but we know that Parlan must be readying his men to leave for Perth."

"Aye, so Andrew and I will talk more after supper. This information coupled with what my father said about the number of men Parlan is raising, plus his order to ignore Jamie's restrictions, should provide at least some of the evidence his grace seeks to convict the plotters. But Pluff's testimony would mean nowt to the lords of Parliament. To be useful to Jamie, we need to find *adult* witnesses and also think of a way to stop or hinder Parlan's army."

"We must also get word to the King, and quickly," she said.

"Aye, sure," Mag said, still soaping himself. "We'll send running gillies to Craggan and Inch Galbraith requesting support for whatever we do, too. I'll wager that Colquhoun will be as adamant as my father is, though, about having a plan that is likely to stop or impede such an army. Andrew is scheming, but it will likely be morning before we can send the lads off. We'll need a plan first."

"You will," she agreed. "Murie told me just today that a good story can divert men from feuding and fratching. But you will need more than that. We have plenty of weapons and our own men to fight, but Parlan has many more men than we do."

"He does, aye," he agreed, sluicing water over himself with the pitcher. "And he knows how many Andrew has here, as well." Finished with the pitcher, he set it down and stood up. "Hand me a towel, will you, lass?"

She did so, and as she handed it to him, he pulled her into a wet embrace. Planting a firm kiss on her cheek and another on her lips, he murmured, "You may have given me a wee notion with that tale about Muriella. As I recall it, your father is as skilled as she is when it comes to weaving stories."

Andrena could not deny that. But when she asked him to explain, he said, "Not now, lass. I must think more. Mayhap we'll talk later."

"You can be sure we will, sir," she said.

~

"We have to disrupt Parlan's part of the plot," Andrew said when he and Mag met in his chamber after supper and took their usual places. "If we do nobbut delay the man, it will help his grace." He reached for the whisky jug.

"An attack on Arrochar might delay Pharlain but would gain *us* only defeat," Mag pointed out. "Forbye, we cannot be sure we'll gain enough support to delay him before he departs. I'd liefer we choose our own time and place for any fight."

"I, too," Andrew agreed, eyeing him curiously. "What would you suggest?"

"That we divert Pharlain's attention to another threat, to gain time. Or we bring him to us in some way that will delay him *and* give us the advantage."

"Bringing him to us is easy," Andrew said grimly. "The man would leap at any chance to seize Tùr Meiloach. But he's already gathered and armed his men, so that, too, would gain us nobbut defeat."

"Not if we spin him a tale that makes him think we're vulnerable but only if he acts on a certain day, mayhap even at a certain time. We'd need enough truth in the tale to persuade him that his chance to seize these lands has come at last."

"D'ye have such a tale in mind?"

"Not yet," Mag admitted. "Andrena just put the notion in my head. She said Muriella tried to get a story out of her about our journey. When Andrena said there was nowt to tell, Murie said it depended on who did the telling. She insisted that even a tedious tale told by a good storyteller, with mayhap some exaggeration and such, could become powerful enough to divert men from their feuds and fratching. It occurred to me then that you've spent two decades spinning myths that have kept Parlan and his louts at a distance. Between us, we should be able to devise one that draws him to us whilst keeping him from guessing that we *want* him to come."

"But who would tell him such a tale?"

"Someone from Tùr Meiloach does report to him already," Mag said. "You ken fine that your myths travel everywhere, and we'd often hear talk at Arrochar of goings-on here, celebrations and such. I doubt he kens aught of true import, though, because the men hunting me did not know of your bridge across the south river."

Frowning, Andrew said, "What else does the villain know?"

"He hears when people leave or return and how many warriors you have. Such information is erratic, though, because Andrena told me that men leaving Arrochar have come here through the pass above Glen Luss, and I'd heard nowt of that before. In troth, I thought Pluff might be Pharlain's source when he admitted secretly visiting Arrochar. But if he was just seeking MacNur's daughter—"

"He might have told *her* things and the lass passed them on."

"Pluff cannot be Pharlain's primary source, because Pharlain has been gleaning such information since before I was captured. Forbye, I talked with MacNur after supper, and he assured me that this was Pluff's first disappearance from Tùr Meiloach that was longer than an hour or two."

"Aye, but Pluff may have known the lass for a long time. Or he may have been meeting someone else, nearer home, all along."

"In any event," Mag said patiently, "I think that you and I should devise a tale, most of which we can tell *any*one.

It should perhaps suggest an open door of sorts, a way into Tùr Meiloach that Pharlain will believe might stand unguarded for just a few hours or a day. If I describe what I have in mind, I'll wager that you can make it more intriguing to him, mayhap even impossible for him to resist."

"Aye, sure, I can do that," Andrew said with a grin. "Then, after he steps through our doorway, we shut the door, aye?"

"Aye, right behind him," Mag agreed.

"'Tis a good notion, that. But we'll need more men than I have here to make it work. So it be a good thing that your da and Colquhoun will both support us."

Mag nodded. He just wished that he could be as certain as Andrew and Dree were that Galbraith would keep his word to them.

~

Andrena, having spent her evening after supper with her sisters, had learned that although they'd accomplished much in preparation for Lady Aubrey's birthday celebration, much remained to do. Nevertheless, she had bidden them goodnight at the usual time and then waited impatiently for her husband in their chamber. When more than an hour had passed, she went to bed, leaving candles alight for him.

The room was dark when movement on the bed woke her. She muttered irritably, turned over to see only his shape, and said, "What did you decide?"

"That I have a powerful need for you," he murmured, kissing and caressing her in such a tantalizing way that other needs stirred, shifting the first one into last place. When they lay back at last, replete, she asked him again.

" 'Tis late, *mo chridhe*, and we're both tired. We'll talk more tomorrow."

So, she slept, but when she awoke, sunlight streamed in through the open window and Mag was gone. Dressing without bothering to shout for Tibby, she went in search of him only to learn that he'd left the tower with a number of men, their destination and time of return unknown.

Frustrated but resigned to such masculine tactics, she went for her usual walk with Old Bess, taking the dirk and her eating knife. Finding a place where she'd be unobserved, she tried out some of the tactics Mag had described to her.

She soon realized that no matter how she adjusted the dirk, getting it out of its sheath in anything like a hurry was awkward. Her eating knife, being smaller, was manageable. But the leather-thong loop that kept it in its sheath impeded her efforts.

At last, by adjusting the sheath so she could carry it near her left hipbone with the hilt tilted slightly downward to the right, in much the way that Mag wore his dirk, she could slip the loop off with a finger and draw the knife with her right hand. She could conceal the much smaller knife under her shawl or the jack she wore with her breeks.

Returning to the tower, she spent the rest of the day tending to a list of tasks that Lina had set for the upcoming birthday festivities. When she learned that Andrew had sent lads out to invite cottars and other folks to attend, she began to fear that her father and Mag had decided they could do naught but warn the King of his danger.

"If Mag has gone to Glasgow or anywhere else without

telling me," she muttered as she dressed for supper, "he will soon learn his error."

But Mag returned with the other men shortly after gillies had begun serving the evening meal. Stepping to the dais at the women's end and crossing behind them to his seat, he paused to give Andrena's shoulder a warm squeeze.

Smiling up at him but determined to know what was happening, she waited only until she'd finished eating before excusing herself. Moving to Mag's side, she said quietly, "I would speak with you, sir, when you will."

Nodding, he said, "I'm at your service now, lass, if your lord father will permit me to abandon him."

Andrew nodded and said with a knowing smile, "Aye, sure. Ye can come to me later, lad. I want to hear all ye've accomplished today."

As they left the dais, Andrena murmured, "First, *I* would like you to tell me where you have *been* all day, sir."

Mag put an arm around her and drew her close in a brief hug, then urged her up the stairs before him with a smack to her backside just hard enough to make her wonder if he'd meant it as a warning.

Glancing back, she saw the twinkle in his eyes. Nevertheless, the brief time of wondering had reminded her that she still could tell only a few things about his moods by his voice or demeanor, let alone in any other way.

When they reached their bedchamber, he shut the door and said, "Andrew and I talked long last night and made some plans, sweetheart. I took some men out today and told them what we hope will come to pass."

"What do you hope?" she asked.

"To delay Pharlain if not to defeat him," he said.

"Sithee, since he will lead all of the Loch Lomond lairds who support him, their very number must constitute a large part of the conspirators' army. If we can keep them from joining the rest on time, we'll deal their plans a sharp, perhaps even fatal, blow."

She nodded. "Meantime, his grace is gathering men to his own banner."

"Most certainly, aye," he said. "We sent men with messages to Colquhoun and to my father. And a report will go to his grace, as well, of course."

"You sent a running *gillie* with a message for the King?"

"Nay, nay, I expect that Ian Colquhoun will go if his father agrees. I sent one lad to Colquhoun with both of those requests," he added. "Your father's running gillies are fast. But they cannot run to Paisley—let alone to Stirling or Perth—as fast as a galley can take Ian to Dunglass. From there he can ride after Jamie, if necessary. I'll stay here to aid your father and his men."

"When is all this to take place?"

"We'll see," he said. "We cannot know exactly what will happen or when, only that it must happen before, but near, the day Pharlain *plans* to leave for Perth. We want to prevent his departure long enough for Jamie's supporters to gather round him in Perth. But we must also consider your mam's celebration. We'll want to ensure her guests' safety whilst they're here—also that of you and your sisters."

"What danger could there be for us in the tower?" she asked. "Its walls are impregnable. Forbye, the old tales about Tùr Meiloach still deter sensible people from trespassing onto our lands without Father's permission."

"Nevertheless, when the time comes, we'll want to know that everyone who belongs in this tower is safe," he said firmly. "That means being sure that they will *all* stay inside when we put our plan, whatever it may be, into action."

Such emphasis and the stern look he gave her made his meaning clear if their plan was not. But she got no more out of him about any plan. Although she tried over the next few days, more often than not, he was outside the barmkin wall. So she saw little of him and received little information when she did see him.

Every man in the place seemed focused on what might lie ahead, although no one would speak to her of what he knew. She understood their silence, for men rarely revealed their plans to others, warriors least of all. Understanding them did little to reconcile her to her ignorance of what they were planning, though.

She carried her eating knife now, even when she wore her breeks. And Mag twice found time to show her how she might effectively use it to defend herself.

To her relief, he had not forbidden her early-morning rambles with Bess. So she decided that, despite his earlier comments to the contrary, he did not object to them. However, she had a strong feeling that he *would* object if she tried to follow him or any of the other men when they left the tower.

If he had heard from Colquhoun or Galbraith, she knew naught of that either. But she believed he would tell her if he did hear from either laird.

On the eve of Lady Aubrey's birthday, the Laird of Colquhoun arrived with his lady wife and a tail of six men in time for supper. Ian was not with them. When Andrena inquired about him, Colquhoun said with his pleasant smile that they would all know of his son's return when they saw him.

Andrew and Mag drew Colquhoun away after that. And Andrena renewed her acquaintance with Lady Colquhoun, who was also a close friend of Lady Aubrey's.

The additional company provided a pleasant overture for the next day's festivities. Everyone enjoyed excellent food and wine, amusing conversation on the dais, and musicians who played loudly enough to be heard without disturbing their conversation. Later, Muriella entertained everyone with two new tales she had learned, as well as humorous anecdotes from her childhood.

Andrena decided that Murie had chosen her anecdotes with an eye to making their mother and their guests laugh—and to embarrass her older sisters.

By the time everyone retired to bed, the wine Andrena had drunk had relaxed her so that she was thinking only of how pleasant an evening it had been when Mag suggested that she go on up and get ready for bed.

"Aye, sir," she said with a smile, a nod, and warm anticipation of coupling with him. Half an hour later, she wondered sleepily what was keeping him.

She fell asleep before he joined her, slept soundly through the night, and awoke the next morning to find Tibby bustling about the sun-filled room.

Mag was not there, making her wonder if he had come to bed at all.

"Have you seen Magnus Mòr?" she asked the maid-servant.

"Aye, sure, m'lady," Tibby said. "He were up afore dawn tae break his fast wi' some o' the other men. Then they all went out a-hunting. The laird said it had been a gey long time since he'd had guests for the hunt. So, although it do be her ladyship's birthday, he said he didna mean tae waste such a fine opportunity."

Grimacing at the thought of a hunting party disturbing the forest creatures, Andrena asked no more questions. She assured herself instead that the men would not stay away long on such an important day.

⁓

The men were not hunting.

Mag and Andrew led a large company of men-at-arms into the hills northeast of the tower. They were making their way through dense woodland, toward what Andrew described as an erstwhile pass in the granite heights above them.

"The pass suffered a few bad landslides," Andrew explained as they went.

"Suffered?"

"They didna occur all on their own, withal."

"The wee folk did it, I expect."

"Aye, sure, along with boggles, boggarts, and banshees, to name a few. They do say that the Fates help them wha help themselves, aye?"

Mag shook his head at the man but admired his ingenuity. To have persuaded his enemy that Tùr Meiloach enjoyed strong protection, and maintained his deception for two decades, commanded respect however he had done it.

"You did set men to watch the river, aye?" he asked a few minutes later.

"Aye, sure, but Parlan will choose the pass. The rivers be yet too wild. Forbye, as ye said yourself, we've discerned nae sign that your pursuers knew aught of the south river bridge."

"I did scale the south cliff," Mag reminded him. "On a dark night, in a storm."

"Aye, but your life was in your hands. And the Fates were with ye, too."

Engaged, in the ladies' solar, with last-minute details as she and her sisters had been since breaking their fast, Andrena paid little heed to the first tingling uneasiness she felt. Recalling her father's hunt, she thought she was sensing disquiet of the forest creatures at the hunters' invasion of their territory.

The unease increased to apprehension and grew stronger. Studying her sisters, she saw that both were busy and unperturbed. So neither Andrew nor their mother was cause for the sensation. Moreover, Lady Aubrey and Lady Colquhoun were each still enjoying a rare opportunity to sleep late.

Moving to the south window, she saw several hawks soaring in an overcast sky. Although she knew they might be part of the disturbance she felt, their behavior was different from what she'd seen before. The sensation she felt was different, too. It intensified to a sense of something ominous approaching and then rapidly clarified itself as danger greater than what she had sensed in Dougal MacPharlain's galleys.

She could see naught to explain her feeling. The hawks, instead of clustering as they had before, when she had felt their distress so keenly, ranged widely and might well be reacting to the hunting party. If so, they were not causing the alarm she felt. It seemed to come at her from all directions, from above and below, too.

Moving to the west-facing window, she could see only a portion of the loch beyond the cliffs. She saw no boats. All that she did see looked calm.

"What is it, Dree?" Lina asked. "Is aught amiss?"

"Danger comes," Andrena said. "But I don't know its source or direction."

"It doesn't matter," Murie said with a shrug. "Father has forbidden us to leave the tower, Dree. He and Magnus both told Malcolm to keep us inside whilst they hunt. Not just inside the wall but inside the tower. This time, you cannot investigate."

Andrena barely heard her. The sensation had grown so strong that she could no longer fight it. She turned and strode toward the door.

Lina's voice intruded as if from a great distance. "Dree?"

Shaking her head, she said, "Not now, Lina, I must have quiet to determine what stirs this feeling and why. Don't worry. Naught will happen to me."

"Perhaps not now," Lina said. "But if Magnus said we should stay—"

"Magnus is not here," Andrena interjected. "He, Father, and the others are all out in the woods, hunting. If there *is* danger and they don't see it coming…"

She opened the door as she spoke and stepped onto the landing, pausing only long enough to decide that going up to the ramparts would be useless. The forest's dense canopy would conceal hunters and danger alike. She'd be wiser to slip out if she could and track down the menace that threatened them. The urgency that drove her insisted that she lacked time to argue with anyone. Even Lady Aubrey might try to stop her if Andrew had said they were all to stay inside.

Feeling for her eating knife as she hurried downstairs, she had an impulse to take her dirk, too. But she reminded herself that Mag knew more than she did about such things. She would not change to her breeks, either. The last thing she wanted, if Parlan *had* dared to invade their land, was to look like a man or a boy. Even Parlan, surely, would hesitate to harm a noblewoman—his own cousin's daughter, at that.

Hearing a faint echo in her mind of Murie's saying that Andrew and Mag had both left orders to stay inside the tower reminded her that Mag had warned her that such an order would come when the men put their plan into action. Even so…

Hurrying down to the postern door, she took her shawl and knitted cap from the hook. The heavy iron bar was in its nighttime position across the door. When she moved to lift it, Murie's voice from the stairway above startled her.

"Where are you going, Dree?"

"To see what I can see," she said. "Since Father and the others went hunting, even if I could persuade Malcolm to heed my warning, he'd send no one if Father said to stay inside the wall. I'll take care, Murie, but I must go. If Parlan is coming with an army, the hunters may not see it coming. I must see what the danger is and find a way to warn them, or see enough to persuade Malcolm to do so."

Murie hesitated, but Andrena held her gaze. "Put the bar back when I've gone. Tell no one where I am, save our mother when she awakens, unless something else occurs. If aught does happen to me, you will know it, Murie.

But, even if you do, stay inside this tower. I'll keep to the woods and shrubbery."

Murie shook her head. "Father will be furious, Dree. And Magnus—"

"I am thinking of Magnus *and* Father. Now, no more. I must go."

Opening the door, she stepped outside and pulled it shut. Waiting to hear the reassuring thud of the bar going back into place, she descended to the yard.

Pluff stood guard near the postern gate as usual. The only two guards that she saw on the wall were looking outward.

When Pluff saw her, he gaped.

Putting a finger to her lips, she hurried toward him. "I must go out, Pluff. Danger comes, and I must see what form it takes."

"Coo," the boy breathed. "Did the lady Aubrey *see* it? They do say—"

"Never mind what they say," Andrena said. "With the men away hunting, the men-at-arms they left here must stay and keep the gates and tower shut tight. Yet someone must warn the hunters of their danger. So you must open the gate for me, Pluff. And when I go out, you must distract the guards on the wall long enough for me to run into the woods. Can you do that for me?"

"Aye, sure, though I'll get a leathering when they hear what I've done."

"I will do all I can to prevent that," she promised, well aware that she might face similar punishment when Mag and her father learned what *she* had done. None of that mattered, though, if Mag was in danger.

"Aye, then," Pluff said, and quietly opened the postern gate.

Chapter 20

Mag and Andrew lay concealed in steep woodland near the outflow of a large, deep tarn. The tarn collected snow-melt from the precipitous, encircling heights of tumbled rocky debris and sheer granite cliffs that formed the granite bowl in which it sat. The tarn, with myriad streams and rills that fed it, was the primary source for the river that formed Tùr Meiloach's north boundary. The sheer cliffs curving around the tarn's northern perimeter helped protect the area from intruders.

From where the two men were, they had an unobstructed view of the vee-shaped declivity that—although now filled with loose rocks, strewn with boulders, and treacherously unstable—had once served as the high pass from the west-Lomondside of the peaks to the northeastern part of Tùr Meiloach.

Most of their men had concealed themselves nearby. Others kept watch on less likely approaches. Three more had hidden on the ridge above the pass. The three took turns reporting the slow progress of Pharlain's men as they made their way carefully up the far side, following the ancient route to the pass.

Andrew had sent word out to his captains to begin

converging on the northeast area while taking care to leave a man or two to watch the other approaches. Having received no report of boats on the loch, he and Mag remained confident that Pharlain was behaving as they'd hoped he would.

⁓

Safe in the woods, Andrena turned west toward the loch, only to realize that if she went onto the clifftops to look down along the loch shore, men on the ramparts would see her. Since no part of her plan included drawing notice from the tower or men on its wall, she turned instead toward the steep, wooded slopes in the northeast, where she felt the strongest warning of danger. On the higher ground, she could stay concealed and yet see more while she figured out what was going on.

Taking care to disturb little shrubbery, she moved nonetheless quickly while keeping her senses on full alert, until she realized that her feeling of imminent peril was expanding rapidly. An ominous sense of bellicose intruders from the southwest, where Mag had climbed the cliff, spread to include a pulsing awareness from the south*east* peaks of similarly pugnacious men nearing the high pass there.

She had no time to assess those feelings before more such sensations flowed to her from the northwest. And *where* was the hunting party, if hunting party it was?

Danger from armies of men seemed to be all around her.

Striving for calm, she reminded herself that many of their own people would be coming to the tower to celebrate the lady Aubrey's birthday. That did little to reassure her, though, because she realized that that very fact might have encouraged Parlan to think Andrew might have left the passes unguarded.

Above her, as one went higher along the northern river, one found naught but granite cliffs, boulders, and open, scree-strewn slopes. The pass boasted no discernible, let alone easily passable, trail. Hunters might find a roaming deer or two. Otherwise only wildcats, a few agile sheep or wild goats, ravens, ptarmigan, and eagles inhabited the higher elevations. None save the deer made good eating.

She wondered if perhaps Andrew, Mag, and the other men were seeking a good place to put their plan into action or perhaps even luring Parlan into a trap.

On Lady Aubrey's birthday?

If it was a trap, surely Andrew's men and Colquhoun's would have left watchers elsewhere, keeping a lookout. Yet no one had sounded an alarm.

The sensible thing to do, she knew, was to return to the safety of the tower. But she had her wee pipe in the pocket of her shawl. She also had increasing fear that she alone was aware that the danger lay all around them— and an increasingly overwhelming need to warn Mag and Andrew.

Her decision made, she kilted up her skirts more securely under her narrow leather girdle, felt to be sure that her small knife was in position beneath her shawl, and lengthened her stride. Coming to a wide, boulder-strewn clearing, she hesitated, still sensing danger everywhere but particularly north of the tower from above and below, east and west, drawing nearer and nearer.

Realizing that her senses were being overwhelmed,

she stayed where she was, at the edge of the clearing, and tried to concentrate, to sort the sensations.

Were there men in the forest nearby? There were, aye, and it felt as if *she* were the one they surrounded. But some of them were likely her father's men.

The safest path seemed to lie straight ahead of her. Accordingly, she hurried across the clearing, darting glances right and left. Every instinct told her to run as fast as she could. But doing so on such uneven ground would likely bring disaster.

Halfway across the clearing, as that thought flitted through her mind, a cacophony of men's shouts and clanging swords erupted behind her and to her right. Leaping forward, terrified now and no longer concerned about noise or stumbles, she flew into the woods on the far side of the clearing only to come to a dead halt when a large man clad in mail, with sword drawn, stepped in front of her.

"Let me pass," she said firmly. "Or do you make war on noblewomen?"

"Nay, lassie," he replied, stepping nearer and looking around, his sword still at the ready. "I dinna make war on women. But when this business be done, ye'll make a fine *fortune* o' war, I'm thinking. I'll just bind ye up and slip ye under a bush where ye can keep safe. Likely, ye'll thank me later for looking after ye."

Taking a step backward for every step he took toward her, Andrena exerted herself to look helpless. Looking frightened came easily, because she knew she had erred gravely by not returning to the tower the minute she'd sensed how many invaders there were. If this lout or another didn't kill her, Magnus surely would.

Her heart pounded. Sensible thought stopped in the face of the anger flowing at her from men at battle in the woods north and east of her. Keeping her gaze on the one in front of her, she tried to ignore the rest. Much of the noise to the north seemed to be moving downhill toward the tower. If she could elude this man—

He lurched toward her, holding his sword out away from him with one hand as if he took care not to injure her while he reached for her with the other. She was in the clearing again, if such a rocky place could be called so. When his free hand caught her left arm and gripped it hard, she had all she could do not to panic. But she knew she had to keep her head and move carefully to have any chance at all.

A few minutes earlier

The snail's pace of Pharlain's men in their ascent toward the pass had stirred Mag's suspicions. "What if this is a diversion?" he muttered to Andrew.

That the watchers they had set elsewhere had sounded no alarm could mean that Pharlain, anticipating a trap, had created his own diversion to keep the bulk of their army in one place until *all* of his men were in position to attack.

Andrew twisted around to look downhill toward the river.

"Devil take the man!" he exclaimed. "He's got lads creeping up *our* riverside from the loch. How the devil did he get them across?"

"In the night, perhaps," Mag said. "If they've lost their fear of boggarts..."

But Andrew wasn't listening. To one of his men nearby, he growled, "Take your lads to meet them. And sound the alarm only after ye do. The men we left on watch are too few to engage that lot—if the bastards havena killed them already."

Praying that everyone at the tower—Andrena in particular—had stayed inside and not ventured even as far as the yard, Mag got to his feet. Andrew had begun signaling orders to his other men and would likewise have orders for him.

Motion in a clearing on the hillside below diverted Mag's attention.

The moving figure was female, Andrena.

Thought stopped, and his emotions as he drew his sword left no room for such paltry stuff as surprise. Instead, fury exploded within him, a fury so powerful that it was all he could do to control himself long enough to glance back at Andrew and wonder if the man had been shouting orders to him.

Sounds of battle erupted below them.

"Andrew," Mag bellowed, pointing, "look yonder!"

"I see her, aye," Andrew replied. "Go on, then. Take your men down there. She may have sensed trouble, but dinna fear, lad. She'll be safe enough!"

"Not when *I* get my hands on her," Mag shouted back.

When Andrew—clearly daft—grinned in reply, Mag signaled to his own lads to follow him. Drawing both sword and dirk, he set off downhill through the woods at a lope, leaping shrubbery and skirting boulders in his path as he went.

An image flashed through his mind of Will, trying to fight off Pharlain's ambushers and falling, while Mag was also fighting and too far away to help him.

A brief glance northward showed Andrew signing to some men to stay where they were, to wait for Pharlain. Shouting at Mag to keep south of him, Andrew led his own men in a charge downhill along the river to engage the enemy there.

When he looked back at the clearing below, Andrena had vanished.

To his added horror, as he plunged down the hill at his perilous pace, men fighting the battle below spilled into the clearing from the woods south and west of it. Other men, waving swords and axes, charged uphill toward him and his men.

He was swiftly assessing their strength when Andrena stepped backward into the clearing again, nearly making him choke on his own indrawn breath.

A swordsman grabbed her and yanked her back among the trees.

Shouting for his men to run faster, Mag charged down toward the two, determined to wreak slaughter on anyone who got in his way.

⁓

Overwhelmed by the anger and fury she felt around her, Andrena barely noticed that the battle had enveloped her. Instead, when her captor pulled her back into the woods, she watched every move he made, determined to keep her wits about her.

"Ye're a fool," he snapped. Despite the clash and bellow of battle, she heard him clearly. "They be moving downhill as be natural," he added, leering. "We'll just hide ourselves here till it be safe. I'll look after ye."

"You are nowt but a coward," she said, jerking her left

arm from his grasp as her right hand sought the hilt of her knife. Slipping the sheath's leather thong off with her forefinger, she gripped the knife hilt firmly and raised her left hand as if to try to push him away. As Mag had predicted, the man's gaze followed that hand.

"What's this?" a voice cried from her right. While keeping her gaze on her opponent, peripherally she noted two men running toward them through the trees.

Fixing her gaze on her chief tormentor when he reached again to grab her, and ignoring the others, she slashed his outflung hand, drawing blood. When he cried out and looked in dismay at the injured hand, she darted out of reach behind the nearest tree. He shouted at her. The other two, evidently viewing her as easier prey than any fighting man in the clearing or elsewhere, moved in to help him.

Watching all three now, she kept stepping backward, threading her way between and behind trees as she did. Her every sense heightened until she felt strongly aware of obstacles behind and nearby her, almost as if she had eyes all around her head. Since she had no such extra eyes, when the first deep growl sounded at her heels, she thought vaguely that Old Bess must have followed her and did not look away from the men. A second growl snatched her gaze leftward, where a large wolf stood poised in a gap between shrubs, its teeth bared.

Another glided silently past her on the right and stopped.

She felt no fear but easily sensed sudden terror in the three rogues.

One of the three wildly waved his sword and shouted at the wolves. As he did, a third wolf leapt at him from the shrubbery.

Shrieking in terror as the beast's speed and weight took him to the ground, the man tried desperately to fight the wolf off. The third man raised his sword to attack. As he took a step forward, the surrounding woodland came alive with menacing barks, bays, and deep, threatening growls.

The swordsman turned to flee, his eyes wide with terror, only to see other men with swords drawn rushing toward him. Their leader was a veritable giant with fury in his golden eyes, who apparently lacked any sensible fear of wolves.

Andrena, seeing a warrior intercept Mag and engage Mag's sword with his own, felt her throat close in horror.

The wolf pack surrounded her. When she took an impulsive step toward the two fighting men, the leader of the pack growled menacingly ... at her.

Mag had seen the wolves and the men with Andrena before the warrior's sword clanged against his. Another swift glance, as he parried the blow, showed him that the wolves, although near the lass, seemed all to be facing away from her, threatening anyone who approached them.

He focused fully then on his opponent, and the sounds of battle retreated. Even so, he knew from experience that he would notice anything unusual or threatening. No sooner did he dispatch the man, though, than another took his place.

He realized that MacFarlan's men were fighting an enemy that seemed to increase each minute in size. Images flashed of Andrena and the wolves, but he ruthlessly suppressed them. If he fell in battle, he could do nowt for her.

A horn sounded. His flicking glance revealed a banner flying through the woods as its bearer raced toward him. The three bears' heads on that banner were instantly reassuring. The horn sounded again, and new men-at-arms entered the fray, all bearing the Galbraith badge. In the thick of them was the laird himself.

The battle ended quickly after that.

When Mag recognized the man he had just sent to ground as one of the thugs he'd seen menacing Andrena, new rage surged through him. Hauling the ruffian up with his left hand, he set himself to teach him another lesson with his right.

"Nay, lad."

Snapping his head around, he saw Andrew with a hand raised, palm outward, and determination in his eyes. Mag held his fist in midflight and let the ruffian fall.

"This lout threatened my lady wife, *your daughter*, my lord."

"Aye, well, the lass stands yonder, safe as a mouse in a mill," Andrew said, gesturing toward the woods.

Mag saw her then, standing calmly, alone. The wolves had vanished.

"I have me doots that that chap kens the lass for who she is," Andrew said. "Forbye, if he's a MacFarlan, he'd be one of me own. If so, he deserves the chance to submit to his true chief. Will ye do that, lad?" he asked of the shaken warrior.

The man dropped to a knee and bent his head to Andrew. "Aye, laird," he said gruffly. "I do yield and do swear my fealty to ye, right willingly."

Andrew glanced at Andrena. When she nodded, he looked around, his gaze taking in the defeated warriors and the Galbraith men standing guard over them. "What then of ye other MacFarlans?" he demanded. "D'ye swear to abandon the wicked usurper, Parlan, though he calls himself Pharlain after our own great ancestor? Will ye aid me in taking back me own lands and chiefdom from him?"

One by one, they submitted. After each man who did, Andrew looked to Andrena for a nod. Only once did she shake her head, whereupon, he said to the man, "I have given ye the chance to side with your true chief. But ye've lied to me. Sithee, lad, the true MacFarlan chief, whilst standing on the sacred ground of Tùr Meiloach, kens all that be in any MacFarlan mind and heart. What say ye now?"

Trembling, the man swore his allegiance again, fervently.

"Art sure this time?" Andrew asked him.

"Aye, laird, afore God and the true son o' the ancient Pharlain, I do swear."

Andrew looked at Andrena, who nodded.

"Verra well then, I accept your oath," Andrew said. "See that ye remember it, though. Do ye forget, I've a fine hanging tree to accommodate ye. We'll be going past it, so ye can take a close peek at it as we do—all of ye," he added, scanning the group. Then, to Mag, he said, "We'll collect this lot and take them to the tower. I warrant ye'll want to speak with your da, so—"

"With respect, sir," Mag said, shifting his gaze from Andrew to Andrena, "I would first see my lady wife safe within the tower."

"Aye, sure," Andrew said. "We'll no wait for ye then. But I did tell ye she would keep safe, did I no?"

"Mayhap she *was* safe then," Mag said, still eyeing her. "She is less so now."

Without another word to Andrew or a glance at his own father, Mag strode to his wife, scooped her up bodily, and carried her back into the woods.

               ⌐

For once, Andrena had no doubt about Mag's feelings. His fury flowed through him unchecked and radiated outward to engulf her in a wave that made the sensations she had felt during the battle seem insignificant by comparison.

She did not have to look at him to sense his wrath, which was just as well. She regretted his anger, was even a little afraid of it. But the regret and fear mixed oddly with grateful delight that he had at last opened himself to her emotionally.

"Prithee, sir, put me down," she murmured, laying a cheek against his chest and keeping her eyes hooded, lest he discern her relief. "I am perfectly able to walk."

"I know you can walk," he snapped, his fury with her increasing to rage that seared her senses. "You would be safer now had you *not* been so able and had stayed inside as I commanded you to do."

Had she sensed such rage in him before that day, it would doubtless have made her tremble in the same way that her father's merciless anger had affected Parlan's man. But she did not tremble. She said, "You are gey strong, sir, and can carry me easily. But what if we meet enemy stragglers here?"

"We won't," he said. "My father's men and Colquhoun's will have collected all in their path from the east or the south. I am the only one who need concern you."

"I do wish you would put me down."

"*If* I put you down," he said dourly, "it will be over my knee. Never before has anyone given me such a scare or so thoroughly deserved a hiding."

Moving her face closer to his neck so he would not see the least tiny twitch of a smile, if one stirred, she kept silent, letting his continued fury enfold her until she could trust her voice and demeanor. Now that the dam holding back his emotions had broken at last, she knew it would not easily reconstruct itself.

Drawing a breath, she relaxed in his arms and looked up to say, "You are gey fierce for one who has just done battle, sir. Mayhap you could put such energy to better use with a repentant wife than in skelping her. You do want many sons, I trow."

His pace checked slightly. But he remained silent long enough to make her wonder if she *could* ease his fury before he expressed it as he had threatened to do.

She sensed no cooling of his temper.

At last, he said, "Art truly repentant?"

Aware of his ability to read much in a voice or a facial expression, she said frankly, "I was wrong to come so far, Magnus. But I'd sensed danger approaching, and I was terrified for you and for Father. Tibby told me only that you and he had gone hunting with Colquhoun and some other men. Moreover, it is the anniversary of Mam's birth, the day of her celebration. So I thought what Tibby said was true."

His fury ebbed swiftly then, for he exhaled it in a rush of breath before his gaze collided with hers. To her surprise, she sensed guilt stirring in him.

About to step over a trickling rill, Mag stopped where

he was and set her on her feet. The forest floor there was flat under a thick carpet of pine duff.

Except for the trickling water, the only sound she heard was a distant horn blasting three notes.

"That is a Colquhoun signal," she murmured, eyeing him warily.

"Aye. 'Tis the one we agreed on to let men on the wall and ramparts know that all is well and that whoever approaches has prisoners."

"So our men knew there was to be battle." *Although*, she added silently to herself, *Pluff had not known.*

Mag said, "Malcolm and the captain of Andrew's guard knew. That is all."

Her thoughts raced on. "If we took many prisoners, those who swear fealty to Father may agree to testify for his grace against Parlan and the other conspirators."

"They may, aye."

As he spoke, he took off the leather baldric that held his sword and set it carefully atop a nearby flat rock. Turning back to face her, he unbuckled his belt.

A chill shot through her.

But he set the belt atop the sword, unkilted his plaid, and draped the fabric over an arm. Then he unfastened and took off the chain mail he wore over his sark. Setting the mail aside, too, he said, "Come here to me."

She went without hesitation, sighing deeply as his arms enfolded her and pulled her close enough to feel the length of his body against hers. His body warmth reassured her, although not as much as the warmth flowing to her from within him. She sensed his relief, lingering shreds of his anger, and remorse.

"Andrew did not tell me that he'd said we were going

hunting," he said. "I cannot blame him alone, though. I never stopped to consider what he might tell his people. And, knowing his penchant for telling tall tales, I should have. I also ought to have recalled your ability to sense danger and what *that* might lead to. I thought my command to stay inside would be enough to keep you out of danger."

"You did not consider all the possibilities before you acted, aye," she said. "But I can say naught to that, sir. It is a fault that people more often ascribe to me."

"You deserve that I should accuse you of it now," he said solemnly. "But for me to scold you for something that Andrew and I also did seems unfair."

Concealing a wry smile, she murmured to his chest, "And *most* unwise."

He set her back on her heels then but gave only a warning look in response to those words. Then, abruptly, he said, "How did you summon the wolves?"

"I did not," she said. "The first one was at my heels when it growled. The second appeared from the shrubbery. Then a third sprang at one of the men, knocking him and his sword to the ground. When the woods erupted in battle, other beasts gathered round me. I felt no fear, though, because the warriors kept well away from us. Once, when I tried to stir from where I stood, the wolves stopped me. Still, I was not afraid of them. 'Tis gey odd, is it not?"

"Just part of the magic of Tùr Meiloach's sacred grounds, I expect," he said, looking into her eyes. "Word of their behavior will spread fast, lass. As it should."

"Aye," she said, returning his gaze and licking suddenly dry lips. "Father will encourage the tales, especially if Parlan is not amongst the prisoners."

"We'd have heard straightaway if he was," he said.

He put a hand to her chin, tilting it up more. His fore-finger traced a line along her jawbone, then moved to touch her lips. "It did terrify me to see you in such danger, especially when that lout grabbed you and jerked you out of my sight."

"It made you gey angry with *me*, too," she said. "I ken that fine."

"Who let you outside the wall?"

She pressed her lips together, determined to protect Pluff. At last, she said, "Most of our men are accustomed to following my orders, sir."

"The men I've commanded follow mine, too," he said. "The only person who does not is my lady wife."

"Then I am the one you should punish if you punish anyone," she said. "I remembered what you told me, though," she added. "I had my wee knife, and I used it. When the man who grabbed me tried to do it again, I slashed his hand and got away by weaving amongst the trees. He tried to catch me, but the wolves came. By my troth, sir, I never felt as if I were in danger, except from you when I sensed how angry you were. I did know earlier that danger threatened you and my father. But when the battle broke out, I had every confidence that our people would win."

"They'd likely have lost had my father and Colquhoun not come to our aid."

"I told you that your father would come," she reminded him.

He bent nearer, his lips almost touching hers. "Would you argue with me, lassie mine? Or will you honor that so-enticing invitation you extended a while ago?"

⟳

Her beautiful eyes widened. "Here?"

"Aye, here, why not?" Mag demanded, giving her another stern look to see how she would react.

"But what if someone comes?"

"I will know if someone is coming. And, unless you have deceived me, you will sense any such approach before I do."

Her lips parted, and he brought his down on them possessively and hard. Thrusting his tongue into her mouth, possessing it, too, he caressed her back and breasts thoroughly before moving his fingers to her lacing. In scant moments, at his command, she stood naked before him while he spread his plaid on the ground.

Straightening slowly, he feasted his eyes on each tantalizingly soft curve. Then, in his own good time, he moved to her, picked her up again, and laid her on the bed of softly yielding, wool-sheeted pine duff.

"Now, *mo chridhe*," he murmured, stretching out beside her as he yanked his sark off over his head, "I'll teach you a few new lessons."

⟳

Andrena gasped at her body's response to his masterful tone, as if every nerve in her leaped unbidden to be possessed.

When she moved to return his caresses, he caught her hands and put them above her head, pinning them together under one of his. The warning look was back in his eyes, but the Galbraith twinkle replaced it before his lips claimed hers again. He eased one knee and then the other gently between her legs, used his free hand to see if she was ready for him, and thrust himself deep inside her.

For the first time, she could sense his every emotion. His passion for her filled him, but she sensed protectiveness, too. Just as he had taken care before he'd entered her, he now seemed to hold himself back. So, although he began to move more swiftly and powerfully, she knew he was restraining himself.

Using her gift to determine what movements of hers would excite him most, she exerted herself to stimulate him more, and then more yet. So intent was she on learning the extent to which she could influence his responses that when he moaned, her own response to it caught her off guard.

Heat surged through her, burning hottest at her core, until in a pulsing climax, she reached the dizzying heights that he had revealed to her at Inch Galbraith and cried out just as she had then. His reactions were noisier, too, but she didn't care. What was happening was too intense, too incredible, too sensually explosive for her to care about noise or anything else.

Epilogue ─────────────────

Two months later

He had wanted to run, but the plain fact was that he was too exhausted. His head ached, and the sword cut in his forearm, where his chain-mail sleeve failed to meet his glove, still stung. And wasn't it just like his lass to be gone when he wanted her, rather than awaiting him at home, where a wife ought to be?

That he'd had to ask Muriella where Andrena was had delayed him, too. Murie had wanted to hear about his time away and had been disappointed when he'd insisted on finding Andrena first.

He had not stayed on the path they'd followed the first time, to reach her spear-fishing rock, but had angled uphill before reaching the burn, aiming to come out above the jutting granite slab and its nearby boulders. That way he'd get a look at it from the side opposite the slope he'd climbed that day to look southward.

Then he saw her, and his heart began to pound, banishing his exhaustion.

She sat below at the edge of the rock slab, well to his right and looking away from him. She had rucked her skirts halfway up her thighs, providing a fine view of her slender, shapely legs while she dangled her bare feet in the water. Her head was bereft of veil or coif, her tawny plaits hanging down her back to her waist, one threatening to slip over her shoulder. She had no spear in hand today. If she'd brought the dirk, as Murie had told him, she had already stowed it in her cache.

Surely, she had sensed his approach. Even had she been lost in thought, she ought to sense his presence now. Sakes, the one unusual thing that she *had* done was to tell Muriella where she meant to go. Cryptically, aye, but—

Andrena turned her head and looked right at him. Smiling, she said, "Are you coming down here, or do you mean to stand gawking at me until suppertime?"

"I like gawking at you. How long have you known I was here?"

"I knew you were coming home and this morning that you were close. But I wanted to meet you alone, not with your men or others. Murie told you I was here?"

"She said you had gone to stow your dirk in your cache," he said, making his way quickly down the slope.

"I knew you would remember where it was. Come and sit. You look tired."

"Mayhap I do, but I no longer feel tired. It is good to see you, *mo chridhe*. Are you not going to welcome me as a wife should properly greet her husband?"

"Nay, for I want to hear everything that happened, and I ken fine that if I kiss you and feel your arms around me, I will learn naught. You have been a gey long time from home, sir. Explain yourself. We did hear of a battle near Perth and that rebels had taken Stirling, but no more. Still, I trust you were in time to warn Jamie."

"We were, aye," he said, taking a seat near her where he could lean against one of the boulders. He wanted to take her in his arms. Sakes, he wanted to do more than that. He would be talking about his journey for days to come, but he knew that he'd be wise to give her the gist of it now. She had played an early part in it all and deserved to know its outcome before everyone else did.

"Parliament met on the twelfth of March, as you know," he said. "We nearly did not reach Jamie in time, because although we did delay Pharlain and reduce his own force significantly, he and the other rebel lairds had a head start on us. Also, we had to skirt Murdoch's castle in Doune, where the rebels were gathering."

"One of Parlan's men told you they would go there, aye," she said. "But you did get to Perth in time."

"In time, aye, but barely. Sithee, this meeting of Parliament had lasted days. Before Jamie became King, meetings lasted an afternoon or a day. But he had much to discuss, including one gey controversial notion. To aid him in establishing his rule of law, he wants to appoint advocates for the poor without cost, to plead their cases in his courts. There was long discussion and much dissent, because not one lord or anyone else had ever heard of such a thing. But, in the end, Jamie prevailed."

"When did you and Ian, and the others, get there?"

"Late on the evening of the eighth day, only a day before the rebels, who had waited near Doune for others besides Pharlain. Thanks to the men from Arrochar who yielded to your father, we had gathered enough evidence and testimony for Jamie's needs. But the rebels had a huge army, including Highlanders, Islesmen, most of Lennox's Lomondside lairds, as well as Bishop Finlay of

Argyll and a host of Campbell-MacGregors, Grahams, and others."

"Still, his grace had allies of his own."

"Aye, sure, the Douglas, Scotts, Angus, the Bishop of St. Andrews, Lauder, and others. All of them had followed his command, as we did, and brought small tails of men with them. Only his cousin Alex Stewart, who is Lord of the North and Earl of Mar, ignored the royal restrictions on noblemen's tails. Sithee, Alex sees himself as Jamie's equal, but his refusal turned out to be a good thing, because he is also one of the few Stewarts loyal to his grace. So, it was Alex who took Stirling Castle and Stirling Bridge back from the rebels. He did it with a ruse, which impressed our friend Ian Colquhoun. Alex also arrested Murdoch and his son, Lord Alexander Stewart. There *was* great battle, though, before we defeated them all."

"Did Murdoch lead the rebels?"

"Nay, Lord Alexander did. Sithee, their plan was to cut Jamie off from his allies in the south, kill him, hold Stirling—castle and bridge—and seize Dumbarton. On Jamie's death, Murdoch was to become King of Scots, and Lord Walter Stewart was to become Governor of the Realm."

"Murdoch's reign would not have lasted long then, I'd wager."

"I agree, and so does Jamie. Walter would likely have eliminated Murdoch at the first opportunity and taken the throne. But the possibility that either Murdoch or Walter will become King of Scots no longer exists."

"They are both dead, then."

"Aye, but Jamie adjourned Parliament because of the rebellion."

"Adjourned?"

"The lords of Parliament had the same reaction, since no King of Scots had done that before. But Jamie said that he still had work for this Parliament to do and that no one could attend to business with a rebellion going on. So, they reconvened just days ago in the great hall at Stirling Castle. Jamie and others presented their case there against Murdoch, Lennox, Lord Walter Stewart, and his brother, Lord Alexander. When the lords of Parliament found them all guilty of high treason, Jamie ordered Walter beheaded straightaway, the others the following morning."

"But not James Mòr Stewart," Andrena said thoughtfully. "One wonders how he came to be so different from the other Stewarts of Albany."

"Apparently *not* so different after all," Mag said grimly.

~

Andrena stared at him with instant concern for the bleakness she sensed in him. "What is it, sir? Not Ian or Colquhoun, I hope. What happened?"

"More than a sennight before the rebels gathered near Doune, Murdoch and Lennox arrived in Perth, hoping to look innocent," he said. "But when we met the rebels in battle, Lord Alexander Stewart was leading them with James Mòr at his side. By my troth, lass, James Mòr rode right at Jamie and tried to murder him."

"Jamie led his own army, then."

"Aye, sure, he did. The man is an expert horseman and a veritable fiend with a sword in hand. He took three men down by himself and was lunging for James Mòr when the royal charger slipped and fell with him."

Andrena gasped. "Did you see that?"

"I did, for I was riding close behind him. I'd reined toward James Mòr, but when I saw the King fall, I rode up to him instead, to keep others away whilst he remounted. I expected him to blame me for letting James Mòr get away, but..."

"Surely not!" she exclaimed, ignoring the strange uncertainty, even sadness, that she felt emanating from him then.

"Nay," Mag said with an astonishingly sheepish look. "He knighted me, lass. Ye'll be Lady Galbraith-MacFarlan now, I fear."

"*Both* names?"

"Aye, sure, and by his grace's command, for he dubbed me so, with both."

"Does my father know that yet?"

"Nay, it will be a wee surprise for Andrew. But I trow he won't hold it against me. I came to find you before I told anyone else, *mo chridhe*. Do I get nae reward for such thoughtfulness?"

"There is doubtless much more that you've not told me," she said. "What of your brother Patrick? If you saw James Mòr, did you see Patrick with him?"

He hesitated, his sadness and disappointment making his answer for him. Then he said, "He was there, aye, and Pharlain escaped during the battle. But I can tell you the rest later. There is nowt to dread for anyone close to you or your family. Moreover, my father, Colquhoun, Ian, and I all survived without serious injury."

"But there is something more that you fear will trouble me," she said.

"I can see that this *gift* of yours is going to cause trouble," he muttered.

She was silent.

"Very well, I told you that James Mòr, Patrick, and Pharlain escaped. What I did not tell you is that they and their men captured Dumbarton. Ian's cousin, Gregor Colquhoun, is dead, and Ian has returned to Stirling to take the news to Jamie."

She sensed there was more and that he would somehow be much involved in whatever was to come. But if the royal burgh and castle of Dumbarton were in rebel hands, she also knew that what he needed most right then was a welcoming kiss and loving attention from a wife grateful beyond words for his safe return.

Accordingly, she scooted close to him, dried her feet with the hem of her skirt, and let him pull her into his arms.

"Ah, lass," he said, bending to possess her lips with his own.

Soon his plaid was off and spread beneath them, and he was feasting himself on her eager body, caressing all of it that he could reach, unlacing her and baring her breasts to his impatient hands and lips.

"How I have missed you, my love," she murmured, when one of his hands moved to touch her below.

"It is good for a wife to miss her husband," he said with a smile in his voice. "Show me how much you have missed me, *mo chridhe*."

Since she could detect every change of feeling in him now, she quickly discovered that she could stir him to a certain point and then try something else. Such wee frustrations as these tactics caused seemed to enflame his senses.

Recalling next how his lips and tongue had driven her

nearly mad at times, she tried similar techniques on him, with exceptionally satisfactory results.

"Lass, lass," he said breathlessly, "I can see that there are benefits to your gift, but we *must* find a more comfortable place."

"But I don't want to stop," she said. "Come inside me now, love."

Mag needed no further invitation than that, nor would he...ever.

Dear Reader,

I hope you have enjoyed *The Laird's Choice*, the first book of my new "Lairds of the Loch" trilogy. Ideas for this book began to flow when I found myself eyeing a particular area of the western Highlands between Loch Lomond and Loch Long, and studying the clans there. I wanted something different that would retain the mystical quality of the Highlands but explore a few "gifts" that many of us still have today, and perhaps exaggerate them into protective abilities or gifts in my characters.

I knew that I wanted my heroines to be part of a feuding clan. Choosing the ancient MacFarlanes was easy, because not only are they a historically wild and woolly bunch (and one of my favorite and most supportive clans at Scottish games), but they also controlled a particularly important gateway to the western Highlands.

I also soon realized that my MacFarlan characters would need to live in an area that would provide some sort of protection from the villain who usurped Andrew MacFarlan's chiefdom and primary estates. The landscape offered rivers and mountains, but the MacFarlans needed a little more help than that.

In looking for things that would stir the creative juices, I began rereading some of my favorite ancient myths, and when I reached the story of Camilla, the opening for *The Laird's Choice* was born, and so was Andrena's special connection to wolves. The rest came mostly from the author's always inventive imagination.

As for elements that are true or definitely Scottish, until the nineteenth century, Clan MacFarlan(e) was called Clan Farlan. The tale of the horseshoed woman is true. And just as a vocabulary note, giving someone the "dichens" is an ancient Scottish phrase and likely ended up being "giving one the dickens" today.

A note about Clan Galbraith: Authority George Eyre-Todd does not include them as a clan in his *Highland Clans of Scotland: Their History and Traditions* (New York, 1923) except as a sept of Clan Farlan (vol. 1) or of Clan Donald (vol. 2). However, Sir Iain Moncrieffe of that Ilk, erstwhile Albany Herald of Scotland, does include them as an independent clan in *The Highland Clans* (Bramhill House edition, New York, 1977).

Also, for those who might question the Galbraith bears' heads (many sources do say they are boars' heads), Moncrieffe includes a picture of their crest, which clearly shows a muzzled bear, not a boar. Campbells do have a boar's head.

According to online sources and specifically, *The History of the Rosary by Fr. William Saunders* (http://www .ewtn.com/library/answers/rosaryhs.htm), the origins of Lady Aubrey's prayer beads are ancient but rather vague. The use of prayer beads and multiple recitations of short prayers to aid meditation stems from the earliest days of the Church, with roots in pre-Christian times. During the Middle Ages, the devout used such strings of beads—known as Paternosters, from the Latin for Our Father—to count their "Our Fathers" and "Hail Marys." The structure of the rosary itself evolved gradually between the twelfth and fifteenth centuries.

By most accounts, Jamie was an English captive for nineteen years, although the dates given by his biographers vary considerably. If he was captured in 1403, the earliest date I've seen (and the year in which I set *Highland Lover*), his release at Easter in 1424 gives him twenty-one years. James himself wrote that they captured him in 1405, which does add up to nineteen years by Easter 1424, the date on which nearly all accounts and the records agree. As I noted in *Highland Lover*, the entry for James I of Scotland in the English *Dictionary of National Biography* makes a logical argument for his capture in 1406 but undermines that argument by declaring that the capture could not have come earlier due to a truce then in force between England and Scotland (a truce we know Henry IV of England broke regularly).

This sort of stuff is great fun for any author of historical fiction, because gaps, questionable data, and historical mysteries provide free flow for one's creative juices and energy for the gray cells to leap hither and yon.

I would like to extend special thanks to Donal MacRae for his help in naming Tùr Meiloach and explaining about its giants, and to Michael MacFarlane, Matthew Miller (California Commissioner for The International Clan MacFarlane Society, Ltd.), and everyone who contributed to www.clanmacfarlane.org for their valuable assistance, helpful commentary, and excellent resources.

As always, I also thank my wonderful agents, Lucy Childs and Aaron Priest, Senior Editor Selina McLemore, Senior Managing Editor Bob Castillo, master copyeditor Sean Devlin, my publicist Jennifer Reese, Art Director Diane Luger, cover artist Larry Rostant, Editorial Director Amy Pierpont, Vice President and Editor in Chief Beth de Guzman, and everyone else at Hachette Book Group's Grand Central Publishing/Forever who contributed to this book.

If you enjoyed *The Laird's Choice*, please look for Book 2 of Lairds of the Loch. *The Knight's Temptress*, in June 2013. Meantime, Suas Alba!

Sincerely,

Amanda Scott

www.amandascottauthor.com

When Lady Lina MacFarlan
is captured by her father's
sworn enemy, it's up to roguish
royal warrior Sir Ian Colquhoun
to save her.
But can anyone save Ian from his
all-consuming desire to make the
lovely Lina his own?

Turn this page for a preview of

The Knight's Temptress

Available in June 2013

Chapter 1 —————————————————

Scotland, Loch Lomond, Summer 1425

Lizzie, no! Come back!"

Dismayed to see her young companion spur the bay gelding she rode to a gallop and rapidly disappear southward—the opposite direction from the way they were supposed to turn when the Glen Fruin path met the one along Loch Lomond's southwestern shore—eighteen-year-old Lachina MacFarlan gritted her teeth, warned herself to remain calm, and urged her own dun-colored horse to a faster pace.

A male voice from behind and above her on the glen path shouted, "Lady Lina, wait!"

Glancing back at the gillie who followed her, Lina did not reply or slow her mount. Nor did she give more than fleeting thought to the likely reaction her good-brother, Sir Magnus Galbraith-MacFarlan, would have when he heard—as he certainly would—that his little sister had broken her word yet again.

Although Magnus was the largest man Lina knew—or had ever seen, for that matter—she did not fear his wrath. For one thing, he and his wife—Lina's older sister

Andrena—were visiting Mag's sister Wilhelmina and her husband, in Ayrshire. For another, Lina knew that Mag was astute enough to deduce that the blame for this mischief, if he learned of it, lay entirely with the irrepressible Lizzie.

Reaching the shore path, Lina scarcely heeded the sparkling blue expanse of the splendid loch spread before her but deftly turned the dun gelding onto the main track and felt mixed relief and exasperation when she saw Lizzie ahead of her again.

The slim, fourteen-year-old scapegrace rode as if she were part of the horse, Lina thought with a touch of envy. She was a competent horsewoman, but Lizzie was spectacular, especially riding astride in her mossy-green cloak with her mass of long, curly red hair—confined only by a white ribbon at the nape of her neck—billowing behind her in a great cloud of light red and sunny, gilding highlights.

Lina's own honey-gold hair lay smoothly coiled against the back of her head under a white veil held in place with a narrow band that she had embroidered with pink roses. Her hooded cloak was of fine gray wool that her sister Muriella had spun from their own lambs' wool and that Lina had woven into fabric.

The day was cool, thanks to the chilly breeze blowing off of Ben Lomond, just northeast of them and still snow-capped. The breeze rippled the waters of the loch, but the sun was shining in a clear sky. While riding down the glen, had Lizzie not been riding ahead of her, eager to reach the loch, Lachina might have paused to doff her cloak. Now, in the chilly breeze, she was glad she had not.

Before seeing Lizzie turn south, she had assumed that

the younger girl might ride north to the cluster of cottages, or clachan, on the west shore of the loch, opposite her father's tower on the islet known as Inch Galbraith. Lizzie had said earlier that she wanted to do so and had paid no heed when Lina had suggested that such a distance might mean they would worry Lizzie's aunt, the lady Margaret Galbraith of Bannachra Tower. The tower, an ancient Galbraith possession, stood on a rise above Fruin Water, a mile and a half up the glen.

That Lizzie had turned southward instead meant that she'd had a destination other than the clachan in mind all along. The ever-present, self-critical voice in Lina's head suggested that she ought to have guessed that the younger girl was up to mischief, that she'd seen enough of Lizzie in the past few days to be aware of the lengths to which she would go to get her own way. Lina also knew that Lizzie must have heard her shout, although Lizzie had not paused or looked back.

Hoping that no one else would hear her, Lina shouted again, "Lizzie, stop!"

But Lizzie pounded on, making Lina wish that Sir Magnus were with them, because he would doubtless...

That thought slid away of its own accord. Useless to speculate about what anyone might do who was miles away. Moreover, had Mag or the Laird of Galbraith been with them, Lizzie would not have dared to ride on ahead as she had.

Lina pressed her lips together. No use to repine about what Lizzie was doing, either, because repining would do naught to stop her. Had she been Lina's younger sister, Muriella, Lina would have reined in and waited for her to come to her senses.

But the only traits that Lizzie and Murie shared were their occasional lapses of good judgment and a desire—common to many people of their age and experience—to enjoy more freedom than they had and to make their own decisions.

Murie could also take the bit between her teeth from time to time, but she would not go dashing off into unknown territory, as Lizzie was doing—territory unknown to Lina, at all events. Lizzie was a mystery to her in other ways, too, because they scarcely knew each another. Although Magnus and Andrena had been married for nearly six months, Lina had known Lizzie for only six days.

"Lady Lina, dinna ride any further! Ye mun turn back!"

Realizing that while she was lost in thought, the gillie had closed the distance between them, Lina glanced back at him and said, "I think Lady Elizabeth wants to see if Duchess Isabella's banner flies over Inchmurrin yet, Peter. She was with me when the laird told us that his grace, the King, had given her permission to return."

"We'd ha' heard summat more if the duchess were coming so soon, m'lady."

"Aye, perhaps, but we cannot just turn back and abandon her ladyship."

"But the pair o' ye mustna ride south!" Peter exclaimed. "There be danger there. The rebels! The laird gave strict orders about that. Ye ken fine that he did."

Lina did know about those orders, because she had heard the Laird of Galbraith issue them herself, and so had Lizzie. But Galbraith had issued a number of orders before departing the day before, without much more explanation than to say he was responding to a summons from the Colquhouns of Dunglass Castle, which lay some ten miles south of Loch Lomond, on the river Clyde near Glasgow.

Suppressing a sigh, Lina said, "We must catch up with her ladyship, Peter." Leaning forward, she urged her mount to a faster pace. Thickets of shrubbery and copses of trees dotted the loch shore and the hillside above them, but denser woodland lay ahead, and the track disappeared into it. Surely, Lizzie would not...

"That hibbertie-skippertie lass be a-heading right into them woods, m'lady!"

"I can see her, Peter," Lina called back to him. "Just ride, and mind your tongue when you speak of the lady Elizabeth!"

"'Tis what Sir Mag calls her," Peter said. "I ken fine that I should not, but—"

Evidently deciding that he had said enough, he broke off.

Having turned her head slightly when he'd begun talking again, Lina turned back to see that Lizzie was slowing her mount. Perhaps, she'd come to her senses. Even as the thought flitted through her mind, a sense of unease stirred.

The woods ahead seemed suddenly and ominously to darken.

"Was that not a grand gallop?" Lizzie called out cheerfully as Lina and Peter drew near and slowed their mounts.

"What you want, my sweet, is a taste of your brother's temper," Lachina said evenly, reining in some yards away and keeping her eyes on the woods, aware that her unease was increasing. "What were you thinking to hare off like that?"

Lizzie shot a glance at Peter and then looked back at Lina with one eyebrow raised before saying, "Even Mag would not scold me in front of a gillie, Lina."

"You chose the setting," Lina said. "And you might at least have considered the fact that your father will likely blame me if he learns about this, since I am four years older than you are."

"Nay, then, he will not. If he were here, he would scold, to be sure. But he is not here. And by the time he comes home again, everyone else who may learn of it will have forgotten it. So, you need not fret or fratch with me, Lina. By my troth, I want only to see if the Duchess of Albany is in residence yet."

"We can see Inchmurrin's towers from here, Lizzie. No banner flies above them, let alone a ducal one. Moreover, we are disobeying your father's orders. Do you truly believe that he will not hear about what we have done?"

Lizzie shrugged. "Peter is *your* gillie, Lina. He will not carry tales about me to my father. Will you, Peter?" she added, flashing her beautiful smile at him.

"It will not matter who tells him," Lina said.

"No one will, and we are quite near Balloch now. Since the duchess inherited all of her father's properties, and Balloch is yet another of them—"

"The King is unlikely to let her keep all of the Earl of Lennox's properties," Lina said, trying to ignore her growing sense of urgency and at least *sound* patient. "Balloch was, after all, a royal estate before the first Duke of Albany gifted it to her father when Isabella married Albany's son. In any event, we are turning back."

"But I have never seen a duchess," Lizzie said. "Nor have I—"

"Listen, m'lady!" Peter interjected.

Lina heard immediately what he had heard and wished that she had been born with her older sister's ability to sense when others were near her in the woods.

"Horsemen," she said, looking at Peter, who nodded.

"Armed men," he added knowingly. "Ye can hear weapons clanking, and they dinna be trying tae keep silent, neither."

"Then likely they are royal men-at-arms, escorting the duchess," Lizzie said.

"Or rebel forces in such numbers as to fear no one," Lina replied, feeling in her bones that that was more likely than the duchess.

"It could as easily be my father, returning from Dunglass," Lizzie said.

"I hope it is," Lina said roundly. "You will be well served if he finds us here, will you not?"

Lizzie grimaced.

Peter said, "We mun turn back, m'lady. If we set our horses tae a gallop—"

"They will give chase," she said flatly. "We cannot outrun them, Peter. Our horses are not fresh, and those others may be."

"We are noblewomen," Lizzie said, with a toss of her head. "No one will dare to harm us."

Lina nearly contradicted her, but a sixth sense told her that she would be wiser to let Lizzie believe what she wanted to believe.

Instead, Lina met Peter's worried gaze and said, "Ride into that copse above us yonder, Peter, and quickly. They won't hear just one horseman on that grassy hillside, but they would certainly hear three of us. Nay, do not waste time arguing," she added firmly. "The copse is dense enough to conceal you and your horse, and they have not yet seen us. If aught goes amiss, you must ride for help. Lizzie is right, though. They are unlikely to interfere with us, whoever they are."

"But, m'lady—"

"Go," Lina said. "If they are enemies, you may be our only hope of rescue."

Without another word, Peter wrenched his horse's head toward the hillside and spurred hard, disappearing amid the trees there just as Lina caught sight through the woodland foliage of the first mounted riders ahead on the path.

"Don't you dare look at that copse again, Lizzie Galbraith," she said fiercely, trying to think. "That is a Stewart banner they fly, but it is *not* a royal one."

"Oh, Lina, what have I done?" Biting her lip, Lizzie fell silent.

Minutes later, rebel men-at-arms surrounded them.

Dunglass Castle, that afternoon

"We must plan any attack on Dumbarton for well after midnight, when they'll least expect it," eighteen-year-old Adam Colquhoun said eagerly. "We should be able to secure the town, Ian, but I cannot think how we'll get up that devilish rock to win back the castle. It's two hundred feet high!"

Sir Ian Colquhoun smiled but shook his head at his younger brother, whose dark hair and light-blue eyes mirrored Ian's own. "We'll think of a way, lad. In troth, my most successful gambits have been carried out in broad daylight," he added lightly, letting his gaze drift from Adam to the two older men seated at the high table with them. The rest of the cavernous great hall was empty.

"In broad daylight!" Adam exclaimed. "But—"

"Hush now, Adam," the Laird of Colquhoun interjected. "Ye've put your finger on the most vexing obstacle to retaking Dumbarton from James Mòr Stewart and his nest of villains, but let Ian have his say. After all, he's the one his grace has ordered to reclaim the royal burgh and castle, and return them to royal custody."

Smiling this time at his father, Ian said, "Jamie did order me to do it, aye, sir, but I'll expect to draw considerably on your wisdom. And that of Sir Arthur," he added, looking at the Laird of Galbraith, who acknowledged his words with a dignified nod. "Sithee, the enemy is *much* stronger than we are," Ian went on. "So, we must avoid head-on battle, and we don't know who amongst the Loch Lomond lairds and their tenantry is truly with us and who is not, whatever they may tell us."

Galbraith said, "I own, lad, I'm of a mixed mind, myself, about this venture. Ye ken fine that my son Patrick has long served James Mòr and therefore stands now against the King, whilst Rory, my heir, serves the Duchess of Albany. And she has even more reason than James Mòr does to loathe the King, because Jamie beheaded not only her husband and two of her three sons but also her eighty-year-old father."

"True, sir," Ian said. "But you do have one son who is definitely loyal to Jamie. So I'm hoping that, even if you believe that you cannot actively support us, you will do nowt to prevent our success."

"My view being still that the King is chief of chiefs, I can make you that promise, aye," Galbraith said. "Forbye, I'm thinking that your own sire may have qualms about this business, too, Ian. He generally puts peace above all else, does he not?" Shifting his gaze to Colquhoun, he added gently, "What say you, Humphrey? Art willing to wage war to reclaim Dumbarton?"

Colquhoun shrugged. "I'm much *less* willing to let James Mòr Stewart seize control of the river that flows by this castle, not to mention the entire Firth of Clyde," he said. "He would then control the route from here to Glasgow and to the sea."

"He has apparently made no such attempt yet," Galbraith pointed out.

"Only because he lacks enough men able to manage Dumbarton's boats against others on the river and the firth," Colquhoun said. "Forbye, the boatmen they do have are nearly all lads who served under our own Gregor Colquhoun and swore fealty to James Mòr only to preserve their own hides after he'd murdered Gregor and seized Dumbarton."

"That is also true," Ian said, no longer smiling. "And the first thing that I shall do when I have reclaimed Dumbarton is to hang any man who served my cousin Gregor whilst he was captain of the guard there but refuses to aid me."

"And, may heaven preserve us, I'll help you do it," declared a deep voice from the rear of the hall.

Recognizing that voice, Ian leaped to his feet. "Maggy, you're back! I expected you'd be gone for a fortnight or more, and nobbut six days have passed since you left us. You did not bring the lady Dree back here, too, did you?"

"Andrena is content for the nonce with my sister Mina," Sir Magnus said as he strode to the dais. Shaking Ian's hand, he said, "You said you were summoning local lairds and knights to a meeting here, so I expected to see a number of men."

"Sakes, I sent messages out only three days ago, but Rob MacAulay will be here, and at least one or two Buchanans will come, if only to see what we're up to. Jamie told me we might count on a few Border lords to aid us, as well."

Mag nodded, then turned to shake hands with Colquhoun and Adam, leaving his father for last. Galbraith was standing when Mag moved to greet him, and clapped him on the back.

"'Tis good to see ye, lad," he said. "We've a dilemma here, I can tell ye."

"I know that Jamie wants Ian to take back Dumbarton, sir," Mag said. "I know, too, that our Patrick is there with James Mòr. But the pair of them chose their road, and if Patrick knew that James Mòr was of a mind to act against the King, I ken fine that he said nowt of it to you. Moreover, Rory sets us another dilemma."

"He is my heir," Galbraith said. "But at present, his loyalties are divided between Clan Galbraith and what remains of the House of Albany."

"Which is nobbut the Duchess of Albany," Mag said.

When Galbraith nodded, Mag turned back to Ian and said, "What do you hope to accomplish with your meeting? From all that I've heard and was able to see for myself on my journey to the Ayrshire coast and back, James Mòr controls the royal burgh, its harbor, and the castle. His position must be well-nigh impregnable."

"There is a way to undo that," Ian said confidently. "We must simply figure out what it is. Forbye, before we can act, we must know more. But I do have some ideas to put before you all, so that we can discuss them."

Accordingly, the men put their heads together and talked over Ian's ideas, dismissing several out of hand as being typical of Ian, who the others all knew was a notorious risk-taker. They deemed three, possibly four, of his ideas sufficiently plausible to warrant further discussion. They were still talking of how they might best broach those possibilities to the others who would join them, when one of the Colquhoun men-at-arms entered with a younger lad and said to Colquhoun, "Forgive us, laird, but this lad begs urgent speech wi' ye."

Ian did not recognize the newcomer, but Mag leaped up, exclaiming, "Peter! What brings you here, lad? What's amiss?"

Noting the dismay on the lad Peter's face, Ian realized that he had not expected Magnus to be there. But Peter recovered swiftly, saying, "'Tis glad I am tae see ye, sir. This were the nearest place I knew tae come. But..."

When he hesitated, Ian said impatiently, "What is it? Who are you?"

"I be Peter Wylie, Sir Ian, from Tùr Meiloach. But mayhap I should speak privately with Sir Magnus."

"Tell us, lad, whatever it is," Mag said. "We're all friends here."

"It be their ladyships, sir," Peter said, darting a glance at Galbraith.

"Which ladyships?" Ian demanded, thus recalling the lad's gaze to himself.

Swallowing visibly, Peter glanced at Galbraith again

and then back at Mag before he met Ian's gaze and said, "The ladies Elizabeth Galbraith and Lachina MacFarlan, sir. They rode too near the woods at the south end o' Loch Lomond, and rebels seized them."

"The devil they did!" Ian exclaimed.

"Where were you, Peter?" Mag asked ominously.

Looking utterly wretched but speaking nonetheless firmly, Peter said, "See you, sir, we were to ride only to the loch, but the lady Elizabeth wanted to see if the duchess had arrived at Inchmurrin yet. Lady Lina shouted for her to—"

Noting Mag's frown, Ian said hastily, "We all know the lady Elizabeth, Peter. But you fail to answer Sir Magnus's question. If you were with them…"

More wretchedly than ever, Peter chose to address a point midway between Ian and Mag, saying, "See you, we heard men and horses ahead in the woods, and the lady Lachina ordered me to take cover, lest they be enemies."

"Then why not all take cover?" Galbraith asked grimly.

"She said we must not, that they'd hear three horses but mayhap not hear just one. And, by my troth, laird, them villains never even glanced my way. They had eyes only for their ladyships. Come to that, they turned straightaway back into the woods, too, so I followed them."

"What else did you see?" Mag asked. "Did they harm them?"

"I saw nowt except that they went to Dumbarton. When we reached the flats before the castle rock, I stayed in the woods, but they rode right up that steep track to the castle."

"This changes things," Ian said, looking at the other four men.

"It does, aye," Mag agreed, giving Ian a measuring look.

"We need more information and straightaway," Ian said. "You and I—"

"Nay, lad, I'm for Ayrshire again," Mag said.

"For Ayrshire!" Ian and Galbraith exclaimed in one voice. Glancing apologetically at Galbraith, Ian said, "Lizzie's *your* sister, Mag. Moreover, you and I can sneak over there tonight…"

But Mag was shaking his head, and Ian noted the twinkle in his eye before Mag said, "You're daft if you think that I'm likely to sneak anywhere, lad. I'm too big for sneaking about. And there's a thing I'm guessing that you don't know or have never credited if you do know. That is that my Andrena shares so strong a bond with her sisters that each knows when one of the others is in trouble. If she is not already on her way back here, I'll be much amazed."

"But surely, your good-brother would not allow her—"

"She will come despite him," Mag said. "Forbye, just before I left, she informed me that I'm soon to become a father. She didn't tell me before, because she knew I wanted her to meet Mina. The only thing that might prevent her from leaving at once is that she will be sure that I'll come for her. So I must." He shifted his gaze next to his father. "You will recall, sir, that young Muriella is also at Bannachra. If my aunt Margaret and the lady Aubrey have not locked her up or tied her down, she, too, will be seeking a way to learn what has happened to Lina."

"I'll send someone," Galbraith said. "You go on and collect Andrena. We'll see to things here. If Patrick has allowed anything to happen to Lizzie—"

"He won't allow that, sir," Mag said.

But Ian could tell that Mag was not as sure of that as he sounded, and a glance at Galbraith told him that he wasn't sure about Patrick either.

Firmly, Ian said, "I'll find out what's going on there, Mag."

"I know you will."

~

Dumbarton Castle, that night

"Do you think we'll be able to sleep on these pallets, Lina?" Lizzie asked.

"Eventually, aye," Lachina said.

"Well, I'd sleep better if I were warmer. I wish someone had built us a fire on that wee hearth or brought us some proper blankets, not to mention food."

"I don't care about food yet. I'm just surprised that no one has been near us since they put us here, and I'm glad that they did leave that pitcher of water." She was also glad that Lizzie had surprised her by not complaining about their situation.

The younger girl seemed to have little fear and almost to treat the whole affair as an adventure. As a result, Lina's initial terror, when the men had informed them that they were to be "guests" at Dumbarton Castle, had faded to plain fear and trepidation. She hoped that Peter had escaped but feared he would ride all the way home to Tùr Meiloach and her father, Andrew Dubh, to seek help. He knew no one at Bannachra, and since the lady Margaret had never married...

A light rap at the door ended that train of thought, and

she turned to see the door open to reveal two men, a short, stocky one in what she assumed to be the attire of the castle servants and the other much more ill-kempt with shaggy hair hanging over his face and his clothing in tatters. The latter carried a hodful of peat topped with straw, which he took to the hearth. While the first man stood silently by the door, the hod-carrier knelt, set down his load, extracted a tinderbox from a pocket amid the tatters, and muttered, "We thought ye'd like a fire, the pair o' ye."

"Thank you," Lina said with sincerity.

"'Tis nowt," the man said. Deftly arranging peat and straw, he dealt as deftly with lighting it, then stood and turned away, evidently confident that it would burn.

"Some'un comes," the man at the door murmured.

The shaggy man looked right at Lina then, his light-blue gaze holding her startled one with ease. "Dinna squeak, lass. Just tell me, ha' they harmed ye?"

"No," she said. "But—"

A quick shake of his head silenced her, and he moved toward the door. Just then, a tall figure appeared behind the silent guard, and Lizzie shrieked, "Patrick!"

Terrified that Lizzie might also have recognized the shaggy man as Sir Ian Colquhoun, and betray him to her brother, Lina was grateful to see the other two men slip quickly past him and away down the stairs.

THE DISH

Where authors give you the inside scoop!

From the desk of Katie Lane

Dear Reader,

Have you ever pulled up to a stoplight and looked over to see the person in the car next to you singing like they're auditioning for *American Idol*? They're boppin' their head and thumpin' the steering wheel like some crazy loon. Well, I'm one of those crazy loons. I love to sing. I'm not any good at it, but that doesn't stop me. I sing in the shower. I sing while cooking dinner and cleaning house. And I sing along with the car radio at the top of my lungs. Singing calms my nerves, boosts my energy, and inspires me, which is exactly how my new Deep in the Heart of Texas novel came about.

One morning, I woke up with the theme song to the musical *The Best Little Whorehouse in Texas* rolling around in my head. You know the one I'm talking about: "It's just a little bitty pissant country place..." The song stayed with me for the rest of the day, along with the image of a bunch of fun-loving women singing and dancing about "nothin' dirty going on." A hundred verses later, about the time my husband was ready to pull out the duct tape, I had an exciting idea for my new novel.

My editor wasn't quite as excited.

"A what?" she asked, and she stared at me exactly like the people who catch me singing at a stoplight.

She relaxed when I explained that it wasn't a functioning house of ill repute. The last rooster flew the coop years ago. Now Miss Hattie's Henhouse is nothing more than a dilapidated old mansion with three old women living in it. Three old women who have big plans to bring Miss Hattie's back to its former glory. The only thing that stands in their way is a virginal librarian who holds the deed to the house and a smokin' hot cowboy who is bent on revenge for his great-grandfather's murder.

Yes, there will be singing, dancing, and just a wee bit of "dirty going on." And of course, all the folks of Bramble, Texas, will be back to make sure their librarian gets a happy ending.

I hope you'll join me there!

Best wishes,

Katie Jane

♥ ♥ ♥ ♥ ♥ ♥ ♥ ♥ ♥ ♥ ♥ ♥ ♥ ♥

From the desk of Amanda Scott

Dear Reader,

What happens when a self-reliant Highland lass possessing extraordinary "gifts" meets a huge, shaggy warrior wounded in body and spirit, to whom she is strongly attracted, until she learns that he is immune to her gifts and that her father believes the man is the perfect husband for her?

What if the warrior is a prisoner of her father's worst enemy, who escaped after learning of a dire threat to the young King of Scots, recently returned from years of English captivity and struggling to take command of his unruly realm?

Lady Andrena MacFarlan, heroine of THE LAIRD'S CHOICE, the first book in my Lairds of the Loch trilogy, is just such a lass; and escaped Highland-galley slave and warrior Magnus "Mag" Galbraith is such a man. He is also dutiful and believes that his first duty is to the King.

I decided to set the trilogy in the Highlands west of Loch Lomond and soon realized that I wanted a mythological theme and three heroines with mysterious gifts, none of which was Second Sight. We authors have exploited the Sight for years. In doing so, many of us have endowed our characters with gifts far beyond the original meaning, which to Highlanders was the rare ability of a person to "see" an event while it was happening (usually the death of a loved one in distant battle).

It occurred to me, however, that many of us today possess mysterious "gifts." We can set a time in our heads to waken, and we wake right on time. Others enjoy flawless memories or hearing so acute that they hear sounds above and/or below normal ranges—bats' cries, for example. How about those who, without reason, dream of dangers to loved ones, then learn that such things have happened? Or those who sense in the midst of an event that they have dreamed the whole thing before and know what will happen?

Why do some people seem to communicate easily with animals when others cannot? Many can time baking without a timer, but what about those truly spooky types who walk to the oven door just *before* the timer goes—every time—as if the thing had whispered that it was about to go off?

Warriors develop extraordinary abilities. Their hearing becomes more acute; their sense of smell grows stronger. Prisoners of war find that all their senses increase. Their peripheral vision even widens.

In days of old, certain phenomena that we do not understand today might well have been more common and more closely heeded.

Lady Andrena reads (most) people with uncanny ease and communicates with the birds and beasts of her family's remaining estate. That estate itself holds secrets and seems to protect her family.

Her younger sisters have their own gifts.

And as for Mag Galbraith… Well, let's just say he has "gifts" of his own that make the sparks fly.

I hope you'll enjoy THE LAIRD'S CHOICE. Meantime, *suas Alba!*

Amanda Scott

www.amandascottauthor.com

From the desk of Dee Davis

Dear Reader,

Sometimes we meet someone and there is an instant connection, that indefinable something that creates sparks between two people. And sometimes that leads almost immediately to a happily ever after. Or at least the path taken seems to be straight and true. But sometimes life intervenes. Mistakes are made, secrets are kept, and that light is extinguished. But we rarely ever forget. That magical moment is too rare to dismiss out of turn, and, if given the right opportunity, it always has the potential to spring back to life again.

That's the basis of Simon and Jillian's story. Two people separated by pride and circumstance. Mistakes made that aren't easily undone. But the two of them have been given a second chance. And this time, just maybe they'll get it right. Of course to do that, they'll have to overcome their fears. And they'll have to find a way to confront their past with honesty and compassion. Easily said—not so easily done. But part of reading romance, I think, is the chance to see that in the end, no matter what has happened, it all can come right again.

And at least as far as I'm concerned, Jillian and Simon deserve their happy ending. It's just that they'll have to work together to actually get it.

As always, this book is filled with places that actually exist. I love the Fulton Seaport and have always been fascinated with the helipads along the East River. The buildings along the river that span the FDR highway have always been a pull. How much fun to know that people are whizzing along underneath you as you stare out your window and watch the barges roll by. The brownstone that members of A-Tac use during their investigation is based on a real one near the corner of Sutton Place and 57th Street.

The busy area around Union Square is also one of my favorite hang-outs in the city. And so it seemed appropriate to put Lester's apartment there. His gallery, too, is based on reality—specifically, the old wrought-iron clad buildings in SoHo. As to the harbor warehouses, while I confess to never having actually been in one, I have passed them several times when out on a boat, and they always intrigue me. So it isn't surprising that one should show up in a book.

And I must confess to being an avid Yankees fan. So it wasn't much of a hardship to send the team off to the stadium during a fictional World Series win. I was lucky enough to be there for the ticker-tape parade when they won in 2009. And Boone Logan is indeed a relief pitcher for the Yankees.

I also gave my love of roses to Michael Brecht, deadheading being a very satisfying way to spend a morning. And finally, the train tunnel that the young Jillian and Simon dare to cross in the middle of the night truly does exist, near Hendrix College in Arkansas. (And it was, in fact, great sport to try and make it all the way through!)

Hopefully you'll enjoy reading Jillian and Simon's story as much as I enjoyed writing it.

For insight into both of them, here are some songs I listened to while writing DOUBLE DANGER:

"Stronger," by Kelly Clarkson
"All the Rowboats," by Regina Spektor
"Take My Hand," by Simple Plan

And as always, check out www.deedavis.com for more inside info about my writing and my books.

Happy Reading!

Dee Davis

♥ ♥ ♥ ♥ ♥ ♥ ♥ ♥ ♥ ♥ ♥ ♥ ♥ ♥

From the desk of Isobel Carr

Dear Reader,

I have an obsession with history. And as a re-enactor, that obsession frequently comes down to a delight in the minutia of day-to-day life and a deep love of true events that seem stranger than fiction. And we all know that real life is stranger than fiction, don't we?

RIPE FOR SEDUCTION grew out of just such a real-life story. Lady Mary, daughter of the Duke of Argyll, married Edward, Viscount Coke (heir to the Earl of Leicester). It was not a happy marriage. He left her alone on their wedding night, imprisoned her at his family estate, and in the end she refused him his marital rights and went to live with her mother again. Lucky for her, the viscount died three years later when she was twenty-six. And while I can see how wonderful it might be to rewrite that story, letting the viscount live and making him come groveling back, it was not the story that inspired me. No, it was what happened after her husband's death. Upon returning to town after her mourning period was over, Lady Mary received a most indecent proposal ... and the man who made it was fool enough to put it in writing. Lady Mary's revenge was swift, brutal, and brilliant. I stole it for my heroine, Lady Olivia, who like Lady Mary had suffered a great and public humiliation at the hands of her husband, and who, also like Lady Mary, eventually found herself a widow.

And don't try finding out just what the poor man did or what Lady Mary's response was by Googling it. That story isn't on Wikipedia (though maybe I should add it). You'll have to come let Roland show you what it means to be RIPE FOR SEDUCTION if you want to find out.

www.isobelcarr.com